Books by C.C. Warrens

The Holly Novels
Criss Cross
Winter Memorial
Cross Fire
Crossed Off

Seeking Justice Series
Injustice for All
Holly Jolly Christmas

This novel is a work of fiction. Situations, scenarios, and characters in this book are a reflection of creative imagination and not representative of any specific person, group, situation, or event.

Cover art is from depositphotos.com and Shutterstock.com.

Editing by Deb Hall at TheWriteInsight.com

A Caffeine Conundrum, mentioned in chapter 14, is a novel written by Angela Ruth Strong (White Salmon, WA: Mountain Brook Ink, 2018).

All scripture quotations, unless otherwise indicated, are taken from the Holy Bible, New International Version®, NIV®. Copyright ©1973, 1978, 1984, 2011 by Biblica, Inc.™ Used by permission of Zondervan. All rights reserved worldwide. www.zondervan.com The "NIV" and "New International Version" are trademarks registered in the United States Patent and Trademark Office by Biblica, Inc.™

Acknowledgments

A special thank you to everyone who has prayed for me and gone out of their way to brighten my days during the writing of this book. Your encouragement, support, and prayers inspired me to push forward.

. . .

A special thank you to Colleen, for her giving heart and thoughtfulness, both of which kept this book from being delayed any further!

. . .

A special thank you to Val, who answered many of my questions about the justice system and courtroom etiquette.

. . .

And last but by no means least, thank you to my local law enforcement officers, who were kind enough to answer some of my spontaneous questions when I caught them out and about!

This book contains subjects and situations that might be difficult for some readers.

IMPERFECT
JUSTICE

A Seeking Justice Novel

IMPERFECT JUSTICE is the second book in the Seeking Justice series. This series ties in with the Holly Novels. To see where it all began, check out *Criss Cross: A Holly Novel*.

1

 $\mathscr{T}$ he bloody footprints materialized on the sidewalk as the rising sun crept slowly over the city— small, feminine, and uncoordinated.

Liam's blue eyes lingered on the gruesome trail that had led him to the front door of a rundown duplex, his mind drawing details from the photograph in his pocket to paint the scene:

A girl, bruised and terrified, stumbling out the door and down the sidewalk as she desperately tried to escape whatever horror had happened here.

That girl had staggered into the emergency room several hours ago, but just before Liam arrived to take her statement, she vanished. He searched for her, but with no name or picture ID, he had to pull a black-and-white photo of her from the hospital security camera. She was young—late teens to early twenties—with soulful eyes, and delicate features.

Although Liam knew he was supposed to remain professionally detached, the anguish in the girl's eyes had sunk barbed hooks into his heart. Maybe he needed to compartmentalize better, but he didn't understand how anyone could see that level of pain in another human being and feel nothing.

This was going to be one of those cases that consumed him, and he prayed the crime scene offered some clue as to where the girl might be.

He pulled his police badge from beneath his T-shirt, letting it dangle on the chain against his chest, and drew his sidearm. A part of him—the part that frequently landed him in hot water with the department—hoped the girl's attacker was still inside, because he really wanted to punch him until he cried.

The guy had beaten a girl so badly she nearly passed out before making it through the emergency room doors. In Liam's opinion, he deserved the same treatment, but if he brought in one more suspect with a concussion, he would be assigned desk duty.

Still, it was tempting.

He listened for movement inside the duplex, then nudged the door inward. "Police!" His deep voice ricocheted off the dark walls, and he clicked on his flashlight.

The duplex appeared as vacant as it sounded—chipped and peeling walls, patches of tile worn through to the cement beneath, and a staircase on the verge of collapse. The building was one windy day away from folding in on itself. It had to be condemned, but the tiny pink sneakers placed neatly along the wall suggested *someone* was staying here.

He swept his flashlight over the foyer, absorbing details that he had glossed over the first time. A small pool of crimson liquid at the bottom of the staircase grabbed his attention. It was smeared and streaked across the tile from where someone, likely the victim, had slipped through it.

But whose blood was it?

He filed that question away for later. Right now, he needed to focus his attention on searching the house for anyone who might still be inside.

He stepped carefully around the evidence and into the connected room. The living area was nearly empty, with only an old stereo, a floor lamp, a stack of worn books, and a beanbag chair patched with duct tape tucked into one corner. The kitchen was just as sparsely furnished, boasting a card table and folding chair with a few clean dishes resting on the counter.

Where were the knickknacks and family photos? Every woman he dated had "stylish" picture frames on nearly every horizontal surface. So did his mother, but this girl . . .

She had nothing but the bare necessities. But then, maybe she was content with books, music, and hot tea.

He could envision her sitting at the kitchen table, knees drawn up and toes curled over the edge of the seat, as she quietly turned the page of her book and sipped tea from the chipped mug that read, "Solving mysteries one sip at a time."

Except in this case, she *was* the mystery, and she wasn't leaving him any helpful clues as to her identity.

Satisfied that the lower level was clear, Liam made his way back to the foyer and tried to visually gauge whether or not the staircase would hold his weight. At six foot five, he was easily 120 pounds heavier than the girl who probably bounded up and down these steps every day. He placed his boot on the first one, and it let out a troubling creak, but held. He bypassed the fourth step entirely, deciding it was best not to test the bowed and cracking board.

By the time he reached the top floor, he realized that there was no way anyone could make it up those steps without giving themselves away. That meant the attacker had surprised the girl downstairs or he'd been waiting upstairs for her when she got home.

He cleared the second floor more quickly than the first, finding no one else inside. He slid his gun back into its holster as he stood in the doorway of the girl's bedroom.

This was where the victim's nightmare began.

Liam rubbed his thumb and forefinger together, missing the stress outlet of a cigarette, as he crouched at the edge of the scene. With the evidence scattered around him, it didn't take much imagination to envision what happened in this room.

How was he supposed to remain objective when he knew what had been done to this girl? He'd reviewed her medical report, and he'd watched the security footage of her limping out of the hospital.

The fact that she fled while in excruciating pain told him that she didn't believe anyone could or would protect her from the man who did this to her. But *he* would've protected her, if she had just given him a chance.

He rose and called in forensics to collect the evidence and process the scene, while he searched for anything that would help him identify his victim.

By midafternoon he was no closer to putting a name to her face. He had searched every crack and crevice of the home, but he had more questions now than he had before.

He ducked under the crime scene tape strung across the front door of the duplex, and out onto the sidewalk, expelling a frustrated breath into the chilly air.

This neighborhood was the equivalent of a pothole: something everyone went out of their way to avoid. The shadows were crawling with junkies, drug dealers, sexual deviants, and anyone else who needed a dark hole to hide in.

And then there was his victim, a girl who loved hot peppermint tea, inspirational books, and '90s Christian pop music.

He suspected she was a runaway, trying to keep her head above water, but how was she making ends meet? It was possible she'd found a job or had some artistic skill that put the food in her cupboards and the clothes in her closet, but he doubted it.

She was young, pretty, and probably desperate, all of which made her an ideal mark for sex traffickers.

Once victims were enticed or forced into prostitution, it was nearly impossible to escape. If this young girl had been dragged into that world and tried to claw her way out, there would've been violent consequences.

"You got a name for this girl yet?"

The voice came from behind him, and he glanced over his shoulder at Mags, who readjusted the ruler beside the bloody footprint before capturing a photo.

"No." He sighed. "Nothing yet."

"If you don't find out her name soon, I'm sure you'll come up with a good one for her."

"Am I that predictable?"

"You're the only cop I know who refuses to use the appropriate terminology."

He hated calling victims Jane or John Doe; it made him think of corpses on a slab in the morgue, and he wasn't willing to go there yet. In his mind, until he found a body, his victims were alive and waiting to be found.

Until he discovered this mystery girl's name, he needed something to call her. He pulled her picture from his pocket and studied it, turning over possible names in his mind until he landed on one that suited her.

Purity.

He couldn't wait on the crime lab to provide him with leads to follow. They were backlogged, and it could be months, even years, before they got around to running DNA from the sexual assault kit. Even then, the results might be inconclusive.

His best chance at information was out there on the street. Someone had to know this girl; the problem was, the people who lingered on the street day in and day out weren't likely to confide in a cop.

11

His gaze strayed to the bloody footprints, and his heart twisted in his chest. He would find Purity, no matter how long it took, and then he would track down the man who did this to her and make him regret it.

2

$\mathcal{H}$olly pulled on her winter boots and straightened, her honey-brown eyes snagging on the garment bag hanging on the back of her bedroom door.

The outfit inside was stunning—black skinny slacks and an emerald sweater with threads of silver woven into the fabric—but the reason for its presence left an anxious knot in her stomach.

She would rather wear her paint-splattered overalls and an oversized sweatshirt—or three—when confronting her foster brother in court. But Shannon, the prosecuting attorney, had flipped through her entire wardrobe, the crease of dismay in her forehead deepening with every hanger she swept aside.

Shannon was an elegant woman who exuded confidence and grace with every breath. Holly felt more like one of those stumpy donkeys, the ones with the short legs and oversized ears that tripped over their own feet.

It didn't matter how nicely Shannon dressed her; the outfit might create a temporary illusion of confidence and grace, but the illusion would shatter the moment the courtroom doors opened. She doubted she would make it up the aisle to the witness box before her outsides began trembling as violently as her insides.

Ten months had passed since she last saw her foster brother, three hundred and eight days since he tried to break her into thousands of irreparable pieces, and thinking about him still made it hard to breathe.

She wanted to be fierce like David, to walk into battle with nothing but stones and a slingshot and trust that God would use them to slay her giant. But she couldn't seem to smother the voice whispering fear into every fiber of her being.

What if something goes wrong? What if the jury doesn't believe my story? What if the judge decides to let him go?

The marshmallows in her stomach melted into nauseous goo. If the judge set her foster brother free . . .

She dropped onto the edge of her bed and sank her trembling fingers into Riley's coarse fur. Her canine companion shifted, but he didn't wake; snout still buried in the ballet flat he'd dragged onto the mattress, he snored wheezily.

She wished the judge would let her bring him to court during her testimony. He helped soothe her panic, and the feeling of his fur between her fingers grounded her when the memories tried to sweep her into the past.

Unfortunately, Riley was a former police dog who suffered from post-traumatic stress, and he tended to overreact when he thought Holly was being threatened. For that reason, her request to bring him to court had been denied.

A gentle tap on the outside of the door pulled her from her thoughts. "Yeah."

The door inched inward, and an older man with salt-and-pepper hair filled the opening. The shade of his eyes reminded her of the bright green moss that coated the roots of the forest trees in her hometown.

"Hey, peanut," he said, his voice still carrying a touch of his Southern upbringing.

She scrunched her nose at the endearment. "I don't even look like a peanut."

"At five foot one, you're close enough."

"Five one and a *quarter*, thank you very much." And if she wore her hair in a bun on top of her head, she was almost five three.

Marx smiled and nodded to the hoodie she was wearing, the one he'd given her as a gift for her birthday two days ago. "Glad to see it fits."

It was a size smaller than she preferred, and the phrase stamped across the front in hot pink letters was ridiculous: "I put the 'she' in shenanigans." But it was purple, and it had a pouch where she could stash her snack bag of marshmallows.

"You about ready?" He glanced at his watch. Unlike most people nowadays, who relied on their smartphones and fitness bands to keep track of time, he still wore an old leather watch with a hand dial. "If we don't get goin', you're gonna be late for your appointment."

Every week, sometimes twice a week if she was having a particularly rough few days, Marx drove her to the counseling center downtown. The older woman she met with was nice enough, but she was frustratingly determined to stay on topic, even if that topic was one Holly would rather avoid.

Holly blew out a breath and dragged herself off the bed, dreading the inescapable conversation about her upcoming testimony.

Marx lifted an eyebrow at her obvious lack of enthusiasm. "What, did she tell you she's out of chocolate this week?"

Holly rolled her eyes. After her third visit, her therapist always made sure to have a bowl of candy in her office. Instead of offering a tissue in response to Holly's tears, she slid the bowl of chocolates toward her. "No, but I do think I ate all the caramel ones on Wednesday. And the cookies 'n' cream. And maybe the cherry ones."

It had been a rough conversation.

Marx smiled and shook his head. "I do not understand how you're still so scrawny."

Indignant, Holly mounted her hands on her hips. "I am not scrawny."

"Mmm hmm." He reached out a hand and tickled her ribs, drawing a surprised squeak from her. "Practically a xylophone."

She scampered out of his reach and pointed a threatening finger at him. "I will tickle you back."

"I'm terrified." He grabbed her fluffy white hat from the hook beside the door and tossed it to her. "Now come on."

She tugged her hat down over her ears and followed him out of the bedroom. "Can I drive?"

"No."

She frowned at his quick response. He hadn't even hesitated. "Why not?" She might not officially have her license, but she had her permit. "I'm not that bad of a driver."

He gave her an incredulous look as he grabbed his car keys from the side table by the front door. "You hit a handicap sign."

Oh, right, she had done that. "At least it wasn't a handicap person."

"No, there is no 'at least.' You hit a stationary object. *With my car.*"

Given how attached he was to his car, it was a wonder she was still allowed in it. "I can pay to fix the dent if—"

"It has nothin' to do with the dent." He shooed her into the hall so he could lock the door. "You've barely slept the past few nights, and I don't wanna die in a ten-car pileup."

"But—"

"The answer's still no." He started down the steps. "And don't give me that face. You are not gonna win this argument with cuteness."

She scowled, hoisted her sliding bag back up onto her shoulder, and bounded down the steps after him.

3

*S*hannon paced the length of her office, her gray eyes flicking back and forth across the yellow legal pad in her hand as she retraced every line that she'd written. Her opening statement would set the tone for the trial, and she needed to paint a vivid picture for the jury.

"This man abducted a young woman and imprisoned her in . . ." She trailed off, her stockinged feet coming to a standstill on the cool tile, then scratched out the word *imprisoned* with her pen. It brought to mind images of convicts and guilt, not victims.

She needed to be extremely selective about the words she used. She didn't want to give the defense an opportunity to twist her statements to their own advantage.

Tapping a foot on the floor, she shuffled through her mental rolodex of alternative phrases. *Held captive.* She jotted it down, pinched the pen between her lips, and resumed pacing.

The trial started in two days, and after the judge granted the defense's request to suppress all three of the videos she'd submitted into evidence, she had to rework some things.

During the span of Holly's captivity, Collin recorded three homemade videos, each one depicting hours of violence and psychological torment.

The first two videos were digitally distorted, irreparably disfiguring Collin's face and voice. She expected those two would be excluded, but losing the third video had caught her off guard.

Collin didn't have a chance to manipulate the recording before the police raided the warehouse where he was keeping Holly, and it clearly depicted his face as well as his brutality.

The defense argued that the footage was too violent to subject a jury to, and that viewing it could unduly traumatize them. Shannon pointed out that they needed to see the brutality to understand what the defendant was capable of.

Ultimately, Collin decided to plead guilty to sexual battery and misdemeanor assault, making the video "unnecessary," according to the judge. Shannon had been stunned speechless. No other judge would've been so easily persuaded by Collin and his lawyer.

When the judge sided with the defense to dismiss the third video, it felt as though he'd stripped away Shannon's arsenal and was sending her into battle with sticks. She would have to whittle those sticks until they were deadly sharp.

A not-guilty verdict wasn't an option. The lives of people she cared about would be at risk if she failed to prove beyond a shadow of a doubt that Collin Wells deserved to spend the rest of his life behind bars.

"He stalked Holly, making several appearances and phone calls, until eventually she was forced to move in with a friend."

Shannon's ex-husband, Rick—or Richard, as most people called him—had a unique bond with Holly, and he opened his home to her after her foster brother showed up on her doorstep. It was the only way to protect her—from Collin and from a life on the run. But their living situation, while completely innocent, could present its own problems during the trial.

She wasn't sure how Collin's lawyer would spin it, but no doubt it would involve some indecent relationship between the two of them. If necessary, the defense would create an entire narrative to discredit one or both of Shannon's witnesses during cross-examination.

The truth was, Holly was as skittish as a kitten when it came to intimate relationships with men. Even the suggestion of romance was likely to send her scampering into her bedroom and locking the door.

Rick had earned her trust by respecting her boundaries and showing her the kindness and love she had been deprived of for most of her twenty-nine years. He might come across as gruff and sarcastic, but Holly brought out the softer side that Shannon remembered.

She made a note to compile a list of examples that would prove their relationship was platonic, just in case the defense decided to take things in that direction, then continued to review her statement.

"She felt so threatened that she took out an order of protection against him that stipulated no contact."

She tapped the pen against her lips, then circled the sentence. She could phrase that better.

After hearing Holly's story, it was clear that Collin Wells had no intention of leaving her in peace. Shannon requested an order of protection, despite Holly's insistence that the legal motion was pointless. Her foster brother had ignored every boundary she'd ever had, and Holly didn't believe a piece of paper would make a difference.

The ink on the document was barely dry before Collin grabbed Holly and disappeared.

"He took her from the apartment of—"

A knock on the door shattered Shannon's focus. What good was putting her phone on Do Not Disturb if people were just going to bang on the door?

"I asked not to be disturbed."

The door cracked open and Hazel, the elderly woman who recently started working at the reception desk, popped her head in. "I'm sorry, but there's been a delivery for you." She hip-bumped the door the rest of the way open and carried in a vase of flowers. "Someone's sweet on you."

Shannon frowned as Hazel set them on the corner of the desk. She wasn't seeing anyone, and Rick knew she didn't care for daisies. "Is there a card?"

Hazel handed her a letter-sized envelope, then pressed her nose to one of the daisies and drew in a deep breath. "I just love flowers. They're so romantic." She smiled brightly, then swept out of the office.

21

Shannon's attention returned to the envelope in her hand, and she pulled the sheet of paper from inside, unfolding it:

Let this case die.

Well, that was straightforward, if a bit melodramatic. Did the sender really expect a vase of cheap flowers and a warning to "Let the case die" to discourage her from pursuing justice?

She flipped the sheet of paper over, on the off chance the sender was dimwitted enough to sign it, and found a second message.

"PS Burgundy is a good color for . . ." She looked down at the burgundy skirt and blazer she wore, and unease skittered across her nerves.

Her gaze immediately darted to the wall of windows in her office, and she rounded her desk to peer through the slatted blinds.

Collin Wells had to be the one behind this. He enjoyed instilling fear through mind games. The only hitch in that theory was that he was sitting in a cell, awaiting trial. Was he working with someone on the outside?

She scanned the street for anyone who might be watching her. The man on the corner smoking a cigarette? The old woman sitting in the café window with a book? Maybe the man with the . . .

"Stop it, Shannon," she told herself, realizing that she was responding exactly the way the sender intended—looking over her shoulder in fear.

She snapped the blinds shut, turning away from the window, and sucked in a startled breath when she found a man standing in her doorway.

"Am I interruptin' a private conversation?" he asked.

She pressed a hand to her thundering heart and fixed her ex-husband with an exasperated look. "Would it kill you to knock, Rick?"

He smiled, the skin around his eyes crinkling in a way that made her heart flutter, and tapped his knuckles on the door frame. "Better?"

She sighed and discarded the eerie letter and her notepad on the desk before folding her arms. She couldn't decide if she was more relieved or flustered by his presence. After the unsettling message, she appreciated the sense of safety he brought with him, but even three years after the divorce, her feelings for him were . . . complicated.

"Hazel didn't tell you I was busy?"

"No, but she did ask me to dinner."

Shannon released a sigh. Rick had mesmerizing green eyes, and they melted the spine of nearly every woman over thirty in the office. "I need a male receptionist."

"I would just use my badge."

Rick was a detective with the NYPD, and he carried his badge and gun even when he was off duty. "I hate when you use that thing to get your way. It's an unfair advantage."

"You wanna talk about unfair advantage." He pushed away from the doorway. "Let's talk about this look women have that reduces a man's willpower to dust."

Shannon leaned against her desk. "Sounds like you had an interesting morning."

"Holly asked if she could drive today, and I knew as soon as I told her no that she was gonna give me that face."

"Those big, disappointed eyes."

"Mmm hmm. I had to look away."

Shannon crossed her arms, amusement tugging at the corners of her lips. "You caved, didn't you?"

"I let her drive for five minutes, and she nearly took out a mailbox on a corner. The girl has no concept of a turn radius."

Shannon laughed. Holly had been too busy running for her life to learn to drive. Rick agreed to teach her—an offer he was no doubt regretting—but they hadn't had much time for lessons before the situation with Collin escalated.

"Maybe you should postpone the driving lessons until after the trial. I'd rather not lose two of my witnesses in a fiery crash."

"Your concern is overwhelmin'."

Shannon smiled at his sarcasm. "What brings you by?"

He nodded toward her cell phone lying on top of a stack of folders. "I take it you didn't get my message."

She tapped her phone screen and saw the missed call and voice mail notifications. "I had it on silent so I could practice my opening statement."

He lifted an eyebrow and visually scanned the room. "You forgot to bring the jury."

Heat crept up her neck. When she first started practicing law two decades ago, she had a difficult time envisioning the jurors as she prepped for her opening statement and closing arguments. She would prop twelve pillows on the living room couch and practice making eye contact with each one as she spoke, just as if she were locking eyes with members of the jury. It helped her create a habit; it also made her look insane. She'd been mortified the first time Rick walked in on her talking to a row of pillows. Instead of politely ignoring the oddity, he decided to play along by dubbing them "the jury" and assigning them ridiculous names.

"Thank you . . . for . . . bringing that up."

He smiled. "Didn't somethin' happen to Foreman Francis?"

"Yes, you knocked him off the couch onto a burning candle and caught him on fire. I happened to like that pillow, by the way."

He grunted unapologetically. "I figured you were busy gettin' things pulled together, and since I was in the area, I brought you a little somethin'."

25

He offered her a covered mug, and the moment she popped the lid, the sweet scent of vanilla, cream, and chai flooded her office. It might only be the end of January, but it smelled like fall. Her favorite.

"I don't suppose you asked for—"

"Full fat cream. None of that skim nonsense."

It warmed her that he still knew her so well, that he remembered such small details about her. "Thank you."

He nodded. "How is everythin' comin' together?"

She drew in another breath of spicy sweetness before answering. "I'm still working some things out. I know you're concerned about not having the videos, but plenty of trials have been won without any camera footage."

"Yes, but losin' the videos puts a pretty large dent in your evidence."

"I have plenty of witnesses and forensics. And there are a lot of other charges against Collin—assault, Jace's abduction and abuse, Rachel's murder." She set aside the latte. "I need you to trust that I can do my job."

"I do trust you, but we both know Collin is not gonna go down without a fight, and he's not gonna fight fair."

Shannon's gaze flickered to the bouquet and then away. No, Collin was not a man accustomed to losing, and he was going to utilize whatever means necessary to walk away from these charges.

"He can fight as hard as he wants in the courtroom, but the moment Holly takes that stand and tells them what happened, the jury will bury him."

She hoped.

Putting victims on the witness stand was always a risk; there was no way to know how they might react when forced to confront their attackers.

Shannon had recommended an excellent trauma counselor to help Holly work through the aftermath of her abuse, but the young woman's fear was so ingrained that a few months of therapy might not be enough. There was a very good chance her fear would trigger a panic attack on the witness stand.

"How's Holly doing?"

Shannon tried to maintain a professional distance between herself and the victims she worked with—it saved her a lot of heartache—but she'd spent a lot of time with Holly over the past six months, and she'd grown fond of her.

Rick tilted a hand back and forth in a so-so gesture. "She's determined to be positive. I know she's scared—she's barely slept in days, hasn't eaten a solid meal in longer than that, paces the apartment at all hours of the night—but she just keeps smilin' and bakin' . . . things."

A trial was stressful on everyone involved, but more so on the victims. Not only would Holly have to see her foster brother again, but she would have to relive the details of her assault in front of a roomful of strangers.

"Honestly, I wish I could just take her back to Georgia. I've never seen her more carefree and happy than when she was dancin' around the kitchen, bakin' cookies with Mama." Rick's expression clouded. "I watched that happiness fade as we drove back to New York, replaced by anxiety and fear."

Georgia was probably far enough from Collin that she felt safe, but her foster brother wasn't a problem she could run away from. Not if she ever wanted a normal life.

"Is the counseling helping at all?" Shannon asked.

"You know Holly. She's not very good at verbalizin' her pain. The only sound in the therapist's office right now is probably the crinkle of candy wrappers."

A surprised laugh bubbled out of Shannon. Holly was addicted to sweets, and setting a bowl of candy in front of her was a surefire way to make her more agreeable. "Oh, speaking of Holly. I picked up an extra outfit for her when I went shopping yesterday."

She'd tried to convince Holly to go shopping with her on several occasions, but even a bribe of hot chocolate and freshly baked cookies wasn't enough incentive. The girl despised shopping.

Shannon walked to the coatrack by the door and grabbed the garment bag from one of the pegs. She unzipped it to show Rick the outfit she'd found on a sale rack at an upscale boutique. The design was both professional and bright.

"What do you think?"

Rick rubbed his jaw, and she recognized the mannerism. He was concerned that his opinion would offend her, and he was hoping to escape without comment.

"Quit stalling."

"Who says I'm—"

"We were married for twenty years, Rick. I know your tactics, which is why you're not going to evade my question by asking a question. Now tell me what you think."

He made a sucking sound with his cheek. "Okay fine. I hope you kept the receipt."

She frowned. "You don't think it would look good on her?"

"Oh, I think she'd look downright adorable, but she'll never wear it."

"Why? What's wrong with it?"

"For starters, it's yellow. Holly hates yellow."

"It's a cheerful color."

"Cheerful," he repeated slowly. "What victim in their right mind is cheerful while describin' their assault to a dozen strangers?"

Shannon opened her mouth, closed it, then said, "Point taken, but she doesn't have to wear it for her testimony. She can where it during the verdict announcements or sentencing."

"It's a dress, Shannon."

"I am observant enough to notice that, Rick, but thank you for clarifying."

29

"Holly won't even wear a dress to church because it makes her feel too vulnerable. And you expect her to wear one when she's in the same room as her attacker? You'll be lucky if you can get her into that courtroom without body armor."

Shannon regarded the dress from a new perspective. Why hadn't she considered that? Holly hid inside layers of clothing; she would never be comfortable in something that left her so exposed. "I'll figure out something to do with it." She doubted she could take it back, but she could always donate it to charity.

"I suppose I should let you get back to work."

Disappointment threaded through her at his words, but she suppressed it before it could settle too deeply. Her interactions with Rick needed to remain professional, regardless of how much her heart longed for more.

"That's probably a good idea." She brushed a polite kiss across his cheek, her usual parting gesture, but this time it was harder to break the connection and step back. She was spending too much time with him, and it was making it impossible to remain professionally distant, but there was nothing she could do about that until this trial was over.

"I'll see you tomorrow then."

He stepped out, and she shut the door, resting her forehead against it. She needed to pull herself together and refocus on the task at hand.

4

A familiar ache expanded behind Shannon's eyes as she stared at her trial notes. She sighed, resting her elbows on the desk, and massaged her temples.

She'd struggled with migraines ever since she was a child. Doctors told her it was likely hereditary, but her mother never suffered from headaches. The unfortunate condition must have been passed down by her father—whoever he was.

As far as Shannon was concerned, he didn't exist. He was nothing but an imaginary figure created by her six-year-old mind, a faceless hero who would someday swoop through her bedroom window and carry her away from the emotional starvation of her childhood. It was easier than the truth, which was that he was probably just one of the nameless men who visited her mother through the revolving front door of their house.

Shannon opened her desk drawer and considered the bottle of prescription migraine medication. She preferred not to take it unless all other avenues had failed.

With a frustrated huff, she closed the drawer and switched on the electric kettle. Peppermint tea with a splash of honey might take the edge off. She stood and searched through the box of flavored tea she kept on the bookshelf, finding the last bag of peppermint. She unwrapped it and dropped it into her favorite mug just as someone tapped on the door.

Oh, for heaven's sake, what now?

"Yes."

Hazel popped her head in, the movement sending one of her gray curls tumbling down over her forehead. "There's a lady here to see you."

"I don't have any appointments scheduled for this afternoon."

"She said it's important that she speak with you. Something about the trial."

"What's her name?"

"She didn't give one."

Shannon frowned. She didn't appreciate surprise visitors, especially ones who refused to give their names, but if the woman had important information regarding the trial, she couldn't very well turn her away. "Send her in."

Hazel disappeared from the doorway, and a moment later, the quiet click of heels followed her back down the hall to Shannon's office. She ushered the visitor into the room before closing the door to give them privacy. Shannon's unexpected guest was a woman somewhere in her midfifties, her black hair streaked with gray, and her pale skin creased with lines of stress.

Shannon straightened. Even though they had never met, the woman's pale blue eyes were unmistakably familiar. "Mrs. Wells. This is a surprise."

Agatha Wells shambled forward almost timidly. "I hope you'll forgive me for showing up without an appointment, but I was hoping to discuss my son's case."

Shannon gestured to one of the guest chairs. "You do realize I'm the prosecutor, not his defense attorney."

"Of course, yes." She sat down and gripped her oversized handbag in her lap. "But my son is innocent."

"That's for a jury to decide."

"I brought pictures." She rummaged through her bag and pulled out a handful of photos. "If you could just see how sweet my boy is, you would understand."

"Mrs. Wells, I'm aware of how difficult this must be for you, but pictures aren't going to exonerate your son."

"Please just look at them." Her eyes glistened with desperation as she held them out.

Begrudgingly, Shannon took them from her. The young man in the first photograph couldn't have been more than fifteen, and he flashed a dazzling smile at the camera. Even then, he'd had the kind of looks that belonged on a magazine cover.

She flipped to the second photo and her breath caught. It was that same boy, maybe three or four years later, sitting on a picnic table with his arm around a red-haired girl.

"My Collin and Holly were so close back then," Mrs. Wells said. "Practically inseparable."

Shannon stared into the little girl's eyes, so completely devoid of hope, and her stomach turned. She knew the string of terrible events that played out in that house, but seeing the shattered soul of a child right in front of her . . .

She wished she could reach back through time and hug that broken little girl, to reassure her that someday her life would be whole, that she would be surrounded by love. It broke her heart to know that this picture captured the beginning of Holly's suffering, not the end.

Why had no one protected her?

Mrs. Wells leaned forward. "You can see that he's a good boy, can't you? You can take it easy on him. He's been behind bars all these months. It isn't right that he should have to suffer so terribly."

Shannon's fingers tightened on the pictures. This woman's son had inflicted unimaginable suffering, and the jail cell he currently occupied was extravagant compared to the room where he imprisoned Holly. "If he's displeased with his accommodations, he's welcome to take it up with the jail administrator."

Irritation flickered through Mrs. Wells's eyes, but she quickly masked it. "Are you really so heartless?"

"Mrs. Wells, when your son was granted bail after violating Holly's order of protection, he neglected to show up for his court date. No judge was going to grant him bail again. The fact that he's been behind bars since his arrest is entirely his fault." Shannon handed the pictures back to her, and Mrs. Wells's shoulders slumped.

"You're pitting my son and daughter against each other."

"You don't have a daughter." The electric kettle clicked off, and Shannon poured steaming water over her tea bag.

"Just because it's been fifteen years since Holly lived under my roof doesn't mean she's no longer my daughter. We fostered her for nearly a year."

Now she wanted to play the mother? She had been nothing but cold and neglectful to her foster children, and she had allowed her son to abuse Holly. The evil in that household ran so deep that Shannon felt it on the back of her neck when Holly described her time there.

Mrs. Wells nodded to the kettle. "Oh, tea would be wonderful, if you have extra. Obviously I don't want to impose."

Yes, obviously.

Not wanting to be impolite, Shannon walked over to grab the box of tea bags and a spare cup from the windowsill. When she turned back to the desk, she noticed that Mrs. Wells was sitting closer to the edge of her chair. Unease and suspicion threaded through Shannon, but she said nothing as she poured hot water over a bag of black tea for her *guest*.

"Thank you so much," Mrs. Wells said, accepting the mug.

Shannon sat down in her chair and crossed her legs, studying the woman across from her. She appeared to be nothing more than a mother who was desperate to save her son, but Shannon had never been one to trust appearances.

"Aren't you going to drink your tea?" Mrs. Wells asked, and Shannon glanced at her cooling beverage.

She'd been looking forward to it, but from what Holly had told her about this woman, Shannon didn't trust her not to slip something into her tea while her back was turned. "Why are you really here, Mrs. Wells?"

"Because I'm worried about my children. Holly has always been so emotionally fragile, and I don't think testifying will be good for her mental health."

"I find it interesting that you're suddenly concerned about her well-being."

Mrs. Wells's shoulders straightened with indignation. "I don't know what you're insinuating, Ms. Marx, but Holly's well-being has always been important to me. You're the one subjecting her to unnecessary emotional distress. Surely you can manage this trial without her."

Shannon smiled at her less than subtle attempt to gauge the stability of the state's case. "With respect, what the prosecution can or can't manage is none of your concern."

"My children—"

Shannon sat forward and leveled a hard look at her. "You can retire the charade, Mrs. Wells. You and I both know that you don't care about Holly. You never did. The only reason you're concerned now is because she's going to tell the truth, and your son will be held accountable for his crimes."

Mrs. Wells's eyes turned icy, and the sweet-old-lady façade vanished. "My boy did nothing wrong."

"Is that what you taught him growing up? That he could do as he pleased without consequences?"

"Good boys don't need consequences."

"Your son is a sexual predator."

Mrs. Wells's face reddened, and she slammed her mug down on the edge of the desk, hot liquid splashing over the rim. "Is that what that manipulative little liar is telling everyone? That he forced her? It couldn't be further from the truth. She teased my son, seduced him. And now you're giving her a stage so she can seduce a jury with her lies."

This woman was as deranged as her son. "We're done here."

Mrs. Wells stood and leaned over the desk. "I won't let that lying tramp humiliate my boy."

Shannon didn't miss the threat in her words, and she rose from her chair, sinking authority into her voice. "You go near any of my witnesses, and I'll have you arrested. Now get out of my office."

"Who said anything about going near your witnesses?" She fixed Shannon with a smile that raised the hairs on the back of her neck. "I do hope you have a nice, safe evening all alone in that big house of yours, Ms. Marx."

. . . .

Shannon looked up toward the light fixture on her front porch as she climbed the dark steps; she could've sworn it was on when she left this morning.

Maybe the bulb blew out, she reasoned, but even as the thought fluttered through her mind, a counterargument followed: *Just hours after that insane woman suggested you might not be safe in your own home? Unlikely.*

She looked over her shoulder and scanned the shadows that stretched between the streetlights. The sidewalks were empty, and the only cars parked along the curb belonged to the neighbors.

Reaching into her purse, she groped for her keys. She should've searched for them before exiting the cab, but her mind was preoccupied. Now, with her porch light out, it would take her forever to find them.

She shifted, and something crunched beneath her shoe. She stepped back and pulled out her phone, shining the flashlight toward the porch floor. Glass sparkled, and she quickly shifted the beam of light toward the socket on the ceiling. All that remained of the bulb was jagged slivers.

Her heart lodged in her throat.

Someone had broken the bulb. This was a story she heard too many times in the courtroom—an attacker disorienting his victims with darkness and then lying in wait.

A rustling sound from somewhere to her right had her frantically digging for her keys. She was a second away from dumping her purse's contents onto the porch when her fingers closed around the metal ring. She jammed the key into the lock, twisted it, and practically flung herself into the house.

She locked the door and leaned against it, her trembling fingers still gripping the dead bolt. What had she been thinking getting out of that cab without her keys in hand? She could've easily become a statistic.

As she remained still, listening for any more unsettling noises over the rapid staccato of her breathing, a thought drifted through her mind: Was this how Holly had lived for the past fifteen years? Wondering if every dark bulb or mysterious noise was a sign that her foster brother was just steps behind her?

The thought ignited a spark of righteous anger in Shannon's chest. No one had the right to inflict that kind of mental torment on another person, to force them to live with fear as an ever-present shadow.

She turned, resting her back against the locked door, and stared into the darkness of her home, Mrs. Wells's words gnawing at her nerves.

All alone in that big house.

She was tempted to call Rick and ask him to come over and check things out, but knowing him, he would overreact. Shannon might no longer be his wife, but he still loved her, and he was fiercely protective of the women in his life.

She chewed on the inside of her cheek as she stared at the phone in her hand, debating whether or not to ignore the broken lightbulb and veiled threats.

Deciding to err on the side of caution, she sighed and called Samuel.

. . . .

Samuel shined a flashlight on the light fixture above him, his mouth set in a grim line, and then flicked the beam to the shards of glass scattered around his feet.

He crouched, his dark eyes scanning the length of the porch. "I don't see any rocks."

Shannon lingered in the open doorway, arms folded around her waist to keep her cardigan wrap in place. "Rocks?"

Samuel rose to his full height, putting him even with her five foot eight inches. He wasn't a large man, but his stocky frame paired with his police uniform and no-nonsense attitude gave him an air of authority.

"Sometimes kids throw rocks or other debris at houses after dark—take out a light fixture, break a window. I don't see anything."

"Oh." She tightened her arms around herself. So much for the possibility that it was caused by rowdy teenagers. "It could've been an electrical surge."

Samuel's thick, black eyebrows crept upward. "Typically the bulb blows *out*, not into a hundred pieces."

She shifted against the door frame, a shiver lingering at the base of her spine. The only alternative to the first two theories was that someone came onto her porch with the intention of putting out the light. "You didn't find any sign that anyone was in the yard?"

Samuel flicked the beam of light over the grass. "The ground is frozen and there's no snow, so even if someone *was* out there, there wouldn't be any prints."

She sighed and rested her head against the door frame. Maybe she was blowing this whole situation out of proportion. "I'm sorry I wasted your time."

He slid the flashlight back into his belt and rested his hand on his sidearm, a stance she'd seen more than one officer adopt. "What's really going on, Shannon?"

"What do you mean?"

"You didn't call me just because of a broken bulb. Something else is bothering you."

She could provide him with a bullet point list of things that were bothering her, starting with the fact that the ache in her head was ebbing and flowing like a relentless tide, refusing to completely recede.

"I guess I'm just a bit on edge because of this trial. Things are more complicated than I originally anticipated."

The mention of the trial flipped a switch in Samuel, and a quiet anger ignited in his eyes. She'd seen that look before, when he first learned the details of what happened to Holly. She was under his protection the night she was taken, and he felt responsible.

"Is the case in danger?" he asked.

"No, I don't think so."

"Then what is it?"

She rubbed at her forehead, debating whether or not to share her concerns. Samuel was her friend, but he was also Rick's friend. Anything she told him would likely travel down the grapevine.

She supposed a visit from Rick was inevitable at this point. Samuel would mention the broken bulb and her unease, and Rick would show up tomorrow like a blustery storm.

Shannon sighed, regretting that she had called Samuel in the first place. "I don't have any proof, and I could be wrong, but I think Collin and his mother are trying to rattle me." She explained the flowers and the letter, the unexpected visit from Agatha Wells, and then gestured to her light fixture. "And then I came home to this."

Samuel said nothing for a moment as he processed the details. "I think you need to be more cautious. These people are dangerous."

"Collin is dangerous. His mother is desperate to protect him from the consequences of his decisions. She's guilty of being a terrible mother, an even worse foster mother, and I think she wants me off balance, but I'm not convinced she's a homicidal maniac."

She certainly couldn't rule it out, but there was no evidence to suggest it at the moment.

"I know you have work to do, and I don't want to keep you any longer. I'll call if I hear or see anything else unsettling."

Samuel tapped a finger on his sidearm, still concerned. "Do you want me to check the house before I leave?"

"That's not necessary. All the doors and windows were still locked when I got home, and the alarm was still armed."

Reluctantly, he nodded. "Okay. I'll be patrolling nearby tonight, so I won't be far if you need me."

She thanked him and watched him descend the steps and climb into his squad car. Wrapping her cardigan tighter around herself, she cast the darkness one last wary look and then shut the door.

If the events of tonight were Mrs. Wells's attempt to frighten Shannon into backing off her son's case, the woman only managed to strengthen her resolve. The more intimately she understood Holly's situation, the more determined she was to put Collin away for the rest of his life.

5

*T*he distant sound of a heartbeat filled Shannon's ears as she ran her hands along a rough wooden surface, feeling for a crack that she could widen with her nails.

She couldn't breathe in this coffin-sized box, couldn't capture enough air to scream.

The heartbeat grew louder, hammering against her eardrums, and she woke abruptly, the dark lid of the box dissolving into the creamy white plaster of her living room ceiling. Shannon pressed a hand to her chest and tried to catch her breath.

She must have dozed off on the couch.

It was a wonder she slept at all; after last night, every shifting shadow and creaking board had sent her blood pressure spiking.

She grabbed a fistful of her shirt and puffed the material, letting the air cool her sweaty skin. What a horrid dream. She pushed herself up against the pillows, the sudden shift sending the folder on her stomach sliding to the floor.

Photographs spilled across the area rug, and she leaned over to pick up the one she'd been reviewing before falling asleep: a wooden box.

Shannon wasn't claustrophobic, and she had no fear of being buried alive, but the occasional nightmare was par for the course when becoming intimately familiar with cases this heartrending.

When Holly was just a child, her foster brother would force her down the basement steps and into an old gun chest, where he would lock her in for hours, sometimes days. This wooden crate was his attempt to revive one of his favorite childhood games.

Disgusted, Shannon tossed the photograph onto the coffee table.

A distant knock drew her attention, and she recognized the heartbeat-like rhythm that had woken her. Someone was at the front door.

Pushing back the blanket, she got to her feet. She often forgot how old she was until she tried to move, and then every joint in her body made a sound reminiscent of a herd of children running across bubble wrap.

Fifty was approaching too quickly.

She massaged her lower back as she stepped over her scattered notes and headed down the hall.

She caught her reflection in the entryway mirror and grimaced. Time had stripped the color from her roots and etched deepening lines around her eyes and mouth. A night of restless sleep hadn't helped matters.

She smoothed her fingers under her puffy gray eyes and sighed.

Rick used to call her beautiful; now she was an antique that people would probably describe as gracefully aged or refined. No amount of makeup or anti-aging cream could replenish the youthful glow she'd lost in her thirties. She had tried most of the brands available.

Did Rick still think she was beautiful?

"What a ridiculous question," she muttered to herself, sweeping her unkempt hair up into a ponytail and turning away from the mirror.

Another series of taps, more insistent this time, wore out the last of her uncaffeinated patience. "I'm coming!"

She brushed aside the curtain that covered the narrow window to the right of the door, and squinted into the morning light. The halo of brightness dimmed as her eyes adjusted, outlining the man on her front porch.

Rick.

She groaned inwardly and let the curtain fall shut before swinging open the front door.

He stood with his hands resting on his belt, irritation in every line of his body. "I spoke to Sam."

"Of course you did." She couldn't keep the note of exasperation from her voice. Samuel could go days without speaking—he was a man of few words—but he couldn't keep quiet about this for more than twelve hours? She widened the door and stepped aside. "Come on in."

There was no point in giving the neighbors something to gossip about by arguing on the front porch.

She walked into the living room and stilled, horrified by the clutter. She had left this room just a minute ago, but now that Rick was here, she became aware of every sock, used tissue, and empty dish scattered throughout the room.

And when was the last time she dusted?

She swiped a finger across the table beside her and cringed at the clean streak left behind on the surface. A while. It had definitely been a while.

"Why didn't you call me last night when you got home and found the broken lightbulb? I would've come . . ." Rick appeared in the archway beside her, and the sight of the living room seemed to momentarily distract him. "Did somebody break in too? Or are you still this horribly disorganized?"

She rolled her eyes and scooped up a sock, balling it in her fist. "Not everyone is as neat as you." She had no idea where the other sock was hiding— probably under a cushion. "With my workload, cleaning isn't exactly at the top of my to-do list."

"I can see that." He picked up a decorative pillow, dusted it off, and set it on the couch. He rescued a few more, then frowned. "What is it with women and pillows? Holly's got enough of them to supply an orphanage, and you're not far behind."

"This coming from the man who buys Holly another purple pillow every time he sees one. Her stockpile is your doing. You spoil her."

"Maybe. But why do *you* have so many?"

Because they fill the empty space, she thought. But it didn't seem to matter how many pillows or pieces of furniture she stuffed into each room, there was a gaping void that couldn't be filled by material things. "I'm a woman. I don't need any more reason than that to enjoy pillows."

Rick rested a hip on the back of the couch, watching her with an unreadable expression as she tidied the room. His tone was calmer than she expected when he broached the subject he'd come here to discuss. "Why didn't you tell me about the flowers and letter when I was in your office yesterday?"

She picked up a towel and lined up the corners, folding it into a rumpled square to give herself time to think. "Honestly, there was no point. The letter was disconcerting, but it wasn't threatening."

"There are different kinds of threats and you know it. The fact that they knew what you were wearin' means they were watchin' you."

She tried to smooth the wrinkles from the towel. "I realize that."

"You told Sam the flowers were sent anonymously."

She didn't miss the concern in his statement, and she knew where his thoughts had taken him. Nine years ago, one of her cases involved the prosecution of a man with deep gang affiliation, and several members of that gang sent her anonymous threats and disturbing gifts.

"I don't think it has anything to do with Martinez or his gang." She placed the towel on the chair beside her and crossed her arms. "It's been nine years. And the message suggests it has something to do with one of my current cases."

"How many are you workin' on right now?"

"I don't know the exact number. I'm overseeing several that my ADAs are working, but Collin's case is the only one I'm personally taking the lead on at the moment."

"You think Collin's mother is behind the flowers and letter?"

"Her unexpected visit just hours later certainly makes me suspicious." She picked up an empty oatmeal bowl and looked around, trying to figure out where to put it. "Maybe she was hoping the letter would knock me off balance and leave me more agreeable to her request."

Rick's eyes narrowed. "What request?"

"Leniency for her son. She's convinced that he's innocent, and that Holly is fabricating the abduction and assault to humiliate him. She all but accused me of enabling Holly's so-called lies by allowing her to testify."

"Did she threaten you?"

"Not really. At least not in any way that would stand up in court. She chooses her words carefully." That seemed to be a Wells family trait. "And I'm sure she knows that hurting me would accomplish nothing. If something happens to me, I have ADAs who know Collin's case almost as well as I do, and they'll step up."

"What about Collin's lawyer?"

"Burdock?" He was a highly skilled defense attorney, and she'd come up against him several times in the courtroom. He had a tendency to represent despicable characters with deep pockets. She wouldn't be surprised if the man sought Collin out and offered his services. "He's never taken things beyond the courtroom before, and I can't imagine him jeopardizing his reputation or career for a client."

Rick straightened and rubbed a hand over the back of his neck. "You're sure this is all just a scare tactic?"

"I am. But since checking it out will make you feel better, the flowers came from Pastel Petals, a floral shop about two blocks from my office." She wrote the information down on a scrap of paper and handed it to him.

He studied it, then tucked it into his jacket pocket. An odd expression crossed his face, and when he pulled his hand out, a Ziploc bag came with it.

There were two pastry-looking blobs in it and a note stuck to the outside of it.

"Please give this to Shannon when you see her," he read aloud. "Love, Holly."

Shannon accepted the bag and studied the deformed pastries. "Are these . . . muffins?"

Rick shrugged. "I'm not sure there's a name for them. Some sort of cookie-scone-biscuit."

"Did you try one?"

"I have the . . . privilege of tryin' everythin' Holly bakes. Sometimes the recipes turn out perfect."

"And the other times?"

"My taste buds wanna curl up and die."

Shannon opened the bag and sniffed, recoiling from the unusual scent. Where had she put the Pepto

Bismol? Something told her she was going to need it after eating one of . . . whatever these were. "Any idea what's in them?"

"I can tell you what's *not* in them. No eggs, no butter, no sugar. She used applesauce. *Unsweetened* applesauce and water." He grimaced. "She's findin' recipes on some website called . . . Pinktress or somethin'. These people—they do not know how to bake."

Shannon bit back a smile as he butchered the name of the popular website. "At least she's trying."

She had to admire Holly's spirit of determination in the face of repeated failure. The young woman was not a quitter.

Rick surveyed the room with a pained expression. "You want me to stay and help tidy up?"

She definitely wanted him to stay, but that desire had less to do with housework and more to do with his company. She missed him. Not that she had any right to, considering she was the one who filed for divorce.

"No, I think the cleaning is going to have to wait. I have a lot of trial preparations to get done, and I need to focus."

Rick nodded. "Are we still meetin' at the courthouse this afternoon?"

"Yes, that's the plan."

She needed to make sure Holly was familiar with her surroundings and the process. It would give her less to be anxious about during the days leading up to her testimony.

"All right." Rick tucked his hands into his jacket pockets. "But I need you to grab me a lightbulb, because I'm fixin' up the porch before I go, and I'm not leavin' until you have the alarm set and the door locked."

She expected nothing less.

6

*H*olly pulled her damp hair over one shoulder as she walked out of the bathroom, twisting it into a long braid.

She paused at the end of the hall when her eyes snagged on the television. She'd forgotten to turn it off when she left the room to shower, and the sitcom had been replaced by a local talk show.

Collin's face flashed across the screen as the host discussed the upcoming trial, and the hot chocolate in Holly's stomach congealed into a nauseating mass.

Even from a photograph, her foster brother's frosty eyes seemed to fixate on her, peeling away the protective layers she had wrapped herself in after her shower.

She rushed forward and grabbed the remote, her fingers trembling as she switched off the TV.

It was bad enough that she saw his face every night in her dreams. Now it was in most of the local newspapers, on the television, splattered across the internet. She couldn't escape him.

How are you gonna face him in court when you can't even look at a picture of him, fear whispered. *You can't. You'll fall apart and throw up in front of everyone.*

That was actually pretty likely. She tossed the remote back onto the couch and padded to the living room window in her slippers. She needed a distraction from the worry and fear trying to smother her.

She had tried journaling, baking, reading her Bible, reorganizing the movie shelf—this time by color rather than genre—but nothing had worked. Maybe a run would help burn away some of the anxiety pulsing through her veins.

Her appointment with Shannon at the courthouse was in two hours. She could squeeze in a long, therapeutic jog and a pit stop at the candy store for a bag of sugary deliciousness. She might need another shower afterward, but that's okay.

Riley bumped her thigh as he sat down beside her, and she patted his head. "Wanna go for a run?"

His ears perked up. He had some energy to burn too.

Giving up on the unfinished braid that had unraveled when she lunged for the remote, Holly twisted her hair into a messy bun on the top of her head and went to change. She chose an inconspicuous outfit, complete with an oversized sweatshirt, and her grape-purple sneakers. She did a quick visual check in the mirror.

Nope, no guy was going to look at her twice. Perfect.

She attached Riley's leash and stepped out into the long hallway, stiffening when she noticed one of the other tenants grabbing his newspaper off the hallway floor.

He shot her a dark look as he straightened. "You think maybe you could avoid waking up the whole apartment building at least one week out of the month?"

There were probably twenty people living on this floor, and Holly had disturbed all of them more than once with her screaming night terrors.

Her throat tightened with guilt and embarrassment. "I'm sorry, Mr. Baker."

"Yeah." He tapped the newspaper against his open palm. "You're always sorry." He disappeared back into his apartment and slammed the door.

Holly cringed. If she could shield the people around her from her fear and pain, she would, but there was nothing she could do when anxiety twisted her dreams into nightmares.

She tugged Riley's leash. "Come on, Rye, let's go."

They hit the ground running.

Holly's feet pounded the pavement at a steady pace, the cold air burning down her windpipe into her lungs. She let her body sink into the comforting rhythm, her gaze drifting over familiar shops and faces.

She kept a tight grip on Riley's leash as he trotted beside her, for his protection and the protection of any man who made the mistake of thinking she was approachable.

She turned a corner, and her pace slowed as the scorched ruins of a familiar brick building came into view. The structure—roped off with caution tape—was condemned and waiting to be demolished.

Holly stopped on the outside of the tape and wound Riley's leash tighter, keeping him close. She had knelt right here the night that a raging fire devoured the inside of the building, killing seven women and children.

She could still smell the smoke wafting from her memories, see the ash drifting down from the sky like snow, and her heart panged with regret.

This place had been her safe haven for nearly a year. She'd hidden within its walls, trying to heal along with the other battered women and children.

Riley sniffed the area with excitement as they walked the perimeter toward the back of the structure where a window to the pantry used to be. That part of the building had collapsed, but Holly could still envision it.

About three years ago, she'd broken that window and climbed through it, hoping for a warm and safe place to sleep. The woman who ran the shelter caught her raiding the pantry shelves, but instead of calling the police, she offered her food and shelter.

Accepting that kind offer had been a mistake. She never should've stayed there.

Even though she moved out and into her own apartment, Collin made it his mission to destroy any place where she might feel safe from him. By staying at the women's shelter, she had painted a target on it.

Collin didn't toss the flaming bottles through the windows that trapped the women inside; he left that task for his puppet—a woman he chose for three reasons: because she was desperate and moldable, because Holly cared for her, and because she knew the shelter inside and out.

Like the women and children who burned to death that chilly March night, Rachel Glass had sought refuge in this shelter more than once. She was a victim of prolonged spousal abuse, and when Holly met her, the woman was in so many pieces that she could barely function.

Collin took Rachel's brokenness, her desperation to be safe, and used it to his advantage. He promised to protect her from her husband if she agreed to do everything he asked of her.

And then he sent her after the people Holly cared about. Rachel nearly ran Jordan down in the street. She tried to abduct a little girl Holly was looking after— the sole survivor of the shelter fire—and when she failed to capture eight-year-old Maya, she took Jace instead.

For the longest time, Holly was angry with her for her part in everything that happened. But she had to let that anger go, because she knew how it felt to be so desperate to feel safe that you would do almost anything.

The difference between them was that Rachel's mind and spirit had been shattered long before Collin discovered her. Whatever resilience she had was gone; whatever hope she'd clung to had long faded away.

In the end, Rachel was just another victim of Collin's manipulative games.

Riley's head lifted from the spot he was investigating, and his ears cocked.

"What is it, Rye?" Holly scanned the area around them, searching for whatever had drawn his attention.

A growl rumbled in his chest, and he took a step forward.

Something shifted behind a dumpster, and Holly gripped his leash tighter. "I think maybe we should go." She had no interest in meeting whatever or whoever was lurking behind the large metal bin. "Come on." She gave his leash a tug and started in the direction of home.

7

*M*arx opened the door to Pastel Petals, and his gaze swept over the rows of colorful blooms before landing on the employee seated behind the counter.

The kid, with his facial piercings and black lipstick, was not who he expected to find wrapping up cheerful bundles of flowers.

"Excuse me . . ." He checked the name tag, pinned over the screaming face of a rock star on the kid's T-shirt. "Robbie."

The boy behind the counter looked up from his cell phone and shook the dark bangs from his eyes. "That's not my name."

"It's on your name tag."

"Who says it's my name tag?"

"It's on your shirt, so either it's yours or you stole it, in which case I should inform you that theft is a crime." He unclipped his badge from his belt and propped it on the counter.

The kid sighed with shoulder-sagging exaggeration. "Did my parents send you? Is this one of those scared straight things?"

"No, this is a flower thing."

Robbie straightened with interest. "Was someone stabbed through the heart and a bundle of black roses left on their corpse?"

Marx stared at him for a long second, unsure how to respond to the alarmingly specific, morbid question. "No, nobody was stabbed through the heart today, but I'll keep you in mind if that particular body turns up."

The kid blew out a disappointed breath. "Nothing exciting ever happens."

"Is the owner or manager available?"

"Nah." He grabbed a notepad and pen. "So, what kind of flowers do you want?"

Marx tapped his fingers on the countertop as he considered trying back later, but there was no guarantee a manager or owner would be available then either.

"I have a question about an arrangement delivered yesterday mornin'."

"Was something wrong with the flowers?"

"They were unwelcome."

Robbie's pierced eyebrows knitted. "Oh, well that's not my fault."

"I never said it was."

"Unwelcome flowers usually mean an ex. If she has an ex-boyfriend or husband . . . or both, you should look at them." He threw up his hands. "Just like that, solved your case for you."

"*I'm* the ex."

"Oh, well, that's awkward."

Marx exhaled an irritated breath through his nose. "Could you check on the order for me? They were delivered to Shannon Marx."

Robbie sighed and turned toward the computer, his fingers tapping across the keyboard. "Shannon Marx, Shannon Marx. Yeah, there she is. I delivered the flowers to a building downtown. The old lady at the reception desk didn't even tip me."

"Was the order placed yesterday or was it ordered in advance?"

"Yesterday."

"In person or by phone?"

"In person."

Marx scanned the corners of the shop. "Where are your cameras?"

"Uh, we sell flowers, so . . ."

"No security system?"

"We got locks on the door." He snapped an imaginary dead bolt. "Most people pay by card, so unless someone really wants some tulips, robbery's kind of pointless."

"Did the person who purchased the flowers pay with a card?"

Robbie clicked the mouse a few times. "Yeah, but it was one of those prepaid Visa cards. No name, so . . ."

Marx tried to keep the frustration from his voice. "You said you took the delivery. Did you also take the order?"

"Yeah. She handed me an envelope to pass along and then . . . you know"—he tapped his phone and checked a notification before flicking it away with a finger—"I dropped the order off."

Marx wasn't going to be able to hold the kid's wandering attention much longer. He pulled out his notepad and pen, prepared to take down details. "Can you describe the woman?"

Robbie shrugged again. "Old. Like my grandma. But she had a hat on and a scarf around her face, so ..."

If this kid ended a sentence with "so" one more time, Marx was going to snap. "Was she tall, short, fat, thin?"

"My mom says I'm not supposed to call people fat because it's anti body-positive."

Marx stared at him. What in the world was anti body-positive? "How would you describe her then?"

"Round, I guess."

"Short? Tall?"

Robbie held out a hand level with Marx's nose. "Like somewhere in there."

Marx was five ten, which put the woman around five feet five inches. He made a note. "Could you tell if she was white, black, Hispanic, Asian?"

Robbie squirmed in his chair. "I'm not comfortable with that question."

"People come in a wide range of colors, Robbie. There is nothin' to be uncomfortable about."

"My mom says it's racist to identify people by their color."

"Racism is a prejudice against people with a different skin color. Are you prejudiced against people who look different than you?"

"No."

"Then it's not racism. It's an unbiased observation. And the customer was . . . ?" He waited for the kid to fill in the blank.

"White, I guess."

"What about her eye color and hair color?"

"She had a hat on, so I couldn't see her hair. But she had blue eyes." Robbie tapped his phone again, checking another message. "Can we be done now? I have a video date with my girlfriend."

Marx scribbled down the last detail and closed his notebook. "We're done for now. Enjoy your . . . date."

He stepped out into the wintery air and sighed, his breath disappearing in a cloud of steam.

The woman who purchased the flowers sounded like Agatha Wells, but even if he could prove it, he couldn't arrest her. Sending flowers with unsettling messages wasn't a crime.

The only thing he could do was find out where she was staying and make sure she didn't come anywhere near his girls. He pulled out his cell and dialed Sully, the computer analyst who worked with the department.

The man answered just before the call went to voice mail, his words mangled by a yawn. "It's Sunday. I'm sleeping."

"I guess it's a good thing you can talk in your sleep."

There was a pause. "Should I be creeped out that you know I talk in my sleep?"

Marx had walked in on him more than once while he was asleep at his desk. The man could carry on a conversation while asleep and not remember a word of it.

"Creeped out, no. But you should probably be embarrassed by some of the bizarre nonsense you say."

Sully grunted. "I wish I could remember. What do you need?"

"I need you to find out everythin' you can on Agatha Wells, Collin's mother. She paid Shannon a visit, and I'm concerned she might be up to somethin'."

"I'll see what I can find out."

Marx thanked him and disconnected. There was nothing more he could do with this investigation until Sully got back with him.

He checked the time. He needed to pick up Holly and take her to the courthouse.

8

*H*olly tucked her cold fingers into the pouch of her sweatshirt as she stepped into the courtroom.

Marx had arrived to get her from the apartment just minutes after she returned from her run, and she didn't have time to change. Her ponytail was still damp with sweat, and ash still clung to her sneakers.

Shannon had lifted an eyebrow at her appearance when she walked into the courthouse, but she didn't comment.

Holly took in the details of the expansive courtroom from just inside the doorway. The high walls were paneled in a dark wood, and there were rows of benches.

Over the past few months, she had watched every fictional courtroom drama she could find, trying to prepare herself for the day she would be in this room. Marx made her promise to stop watching Law & Order, though, because it was only making her more nervous.

She stared at the rows of benches, imagining them filled with strangers—an audience waiting for the show to begin.

Voicing the events of her abuse in front of the judge and jury would be difficult enough, but if there were going to be spectators and reporters . . .

"Shannon."

The rapid clacking of Shannon's heels on the hardwood floor stopped halfway down the aisle, and she turned to look back. "Is something wrong?"

"Are there gonna be a lot of people?"

Shannon gripped her briefcase with both hands as she considered the question. "It's an open trial, meaning there will likely be photographers and journalists present for most of it."

Holly's stomach cramped at the thought of people wandering in off the street to watch, journalists scribbling down every painful, humiliating detail.

"But in nearly every case involving sex crimes, the judge clears the courtroom for the victim's testimony," Shannon said, her voice breaking into Holly's thoughts.

"So, when I testify . . ."

"The only people in the courtroom will be your loved ones and individuals essential to the proceedings."

Holly's attention drifted toward Marx, who lingered in the hallway on his phone. He'd promised to be in the courtroom during her testimony.

"I know all of this can be a bit overwhelming at first, but it gets easier," Shannon said.

Holly doubted the second time walking down this aisle would be any easier than the first. Collin would be present the second time, and his cold eyes would be on her the moment she stepped through the door.

"Come on up here with me." Shannon motioned for her to follow before starting forward.

She walked with such poise—spine straight, eyes up, feet gliding gracefully across the floor. Holly straightened her shoulders and tried not to shuffle her feet as she approached the front of the room, hoping to mimic at least a fragment of Shannon's confidence.

Shannon pushed open the small gate that divided the courtroom and waited for Holly to join her. "The Clerk will have you raise your hand and swear to tell the truth, and then you'll have a seat here." She placed her hand on the witness stand.

Holly stepped into the small cubicle and sat down in the wooden chair, biting back a sigh of frustration when only the tips of her toes grazed the floor. It was difficult to project confidence when her feet were dangling above the floor like a nine-year-old's. She wiggled her way to the front of the seat.

Shannon smiled. "We can add a stool for you to rest your feet on if that's more comfortable."

Asking for a shorter chair was probably out of the question, so the stool would have to do. "Yes, please."

Shannon nodded, apparently making a mental note of it. "This is where you'll be when you give your testimony."

Holly could see the entire courtroom from this position, which meant everyone in the courtroom would be able to see *her*. That was an awful thought.

"Rick and I will be right over there." Shannon gestured toward the table behind her. "You'll be able to see both of us the entire time."

Holly's gaze shifted to the opposite table, where Collin and his lawyer would probably sit, and her palms began to sweat. It was closer than she expected. It was . . . how many feet was that? Seventeen? Twenty? Maybe it was only fifteen. A stretch of open space that offered no protection. Collin could cover that distance in seconds, and she would have nowhere to go.

"Holly."

A hand covered hers, and she jerked, swinging her gaze to Shannon, whose gray eyes regarded her with compassion.

"Even if Collin wanted to attack you, he would never get to you."

Holly had heard those words before, but she'd learned over the years that if Collin wanted to get to her, he would always find a way.

Shannon squeezed her hand, trying to reassure her. "There will be security officers in the room, and if he tries anything, they'll intervene."

"I bet I get to him first," Marx said, walking down the aisle to join them.

Shannon cast him a reproachful look and then gave Holly's hand another comforting squeeze. "But you're not going to have to worry about any of that, because nothing is going to happen."

Holly's attention drifted to the jury box lined with empty chairs. Those chairs would be filled with strangers during her testimony, people ready to dissect her words and question her actions: why didn't she fight harder, what did she do to attract his attention, why were her details so vague?

Much of those four days were a haze of pain and exhaustion. She couldn't remember how many times Collin came into the room, how many times he hit her, choked her. The defense attorney would probably use the gaps in her memory against her, but she didn't want to remember every detail. What she did remember was hard enough to cope with.

Her gaze moved back to the defense table. It was close to the aisle, which meant she would have to pass within just a few feet of her foster brother.

"Marx."

"What, sweetheart?"

She tried not to sound as anxious as she felt. "You're gonna walk me down the aisle, right?"

He lifted an eyebrow. "If you ever meet a man worthy of you, I will gladly walk you down the aisle."

Heat crept into Holly's cheeks. "That's . . . not what I meant."

He smiled. "Yes, I'm gonna escort you to and from the witness stand, and I'm gonna sit right here behind Shannon while you testify."

That, at least, was a small comfort. She returned her attention to the empty chair where Collin would likely sit throughout the trial. The thought of seeing him again, of being so close to him, made her want to puke. But if she was ever going to reclaim her life, she needed to take a stand and speak the truth.

9

Home at last.

Shannon closed the door with a grateful sigh and kicked off her heels. She still had a lot of work to do, but she was going to do it from the comfort of her couch with a glass of wine in her hand.

And maybe some chocolate. She still had a few raspberry truffles left that would pair nicely with a rich Merlot.

Pulling off her leather gloves, she punched in the alarm code—the date of the first day she met Rick. No matter how strained their relationship was now, remembering that day always made her smile.

She'd been studying at a café, when a man decided to invite himself to her table. She dismissed his repeated advances and asked him to leave, but he seemed to take her rejection as a challenge, and sat down in one of the empty chairs.

Before the uncomfortable situation could escalate any further, a shadow descended over her corner booth. She looked up to see the handsome, green-eyed man who had caught her attention earlier.

He'd stepped out of the line he'd been waiting in for almost ten minutes, and fixed her unwelcome breakfast companion with a hard look. "Is there a reason you're botherin' my girlfriend?"

Shannon blinked, more surprised by the Southern drawl than his words. Where on earth was he from?

The uninvited breakfast guest, whose breath reeked of coffee, sat back in his chair with a frown. "You two are together?"

"What part of the word *girlfriend* did you not understand?"

Clearing his throat, the man pushed back from the table and stood. "I'll just leave you two to your breakfast then."

Her handsome rescuer visually stalked the man until he left the café, then turned back to her. "Sorry for the intrusion. Just looked like you needed a little help. I'll let you get back to your book now."

When he turned to leave, she released a frustrated breath. "That's it? Apparently we're dating and I don't even get to know your name?"

He smiled, the expression sending warmth flooding through her stomach. "Rick."

"Well, how long have we been seeing each other, Rick?"

He folded his arms. "Since I walked through the door, so . . . at least ten minutes."

She laughed and gestured to the now empty chair. "Join me for breakfast and maybe we can make it thirty?"

They spent two hours at that table, getting to know one another. He was a rookie officer at the time, she was in law school. And oh how he made her laugh.

71

The smile faded from her lips as she punched in the last digit of the code and armed the alarm. Rick was the love of her life, and letting him go had been the most painful thing she'd ever done.

She thought it was the best option at the time, but she was beginning to doubt that decision with every passing day. Time and distance were supposed to help both of them move on, but she had no interest in dating, and Rick still wore his wedding ring.

A heavy thump on the front porch wrenched her from her thoughts, and she stepped back from the door, her eyes dipping down to check the dead bolt. Locked.

Was the person who broke her lightbulb back with more violent intentions?

She fumbled her phone from her purse, but just as she was about to call for help—her thumb hovering over Rick's speed dial—it rang. She frowned at the caller, and then swiped her thumb across the screen to answer. "Mr. Burdock."

"I'm sorry to bother you so late, Ms. Marx, but it's important."

"Unless your client has agreed to plead guilty to all charges, we have nothing more to discuss."

"If we could speak face-to-face, that would be better." A quiet tap of a knuckle came from the other side of the door.

Shannon padded forward and peered through the peephole, disconcerted to find Collin Wells's defense attorney standing on her porch. Rick had asked if the man might be involved in the intimidation tactics against her, and she hadn't thought it likely until now. "Mr. Burdock, this is highly inappropriate."

"I realize that, and I apologize, but your office is closed, and I don't think this can wait until morning."

Shannon disconnected the call and gripped the dead bolt, debating the wisdom of opening the door, then unlocked it and pulled it inward.

She fixed the young man on her porch with a distrusting look. Judging by the way he was massaging his knee, the thump she heard was him tripping up the steps in the dark. Served him right for showing up uninvited at nine o'clock at night.

She switched on the porch light Rick had fixed, the sudden brightness causing her unwelcome visitor to squint. "What's so important that it can't wait until morning?"

He gestured to her house. "Could we talk inside? It's cold out here."

She bit back a scoff. "Mr. Burdock, you're defending a man you know to be a violent criminal, which makes me question whether or not you have a conscience. You show up on my doorstep after dark and expect me to let you into my home?" She crossed her arms. "That's not a courtesy I feel inclined to give you."

Indignation sharpened his reply. "Of course I have a conscience, but you and I both know the income is better for defense attorneys. You could make a lot more money if you switched sides."

"Is this a sales pitch? Because I would rather be financially bankrupt than morally bankrupt."

"Obviously we aren't going to agree on this particular subject, which is fine, because that's not why I'm here. I'm here to warn you."

Shannon tried not to react to the alarm that expanded in her stomach. "I've had my fair share of warnings for the weekend, Mr. Burdock, so if this is another intimidation tactic—"

"I don't know what intimidation tactics you're referring to, but they didn't come from me. I don't operate that way."

"So you had nothing to do with the flowers and taunting letter I received yesterday morning? Or the vandalism of my personal property?"

Burdock blinked. "No. I'm sorry those things happened, but I can assure you *I* wasn't involved." There was something in his voice, a nuance of inflection, that suggested he might know who *was* involved.

"I suppose I'll have to take your word for it, but I think we both know your client and his family aren't so uninvolved."

"I can't speak to that."

She sighed, her patience wearing thin. It had been a long day, and she just wanted to unwind. "I don't know what this visit is about, Mr. Burdock, but if you're here to try to strike a deal at the last minute and plead for leniency, you're wasting your time and mine. I'm not interested."

"On the contrary, I think you should come at Wells with everything you have."

Shannon couldn't decide if he was being genuine or arrogant. "That's an odd thing to say to the person prosecuting your client."

"He's no longer my client. He fired me this evening."

That caught her by surprise. "Why would he do that?"

"He claims I don't adequately represent him, but I expect it has more to do with the fact that I won't do things his way."

Burdock was an exceptional attorney; if a client could afford him, they didn't let him go. Unless . . . "He asked you to do something you don't agree with, and you declined."

Burdock cleared his throat. "My conversations with him are still bound by attorney-client privilege, so I can't say much, but I informed him that I won't be a party to witness intimidation."

"Go on."

"He's taken up art while awaiting trial, and he wanted me to deliver a sketch to a particular young lady, and before you ask, this request took place before he fired me, so I will not testify to it in court."

"What was the subject of this artistic piece?"

Burdock shifted his feet, visibly uncomfortable. "It was a . . . small . . . bird."

Outrage rolled through Shannon. "A *little* bird?"

Burdock winced and nodded. *Little Bird* was the nickname Collin had given Holly, because when he trapped her, her shallow breaths and trembling body reminded him of a terrified little bird.

"Even if I hadn't recognized the intended reference, delivering that sketch to your witness would've been unethical. The protection order she has against Collin Wells forbids any form of contact outside the courtroom."

"He has no respect for protection orders." Shannon rubbed at her arms, her mind working through the possible consequences of these circumstances. "Is Holly in danger?"

Burdock paused before answering. "Her testimony threatens his freedom. But so does a dedicated prosecutor."

Shannon thought back to the unexpected visit from Mrs. Wells, the way the woman sat forward in her chair while her back was turned. Maybe she should've had her cup of tea tested for drugs or poison after all.

"Regardless of what you may think of me, Ms. Marx, I don't want to see any harm come to this young woman or to you."

"Then give me something to work with. Something I can use against him." When Burdock started to shake his head, she added, "If you didn't think we were in danger, you wouldn't be here."

He sighed. "If he'd made a direct threat of violence, I would be within my rights to tell you, but he made no such threats."

Of course he hadn't. Collin was far too intelligent to make incriminating statements. When he threatened to harm someone, he made certain his words were pointed enough to instill fear in his victim and vague enough to mean nothing to everyone else.

If he intended to frighten or harm Holly, he would need to do it through someone else—a hired hand or a relative. "Have you had any contact with Agatha Wells?"

Burdock grimaced with distaste. "She showed up at my office on several occasions, unannounced."

It seemed she made a habit of dropping in on people.

"Did she give any indication that she might threaten the people opposing her son?"

"Not that I recall, but her entire world revolves around her son. I doubt there's anything she wouldn't be willing to do to protect him."

Shannon was afraid of that. "Do you have any idea where she might be staying?" She would feel more comfortable if Rick could keep an eye on the woman.

"I don't."

Maybe his new attorney would have that information. "Do you happen to know who is representing Collin now?"

"He is."

"That's absurd."

Burdock shrugged. "I've gotten to know my former client unfortunately well over the past several months, and I think this move is strategic. The strongest evidence you have against him is your star witness. If she's as terrified of him as you say she is, then what happens when she finds out she has to speak to him?"

"She'll be too afraid to walk into the courtroom." Shannon rubbed at her temples as that possibility sank in.

"I wish there was something more I could do. But all I can do is wish you luck."

"You know he's guilty, don't you?"

Burdock pressed his lips together, visibly measuring his words before speaking. "I'm not sure my beliefs have any relevance at this point, but I truly hope you're able to sway the jury. For Ms. Cross's sake."

Shannon hoped that too.

He nodded. "Have a good night and watch out for yourself." He headed down the steps and disappeared into the darkness.

Shannon closed the door and leaned back against it, dread pooling in the pit of her stomach. How was she going to fix this?

10

*M*orning came too quickly, and Shannon felt ill-prepared as she arranged her notes on the courtroom table.

She'd scarcely slept after Mr. Burdock's visit, and layers of concealer did nothing to soften the dark circles beneath her eyes. It was an appearance of weakness, one Collin Wells would no doubt try to use to his advantage.

She nursed her third cup of overly sugared coffee as she took her seat and surveyed the room.

Few things were as captivating as the dark and twisted stories splashed across newspapers, and this story in particular left the media salivating for more. They lined the rear wall of the courtroom, pens poised to take notes.

An aspiring courtroom artist was already in motion, defining and shading the cheekbones of the defendant, who sat alone at his table.

With his charcoal-gray suit, porcelain skin, and black hair, Collin Wells was a picture of charm and sophistication—quite a contrast to the disturbed man Shannon knew him to be.

Could the artist capture the coldness in his eyes with her row of colored pencils? Was there a particular shade for soulless monster?

"All rise," the bailiff called out as the judge entered the courtroom, and benches creaked as everyone stood. "This court is now in session. The Honorable Judge Tipper presiding. You may be seated."

Shannon sank back into her chair, nerves twisting in her stomach.

"The People versus Collin Victor Wells." The bailiff handed the docket to Judge Tipper, who briefly reviewed it.

Talbot Tipper—an older man with a halo of feathery gray hair and eyebrows as thick as bushes—was not the judge Shannon would've chosen for this case. Or any case, for that matter. Around the prosecutor's office, he was quietly known as Tame Tipper, because he was so laid-back and lenient. He didn't have the backbone to be a T-ball umpire, let alone a criminal court judge, and Shannon had wallowed in a few glasses of wine when she learned he would be presiding.

Not only did he throw out all the videos she intended to use as evidence, but he ruled any mention of abuse between Collin and Holly prior to last January inadmissible. Since the former abuse was unsubstantiated, he believed it would "unduly bias the jury against the defendant."

Shannon had nearly lost her composure during that meeting. With her luck, though, that would've been the moment Tipper decided to spontaneously sprout a few vertebrae and hold her in contempt.

"Members of the jury," Judge Tipper began, "the court is aware that many of you were exposed to publicity concerning this case prior to being selected as jurors. So I will remind you that each of you has agreed to base your verdict solely on the evidence presented in this courtroom, and it is vital that you hold true to that agreement." He turned his attention to the defense table. "Mr. Wells, are you certain you wish to proceed without legal counsel?"

Collin stood, smoothing the wrinkles from his suit jacket. "Yes, Your Honor, I'm certain."

"Very well. The State of New York versus Collin Victor Wells." He listed the charges, then turned his attention to Shannon. "Ms. Marx, are you ready to give your opening statement?"

Shannon rose. "Yes, Your Honor."

"Proceed."

"Thank you." Shannon offered an appreciative nod to the judge, then turned her attention to the jury.

Half of the jurors were women, a fact that hadn't concerned Shannon when Burdock was her opposition. But Collin was an attractive man with a charismatic personality, and she was worried that he might be able to charm some of the younger women.

"Good morning, ladies and gentlemen. I won't reiterate the criminal charges just read to you, but I would like to introduce you to the defendant's victims." She held up a picture of a beautiful family—a mother, father, and two twin girls with carrot-red pigtails. She pointed to the little girl on the left, whose smile had an edge of mischief. "This is Holly Cross when she was just nine years old."

She painted a picture of the young woman's life for the jury, making her as real to them as she was to the people who loved her.

The first nine years of Holly's life were idyllic—days filled with romping through the woods with her sister and best friend, playing catch in the front yard, and eating ice cream sundaes smothered with marshmallows. But Holly's innocent childhood shattered when the unthinkable happened: a man broke into her family's home in the middle of the night and murdered them.

Holly, terrified and desperate, ran through the woods in search of help. A couple picked her up and took her home with them to Maine. That couple, the first people who showed her kindness after everything had been ripped away from her, were criminals. Drug dealers. They were arrested two years after taking Holly in, and again, her life was turned upside down.

Eleven years old and alone in the world, she drifted through the foster care system, one placement after another, until she landed on the doorstep of Agatha and Victor Wells. That was where she met Collin Wells, the only biological child in a home overflowing with foster children.

"Holly ran away from her eleventh foster home," Shannon said. "I'm not allowed to tell you why, but you can draw your own conclusions from the fact that Holly has made herself clear on more than one occasion that she did not want Collin Wells to be a part of her life."

Collin leaned forward in his chair, and Shannon knew he must be seething inside. She hadn't mentioned the abuse, but she had planted the seed.

Shannon revealed a recent picture of Holly. "Holly built a life for herself here in New York City, doing photography to pay the bills, and living in a small basement apartment." She showed them a snapshot of the outside of the building. "Three dead bolts, a metal door fit for a bomb shelter, and windows so narrow that a person can scarcely fit through them. Holly picked the safest place she could find because she was terrified. Not of the man who murdered her family. But of this man."

She gestured to Collin.

"She did everything within her power to remain invisible, and still, Collin Wells tracked her down. He forced his way back into her life, because, ladies and gentlemen, that is what this man does." She paused for emphasis. "When he wants something or someone, he doesn't accept no for an answer. He taunted Holly and the people she'd grown close with, stalking her until she was forced to move in with a friend and take out an order of protection."

She flipped to the next picture in her hand and held it up for the jury. An Asian woman in a wheelchair with remarkable blue eyes and a contagious smile filled the frame.

"This is Jace Walker, Holly's closest friend. She spends her time mentoring children and other disabled athletes, encouraging them to never give up and to push for their dreams even in the face of adversity. Jace

83

Walker was abducted just three days after Holly, grabbed outside her own apartment by one of the two individuals Mr. Wells enlisted as helpers. This particular helper became his third victim."

She flipped to the headshot of a brunette in her late thirties.

"Rachel Glass. Ms. Glass is not an innocent in this brutal string of events, but she *is* a victim. There's no question that she was complicit in the abduction of both Holly Cross and Jace Walker. But Ms. Glass was neither violent nor unlawful by nature. She was a battered wife, desperate to escape the man who abused her for the entire length of their marriage. Collin Wells used that desperation and molded Rachel Glass into what he needed her to be, manipulating her until she was no longer of use. Her lifeless body was discovered in the same warehouse where Holly and Jace Walker were held captive. The second individual Mr. Wells enlisted is a man by the name of Drew Carson. After Wells was arrested for defying the order of protection Holly had against him, he was taken into police custody. While there, he shared a cell with Mr. Carson. The two men conspired to break into the apartment of the police officer who was safeguarding Holly and kill him. On the night of March 18, just hours after Wells posted bail for himself and Drew Carson, the two men broke into Officer Barrera's apartment. Carson shot Officer Barrera, incapacitating him, which allowed Wells to follow through with his intent to kidnap Holly. He abducted her that night and held her captive in an abandoned warehouse for four days, subjecting her to unthinkable cruelties."

Some of the jurors flicked furtive glances his way, searching for the monster beneath the civilized veneer.

"If not for the intervention of the police department, he would have murdered Jace Walker on March 22. And Holly would have died from extensive internal injuries that same day."

She returned the pictures to her desk and interlaced her fingers in front of her, giving her opening statement time to settle, and then she locked gazes with each of the twelve jurors.

"Collin Wells is here today to answer for his crimes, and I need each and every one of you to help me find justice for his victims."

Shannon returned to her seat, and Judge Tipper cleared his throat. "Mr. Wells, if you wish to offer an opening statement, you may now address the jury."

Collin rose, his chilling eyes sweeping over Shannon as she settled into her chair and crossed her legs. She met his gaze, unflinching. She wasn't naïve. He had no sexual interest in her, but he did have an interest in unsettling her. She didn't intend to give him that satisfaction.

Amusement flickered across his face before he turned his attention to the jury. "I'm sorry you all have to be here," he began, his tone passably apologetic. "You look as tired as I feel, and I'm sure there's somewhere else you would rather be. But I do appreciate your time and willingness to listen. I won't bore you by droning on for too long, but there are a few things I need to set straight."

He slid his hands into his trouser pockets, a line of thought forming between his eyebrows.

"Ms. Marx suggested that Holly ran away from my family's home because . . . well, she didn't say why, because she wants you to imagine the worst. What she clearly knows, and didn't tell you, is that Holly ran away from multiple foster homes. Sometimes that's just what kids in the system do. They run—back to their pasts, toward a different future—and some run simply because it's all they know how to do. Interesting that Ms. Marx singled out my family. I don't blame her, of course. It's her job to make me look guilty, and she's got her work cut out for her."

He looked at her over his shoulder, and she lifted an eyebrow, unimpressed.

"During her time with my family, Holly and I became . . . quite close. I tried to look out for her. Even after she moved to her next placement, I worried about her. She was always so . . . fragile and impressionable and desperate for love. Understandable after all the years she was deprived of affection. I worried about the kinds of relationships and situations she would get herself into. So yes, I looked for her, but I never stalked her. Contrary to what Ms. Marx would have you believe, Holly never asked me to leave. Not once."

Because she was so terrified of him that she couldn't speak. Holly could barely speak *about* him, let alone *to* him.

"And these"—he picked up the sheet of paper from his desk, grimaced in distaste, and dropped it back where it was— "these charges make me sound like a monster. I'm glad Holly has people looking out for her, but they're trying to punish the wrong person. I don't doubt that someone took Holly, that they kept her in that warehouse, and that they hurt her in ways that make me sick to my stomach."

Collin Wells was an excellent showman, and he held the attention of the jury like a magician on a stage. They had no idea they were being played for fools.

"I've seen the pictures submitted into evidence. I don't know if Holly was involved in something she shouldn't have been, or if she just garnered the attention of some sick and twisted individual. But someone hurt her. Someone held her against her will. I'm just not that person. And this story that I colluded with this Rachel Glass woman to abduct Holly and her best friend, while creative, isn't something she can prove. I'll tell you why." He leaned forward and lowered his voice to a comical whisper. "Because I've never met the woman."

A few of the jurors smiled at his theatrics.

"And since I've never met her, it's safe to say I didn't kill her."

He paused for just a moment, his expression turning grave.

"I understand that Ms. Marx has a job to do, and that everyone feels obligated to hold someone accountable for what happened this past March, but this theory that I abducted Holly and locked her away in some abandoned warehouse is based on questionable eyewitness testimony. No evidence. Just . . . what someone else thinks they saw. I'm not an innocent man. Like anyone else, I've done things I regret, things I want to make amends for, but I'm not the monster the prosecution would have you believe I am. She'll try to convince you, but if you look closely, her argument doesn't make sense. All I ask is that you keep an open mind and look for the truth. Thank you."

11

*H*olly gazed at the snow-covered cityscape from the rooftop—buildings draped in sparkling white with icicles dangling from fire escapes.

It was a scene worthy of a photograph.

She lifted her camera and snapped a few photos of the quiet neighborhood, capturing the decorated window of the little antique shop that had opened across the street. She loved the twinkling lights and rose-gold ornaments the owner had hung to celebrate the new year.

She could see the display from her bedroom window, and sometimes when she couldn't sleep, she curled up with a mug of hot chocolate and watched the lights.

A tendril of sadness wrapped around her heart as she snapped the last photo. She wanted to preserve this, all of this, because if the trial didn't go as planned, she would have to leave it all behind.

She was trying to trust that God would work things out, but she couldn't shake the little voice whispering doubt in the back of her mind:

He didn't stop Collin from taking you, from hurting you. What makes you think He'll stop him from getting away with it either?

Her foster brother's fate—and consequently her life—was now in the hands of twelve strangers. If they let him go, he would hunt her down and lock her up in another dark, windowless room until she died.

Run, that terrified little voice whispered. *Run while there's still time.*

The instinct to flee, to protect herself the best way she knew how, was almost overwhelming. She'd packed her travel bag with the essentials this morning, but she prayed she wouldn't have to leave.

She'd built a life here, surrounded by people she loved, and she wasn't ready to give that up. Scrapbooks and photographs would never be enough to fill the void their absence left behind.

With a sigh, she lowered her camera and massaged her throbbing wrist. The cold weather reminded her of every bone that had ever been broken; her wrist, fingers, even her ribs ached.

She sank to her knees on the blanket she'd brought out, and searched through the recent pictures. She squinted and zoomed in when she noticed a person loitering on the street outside Marx's apartment. A mixture of alarm and annoyance flitted through her when she recognized the figure.

It was the big, red-haired man who kept popping up every time she left the apartment. He was pushy and rude, and all he seemed to care about was material for his blog.

The metal door to the roof squeaked open, and Holly stiffened as she twisted to see who'd caught her.

C.C. Warrens

The roof was off limits . . . to anyone who paid attention to signs and locks.

Marx shut the door behind him. "Hey, sweetheart."

His hair was still rumpled from sleep, and he hadn't shaved yet. He'd been asleep on the couch when she snuck out of the apartment. Unbolting the door without waking him should've earned her some kind of stealthy ninja badge. The man could hear a pea hit the floor.

Holly relaxed. "Hey."

He carried a blanket and a coffee mug as he trudged toward her through the snow. "Here."

She tucked her camera into her leather bag and accepted the mug. She peered into it, expecting to find it filled with his nasty coffee, but found tiny chunks of chicken and noodles floating around. "You're having soup for breakfast?"

He dropped down beside her on her blanket. "*You're* havin' soup for breakfast."

She scrunched her nose in disgust. Soup had never bothered her until after she came home from the hospital. She couldn't keep down solid food, and Marx made her various broths and soups every couple of hours.

"Don't you wrinkle your nose. There is nothin' wrong with chicken noodle soup, and don't think I haven't noticed you stopped eatin' days ago."

He pinned her with a look of disapproval, and her shoulders slumped. How did he always know?

91

"I'm just . . ."

"Anxious about the trial, I know. But nauseous or not, you need to eat, sweet pea."

She lifted the mug to her lips, resisting the urge to pinch her nose, and took a sip. She nearly spit it back into the cup. Who decided slimy, chicken-flavored water was a good idea?

She forced her throat to swallow. "Ew."

Marx chuckled. "It'll help warm you up." He wrapped the spare blanket around her and rubbed her shoulders. "You know you're not supposed to be up here, right?"

"Maybe."

"But you picked the lock anyway."

She squinted up at him in mock challenge. "Prove it."

He laughed.

"How'd you know I was up here?" She tried to take another sip of the soup, but she just couldn't do it.

"Turns out nosy neighbors are good for somethin'. Mrs. Neberkins saw you headin' up the steps instead of down, and that had her all out of sorts."

Mrs. Neberkins was the elderly woman across the hall, and she was convinced Marx was some kind of criminal mastermind. She'd called the police on him more than once.

Holly set aside the soup and leaned against him, burrowing beneath his arm to steal some of his warmth. "Maybe she'll follow the trial and realize you're one of the good guys."

"I doubt it."

Marx rested his chin on the top of her head, exhaling a warm breath that ruffled her hair. "Promise me you're not gonna watch the trial on TV today."

The last thing she wanted to do was watch people discuss her abduction and torment in haunting detail. "I won't."

"Good." He kissed the top of her head. "I know you're worried about how things are gonna go today, but you don't need to be. It's all gonna work out."

She wished she shared his faith in the justice system, but in her experience, Collin always escaped consequences.

12

*S*hannon caught herself picking nervously at her nails as she waited for her first witness to enter the courtroom, and she curled her fingers into her palms.

It wasn't the witness examination or even the cross-examination that concerned her; it was the witness.

Sullivan Banderman was, to put it mildly, a free spirit. Much of his free-spirited nature was tattooed across his skin or pierced through his ears, eyebrows, and nose. Combined with his outlandish wardrobe choices, the jury didn't always know how to react.

She was certain he did it on purpose. He enjoyed tipping people off balance.

The rear doors opened and a lanky man in a robin-egg-blue suit strode into the courtroom.

At least he's not wearing the pink one, Shannon thought.

His blond spikes had been tamed with a side part, and he had removed the piercings from his nose and eyebrows, but his choice of shoes—iridescent blue—made Shannon cringe inwardly.

He gave her a small wink and a smirk as he passed by, and she flashed him a censuring look.

They had worked enough trials together to be comfortable with one another, and Shannon fully intended to give him a piece of her mind about his suit and shoes the moment they were alone.

"Mr. Banderman," she said after he took his seat on the witness stand. "Can you tell us a bit about yourself?"

He leaned forward. "Well, first off, ma'am, you can call me Sully. Mr. Banderman makes me sound seventy-five, and uh . . . I'm not quite there yet."

A few members of the jury laughed, and Shannon arched an eyebrow at his use of the word: ma'am. She wasn't that old yet. Though it was getting harder to see past the deepening wrinkles around her eyes these days.

"I'm a computer forensics analyst, and I work with the NYPD," Sully said, returning to the question she had asked. "Which is basically a fancy way of saying I dig up information pertaining to their cases. But I'm not a cop."

"And you're good at your job?"

"Well, I haven't been fired yet," he teased, eliciting a few more chuckles. "But yes, I take a lot of pride in my work and the number of cases I'm able to help solve."

Shannon nodded. "I imagine your skills are frequently put to the test, but I'm interested in one case in particular."

"Yeah, the mystery girl who had me stress-eating a bag of Cool Ranch Doritos." There was a hint of frustration in his voice as he leaned back in his chair.

He hadn't mentioned the Doritos when they were prepping for his testimony, and Shannon wasn't sure how to respond. "I suppose we all deal with our stress differently. I hope they tasted good."

"I didn't really taste them." He leaned forward again, interlocking his fingers on the edge of the witness stand. "I was focused on trying to unravel the mystery Detective Marx dropped in my lap. The night of October 2, he called me from a crime scene and asked me to look into his victim, Holly Smith, who was attacked in the park while walking home. It wasn't the first time a victim was reluctant to talk to the police, so I figured it would be pretty routine."

"But it wasn't?"

"Not by a long shot. At the very least I was expecting to find a driver's license or state ID, an address, a phone number. But there was nothing. I even checked social media sites. The only record I could find of a Holly Smith even remotely close to her description was of a girl who disappeared from her foster home in Maine when she was seventeen. So I contacted the precinct where she was reported missing and had them email me a picture of the girl. Detective Marx confirmed it was her, and then we were able to get her foster placement records. It wasn't until later that we learned her real name is Holly Cross."

"Is it unusual for someone to be so . . . invisible?"

"It's more than unusual. It's practically impossible. Most of us"—he gestured toward the spectators— "leave a digital footprint without even thinking about it. We pay bills, we use a debit card at McDonald's, we post a picture to our Facebook with a GPS tag, we borrow a book from a library."

"So you think this lack of data was intentional?"

"Without a doubt, yeah. I've only encountered two other similar cases. One was a man in witness protection who had been issued a new identity by the government. The second was a woman we later found out had been hiding from an abusive husband, and she dropped off the radar to keep him from finding her."

Shannon folded her arms behind her, gripping one wrist. "Was Holly in witness protection?"

"No. I believe she was hiding. There's no way a person can be that invisible by accident. She had to be making a conscious effort to avoid any traceable records. Up until she gave us a statement the night she was attacked in the park, she was a virtual ghost. That statement put her back on the grid."

"And were her concerns about having traceable records valid?"

"I believe so," Sully said with a bitter twist of his lips. "Because for the first time in my fourteen years with the NYPD, our system was hacked. Someone wormed into our secure database and accessed files, and it wasn't until after the threat was over, that I realized the only files accessed were hers. Someone was looking specifically for Holly Smith."

Shannon made a thoughtful noise. "Using just the information in the police database, would the person looking for her have been able to track her here, to New York City?"

"Absolutely. We didn't have a home address for her, but the park and the café, which came into play later, were noted in the file. People generally eat and shop close to home, so her cyber stalker simply would've had to search the area between those two locations until he found her."

"A process that could take weeks to months?"

Sully puckered his lips in thought. "I've never searched door to door, but even when I have a digital trail to follow, it can take weeks to months to find the person we're looking for."

"And when was the database breached?"

"The end of November 2016."

"Interesting. And Collin Wells showed up less than three months later outside Holly's apartment, which if I'm correct, doesn't have an address of its own?"

"No, it doesn't. It was originally an unattached basement. According to the blueprints I found, the plan was to connect it to the apartment next to it, but it was never completed. The basement address is the same address as the main building. When it was converted into an apartment, no apartment number was registered with the postal service. It's just . . . there."

"So Collin Wells couldn't have figured out where Holly was living by looking it up in the phone book?"

Sully laughed. "No one uses phone books anymore. But no, he would've had to physically search for her residence."

"Thank you, Sully. No further questions at this time."

"Mr. Wells, would you like to cross-examine the witness?" Tipper asked.

Collin stood and approached the witness stand. "What you do is amazing, Mr. Banderman. I can't imagine trying to wade through all that digital information to find a person."

Sully leaned back in the chair and crossed his arms, offering Collin a flat stare. "I'm sure you can imagine it quite well."

Collin's lips curled at the corners. "Tell me, did you ever identify the person who breached the police department's computer system?"

"No, he was careful."

"So, Ms. Marx's imagination aside, there's no evidence that actually connects that breach with my appearance on Holly's doorstep three months later?"

"Nothing solid."

"Meaning the two events could be completely unrelated. Of course, if you're creative enough, you can string a thread between them and make a tenuous connection, as Ms. Marx has demonstrated."

Shannon pushed her tongue between her teeth to keep from grinding them together.

"Thank you for your time, Mr. Banderman," Collin said, returning to his seat.

Sully stared at his feet as he walked away, fixated on something. "You walk like him."

Collin paused and turned back. "Sorry?"

"The man in the videos, whose face is distorted. The man who attacked Holly. You walk like him."

Sully had watched the videos of Holly's abuse countless times, trying to clear up the digital distortion that left them inadmissible. In that time, he learned to care about the girl he'd never met.

Collin's eyes narrowed. "Your Honor, I object to—"

"Ms. Marx," Tipper broke in, lasering her with a look of outrage, as though she could control what came out of her witness's mouth during cross-examination.

Shannon held up her hands. "This was not in my line of questioning, Your Honor. He's speaking of his own accord."

"Mr. Banderman. That will be the last thing you say on that subject. Jury will disregard the witness's last two statements."

But it was too late. Murmurs of videos swept through the courtroom, questions spawning, and several of the jurors watched Collin more closely as he returned to his table.

Tipper shifted his jaw, as though he were pushing a wad of tobacco from one cheek to the other. "Mr. Banderman, you may step down. At this time, we will take a short recess and reconvene in thirty minutes."

He thumped his gavel once, then rose and swept out of the courtroom.

13

Shannon paced the length of the conference room, mentally rehearsing the impending conversation with Rick. She had spent most of last night and this morning searching for any means of opposing Collin's legal maneuver, but he was within his rights.

She'd called Rick as soon as the judge announced a recess, and now she was just waiting for him to arrive at the courthouse.

She wasn't sure how he would react to the news, but she doubted he would absorb it with quiet acceptance.

The conference room door opened and Rick popped his head in, brow furrowed with concern. "Your call sounded urgent. Everythin' okay?"

She folded her arms. "There's something important we need to discuss."

He slipped in and shut the door behind him. "What's wrong?"

She was dreading this conversation, but there was no avoiding it. "I received a visit from Mr. Burdock last night. It seems . . . Collin fired him and has decided to represent himself."

Straightforward and to the point seemed like the best approach, but when silence stretched throughout the room afterward, she questioned whether or not she should've been more delicate.

"You understand that this means there will be no attorney acting as a buffer between Collin and the witnesses," she said.

"No."

She frowned at the ambiguity of his response. "No, as in you don't understand, or no, as in . . ."

"No, as in he does not get to cross-examine Holly."

She understood his feelings, but this wasn't the kind of situation where they could simply take a vote and alter the circumstances.

"Unless he changes his mind and decides to hire another attorney, he *will* be cross-examining all of you. There's no avoiding it."

"I'm not worried about all of us. We're cops, we'll be fine, but I don't want that man anywhere near Holly."

She had already considered that, and she would petition the judge to limit Collin's movement during Holly's testimony. He couldn't be allowed to roam freely through the well of the courtroom like he had this morning. "I'll request that he be required to remain by his desk while Holly's on the stand."

Rick pressed both hands to the table, resting his weight as he considered it, then shook his head. "That's not good enough. He has no business talkin' to her."

"I know it complicates things. I'm the one who promised her she wouldn't *have* to talk to him."

She just hoped that this situation wouldn't undo all of the trust she'd built with Holly over the past six months.

"You don't understand, Shannon. When he speaks to her, he messes with her mind."

Collin had a sixth sense about people's insecurities, and with a single word or phrase, he used them to instill doubt and fear. Something he said to Holly in one of the videos still lingered with Shannon.

You're like the kicked puppy everyone feels sorry for but nobody really wants.

In that one phrase, he reminded Holly of years of rejection, of every foster family that passed her along with a sympathetic smile and best wishes. And he made her doubt that anyone could ever love her and truly want to keep her around.

"You have no idea how long it took to undo the damage he caused with just his words," Rick said.

"That's not going to happen again. She knows now, without a doubt, that you love her. There's nothing he can say to make her question that."

"It's not worth the risk."

"I understand your frustration and concerns, Rick, I do. But you need to accept that he has the right to—"

Rick slammed a hand on the table hard enough to rattle the glass centerpiece. "I don't care about his rights! He didn't afford Holly any rights when he locked her up like an animal for four days!"

Shannon pressed her lips together and waited for his anger to pass.

"He tortured her, Shannon, and now you're tellin' me he has the right to ask her questions about what he did to her?"

"The justice system is imperfect, Rick. You know that. It treats the innocent and the yet-to-be-proven guilty with the same regard."

Rick pushed away from the table and walked to the wall, staring at the plaster as though it might offer a solution to their current predicament. "Can't Holly write her testimony and have it delivered by proxy?"

"It doesn't work that way."

"What about a video? Can we have her record her testimony in a private room so she doesn't have to see him?"

"Assuming she could even tolerate being recorded, which I highly doubt, considering Collin recorded her abuse, he has the right to face his accuser. And as his own counsel, he has a right to challenge her testimony."

Rick swore beneath his breath. It had been a while since she heard him swear like that; it was a testament to the depth of his anger.

"It won't be as bad as you're thinking, Rick. Collin might be a despicable person, but he wants the jury to believe he's innocent. He's not going to accomplish that by demeaning or terrorizing Holly on the stand."

"I'm sure he'll find a way."

"She's a sympathetic witness, and the jury is going to adore her. Even I adore her, and you know I don't bond with people easily."

Rick was Shannon's first real connection. She kept everyone at arm's length—in part, because she didn't know how to connect with people, and in part, because she didn't want anyone to know where she'd come from.

Her colleagues had no idea that she grew up in a home where drugs were more prevalent than food or that her mother was well-known by nearly every man in the town. Shannon clawed her way out of that life and into this one, determined to leave her past behind her.

That was part of the reason she adored Holly. The young woman was determined to escape her past and rebuild an entirely new life, to forge the kind of unbreakable connections her childhood lacked, to make something of herself despite a history of being told that she had very little worth.

They grew up in different times and different circumstances, but Shannon understood Holly, and she even admired her strength.

There was nothing she could do to spare Holly from having to speak with Collin, but she would do everything humanly possible to win this trial for her.

She stepped toward Rick, needing him to listen. "I know you're concerned, but keep in mind that Holly is young, petite, and sweet-natured. When the jury looks at her, they're going to see what you saw the night you met her."

"An innocent girl who needs to be protected."

"Precisely. He won't vilify her, and he won't try to verbally abuse her on the stand. He's smart enough to know that it will turn the jury against him."

"Even if you're right, she's gonna be too terrified to take the stand."

"I know she's going to be scared, and she might try to back out, which is why we need to handle this carefully. We need to prepare her."

"You mean I need to prepare her."

"She trusts you more than she trusts me. But the sooner you tell her, the more time she'll have to adjust."

Rick scrubbed his hands over his face and stared at the ceiling. "Until I'm sure there's no way around this, I won't give her another reason not to sleep at night."

Shannon started to protest, but he muttered a brusque good-bye, wrenched open the door, and walked out. She leaned against the end of the conference table with a sigh.

Maybe relying on Rick to deliver the news was a mistake. If he didn't handle it properly, or he waited too long and Holly refused to testify out of fear, Shannon would be forced to compel her testimony by other means. Means that she didn't want to use.

14

*H*olly's fingers trailed along the spines of the books as she wandered the aisles of the library.

There was something comforting about the scent of books—the way the crisp, inky smell of new pages mingled with the musty sweetness of old.

It reminded her of home, of the dusty collections that lined the shelves of her father's bookstore.

Her fingers dipped into a hollow, where someone had removed a book from the library shelf, and a memory tugged her lips into a smile.

As children, she and her twin sister, Gin, used to race up and down the aisles of the family store, playing peekaboo in the gaps between books. They had spent so many hours there, captivated by leather-bound adventures.

The smile faded from Holly's lips. Sometimes she missed her family so fiercely that her entire body ached. But she was grateful for every memory, even the ones that came with a twinge of sadness.

She toyed with the locket at her chest, the silver pendant holding a precious picture of her family, as she studied the rows of stories waiting to be devoured. She plucked the nearest book from the shelf, a book entitled *Peppermint Peril*, and flipped it over to read the information on the back.

Ooh, a cozy mystery.

She cracked the book open to skim a few paragraphs, and could hardly contain her laughter when the main character began searching her closet for teeny, tiny spy cameras. She reminded Holly of Marx's odd elderly neighbor, Mrs. Neberkins.

She closed the book and started to tuck it into her shoulder bag alongside the manual on driving when the hairs on the back of her neck prickled, sending a whisper of warning down her spine.

Someone was watching her.

She walked stiffly to the end of the aisle and peered out, searching for the source of that familiar unease. When she was living on the run, she'd learned to trust that instinct implicitly, but as her gaze bounced around the quiet library, the only person she saw was another woman typing at a computer.

Maybe her nerves were just playing tricks on her. She chewed on her lower lip and returned to hunt for another book.

She needed something lighthearted and funny. She spotted an interesting-looking book on an upper shelf, a pretty green cover with the title *A Caffeine Conundrum*. That sounded cute.

She stretched onto her tiptoes, but her fingertips fell inches short of her goal. With an annoyed huff, she dropped her heels back to the floor.

Climbing the shelf would probably get her banned from the library, so she needed to find another way. Where were the ladders and step stools?

Didn't the library staff know that not everyone was tall?

She eyed the book, debating her options, when an unexpected male voice from her right made her stiffen. "Need a hand?"

She grabbed the thickest book within her reach, ready to hurl it at the journalist or creep hoping to badger her for details about her abduction. She was tired of being hounded and harassed.

The man raised his hands, but his tone was teasing rather than concerned. "I'm sure tossing books is fun, but if you wanna play catch, I suggest a football."

Recognizing him, the tension melted from her limbs, and she dropped the book back onto the shelf with a thump. "Sorry."

Jordan smiled. "Usually you just throw apples at me."

She rolled her eyes. "I haven't thrown an apple at you since we were kids."

They had been best friends as children—partners in mischief—though Jordan looked nothing like the skinny, nervous boy she remembered. *That* boy would've ducked for cover if she brandished a book, his knees knocking together as loudly as tree limbs on a stormy night.

The man her childhood friend had grown into seemed unshakable. He never hesitated to step between her and danger, and his crystalline blue eyes danced with amusement rather than fear.

Being six feet tall and trained in martial arts probably helped keep his knees from knocking together these days.

"How long were you standing there before you said something?" She hadn't heard or sensed his approach.

"About five seconds. Why?"

She shook her head. "Never mind."

His eyes narrowed suspiciously. "Why, Holly?"

She shrugged a shoulder. "I just . . . felt like I was being watched, but I didn't see anyone."

The amusement left his eyes, and he stepped out of the aisle to scan the area. He must not have seen anything that concerned him, because he rejoined her. "Looks clear."

"I'm probably just anxious." She returned the big book to the vacant space where it belonged. "Are you here looking for more reading material?"

He practically had his own library at home, but his books were stacked in piles against his living room wall rather than organized neatly on a bookshelf. She'd perused the titles the first time she visited, and they all addressed different aspects of the same issue: abuse. Jordan had never been abused, but he wanted to understand her—how she thought, how she felt, why some days were harder than others.

"No, actually I was looking for you. I called a few times, but you didn't answer. I was starting to worry, so I went over to Marx's place."

She groped around in her bag, but her phone wasn't there. "I must have forgotten it." Which was weird, because she always brought it with her when she left the apartment. Of course, she hadn't slept much lately, so occasional forgetfulness wasn't unexpected. Then something occurred to her. "How exactly did you find me?"

"You're a creature of habit. You go to the park to jog, your favorite coffee shop, and the library. I stopped by Marx's apartment, and his nosy neighbor said you left in boots, not jogging shoes."

Mrs. Neberkins, Holly thought with frustration. What did she do, sit by the door all day, waiting for a floorboard to creak so she could spy on people through the peephole?

"And I checked the coffee shop. You stopped there before coming here."

"How do you know that?"

He smiled. "You're the only redhead who always orders hot chocolate with extra, extra, extra marshmallows. The barista remembers you."

"Snitch."

He laughed. "Yeah, she's not exactly a sealed vault."

He was certainly a good private investigator. She had no idea she was so predictable. She would have to go to a tattoo parlor next time, just to throw him off.

"So why were you calling? Is everything okay?" She turned her attention back to the book on the upper shelf as she asked the question.

111

"I just wanted to see if you were interested in tacos for lunch."

Her uneasy stomach rebelled at the thought of food, but she couldn't say no. He'd already accused her of having a "don't eat enough disorder," which was ridiculous. She ate plenty . . . of marshmallows.

"Maybe." She stretched onto her toes, reaching for the green book. If she could manage a few more inches, she could get her hands on it.

"You want me to grab it for you?" Jordan offered.

"No, I can get it." She jumped and her fingertips brushed the edge of the shelf holding the book hostage.

So close . . .

Humor colored Jordan's voice. "I could give you a boost."

She pinned him with a threatening look. "Don't even try it."

He was not picking her up, and she wasn't about to sit on his shoulders like a toddler. She could do this on her own; she just hadn't figured out how yet. She jumped again, her fingers connecting with the spine. The book slid backward, and she released a groan of frustration.

Just as she was reconsidering climbing up the bookcase, Jordan reached over her head and grabbed the book.

"Hey! I almost had it."

"We define *almost* very differently." He handed her the paperback. "It was cute watching you hop for it, though."

Heat pooled in her cheeks, and she stuffed the book into her bag without bothering to read the cover description. After all that effort, it better be good.

Jordan walked alongside her as she headed to the checkout counter. "What are your plans after the trial ends?"

She stilled, fingers wrapped around one of the books in her bag. Did he know that she had packed her travel bag, just in case the justice system failed as spectacularly as she expected?

No, he couldn't possibly know that. He was just asking a polite question.

She pulled the books from her bag and started scanning them, striving to appear relaxed. "Um . . . I guess I don't really know."

"Are you gonna move back into your apartment or stay with Marx?"

Living with Marx was wonderful—he made her feel safe and loved, and he watched goofy movies with her—but she missed the sense of independence that came with having her own place and paying her own bills.

Marx wouldn't let her pay for anything—not just because her crumpled, disorganized money gave him anxiety, but because he believed in taking care of anyone living under his roof.

And then there was the issue of his neighbors being so close that her frequent nightmares disturbed them.

"It would be nice to have my own place again, but I think all the windows are broken."

Collin had broken into her apartment the month before . . . everything happened. She hadn't been back since, but she'd seen it from the outside. All the window frames were boarded over, and bits of glass still glittered around the perimeter.

"Windows are fixable, if you really wanna move back."

Did she? The number of awful things that happened there should've left it feeling tainted, but it still felt like home. It was hers—the first place where she'd truly built a life for herself, where she adopted a pet, where she met the woman who became one of her closest friends.

"I think I do wanna go back eventually. I wanna plant flowers all around the building, and then open the windows—when there *are* windows—and let the sweet smell fill every corner, let the breeze blow through."

Now that she spoke the words aloud, she realized how much she longed for that future, for a life where she could throw open the windows and doors without fear, where she could lie in the grass with her eyes closed and not worry that Collin might grab her while her guard was down.

That future seemed like a fantasy.

"Why don't I go over and check things out when I have time, see how much work there is to do," Jordan said.

She didn't want to tell him that the effort would likely be wasted. Instead, she pulled the key ring from her pocket, removed the apartment key, and placed it in his palm.

He smiled and closed his fingers over it. "Are you ready for tacos yet?"

She pressed a hand to her stomach, trying to decide if she was too nauseous. "I could eat some cheese dip."

"You're gonna eat chips with that cheese dip, right? Maybe a burrito? Something substantial?"

"They have spoons."

He blinked slowly. "You can't eat cheese dip with a spoon, Holly."

She started for the door. "Watch me."

15

$\mathcal{M}$arx placed a magnet over the last photo, affixing it to the whiteboard in the department conference room, then stepped back.

He sat on the edge of the table, his eyes roving over the details surrounding Holly's abduction.

If he could shore up this case another way—find something vital that they overlooked—then maybe Holly wouldn't have to testify. To ensure that, he needed to make certain there wasn't a speck of doubt for Collin to shine a light on.

Unfortunately, the man was manipulative and meticulous, and solidly linking him to his crimes was like trying to fill a colander with water: there were too many holes.

Marx tapped the dry erase marker against his palm in an agitated rhythm as he stared at the list of names under the heading "Deceased."

Collin orchestrated the deaths of seven innocent people before he took Holly, and his weapon of choice had been a broken woman so desperate to escape her abusive husband that she was willing to do anything. With a few carefully crafted lies, he aimed Rachel Glass at the women's shelter where Holly had once sought refuge, and she killed nearly everyone inside.

Marx sighed and erased the names of the women and children who died in the fire.

There was no evidence to connect Collin to those murders, and the only person who could corroborate his involvement—the woman he manipulated into setting the fire—was dead.

According to the medical report, Rachel had fallen to her death, the impact with the cement floor killing her instantly. What the medical report *didn't* say was that Rachel had help falling to her death.

Marx studied the crime scene photo that preserved the woman's murder with disturbing clarity. He hadn't seen her fall, but from Holly's description of events, he could envision it. It infuriated him that Collin forced Holly to watch Rachel die, a moment that still haunted her.

A quiet tap on the door drew his attention, and his partner pushed into the room.

Michael was one of the few detectives in the precinct Marx could tolerate, which was probably why the lieutenant saddled them together. The younger detective's calm and compassionate disposition balanced Marx's irritability and suspicion, and he understood Marx's relationship with Holly in a way that many of the other officers didn't.

Michael grimaced at the whiteboard. "Questioning my work or just torturing yourself?"

Michael had been assigned as the primary detective on Holly's case, a decision that irritated Marx at the time, but Michael had handled Holly's abduction and assault with admirable discretion and thoroughness.

Marx sighed and sat back down on the table. "I don't need the pictures to torture myself."

Ten months had passed since he found Holly's battered body lying on that warehouse floor, but he remembered every gut-wrenching detail as if he'd just left the scene.

"So you just felt like creating a gruesome collage?" Michael took a sip of his coffee as he sidled up to the table, studying the board.

"I need to find somethin' we missed."

"We've been over this material dozens of times. We didn't miss anything."

Marx pointed the marker at a grainy image of someone stepping out of Sam's apartment building after dark, a rolling suitcase trailing along behind him. "We never did find that suitcase, did we?"

"No." Michael sat down beside him. "We looked everywhere around the abduction site and the warehouse. Chances are, Collin had Rachel Glass dump it somewhere we'll never find it."

Like a landfill or a junkyard. Finding it and recovering prints and DNA would take a miracle at this point.

Michael shook his head in disgust. "I still can't believe he stuffed her in a suitcase."

Collin couldn't just carry Holly's unconscious body out of Sam's apartment building without drawing attention. The only option was to conceal her, and she was small enough that he could pack her into a large rolling suitcase.

"Holly isn't a person to him. She's just somethin' to play with." And if Holly had woken up in that cramped piece of luggage, her panic would've only amused Collin more.

Michael set his coffee aside and crossed his arms. "Okay, so what are we hoping to find?"

"I don't know. Somethin' that can help us convict Collin without Holly's testimony."

"Does she know about him representing himself?"

"No, and I'm not tellin' her unless there's no other option."

"What about the other victim? The one who lives a couple hours away?" Michael snapped his fingers as he tried to recall the name. "Melanie?"

Melanie Bordeaux bore a striking resemblance to Holly, so much so that they could've been sisters, and it was her similarities that caught Collin's eye. He'd been months away from finding Holly, so he settled for someone who looked like her.

"She refused to identify him as her attacker."

When they first tracked Melanie down, she was so distraught that she was seconds from ending her life and the life of her unborn baby. Holly sat and talked with her, speaking hope and life into her with every breath.

Despite everything Holly shared with her, Melanie still refused to come forward and make a statement that would've helped them get Collin off the streets. Even after she knew that Holly's life was in danger, she chose silence.

Holly and Melanie might share some physical features, but that was where the similarities ended.

Michael took a gulp of his coffee. "She's still not willing to come forward?"

"No, and askin' her to is a waste of breath." Marx turned his attention to the crime scene photos, but no matter how long he studied them, no answers leaped out at him.

The sense of helplessness he'd felt since speaking with Shannon expanded, the weight of it almost overwhelming. Why couldn't he find another way to strengthen this case?

He tossed the marker on the table. "I don't know what to do, Michael. I don't know how to protect Holly from this."

"Maybe you don't have to." Michael seemed to consider his words before continuing. "I know you *want* to protect Holly, but there are some battles you can't fight with your fists or your wit."

"Meanin' what? I'm supposed to stand aside and do nothin' while she faces this monster in court?"

"Not *nothing*. Prayer is a powerful weapon on every battlefield—the physical ones and the spiritual ones. All you have to do is use it."

"And what exactly am I supposed to say? God, please fix this?"

Michael shrugged. "Sure, why not? God hears us, even if our words are inelegant and jumbled."

"I wish He would share His plan for justice in all this mess." He waved a hand at the violence and bloodshed on the board in front of them. "Because I just don't see it."

Michael stood and picked up his coffee. "When God wants us to know what His plan is, we'll know. Until then, trying to puzzle it out will just drive us all crazy. And if you don't mind me offering a bit of advice about Holly . . ."

"Knock yourself out."

"Stop trying to protect her from things you can't protect her from and start trying to strengthen her with prayer. The trials of life come at us whether we're prepared or not, so do the dad thing, and prepare her for what's coming."

. . . .

Marx spent the rest of the evening sifting through files and statements, determined to uncover something, but Michael was right: there was nothing to find.

By the time he reached the second floor of his apartment building, it was late, and he was mentally and physically exhausted.

He slid his key into the lock of his apartment door, but before he could twist it, the door behind him creaked open, the scent of old lady and soap wafting into the hall. He turned to see his elderly neighbor watching him through the slight opening, distrust deepening the wrinkles around her eyes.

He didn't have the patience for her outlandish accusations tonight. "Mrs. Neberkins." He nodded for the sake of politeness.

"You think you can poison me!" She widened her door and flung something at him.

He sidestepped, narrowly avoiding the roundish object that smacked into the wall and bounced to the floor. "What is the matter with you?! You can't just throw things at people."

"I found that blueberry brick outside my door this afternoon."

Marx looked down at the muffin, then bent to pick it up. It was heavy, hard, and wrapped in plastic with purple ribbon tying it shut. He sighed at the sparkly purple spirals dangling down the sides. Holly.

"I'm deathly allergic to blueberries," Mrs. Neberkins snapped.

"I'm sorry to hear that, but I—"

"I know about your illicit activities, and you want me silenced."

Oh for the love of . . .

"I am not a drug dealer or a sex trafficker or whatever else you've dreamed up. Holly is my guest, not my prisoner. And I didn't try to poison you." What would be the point in poisoning a woman so old she had one hip in the grave? "This muffin is from Holly."

"You expect me to believe that sweet girl tried to kill me? That's preposterous! Besides, I didn't hear any smoke alarms."

"I didn't say she tried to kill you. I said she made you a muffin." Though, with Holly's cooking, those two weren't necessarily mutually exclusive. "There's a note taped to the bottom that says, 'To Mrs. Neberkins, from Holly.'"

"I would've seen it."

"Were you wearin' your glasses?"

"I don't wear glasses."

"They're around your neck."

She blatantly ignored the glasses resting on a chain against her chest and lifted her chin even higher. Much higher and she was going to get a neck cramp. "I'm not blind."

"I never said—"

She slammed her door before he could finish speaking.

He sighed. "God save me from tiny women."

Stepping into his apartment, he placed his keys and the muffin brick on the side table before resetting the alarm. After the break-in last spring, he had a security system installed. If he were living alone, he wouldn't have bothered, but he wasn't taking any chances with Holly's safety.

"Sweetheart?"

Colored candy was scattered across the countertop. Holly loved M&M's, but she had a peculiar aversion to the brown and yellow ones, and every time she opened a new bag, she separated them from the rest.

There were two glass jars on the counter, one labeled "Holly's" and the other . . .

He turned the jar to see the new label she had added, and nearly burst out laughing: "For a rainy day to flick at people's heads." Well, he did tell her that was what he would use them for.

Holly's jar had a few red, green, orange, and blue M&M's—she must have been eating them while she was sorting—and his rainy-day jar was filled to the brim with the *unwanted*.

He popped one of the scattered pieces of candy into his mouth as he turned to look down the hall, and his eyes caught on the picture frames on his wall.

"How in the . . ."

Holly had gotten him a picture frame for Christmas that was deliberately designed to be crooked, and at the moment, it was the straightest one on his wall.

He shook his head in amusement and readjusted the frames until they were back in their original positions. At one time, the permanently crooked frame—at odds with his tidy, organized apartment—would've made him cringe. Now it just reminded him of Holly.

He ran his fingertips over the message she had engraved in the wood: "To the dad of my heart." The words warmed him. He wasn't her father in any legal sense of the word, but she was the closest he would ever come to having a daughter, and in his heart, she was his baby.

Some people would look at all the hardship and danger that came with loving Holly and run the other way, but he saw her for the blessing that she was. He would happily face the challenges if it meant keeping her in his life.

Even if she did tilt his pictures and reorganize his movie shelf by color.

"Holly?" He walked down the hall and peered into her open bedroom.

He found her curled up on the bed, head resting on Riley's back, with a pillow hugged to her stomach. Her eyes were closed, and the relaxed rhythm of her breathing suggested she was asleep.

"It's about time."

Endless nights of pacing and baking had finally worn her out. And the faint sound of praise music drifting from the wireless headphones in her ears must have drowned out the sound of him coming home.

He entered the room on soft feet and grabbed the blanket wadded up at the head of the bed. He paused when he found Holly's journal lying open beneath it, the short entry catching his eye.

Dear Jesus,

Today I'm thankful for all the amazing people you gave me to love. Please, whatever happens with this trial, let me keep them.

Marx's heart swelled with love. This girl.

Every day, she took a moment to write to Jesus, letting Him know what she was thankful for. Sometimes it was something as small as chocolate, and other times it was something more heartfelt.

Each journal entry helped her to look past the darkness of the world and keep her eyes on Jesus, and all the blessings He gave her. It wasn't always easy to see the light in the world, and sometimes even Holly sat at the kitchen counter, tapping her pencil in thought.

He'd asked her once why she didn't just skip those days. She set down her pencil and gave the question some serious thought before explaining, "God blesses us every day in ways that we're too busy or too overwhelmed to see. There's always something to be grateful for. We just have to look a little harder and dig a little deeper to find it."

Then she popped a handful of colorful marshmallows into her mouth and returned her attention to her journal. She taught him something more about resilience and faith every day.

He draped the blanket over her, and she murmured beneath her breath, curling tighter around the pillow. He leaned down and pressed a feather-light kiss into her coconut-scented hair as he sent up a silent prayer:

Lord, today and every day, I am thankful for this sweet girl.

16

*S*hannon stared out her office window at the morning sky. A sheet of solid gray clouds stretched as far as the eye could see, spitting freezing rain over the city. The weather was as dismal as her mood this morning.

Between the throbbing behind her eyes and the moral quandary she was wrestling with, all she wanted to do was go home and crawl back beneath the duvet on her bed. Unfortunately, mental health days didn't exist during an ongoing trial.

She'd called Rick this morning to ask if he'd spoken with Holly. He hadn't. There were only four days until her testimony, and Shannon had no idea whether or not her star witness was going to be willing to testify.

Her gaze drifted to the unfinished subpoena on her desk. She tried never to force a victim to take the stand, especially a victim of abuse. After the trauma they suffered, being forced to talk about it against their will could easily re-traumatize them. Their choices had already been stripped away by their attacker, and Shannon didn't want to do the same.

She didn't want to be that person.

But most cases were simpler than this one; they didn't involve a predator like Collin, who repeatedly attacked not only his victim but anyone who tried to protect her.

He tried to have Rick killed by luring him to a building where a former convict lived, a convict with a vendetta against him. He sent Rachel Glass after Jordan, and she nearly ran him down with a car. He conspired with Drew Carson to have Samuel shot.

She couldn't prove most of those things, but she knew they were true, and they weighed heavily on her as she considered the subpoena.

Holly's testimony was integral to the stability of the case against Collin, and if she refused to take the stand, there was a chance everything could crumble. If the jury acquitted him, Holly's life wouldn't be the only one at risk. He would go after her again, and everyone Shannon loved would be in the line of fire. She couldn't allow that to happen.

She turned the pen over in her hands with indecision.

Even if she issued the subpoena, she doubted Rick would let it stand. He'd made it clear on several occasions that testifying needed to be Holly's choice, and if Shannon tried to force the issue, there was a chance he would pack Holly into his car and drive her across state lines. And then neither of them would be here to testify.

The subpoena would put them on opposite sides, and it would shatter every bit of trust she'd built with Holly.

She dropped into her chair. There was no path she could take that wouldn't cause pain and distrust.

She glared at the wretched document waiting for her signature. She would give Rick one more night to explain the situation to Holly, and if he didn't, she would handle the conversation herself. Maybe if she could help Holly process the fear and anger, there would be no need for the subpoena.

Deciding to do nothing for today, she opened her desk drawer and dropped the document into it. She reached for her migraine prescription, but it wasn't where she usually kept it.

She groaned. She'd left it on the nightstand. A quick glance at her watch told her she didn't have enough time to run home and then to the courthouse. She massaged the skin around her eyes and looked at her phone.

Would it be inappropriate to call Rick and ask him to pick up the medication? He still had a key.

It's also a good reason to see him.

She rolled her eyes at the thought and dialed his number.

· · · ·

Marx tipped his head to the reception desk as he exited the elevator. "Mornin', Hazel."

The older woman flushed and offered him her undivided attention. "Well, good morning, Detective."

"And how are you on this chilly day?"

She smiled, her round cheeks pinching her eyes. "I would be better if you accepted my dinner invitation. I know this wonderful Italian restaurant."

"I'm a Southern-bred man. We tend to prefer biscuits and gravy to noodles and sauce."

She brightened. "Breakfast, then?"

Marx laughed at her persistence. "If my heart didn't belong to somebody else, I might take you up on that."

Her gaze flickered to the ring on his finger with disappointment. "Some battles aren't worth fighting, Detective."

"And some battles are worth fightin' until the grave, Hazel."

He noticed Shannon's hesitation Sunday morning when he asked if he should stay and help clean up the house. The air of cold detachment she'd regarded him with for most of the past three years was thawing a little more each day.

He'd tried to stay in touch after the divorce, but she went out of her way to avoid him, including ignoring his phone calls. The only reason they were on speaking terms now was because of this trial.

After the verdict came in, Shannon would probably cut him out of her life again. That gave him about two weeks to win her over, and he intended to take advantage of it.

"Have a good day, Hazel." He tapped the counter with a hand before stepping away.

She popped out of her chair before he could round the corner to Shannon's office. "Oh, but I should tell her you're coming!"

"She knows!"

He was surprised that Shannon called and asked him to pick up her pills. Three or four months ago, she never would've done that. He was even more surprised that she hadn't changed the alarm code. It was still the date of the day they first met in that cozy café. That small detail rekindled the hope that she still cared for him.

He raised a hand to knock on her closed door, but paused when he heard her voice, agitated and impatient.

"I understand that it's a lot to pull together, and I don't want to rush you, but . . ." She trailed off, letting silence fill the air. She was on the phone. "Yes, it's extremely important. If there's anything I can do to help matters along . . ." Another pause. "All right. Thank you. I'll be in touch."

Marx waited for the soft click of the receiver landing in its cradle before knocking.

"Come in."

He opened the door to find Shannon behind her desk, rubbing at her temples.

She breathed a sigh of relief when he entered. "I'm so happy to see you."

"It's just because I'm your drug dealer, isn't it?" He pulled the bottle of prescription pills from his pocket and tossed it to her.

131

She caught it with a smile. "That could have something to do with it." She tapped a pill into her palm and then popped it into her mouth, washing it down with a sip of water. "This case is giving me a splitting headache."

"The day hasn't even started yet."

"Hasn't it?" She sounded weary as she grabbed a file from her desk and tucked it into a drawer before he could read the label. It was obviously the source of her stress.

"Another court case you're preppin' for?"

"One I'm consulting on. You know how it goes. Too many criminals, not enough experienced prosecutors."

The police department struggled with the same problem. It wasn't unusual for him to have five or six open cases demanding his attention. Right now, he only had two, both of which had stalled from lack of leads. That left him plenty of time to focus on what mattered most to him.

"I think you need to unwind a bit."

The pill must have caught in Shannon's throat because she grimaced and took another gulp of water. "I'm not sure unwinding is possible right now."

He gripped one of the low-back guest chairs. "Come here."

"Why?"

"Because I asked you to."

"Technically you ordered me to."

He patted the back of the chair. "Please."

132

Her lips thinned, and she stared at the chair in silent deliberation before rounding the desk. She perched rigidly on the edge of the seat, as though ready to spring to her feet at any moment. When he touched her shoulders, she stiffened even more.

She wasn't afraid of him—he'd never given her any reason to be—which suggested her stiffness stemmed from something else. Reluctance, possibly. Or maybe she was afraid his touch would make her feel something, and feelings inevitably led her down a path she couldn't control.

His fingers lingered on her shoulders for a minute before moving to the base of her neck, the spot where most of her tension gathered before migrating into her head.

She groaned and her shoulders started to relax. "Do you remember when you used to rub my feet like this?"

"Mmm hmm."

Her feet always ached after a long day in heels, and he would massage the arches, then her ankles, and all the way up to that ticklish spot behind her knees. She was the only person he'd ever met who was ticklish behind the knees.

She moaned and tilted her head to the side as he worked on the tight muscles.

This close to her, he could smell her lavender perfume, a subtle fragrance that reminded him of comfort. When they were married, he would come home after a particularly rough case, wrap his arms around her,

133

and bury his nose in that scent. He missed those days. Those moments.

"Shannon."

"Hmm?" Her voice had a dreamy quality to it, her tension melting beneath his kneading fingers.

"Have dinner with me."

Some of the stiffness returned, and she shifted in the chair to look up at him. "What?"

"Dinner, as in a meal."

"I don't think that's a good idea, Rick."

"Why not?"

"Because . . ." She stood and stepped away, deliberately putting space between them. "It isn't."

"'Because' isn't exactly the kind of reasonin' I expect from somebody whose career is built on makin' a good argument."

She folded her arms, trying to appear resolute, but he knew her too well to miss the subtle sign of uncertainty in the way she stood. When she was determined, her toes pointed straightforward—like an unyielding arrow aimed at its mark—but if she was questioning herself, it showed in her duck-footed stance.

She followed his gaze to her uncertain duck feet, and retreated behind the desk so he couldn't see them. "We're not together anymore."

"That doesn't mean we can't socialize on occasion."

She huffed, frustrated by his persistence. He considered letting the matter drop, but something urged him to push just a little more.

"It's a dinner invitation, Shannon, not a marriage proposal. We'll eat, talk about our day, and go our separate ways."

She averted her eyes and shuffled some papers on her desk. "I'll think about it."

That was a step in the right direction.

She gathered her files for the day, tucking them into her briefcase with intentional focus. She was avoiding his gaze.

"Who's testifyin' this mornin'?"

"Ella Foster, the medical examiner." She pulled on her high heels. "Not my strongest witness in this case. She's unwilling to say Rachel Glass was murdered because there's no bruising to indicate she was pushed. Her findings leave room for reasonable doubt, but hopefully Holly's testimony will clear that up."

"You want a lift to the courthouse?"

She hesitated at the offer, then shook her head. "I arranged for a cab. It should be here any minute."

"All right."

As much as he wanted to spend those extra fifteen minutes with her on the drive over, he didn't push. His dinner invitation seemed to have flustered her, and she needed to enter that courtroom with her mind focused.

He walked her to her cab and watched the car pull away from the curb. He hoped, after the legal proceedings ended for the day, that she truly would devote some thought to letting him take her out for a nice dinner.

17

*H*olly eyed the sapphire-blue star on the top of Jace's artificial tree. Her best friend was an avid decorator, and she left her decorations up well past New Year's.

Holly stretched onto her toes, trying to reach the star. The wooden chair wobbled beneath her, and she clutched at the wall for balance, wrapping one hand around a flimsy light fixture. She was not going to fall face-first into this spiny, oversized Christmas tree.

Why did Jace even need an eight-foot tree? She was four feet tall.

The chair unexpectedly stilled, and Holly looked over her shoulder at the man who gripped it with both hands.

Sam was the kind of man who intimidated people simply by being in the room with them. There was a time when his nearness would've triggered Holly's anxiety, sending her scampering backward to put space between them. But not now. He might frighten other people with his permanent cop face, but she'd seen his heart.

She smiled. "You're awake."

"Yes." A hint of annoyance leaked into the flatness of his voice. "Because someone is making a lot of noise."

Holly pointed to herself. "Who? Me someone?" She was trying to be quiet, but the floor was uneven, and standing on this chair was like trying to balance a teeter-totter solo.

"Please get down before you break yourself."

"But I have to get the star."

"I'll get the star."

"You're barely taller than me."

That remark earned her two slowly raised eyebrows. "I'm seven inches taller than you, which means I won't have to tiptoe around on a chair."

Fair point. She hated to admit defeat, but she glared at the star atop the eight-foot tree, then hopped down. "Jace, I think your tree is a little—"

"Stunning, right?" Jace leaned over in her wheelchair, a beaming smile on her face. "It belongs on the cover of a magazine. I love it so much I didn't even wanna take it down."

Stunning was one word for it, though not the one Holly would've chosen. Wrapped in blue and silver garland, with every shade of blue ornament imaginable dripping from the branches, it looked like something a Smurf threw up.

Holly scrounged for an accurate yet not insulting description. "It's . . . vibrant."

"Vibrant." Jace's eyes drifted to the left in thought. "Vibrant. I like that."

Sam climbed off the chair and handed Holly the star. She frowned at how easily he'd retrieved it, but kept

137

her height envy to herself as she placed the star into a box.

"I'm gonna make coffee." Sam leaned down and planted a kiss on Jace's lips, the moment lingering a little too long for Holly's comfort.

She averted her gaze and pretended to be very interested in the tree, lifting a heavy glass snowflake from one of the limbs.

A quiet chirp drew her attention to Jace's open bedroom door. A fat gray cat waddled out of the dark room and made a beeline for Holly.

She gasped and bent down to scoop up her pudgy fur baby. "There's my little sausage."

His purr sputtered before catching, and he head-butted Holly's chin with affection.

She squeezed him with love. She'd adopted him shortly after she moved out of the women's shelter and into her own apartment. He'd lived on the street, just like she had, all skin and bones with a skittish distrust of the world.

When Holly first approached him, he hissed and ran away, but he came back the next night, hunting for food. It was so similar to her own story that she fell in love with him instantly.

She approached him with gentleness, patience, and food, and eventually lured him into her apartment where she fattened him up and domesticated him.

She named him Jordan, and he even shared the same vivid blue eyes as his namesake.

Marx wasn't fond of cats, so when Holly moved in with him, she had to find him a temporary home. Someday, when she moved back into her own place, she would have both of her fur babies. She just hoped Riley wouldn't *eat* Jordan the cat.

"Your cat is obese," Sam said. "Which wouldn't bother me, except he insists on sleeping on my chest and I can't breathe." He brushed at the cat hair that covered the front of his black T-shirt. "And he sheds. A lot."

Holly scratched between the little sausage's ears and smiled. "That just means he likes you."

Sam grunted, clearly unappreciative of the affection, and strode into the kitchen to make coffee.

Holly squeezed between boxes of ornaments and the arm of the couch, finding just enough room to sit so she didn't have to hold Jordan's weight.

"So are you and Sam . . ." Her eyes trailed to the bedroom, but she wasn't sure how to phrase her question, or if it was even appropriate to ask. She really wished she had a better understanding of social etiquette.

"Sleeping together?" Jace asked, completely at ease with the private topic. "Only in the most platonic sense. I've been having nightmares about . . ." She mimed a rope around her neck. "So he's been coming over before and after his night shift and sleeping in the room with me. On the floor."

Heaviness fell over Holly's heart. "Oh Jace, I'm—"

"I swear, Holly, if you apologize for that skeevy Ted Bundy wannabe one more time, I will wrap you up in this garland and force you to watch *The Lord of the Rings* with me."

She threw a wad of garland at her, and Holly caught it, a faint smile curling her lips. "Oh no, not *The Lord of the Rings*."

"The extended edition."

Holly cringed inwardly at the thought. The movie was never-ending to begin with, and someone thought it was a good idea to extend it? "Well, in the face of that threat, never mind." She wouldn't utter the apology aloud, but she felt the weight of guilt just the same.

Jace was only taken because of her. If she'd left the moment she realized he was in the city, everyone she loved would've been safe.

Sam carried his coffee out of the kitchen but paused when someone hammered on Jace's door. A male voice followed the startling knock. "I know Holly Cross is in there, and I have a right to ask her questions."

Holly's heart thumped faster at the sound of her name. "Who is it?"

"I'll check." Sam set his mug on the living room end table and walked to the front door, peering through the peephole. His shoulders bunched with frustration, and he stepped back. "It's Addison Miles."

That was the name Holly couldn't think of yesterday, the journalist lingering on the street outside Marx's apartment.

She felt a rush of anger at the man's nerve. Loitering outside the apartment where she was living was one thing, but to come banging on her friend's door like he had a right to disrupt their lives was unacceptable.

Holly stood, setting Jordan on the floor. "I'm gonna tell him what he can do with his questions."

Sam blocked her attempt to reach the door. "We're not opening this door."

"But—"

"His tactic is to provoke people into engaging with him, and then he twists what they say to suit his purposes. I'd rather you not talk to him."

Addison spoke again, louder this time. "I find it interesting that the suspect in this trial has been more forthcoming with the media than the alleged victim."

Holly's stomach cramped. He'd spoken with Collin?

"I'm gonna publish my article either way, but I thought she might like to counter the claims made by the defendant and his family."

What did Collin tell him? What kind of terrible stories were going to be splashed across the internet by morning?

"I think the people deserve to know that the alleged victim and the defendant used to be lovers, and that Holly Cross became bitter and vengeful when her lover ended things."

Holly's legs turned liquid, and she melted onto the arm of the couch. This was a nightmare; it had to be a nightmare.

Jace rolled forward and placed a hand over hers, giving it a reassuring squeeze. "It doesn't matter what he prints. We know the truth."

"The article is already written," Addison continued. "Unless Holly has something to say, it'll be published by this afternoon, and I have a lot of loyal readers."

Ignoring his own advice, Sam unlocked the door and yanked it inward, blocking the gap with his body. "If you wanna print lies, go ahead. You're the one whose reputation will suffer when the truth comes out. Now leave or I'll remove you from the building."

A sneer twisted Addison's voice. "Go ahead, and I'll slap your department with an excessive force lawsuit before morning."

Sam's fingers tightened on the door frame. "I don't care about lawsuits. I care about protecting innocent people, like the girl you're about to slander with your article."

"It's not slander if it's the truth."

"So you have a source outside of the rapist and his biased family members?" There was an irritated silence in the hallway. "I didn't think so. Before you harass a victim, you should really cement your facts."

Sam slammed the door in his face without so much as a good-bye, and snapped the dead bolt to emphasize the end of the conversation.

. . . .

The judge called a recess for lunch, and Shannon collected her things, frustration gnawing at her nerves. She had done her best to convince the jury that Rachel Glass's death was a murder, but with the medical examiner reluctant to rule it a homicide, it was a waste of effort.

Collin's cross-examination was a theatrical performance about how he was being charged with a murder that wasn't even a murder. He expressed *concern* that the prosecution would take a woman's tragic death and fabricate a gruesome story of manipulation and murder just to try to buoy their case against him.

Shannon had nearly snapped the pencil she was twisting between her fingers.

Unless Holly testified and managed to convince the jury that Rachel's death was a murder—one she witnessed while held captive in that warehouse—they were going to lose the murder charge.

Detecting movement out of the corner of her eye, she looked over to find Collin approaching. He wore a pale blue tie that accentuated his eyes, somehow making them seem less cold by comparison.

"I admire how passionate you are in seeking justice for my little sister, but I don't think your case is fairing too well."

Shannon faced him, all of her fear and disgust tucked into a distant corner of her mind. "That's a matter of perspective, Mr. Wells."

"I'm certain the jury will see my perspective as reality by the time we're through. And the media . . . well, they do seem to like me."

"If only they realized you would push them over a railing to their deaths without a moment of hesitation or remorse."

He smiled, his expression perfectly charming. "You know I'm going to win, don't you?"

"You're awfully confident for someone whose never been to law school."

"I may not know as much as you about how the system works, but I don't need to be a skilled lawyer to win. The burden of proof is on your shoulders, not mine. All I have to do is poke holes in your story, and that should be easy enough."

"I think your guards are ready to return you to your holding cell." She pulled her briefcase off the table and gripped it with both hands. "It's impolite to keep them waiting."

As his own lawyer, Collin was permitted a few minutes to speak with opposing counsel, but he wasn't allowed to linger for too long.

Collin placed his hands obediently behind his back as the guards approached, but his gaze never left Shannon. "This trial must be difficult for you."

"What makes you think that?"

"Your star witness is living with your ex-husband."

"I know the condition of their relationship, so if you're hoping to instill doubt or create conflict, you're wasting your breath."

He smiled. "How *are* things between you and the detective?"

Complicated, Shannon thought, but she had no intention of telling him that.

Rick's dinner invitation had been on her mind all morning. She'd spent so long trying to put distance between them that her instinct was to refuse, even when her heart pleaded with her to accept. Either choice would have consequences, and she needed time to consider them before making a decision.

"I'll see you after lunch, Shannon," Collin said, and the way her name rolled off his tongue sent a shiver down her spine.

She watched stiffly as the guards cuffed him and led him out of the courtroom.

18

*S*am sat on the bench outside the courtroom in his police uniform, sipping his coffee as he waited to be summoned to the stand. He stared at the floor as he turned his testimony over in his mind, searching for points of weakness that could be exploited.

His instinctive response to everything was logic and reason, and it served him well in his career, but even he couldn't completely strip away his emotions. Anger was woven into the memories he would be revisiting on the stand: the searing pain of a bullet between his ribs, his sister's screams, Holly huddled in fear on the floor of his apartment.

He rubbed his hands together and stood, pent-up emotion fueling his steps as he began to pace.

He hadn't seen Collin since March 18—the night Collin conspired with Drew to have him killed—and he wasn't looking forward to seeing him now.

"You look like you need to hit something."

Sam turned toward the voice, his dark eyes taking in the familiar, approaching figure. "Not some*thing*. Some*one*."

Jordan's movements were relaxed and agile, but the hatred smoldering in his blue eyes when he looked at the courtroom door belied his calm demeanor. His feelings for Holly went far deeper than friendship—it was obvious to everyone, except maybe Holly—and the man who attacked her was just beyond those doors.

Jordan dragged his eyes away from the courtroom and folded his arms, doing his best not to look like he was contemplating murder. "I haven't seen Collin since they moved him from the hospital."

"So that's why he's still breathing."

"Yep. And apparently I'm not allowed to visit him in jail because I make him feel *unsafe*."

"Well, you did try to arrange a meeting between him and his Maker."

When Jordan realized Collin had been admitted to the same hospital as Holly, he snapped. If not for the two officers who pulled him off, he would've strangled Collin to death in his hospital bed.

"Why are you here?" Sam asked. "I thought Shannon wasn't putting you on the stand because of that incident."

Shannon didn't want to give Collin the opportunity to paint himself as a victim in court, since Jordan *had* attacked him "unprovoked."

Jordan shrugged. "Just here to support a friend."

"Thanks." He adjusted the left cuff of his uniform. "Did Shannon tell you Collin's representing himself?"

Judging by the stunned look on Jordan's face, this was the first he'd heard of it. "No. Has anyone told Holly?"

"Marx wanted to be the one to break the news to her, but I don't know when he was planning to have

147

that conversation. She seemed okay this morning, so I don't think he's told her yet."

Jordan ran his hands over his hair and gripped the back of his neck. "I really hate this guy."

"I'm not his biggest fan either."

"He's been behind bars all this time, he's on trial for a dozen different charges, and he still has the nerve to play games with Holly."

"He's been playing games with her for almost fifteen years without consequences. He thinks he's untouchable."

One of the courtroom doors opened, and a man nodded to them from the doorway. "Officer Barrera, it's time."

Sam took off his hat, gripping it in front of him, and looked at Jordan. "Are you staying out here?"

"No, I think I'll join you and remind Collin he's not as untouchable as he thinks."

. . . .

Oh, for the love of all things holy, Shannon thought, her frustration drawing on the phrase that Rick used when he was exasperated.

She watched from her table as Jordan Radcliffe strode into the courtroom behind Samuel. She had specifically asked him to steer clear of the trial—she didn't even want him in the same building—but he sauntered down the aisle and slid onto the bench directly behind the defense table.

She seared him with a look of disapproval, and he tipped his head politely, acknowledging her dissatisfaction without apology.

Collin twisted in his chair to see who had sat down behind him, and his pale complexion grew even paler. Jordan crossed his arms and smiled, but there was an edge of warning to that smile.

This was going to be a disaster.

The clerk swore Samuel in, and Samuel took his place on the witness stand, his face almost perfectly blank.

Shannon had known Samuel for a long time, long enough to know that his indifferent expression was not a reflection of his heart. He cared deeply for people. But to someone who didn't know him, he looked like a robot devoid of personality, and the moment he opened his mouth and began answering questions in monotone, it would only solidify that belief.

Shannon stood, twisting the pen in her hand as she considered how to break through his hardened exterior and bring out his softer side.

She started with the basic questions—asking about his years and experience on the force, reassuring the jury that he was a reliable witness—before branching out.

"Officer Barrera, are you familiar with the victims in this case?"

"With two of the three, yes. Jace Walker and I have been dating for about a year and a half. And Holly is a friend."

"Would you say she's a close friend?"

"Holly doesn't really do 'close' with men, Detective Marx being the exception. But I care about her and she seems to trust me."

Samuel more than *cared* for Holly. He treated her like a second little sister—always prepared to lecture her on the dangers of the world, and protective to the point of running off men who were attracted to her, including his former partner.

"Tell us how you first met Holly."

"The October before last, Detective Marx was investigating a murder in connection to a woman who was assaulted in the park. That young woman was Holly. When he became concerned that her life was still in danger, he requested volunteers to take shifts safeguarding her at her apartment. I took the night shift for the first couple weeks."

"What inspired you to volunteer?"

"Detective Marx is a longtime friend, but I also have a personal dislike of men who attempt to intimidate, abuse, or assault women." He slid a pointed look in Collin's direction.

Collin's lips curled into a barely perceptible smile, so subtle that the members of the jury likely wouldn't notice.

"Understandable," Shannon commented, recapturing Samuel's attention. "Why was Holly in so much danger?"

"She was being stalked by Edward Billings, the serial killer who murdered her family when she was nine.

It was a coincidence that their paths crossed again, and the moment he realized who she was, he became fixated on her."

Shannon nodded. "What did you notice about Holly's behavior during this ordeal?"

"She was more afraid of someone from her past than she was the killer hunting her. And that was after he murdered two people."

Jurors shifted in their chairs, interested to learn who was more terrifying than a serial killer.

Shannon didn't make them wait long before gesturing to Collin. "More afraid of this man than the man who was suspected of murdering fifty-one people, her own family included?"

"Yes."

Shannon gripped a wrist behind her back, a dramatic frown on her face. "Well, that certainly seems unusual, doesn't it?"

"It seemed irrational. Until I realized that Holly isn't afraid of death. She's afraid of being trapped and overpowered, and of having her free will taken away."

"Have you ever met anyone with Holly's particular brand of anxiety before?"

"To a lesser degree, yes. As a cop who works the night shift, I respond to a lot of domestic violence situations and assaults."

"And because of those experiences, you recognized something about Holly?"

"Yes."

"Can you . . . expound on that for the court?" She tried to keep the impatience from her voice, but extracting answers from Samuel was akin to having her teeth scraped at the dentist.

"Holly's behavior suggested that she'd been traumatized by a man. Given her uncomfortable and cautious body language around men, I suspected that she had been sexually assaulted. And considering how frightened she was of Collin, it was only logical to assume he was the offender."

Collin started to rise and offer an objection, but he must have reconsidered, because he dropped back into his chair without speaking.

"Can you describe one or more instances when you witnessed these traumatized behaviors in Holly?" Shannon asked.

"On the night of her birthday, January 18th, 2017, I was standing beside her when she received a call from a man she later identified as Collin Wells. The caller said, 'This is the part where you blow out the candles.' We had just lit the candles on her cake."

"So he was within visual distance of her apartment, watching the celebration."

"Yes. There's a window above her kitchen sink that would've allowed him the perfect view from as far as the opposite side of the street. Holly dropped her phone, closed herself in the bathroom, and sobbed. I went out to search the area, and she was still hiding in the bathroom when I came back."

"And when Collin Wells made his first appearance—what happened on that occasion?"

Samuel's eyes grew distant with memory. "I was visiting Jace, my girlfriend, when I overheard agitated voices coming from outside. I went outside to investigate, and found Detective Marx and Collin Wells having a tense conversation in front of Holly's apartment. Holly was sitting in the passenger seat of Marx's car, watching out the passenger window. She looked . . . terrified."

"Did she stay in the car?"

"No. Collin Wells made a remark about staying in New York to visit a few places and become reacquainted with Holly, whom he referred to as an old flame. It was at that moment that she flung open the car door in a panic and fled."

"Did you follow her?"

Samuel nodded. "I found her in an abandoned building, huddled in a corner, crying. She was so scared that she nearly maced me when I came through the door."

"Did she tell you *why* she was so scared?"

"She was afraid of being hurt again. She intended to run and disappear. I tried to talk her into staying and fighting, but ultimately, Detective Marx convinced her to stay. There were several more phone calls and multiple unwelcome visits after that, only some of which I was present for. I believe Detective Marx documented the times, dates, and content of those interactions."

Shannon nodded. "What happened after Detective Marx convinced Holly to stay? Did things go back to normal?"

"No. We— Jordan Radcliffe, Detective Marx, and I—decided that one of us should be with Holly at all times, to protect her. While Collin didn't issue any overt threats during his visits or phone calls, he was antagonistic to the point that we became concerned he would hurt Holly. We also decided that it would be to her benefit to learn self-defense, so Jordan and I held weekly training sessions with her."

"How did she do?"

"She's the most uncoordinated person I've ever met," Samuel said, and laughter trickled through the room.

Shannon let the laughter fade before continuing. "It was after one of those training sessions that things went in an unexpected direction, wasn't it?"

"Yes. I was at home with my sister Evey when I received a call from Officer Theo Rogan. That night, Detective Marx was pulled away on a personal matter, which left Holly alone with Jordan after the training session. Collin showed up at the gym, and there was an altercation that resulted in Jordan being arrested. That left Holly on her own, so I brought her back to my place."

"You're very protective of her."

"Yes."

Shannon gestured for him to elaborate on his vague statement. She couldn't make him personable to the jury if he was monosyllabic.

He sighed and leaned forward. "Holly is like everyone's kid sister. Her determination and irrational decisions are frequently irritating, but she's also sweet and occasionally funny. She has a big heart and she genuinely cares about people, even if she's only known them for five minutes. Her heart makes her vulnerable, her petite size makes her an easy target for predators, and her past sometimes makes her seem fragile. Altogether, it's impossible *not* to feel protective of her."

"So you brought Holly to your apartment to keep her safe, but something happened that put all your lives in danger?"

"Drew Carson, my sister's controlling husband, came looking for her. He picked the lock and shot me before I could get to my gun. He had the gun aimed at my head, preparing for a second shot, when Holly jumped on his back, and the second bullet hit the wall."

Samuel fell silent, his gaze dropping to his lap, and when he finally spoke, his voice was soft and laced with pain. "Holly saved my life and the life of my sister the night she was taken. I was supposed to be protecting *her*, but I let her down."

A moment of silence stretched through the courtroom, broken only by the tapping of the court reporter's keyboard.

"I told Evey to run. She was the only person I was thinking about, the only person I cared about in that

155

moment. But after . . ." When Samuel looked up, there was pain and regret in his eyes. "I just sat there, bleeding out, as Collin walked into my apartment and took Holly."

There was the soft side of Samuel that Shannon knew. The man who brought a giant teddy bear and flowers to the hospital when Holly was recovering. The man who sat in the hospital chapel with red, swollen eyes, praying for his friend to pull through, even though he wasn't a man of faith.

Shannon gave him a moment to regain his composure, then retrieved the wooden bat wrapped in an evidence bag and showed it to him. "Do you recognize this bat?"

Samuel squared his shoulders and smoothed the emotion from his face. "Yes. It's mine."

"Can you share the significance of this bat with the court?"

"It was resting against the wall just inside my apartment door that night. Collin grabbed it and used it to knock out Drew Carson."

"Why would he do that?"

"Drew had his gun aimed at Holly, ready to pull the trigger, but Collin wanted her alive."

"Thank you, Officer Barrera." Shannon returned to her seat.

Collin offered a gleaming smile as he prepared for his cross-examination. His voice rang loud and strong through the overpacked courtroom. "Sam. May I call you Sam?"

"No."

"All right then, Officer Barrera." He slid his hands back into the pockets of his slacks, his posture too relaxed and confident for Shannon's liking. "You stated that, given Holly's fear of me, it was only logical to assume that I had assaulted her in the past."

"That's what I believe, yes."

"Hmm. Tell me, how did Holly react when you volunteered to guard her at her apartment?"

"Defensive."

"Did she let you inside?"

Samuel paused, visibly trying to anticipate where this line of questioning was headed. "She didn't feel safe having men inside her apartment, so we stood guard outside."

Collin's eyebrows lifted with interest. "So what you're saying is, she was afraid of you and whoever else was standing guard simply because you were both male. Do I have that correct?"

Samuel's eyes narrowed.

"Do I have that correct, Officer Barrera?"

"To a degree . . . yes," Samuel gritted through his teeth.

"Did you or this other officer ever sexually assault Holly?"

Samuel's eyes darkened with anger, and Shannon sprang to her feet. "Your Honor, he's antagonizing the witness."

"No antagonism meant, Your Honor. I'm simply trying to establish a pattern for Holly's fear."

157

"Then rephrase your question," Judge Tipper instructed.

"Officer Barrera, if Holly's fear of you was based solely on the fact that you're a man, and not because you've harmed her in some way, isn't it logical to assume that her fear of any man, including myself, stems from nothing more than general male anxiety rather than some supposed past assault?" When Samuel gritted his teeth and remained silent, Collin repeated himself with emphasis. "Isn't it logical to assume—"

"Yes, that would be a logical, if inaccurate, assumption."

"Thank you. Now that we've established that the only thing I'm guilty of is being male, let's revisit the night of March 18. Tell us again what happened at your apartment. Describe only what you remember, no supposition."

Samuel went over the events again, starting from the moment Holly stepped through his door to the moment she disappeared. "You hit Drew on the back of the head and knocked him out before—"

Collin held up a hand. "Let me stop you right there. You gave a statement after regaining consciousness post-surgery—my condolences on the gunshot wound, by the way—and in this statement, you mentioned that you passed out from blood loss at your apartment."

"I faded in and out of consciousness."

"I'm curious—how many times did you fade *out* of consciousness at the scene?"

Samuel frowned. "I don't know. Once or twice maybe."

"Once or twice." Collin looked down at the notepad beside him and tapped his fingers on the desk. "And how long were you unconscious during each of those times?"

"I don't know," Samuel repeated.

"You don't know. Considering you're accusing me of abducting someone, I think your state of consciousness or unconsciousness is something that should be taken into account, don't you?"

"Objection. The witness is testifying to what he *witnessed*, which means he was coherent at the time. Mr. Wells is trying to undermine his testimony with irrelevant details."

"Overruled," Tipper said.

Shannon pressed her lips together in frustration and sat back down.

"In light of the fact that you had just been shot in the chest at close range minutes before, which was a shock to your body and mind, and you were fading in and out of consciousness, let's go over the details one more time," Collin suggested. "I know from previous answers that your instinct is to fill in the blanks and answer the questions by making logical leaps, but set that instinct aside and walk us through those last few moments again, describing only what you specifically remember."

"You swung the bat and struck Drew across the back of the head, knocking him out. He dropped to the floor just inches from where Holly was sitting. You drew the bat back for another swing, aiming it at Holly's head."

Collin waited for a beat, but Samuel said nothing more. "That's it? You didn't see me pick up the gun Drew Carson dropped so he couldn't grab it again? You didn't see me toss the bat on the floor after I supposedly drew it back for another swing? You didn't see me 'take Holly,' as you previously stated?"

"I know you took her."

"I specifically asked for no logical leaps, Officer Barrera."

"You were the only other person in the room."

"The apartment door was open, which means anyone could've come and gone while you were unconscious. My being there one minute and gone the next is proof of nothing."

"You were stalking her."

"So you were told. Inaccurately, I might add, but that's beside the point. I would like you to answer my question. Did you *see* me take Holly?"

Samuel's knuckles cracked in the silence that followed the question. "No."

"So the last thing you actually remember was me saving not only Holly's life but yours?"

"That's not—"

"No further questions." Collin dropped back into his chair with a look of satisfaction.

Shannon barely heard Judge Tipper ask if she would like to redirect; her mind was too busy trying to process the repercussions of what had just happened.

Every time she had gone over the events of that night with Samuel, he confirmed that Collin had taken Holly. She couldn't blame him for a small lapse in memory—he had nearly died that night—but this was far from small, and the jury wouldn't be so understanding. At best, they would think he was confused and unreliable. At worst, they would decide he was dishonest or incompetent and disregard his entire testimony.

19

*M*arx tapped a pencil on his desk as he reviewed the information Sully had gathered on Agatha Wells.

Her driver's license photo depicted a heavyset woman with pale blue eyes and salt-and-pepper hair that fell around her shoulders. She was five foot six and fifty-four years old, which would've put her in her early twenties when she gave birth to Collin.

She didn't look dangerous, but she had the same coldness in her eyes as her son.

He flipped open his notebook to double-check the details he'd gotten from the employee at Pastel Petals. Agatha Wells matched the description of the customer who purchased the flowers, but so did a lot of women in the city.

Sully couldn't find any camera footage from the area without a warrant, so there was no way to be certain.

Marx's phone pinged with an incoming message. He flipped it open to find a text from Holly, letting him know that she would be spending the evening with Jordan.

He typed out a short reply:

Okay. Have fun, and be safe.

He'd been hoping to hear from Sam. He'd called several times to see how things went in court, but every call went to voice mail.

Marx was starting to worry.

He set aside the picture of Agatha Wells and studied the other documents Sully had dropped off before leaving for his costume party. Seeing a grown man in a pirate outfit with an eyepatch was . . . odd, to say the least. But then, Sully wasn't exactly normal.

The second document was a divorce record for Agatha and Victor Wells, dated six months ago.

Why divorce her now?

He found his answer when he flipped to the printouts of Victor Wells's social media account. He read the most recent entry.

> I am ashamed of the things my son has done.
> I blame Aggie for worshipping the ground he
> walks on, for letting him do whatever he
> wanted when he was a boy. She made him into
> the monster he's become.

Marx was surprised that the man would so publicly proclaim his son's guilt. The verdict wasn't even in yet.

Holly had never said much about Collin's father, except that he was present but uninvolved. There was no way he was blind to the abuse going on under his roof. He just chose to ignore it.

"Coward," Marx muttered in disgust.

He didn't understand how a man could witness the mistreatment of innocent, vulnerable people and still choose to do nothing.

He skimmed a few more social media posts, but they were just more of the same—a passive, uninvolved father blaming his wife for raising their son wrong. Nothing pointed to where Agatha Wells might be staying.

The next document was an article printed from a website called the NYC Veritas Journal.

Marx groaned in recognition. This particular online journal was managed by Addison Miles, a self-proclaimed journalist who was well-known for his distrust of law enforcement. He latched on to any hint of wrongdoing in the police force and spun stories of corruption and brutality that drew in thousands of readers.

Last spring, he fixed his sights on Holly—the mysterious girl whose disappearance inspired police to scour the streets. He tried to corner her a couple of months after her rescue, hoping to glean details about her abduction, but he didn't get the chance.

This article was entitled "Victim or Villain." Marx braced himself and began to read.

> A lot of mystery surrounds the alleged victim in this city's latest attention-grabbing trial— The State Vs. Collin Victor Wells. Holly Cross appears to be "the girl next door," but her secretive nature and aversion to the media begs the question: what is she hiding? She might not

be the innocent victim everyone believes, according to her foster mother, Agatha Wells.

Addison Miles had been in contact with Collin's mother. That meant there was a chance he knew where she was staying. Not that he would give up that information easily. He continued reading to see if there was anything helpful in the rest of the article.

"I knew she was trouble the day she landed on my doorstep," Holly's foster mother commented, when asked about the young woman opposing her son in court. "The way she was dressed, like a streetwalker at fourteen years . . ."

"Hey."

Marx looked up from the article to see Shannon crossing the squad room with a takeout bag in one hand and drinks in the other. She had traded in her suit for hip-hugging jeans and a white sweater. "Hey. How's your headache?"

"Better. I had a feeling you would still be here. I brought Chinese. I assume you still enjoy General Tsao's chicken and fried rice."

"Mmm hmm."

She set the drinks on the edge of his desk and pulled up a chair. "What are you reading?"

"Trash." He tossed the article on the desk and helped himself to one of the sweet teas she'd brought.

This wasn't exactly what he had in mind when he proposed a dinner date, but he wouldn't complain. "I've been tryin' to get a hold of Sam, but I keep gettin' his voice mail. How did his testimony go?"

A myriad of emotions played across Shannon's face before frustration settled. "Not well."

20

*S*am sat on the bar stool, regret and worry resting between his shoulder blades like a lead weight. After his father was killed in the line of duty, he swore to protect the people he loved at any cost.

That's working out well.

The sarcastic thought left a bitter taste in his mouth, and he lifted the half-empty bottle to his lips to wash it down.

There were three women he cared about in his life—only three—and he had failed to keep all of them safe. It didn't seem to matter how hard he tried; things always went sideways. If he was a superstitious man, he would think he was cursed.

"You a boxer?" the bartender asked, dragging him from his darkening thoughts.

Sam flexed his left hand, the ache spreading from his raw knuckles down through his fingers. "No."

But he had stopped by the gym after court, and he hadn't taken the time to wrap his hands properly before funneling his anger into the heavy bag.

"Looks like you were wailing on something. Rough day?"

Sam glanced at the middle-aged man behind the counter, whose dark eyes regarded him with mild interest. "Yeah, rough day."

"I can pour you something stronger to take the edge off. Might even help you forget whatever's on your mind."

It was a tempting proposition. But even if he took the man up on the offer, the truth would still be there when he downed the last drop; he would just be less equipped to deal with it. He had seen too many good cops fall into that trap, lured in by the false promise that all their problems would just disappear with a few drinks.

He set down the bottle of beer and pushed it away. "I'll pass, thanks."

There was no crawling into a bottle to hide from the fact that he was the only witness to Holly's abduction, and now that his integrity and his memory had been called into question on the witness stand, their only hope was Sam's weasel of a brother-in-law. Drew had conspired with Collin to break in and kidnap Holly and Evey that night, but he agreed to testify for a reduced prison sentence.

Twelve years behind bars and three years on parole. Shannon hadn't made the deal lightly, but the undeniable truth was, Collin was a greater threat.

The bartender let out a low, appreciative whistle and tipped his chin toward the front door of the pub. "There's a nice-looking lady. Maybe if you buy her a drink, she'll make your night better."

Sam didn't need another random woman trying to "make his night better," but he followed the bartender's attention, his gaze slipping past the brunette in the corner who was still sulking over his earlier rejection, and landing on the woman who had just entered the bar.

He choked on his own spit.

The bartender laughed and slapped his back. "What, she take your breath away?"

She had a slight build, her subtle curves wrapped in jeans, a purple sweater, and a brown leather jacket, and her carrot-red hair fell freely around her shoulders.

Sam stared at her in disbelief, then glanced back at his unfinished beer. He hadn't drunk nearly enough to justify imagining things. It was definitely Holly standing in the doorway, her out-of-place appearance accentuated by her purple rain boots.

But she wasn't a drinker, and she avoided places and situations where men would have the advantage if they decided to hurt her. She didn't just walk into bars. What was she doing here?

She fidgeted under the leering gazes of the men and stepped closer to the door, one hand pressed to the glass.

Sam slid off his stool to intervene before the wolves descended and started offering to buy her drinks.

Relief flooded her face when she saw him. She started forward, then hesitated when a man seated at a nearby table lumbered to his feet, his glazed eyes fixed on her.

"Hey pretty girl, want I should buy you a—"

Sam placed a hand on his shoulder and pushed him back into his chair. "No."

The man's face reddened in outrage, and his words slurred. "I wasn't offering to buy *you* a drink."

Holly wrapped her icy fingers around Sam's wrist and inched closer, surprising him. He couldn't recall her ever touching him before.

"Th-thank you, but I'm not really thirsty."

Disappointed, the big man hung his head and slumped over his drink.

Holly's fingers lingered on Sam's wrist for another moment, then loosened and dropped away. She stepped back from him, her cheeks pink with embarrassment. "Sorry."

"You shouldn't be here."

"Jordan said you were upset." Her eyes flickered to the abandoned beer bottle on the counter. "And at a bar, probably drinking. And I just wanted to make sure you were okay."

"It was one beer, Holly. I don't need an intervention."

"That's not . . ." She made a frustrated noise and crossed her arms. "He said your testimony didn't go the way you planned, and you were really angry when you left the courtroom."

He flexed the ache from his knuckles. "You don't have to worry about me."

"You worry about me all the time."

"Yes, but you're . . ." He closed his mouth just in time to keep the words *small and vulnerable* from escaping, but Holly's eyes narrowed with suspicion.

"I'm what?"

Sam sidestepped the question. "Where's Jordan?"

She lifted one finger from her arm and pointed outside. "We got ambushed."

Sam leaned around her to see Jordan about fifteen feet down the sidewalk, blocking a dark-haired woman with a camera every time she made a move toward the bar. Every reporter, journalist, and blogger was slithering out of the shadows, hoping for juicy details about the trial.

Sam was not looking forward to the blog posts and news updates about his testimony. He was never going to hear the end of it from his coworkers.

"So . . . I'm thirsty now." Holly squeezed past him and strode to the counter.

The big man started to rise. "I'll buy you a—"

Sam gave him a look that stalled him in his tracks. "It's still a no." He waited for the man to drop back into his chair before starting toward the bar. He caught the news broadcast on the television. The sound was muted, but the streaming banner across the bottom of the screen recapped the ongoing trial. A picture of Collin appeared in the upper right-hand corner.

Sam leaned over the counter and whispered to the bartender, "Change the channel please."

The man opened his mouth to ask why, but then Holly's photo flashed across the screen, and he glanced at the redhead sitting at his bar. Without a word, he lifted the remote and switched the channel to ESPN.

Sam claimed the stool beside Holly, who was doing her best not to appear rattled by the eyes still watching her.

She rubbed at her thighs and scanned the counter, her feet bouncing on the rungs of the stool. "I don't see a menu. Are there menus?"

"It's a bar, Holly, not a restaurant."

"Does that mean no food?"

He tipped his head toward the bowl of peanuts. "But I don't recommend eating them."

Patrons grabbed handfuls of peanuts on their way back from the restroom. Who knew if they washed their hands? Sam would need to be starving before he stuck his hand into that petri dish of bacteria.

A vaguely nauseated look crossed Holly's face, and she swallowed before turning her attention away from the bowl of nuts. "I think I'll pass."

The bartender approached with a warm smile. "What can I get for you, sweetheart?"

Holly's eyebrows pinched in indignation. There was only one man she allowed to call her sweetheart, and that man was not a middle-aged bartender she'd just met. After reprimanding him with a glare, she let the offhand endearment go. "Do you have any—"

"If you ask for chocolate milk with marshmallows, I'm leaving," Sam said on a whisper.

She cast him a sideways glance, as if trying to decide whether or not he was serious, then said, "Dr. Pepper and . . . maybe French fries?"

"Sure thing, sweet cheeks."

172

She blinked at the retreating bartender's back, and then rubbed self-consciously at her cheeks. She was twenty-nine, but she had a baby face that made her look years younger, and her short stature only added to the misperception.

With a bite of irritation left over from the bartender's comment, she told Sam, "There's nothing wrong with chocolate milk and marshmallows."

"There is, when you put them together." He played absently with the top of his beer bottle until he noticed her watching out of the corner of her eye.

It wasn't just the roomful of men that made her edgy; it was the alcohol.

She's the one who walked into a bar, he thought, his dark mood resurfacing. *What was she expecting, an AA meeting?*

But then he remembered that this was Holly. She had expected exactly what she walked into, but she had still chosen to walk into it because she cared about *him*. He wished she wouldn't do things like that, but it was just a part of who she was.

He set aside the beer and grabbed his untouched glass of water, wiping down the outside of it with a napkin before thoroughly cleaning the rim. "How are you holding up with the trial going on?"

The bartender placed a glass of Dr. Pepper in front of her and she wrapped both hands around it. "I'm fine, and I came here to talk about you, not me."

"There's nothing to discuss."

"I disagree."

"You're disagreeable by nature, so that's not a valid reason."

She shifted on her stool to face him. "I know you're mad at yourself because you think what happened in court is your fault. But it isn't."

When he spoke, he was careful not to let any of his self-directed anger slip through. "How is it not my fault, Holly? I remembered things wrong."

"If you had remembered things right to begin with, what would've changed?"

"I wouldn't have told the jury that he took you."

"And at the end of your testimony today?"

He opened his mouth, but it took him a moment to reason out his words. "I couldn't tell them that he took you."

Her lips quirked into an impish smile. "So . . . whether you remembered right or you remembered wrong, we would still be in the same position."

He understood her logic, but there were bound to be unforeseen consequences for his mistake. There were always consequences. "I suppose."

"Then please don't be mad at my friend."

Her eyes pleaded with him to let it go. She was so quick to forgive and move on, but it wasn't that easy for him. Still, he nodded in agreement just to appease her.

"Ooh, French fries." She perked up when the massive plate of fries landed in front of her.

"Anything else I can do for you, sweet—"

The fry in Holly's hand came within inches of spearing the bartender before he could finish speaking. "You can stop calling me things that aren't my name. I'm not your *sweet* anything." She plunged her potato weapon into the cup of ketchup next to the mound of fries and popped it into her mouth. "And thank you for the fries."

The bartender chuckled as he walked away, either amused by her antics or by the fact that she wasn't the least bit intimidating.

The front door opened and Jordan strolled in. His gaze swept over the faces in the room as he made his way to the bar counter.

Holly nudged her plate of fries toward him. "Want some?"

"Considering it would take you a week to eat all these, sure." Jordan snatched a fry and dipped it in ketchup.

Holly brushed off her hands and hopped down from her stool, searching the room for something. "Excuse me, Mr., um . . . Bartender."

The man smiled. "Joe."

"Where can I find the bathroom?"

"End of the hall." He indicated a long, dimly lit passageway that led to the back of the building.

A wary look crossed Holly's face as she regarded the narrow, creepy-looking hallway.

Sam considered offering to escort her to the restroom, but that would probably offend her womanly independence. "None of these guys are gonna follow you, and we'll watch to make sure no journalists come in through the back."

The startled expression on her face told him he had nailed the source of her hesitation.

"I'll watch your drink," Jordan assured her.

With that last nudge of confidence, she headed down the hall toward the restroom.

Sam took a gulp of his water and eyed the big man who was so keen on buying Holly a drink. He had seen her go, but he looked about as threatening as a dejected puppy. He wanted companionship, like most people who come to bars.

Sam turned his attention to Jordan. "Who was following you guys?"

Jordan shrugged. "Some journalist. Big guy, reddish hair, in desperate need of a comb."

Sam recognized the description of the same man he confronted just this morning at Jace's apartment. What was the guy hoping to accomplish by hounding a girl who refused to answer his questions?

He pulled his wallet from his back pocket. "I'm gonna pay the bill so we can get Holly out of here. That guy's not gonna give up." He tossed a few bills on the counter, then decided to voice the other issue on his mind. "What were you thinking—sending Holly alone into a bar full of drunks?"

"I didn't send her into a bar full of drunks. I sent her into a bar with you, where there just happened to be a few drunk people. I assumed you'd look out for her."

"Of course I looked out for her, but with her anxiety issues, she has no business being here."

"Holly has business being wherever she wants to be. I don't make her decisions for her. Neither do you. Besides, when I told her you were here, she threatened to come on her own if I didn't bring her. You know how she is."

Cold air wafted through the room, and Sam swiveled on his stool to see someone entering through the rear door.

He half expected Addison Miles or his camera lady to sneak inside, but it was just an old woman bundled up against the cold.

She smoothed her flyaway gray hairs back into place as her gaze passed over the patrons in the bar, then pushed open the women's room door and slipped inside.

21

*H*olly checked her shoes as she shuffled out of the bathroom stall, making sure she didn't have any strips of toilet paper trailing behind her.

This bathroom was disgusting, and she wouldn't be surprised if there was more toilet paper on the floor than on the roll.

She tiptoed to the vanity to wash her hands, but when she tried to turn on the faucet, nothing happened. She wiggled the lever and frowned at the single droplet of water that splashed into the bowl.

Why couldn't Sam have picked a nicer bar? Maybe one with chocolate milk. And employees who cleaned things. She rifled through her purse for her bottle of hand sanitizer.

The door to the bathroom opened behind her, and a plump older woman tried to squeeze through the narrow opening with her bulky jacket and oversized purse.

"Here, let me . . ." Holly stepped forward to help with the door, but when she caught a glimpse of the woman's eyes—as pale blue as snow-covered ice—she froze.

She knew those eyes.

The woman shouldered the stubborn door the rest of the way open and then let it fall shut behind her with a resounding thump.

Holly's heartbeat migrated to her temples, each quickening pulse warning her to back away, but she couldn't seem to unglue her boots from the grimy orange tile.

The woman unraveled the scarf from the lower half of her face and smiled, the expression as condescending as it had been fifteen years ago. "Hello, dear."

Holly swallowed, her throat dry.

Mrs. Wells pulled off her leather gloves and tucked them into her purse. "You seem surprised to see me."

Holly had hoped never to see the woman again, but of course she would be in town for her son's trial.

"We need to talk about the trouble you're causing with that busy imagination of yours."

Bitterness welled in Holly as she remembered how many times her former foster mother had dismissed her concerns and injuries with similar sentiments: *You're just trying to cause trouble. It's only your imagination.*

"I don't . . . wanna talk to you."

Mrs. Wells looked her over, her face creasing with false sympathy. "Still such a little thing, aren't you? Plain and shapeless."

She moved closer, and Holly back-stepped, gripping the edge of the vanity.

"It's a wonder any man looks at you twice. Poor thing." She touched Holly's hair with feigned affection, letting the silky strands slide through her fingers. "And you expect a jury to believe my Collin—my handsome, educated, wealthy son—forced himself on you?"

Holly's stomach cramped. She *didn't* expect the jury to believe her. She was a twenty-nine-year-old nobody with a ninth-grade education, easy to dismiss and forget.

"No, no one's going to believe it. When my boy speaks, people are drawn in by his eloquence and intelligence. He was born to be a politician or a lawyer. You can't even speak without stammering and mumbling. How do you think it's going to look for you when my son asks you a question on the witness stand, and you sit there, stumbling over your own lying tongue?"

It took a moment for the meaning behind her words to sink in. "He . . . he doesn't get to ask me questions."

"Oh, has no one told you? He fired his inept lawyer, which gives him the right to defend himself. He gets to ask you anything he wants."

Holly's fingers tightened on the vanity, and she struggled to draw in a breath as fear squeezed her lungs.

Shannon promised her that Collin wouldn't be allowed to speak to her in the courtroom. Surely she wouldn't lie about something like that.

Lawyers twist the truth, fear whispered, making it even harder to breathe. *It's what they do.*

"Now, don't fret." Mrs. Wells pulled a handful of tissues from her purse and held them out. "You don't have to testify."

Holly stared at the tissues. She hadn't even realized she was crying, but now she could feel the tears burning down her cold cheeks.

"I know your friends convinced you that you're doing the right thing, but really, Holly, look at yourself. Something that has you shivering and crying in a filthy public bathroom is hardly what's best for you."

This woman had never once cared what was best for her. She certainly wasn't going to start now.

"There's no reason for you to embarrass yourself in front of all those people. The judge, the jury, the media . . . they will all see your testimony for what it is— a story fabricated by a girl desperate for attention. The media will eat you alive, now that they know what kind of girl you really are."

Holly licked her salty lips. "What do you mean?"

"I was your foster mother for nearly a year. I'm privy to certain information they would all love to hear."

"I didn't do anything wrong."

Mrs. Wells heaved a sigh. "You were such a harmful influence on the other children. Between your pathological lying and promiscuous behavior, I just couldn't handle you. Always sleeping around with boys at school, trying to seduce my son."

Holly stared at her in horror. "But that's not . . ."

"What really happened? The media doesn't care about the truth, Holly. They care about ratings, and a supposed rape victim who makes a habit of lying and sleeping around, well . . . that's a sensational story."

Nausea crawled the walls of Holly's stomach, and she fought not to lose the few French fries she'd eaten. "Please, don't do this."

"It's already done. The best thing for you to do is disappear. People will forget all about you within a month." Mrs. Wells reached into her purse, trading in the tissues for an envelope. "There's enough money in here to help you start over somewhere else. All you have to do is publicly admit that Collin never touched you and then leave."

Leave, as if it were that simple. So many times, she'd left everything behind and melted away into the shadows, but Collin always found her.

She glanced at the thick stack of bills peeking out of the envelope. There was probably more money in there than she made in a year with her sporadic photo shoots, but it wouldn't protect her.

"I don't want your money." She just wanted to be safe, to live her life without fear haunting her every step. "And I won't lie."

Mrs. Wells's lips tightened. "I don't think you understand, Holly. Either you take this money and disappear, or I will give it to someone who will *help* you disappear."

Icy fear slapped Holly in the face and trickled all the way down to her toes, leaving a tremor in its wake. Would she really send someone after her? "You . . . you wouldn't."

"I will do whatever is necessary to protect what's mine, and I'm not going to let some worthless piece of street trash ruin my sweet boy's life."

"But you know I'm telling the truth. You know what he did to me; you knew it then, too, but you—"

"I took you in when no one else wanted you, gave you a clean bed, new clothes, all the food you could want, and you had the nerve to complain because Collin was occasionally rough with you. There's a word for that, Holly—ungrateful."

Holly choked as fresh tears clogged her throat. "You let him hurt me."

The night that Collin first attacked her, Holly went to her foster mother for help, crying so hard she could barely breathe. Mrs. Wells slapped her and called her a liar.

"You could've stopped it, but you didn't. You just . . . let it keep happening."

The bathroom door opened, and a blond woman staggered inside, glancing at them before stumbling off to a stall.

Mrs. Wells's voice dropped to a whisper. "These terrible things you claim my son did to you—they happen to girls all the time. Pretty little nobodies just like you. One day they just disappear, and when they're found years later—*if* they're found—it's in a shallow grave." She straightened her shoulders and pointedly tucked the money back into her purse. "And since you foolishly declined my offer—"

The band of fear around Holly's chest tightened even more. "Please don't."

Mrs. Wells smiled and patted her cheek. "Enjoy this night of freedom, dear. You never know when your circumstances might change."

She wrapped her scarf around her neck, yanked open the bathroom door, and walked out.

22

*H*olly's voice trembled softly as she described the recent encounter with Collin's mother, and Marx's grip tightened on the mug of hot tea he was preparing in the kitchen.

He'd suspected Agatha Wells might try to intimidate Holly, but he never expected the woman to accost her in a public bathroom. Especially with Jordan and Sam nearby.

He cast both men a glare that conveyed his irritation and disappointment. Sam dropped his eyes to the area rug on Marx's living room floor, but Jordan's stormy gaze lingered on the window as the story spilled from Holly's lips.

Agatha Wells had threatened to have her abducted. And possibly killed.

Marx wanted to throw something, but hurling a mug across the apartment wouldn't make Holly feel any safer. Drawing in a calming breath, he finished preparing the Chamomile tea, and then carried it into the living room where Holly sat, curled into the corner of the couch.

"Here, baby."

She lifted her eyes to his and wrapped shaking fingers around the mug. "Thanks."

The brush with her former foster mother left her shaken, and he wished there was something he could do to soothe her.

He sat down on the coffee table across from her and rested his hands on her socked feet. "It's gonna be all right, sweetheart. I know she said some terrible things, but I'm not gonna let anybody hurt you."

The doubt that flickered across her face before she could look away sank between his ribs like a knife.

He deserved it. When she needed his protection the most, he wasn't there. She had no reason to believe this time would be any different, and there was no promise he could make that wouldn't sound hollow.

He patted her feet. "Drink your tea. It'll help calm your stomach."

She stared into her mug for a long moment, her expression pensive. "She said something else, but I think . . . I think maybe she was just trying to scare me." Her brow furrowed. "She said Collin fired his lawyer, that he gets to ask me questions in court." She looked up, her expression pleading for someone to refute it. "But she's lying, right?"

Marx's gut twisted. This wasn't how he wanted her to find out.

"Right?" she asked again, a quiver creeping into her voice. She looked from one face to the next, but no one spoke up to allay her fears.

"Holly—"

"No." The mug began to tremble in her hands, the steaming liquid sloshing over the brim. "No, she wasn't telling the truth. She wasn't."

Marx gently peeled the mug from her clenched fingers before she could burn herself. "I'm sorry, Holly, but she wasn't lyin' about that."

Her eyes turned liquid with tears. "But Shannon said . . ."

"She had no idea he was gonna do this."

"But he can't."

Marx drew a steadying breath, trying to keep anger from his voice. "Accordin' to the law, he can."

A mangled sound somewhere between a sob and an exhale of disbelief escaped her throat, and she buried her face in her knees. Riley whined and rested his muzzle on her feet, nudging his nose between her ankles.

Her pain and fear pulled at Marx's heart, but he didn't know how to make it better. "I wish there was somethin' I could do to fix this, sweetheart, but all I can do is promise you that—"

"Don't." She lifted her head and smeared the sheen of moisture from her cheeks. "Don't make promises you can't keep, and don't tell me it's all gonna be okay."

"I—"

"No." She shook her head, the fear in her eyes giving way to hurt and anger. "You knew. A minute ago, when you said everything was gonna be all right, you knew it *wasn't* all right. And you didn't tell me."

He'd been waiting for the right moment, but in his heart, he knew there was never a good moment to deliver difficult news like this. He just hadn't wanted to cause her any more pain. "You're right, and I'm sorry for that."

"Sometimes sorry isn't good enough." She climbed off the couch and walked away from him, but before she could leave the room, her anger found a new target. She poked Sam's chest and glared up at him. "You."

Sam looked down at the finger jabbing his chest, seeming more intrigued than bothered. He could've brushed her hand away, but he left it where it was.

"You're supposed to be the friend I can always count on to be honest, to never hide or sugarcoat the truth. I sat there on that bar stool next to you after your testimony, and you said *nothing.*" She didn't give Sam a chance to defend himself before turning on Jordan. "What about you? Did you know too?"

Jordan shoved his hands into the pockets of his jeans and nodded regretfully. "Yeah, I knew."

She blew out an angry breath, swiped the tears from her cheeks, and stormed out of the room. The bathroom door slammed, and a moment later the dead bolt clicked.

Sam plucked at his T-shirt where Holly's finger had connected. "I don't think I've ever seen her that angry."

"She's scared and she's hurt, neither of which she's great at dealin' with. Anger is an easy substitute."

Marx set aside the mug of tea and stood. "How did Collin's mother even find her tonight?" He looked between Sam and Jordan, neither of whom offered an answer to his question. "Holly doesn't make a habit of goin' to bars, so somebody tipped her off."

Jordan's eyebrows drew together in thought. "It could've been the journalist. Maybe he was hoping a confrontation would make a good story."

Marx had an inkling he knew the identity of the journalist before he even asked the question. "Let me guess. Addison Miles?"

Jordan nodded. "He skittered down an alley near the bar like a cockroach. I don't know where—" *Thump*. Something hit the bathroom door, and Jordan paused before continuing. "I don't know where he went, but it's possible he left to contact Collin's mother. I'm not sure how he would have her number, but he strikes me as a resourceful guy."

"He interviewed her, so he has a way to reach her," Marx said. "If he knew Holly was at the bar, then he's Agatha's source."

Jordan sat down on the arm of the couch. "If the incident at the bar was all a setup so Addison could write another sensational story, where was he when it was happening? I didn't see him after he disappeared down the alley."

"Maybe he was waiting outside the back door to corner Holly, expecting her to make a—" *Thump*. Sam looked at Marx, his eyebrows inching upward in question. "Maybe he thought she'd make a break for it."

Jordan folded his arms, his brow furrowed in thought.

"What's on your mind, Jordan?" Marx asked.

"Holly told me she feels like she's being watched, but she never sees anyone actually watching her. I thought maybe she was just stressed and anxious, but now I'm wondering how long this journalist has been following her."

Marx blinked in surprise. Holly hadn't mentioned that to him. "When did she tell you that?"

"When we were at the library the other morning, but it's not the first time I've caught her looking around, like she thinks someone's there."

Holly had a God-given sense when danger was near, and it had helped to keep her alive. If she felt like someone was following her, then there was a good chance she was right. "Until this is all resolved, I want somebody with her anytime she leaves the apartment. And that sociopath doesn't come anywhere near her."

"Which sociopath?" Sam asked. "Agatha Wells or Addison Miles?"

"Either of them. And keep an eye out for anybody payin' too much attention to her. We have no idea who else might be a threat."

"Do you really think Collin's mother would send someone to hurt Holly?" Jordan asked.

"From what I've learned about Agatha Wells, she would sell her soul if it benefited her son. Payin' to have Holly abducted or worse wouldn't give her a moment's pause."

Marx walked to the window and looked out at the city. Somewhere out there, a predator was being paid to stop Holly before she could testify, and they had no way to identify him.

. . . .

Marx let Holly vent for a little over an hour in the bathroom, the muffled *thump, thump* of objects hitting the walls and door becoming a quiet rhythm in the background as he perused Addison's website.

There were plenty of blog posts about corrupt law enforcement and conspiracies within the political hierarchy of the city, but it was the dozen pertaining to this trial that concerned him. The first article dated back to the beginning of August, almost six months ago.

Addison went to see Collin in the county jail, and then wrote an article telling his side of the story. Several of his pieces were littered with speculation about Holly, whom he labeled "the alleged victim."

Marx wanted to throttle this man.

Worse than the articles, though, were the comments from his blog followers. Some of them were vicious and disturbing. Did Addison realize how much hate and anger he was stirring in people, that he was directing those feelings at an innocent girl?

Marx glanced toward the bathroom, thankful that Holly was safely home, where he could protect her.

He clicked through the rest of the posts, but none of them mentioned where Addison and Agatha met for their interviews, or even if they met face-to-face. Hopefully he could find out more tomorrow morning.

He closed Holly's laptop and walked to the bathroom, tapping a knuckle on the door. "Holly."

"Go away." Even through the barrier between them, he could hear the thickness of tears in her voice.

He sighed and rested his head against the door frame. "I'm not gonna do that."

She was angry with him for good reason. He'd withheld the truth, a truth she had every right to know and deal with in her own way.

He wanted to protect her from anything that might cause her pain or fear, but maybe Michael had been right when he told Marx to prepare her rather than protect her. If he had just spoken with her and helped her process the news instead of trying to fix everything, they might not be in this situation.

If only there were a guidebook for things like this, something that could help Marx understand when to protect and when to step back and let her face her challenges. He was fumbling his way through this role as a father figure, and he wasn't sure he was doing a very good job.

Lord, help me be what she needs me to be right now. What you need me to be for her.

Listening to the quiet sniffles coming from inside the bathroom, he knocked again. "I'd like to come in if that's all right. Just me."

He'd sent Sam and Jordan home a while ago. She wasn't as comfortable with them as she was with him, and their presence would make it more difficult for her to let down her guard.

"Holly."

There was a long silence before she conceded. "Okay."

He unlocked the door with the key he kept on top of the refrigerator for emergencies, and nudged it open. What looked to be three dozen rolls of toilet paper were scattered across the floor and countertop.

He'd taught Holly this exercise last spring, when she was struggling to release her pent-up emotions. Every roll she tossed represented one moment of pain, fear, or anger, and she'd been cycling through them for an hour.

He held up both hands in surrender. "Could we have a temporary cease-fire?"

Holly sat against the wall between the toilet and the tub, turning a roll of toilet paper over in her hands. After a moment of consideration, she let it tumble to the floor by her feet.

He navigated his way around the obstacles on the floor and cleared a space beside her so he could sit down. He draped his arms over his knees and looked up at the ceiling, searching for the right words.

To his surprise, Holly spoke first, her voice resigned. "I knew he would find a way to manipulate the system. It's what he does."

"We all expected he would try somethin', but this is an act of desperation on his part. He's scared."

"Collin's not scared of anything."

Marx could think of at least two things Collin feared—death and spending the rest of his life behind bars without access to what he craved. Jordan introduced him to the fear of death, and this trial introduced him to the other. "He's afraid of you, peanut."

She looked up at him, incredulous. "That doesn't even make sense. Even when I try to be intimidating, people just laugh at me."

Because she was about as ferocious as a ticked-off kitten, but voicing that explanation would likely earn him a toilet paper roll to the face.

"It makes perfect sense. For the first time in Collin's life, you hold the power over *his* future. He's terrified that your testimony will bury him alive."

Holly shook her head and halfheartedly tossed another roll of toilet paper. "No one's gonna believe me over him."

"I disagree, and apparently so does Collin's mother. If she didn't think your testimony was a threat to him, she wouldn't want you gone so badly."

Holly made a disgusted noise in the back of her throat. "Hagatha."

"Hagatha?" He choked back a laugh. "That's what you call her?"

"That's what all the foster kids called her behind her back."

"Somethin' tells me that nickname was your doin'."

"If you ever meet her, you'll understand."

He hoped to meet *Hagatha* Wells sooner rather than later. He had a few words and a pair of handcuffs for her. Witness intimidation was a crime.

"I'm sorry, sweet pea. The news should've come from me, not from her. I wanted to protect you from the fear and pain I knew it would cause, but . . ." He'd fumbled the ball on that one. "I'm sorry. I hope you can forgive me."

Holly rubbed at her nose. "On two conditions."

Here we go, he thought with amusement. Holly could be quite the negotiator. One of their first encounters involved him trying to pry information out of her, and she allowed him two questions with conditions. "All right, I'm listenin'."

"I know I still struggle with some stuff, and I probably always will, but I'm not . . . broken or fragile anymore, so . . . stop treating me like I am."

She'd come a long way from the traumatized girl he brought home from the hospital—the girl who didn't speak for weeks, who wouldn't leave the apartment, who sobbed for hours and flinched if he moved too quickly. That girl needed his constant protection, but Holly had outgrown her.

"I need to know when something important is happening. I don't wanna be kept in the dark," she added.

"Just to clarify, you were never broken. A little bruised, yes, but he didn't break you. And I promise I will try to be more open with information. What's your second condition?"

She bit her bottom lip. "I could really use a hug."

That he could do. He stretched out an arm and she scooted closer, burrowing into his side. He wrapped her up tight and kissed the top of her head. "Am I forgiven?"

"I forgave you before you came in the bathroom."

He snorted in amusement. So those conditions had just been to mess with him? *Brat.*

She sniffled and rested her cheek against his chest. "What happens if I don't testify?"

He hesitated to answer, but he'd promised to be more open. "Things aren't goin' as well with the trial as we hoped. If you decide not to take the stand, it could . . . seriously weaken the case against Collin."

She fell quiet for so long that, if not for the occasional hitch in her breathing, he might've thought she'd drifted to sleep.

"I realize confrontin' him is gonna be difficult, but remember we have somebody on our side that Collin doesn't."

She drew in an unsteady breath and then released it. Holly believed that God was always with them, but that didn't necessarily mean things would work out the way they wanted them to.

She looked up at him, her eyes still swollen from tears, and said so softly that he almost couldn't hear her, "I'm scared."

"I know, baby." He wrapped his arms more tightly around her and rested his chin on the top of her head. "I know."

23

*S*hannon slipped her key into the lock of her office door, her eyes trailing to the title emblazoned across the frosted glass: *DA Shannon Marx*.

Her gaze lingered on the gold letters. She'd considered reverting to her maiden name more than once—it made professional sense—but she wasn't ready to let go of that small piece of the man she still loved.

With a sigh, she opened the door to her office and stepped inside. She shrugged off her winter layers and put on some tea, taking comfort in the routine.

She speed-dialed Rick's number. He'd called her last night to tell her about the confrontation in the bar restroom.

She would deal with the fact that her witnesses were in a bar during an ongoing trial later; right now, there were more important matters to handle.

Shannon had warned Agatha Wells to stay away from her witnesses, but the woman had gone straight for Holly. The police were already looking for her and whatever mystery man she'd hired, but if she was anything like her son, she would be difficult to find.

Rick sounded worn to the bone when he answered the call. "Hey."

"You sound exhausted."

"You don't sound much better."

She smiled. "You always know how to compliment a woman." Between every creak and groan of the house and concerns about the trial racing through her mind, she hadn't slept much. "How's Holly doing?"

His sigh filtered down the line. "Agatha Wells rattled her, but I think findin' out about Collin representin' himself scared her more than anythin' else."

She put the phone on speaker so she could button her blazer. "You think she's going to be all right?"

"She just needs some time to adjust."

Shannon hoped that was the case. It was already Wednesday, which meant Holly had three days to make a decision about whether or not she was willing to testify. She would be Shannon's final witness, and the judge decided to squeeze her in Saturday morning before breaking for the weekend. The following Monday would open with Collin calling witnesses for the defense.

"I enjoyed dinner yesterday evenin'," Rick said.

She smiled to herself. "Me too."

Spending time with Rick had soothed the ache of loneliness that seemed to be her only companion these days, and she savored every moment, even when he tried to steal her egg roll. Such a crime should be considered grand theft, but she let him off with a smack of her chopsticks across his knuckles.

And she realized something as she sat beside him at his desk, studying the photographs he kept on display—a picture of her, one of Holly, and one of his parents. She'd seen them all before, but it wasn't until last night that they answered the question that had been nagging at her for the past year:

Why wasn't Rick moving on?

It wasn't just that he still loved her. It was that, in his mind, he had everything he needed—his parents, a woman he vowed to love until death do them part, and a girl he cherished as a daughter. He had a family, and there was no need for anyone else.

"I set up a meetin' with Addison Miles," Rick said, breaking into her thoughts. "The journalist Agatha Wells has been talkin' to. Maybe he can point us in her direction."

"Good. I'll be in court for most of the day, but call me as soon as you find out what's going on with Collin's mother. I want her off the streets."

"Who's testifyin' today?"

"The patrol officers who responded to the gunshots fired in Samuel's apartment. And then Carson this afternoon."

If all went well, Carson's testimony would vindicate Samuel in the eyes of the jurors, supporting his statement that Collin abducted Holly.

. . . .

Addison Miles strutted through the front door of the precinct, his beady eyes flickering suspiciously over the uniformed officers. He would throw every officer in this building under the bus if it increased his online following.

Disgust curled through Marx's stomach. He did not want to work with this lie-peddling fool, but he needed to know where Agatha Wells was hiding. And he was hoping, praying, that the man had a conscience.

The smell of old sweat and grease wafted from Addison when he stopped in front of Marx, and bread crumbs peppered the collar of his shirt. "You said you had some information for me."

Marx gestured to the conference room. "After you."

Addison hesitated. "You expect me to meet with you behind closed doors?"

"We're in a police precinct. What exactly do you think I'm gonna do to you?"

Addison sneered. "I've talked to people who've been attacked by the police behind closed doors."

"I don't have time for this. Either come in or get out."

Addison scratched at his mane of wiry red hair, then strode into the conference room. He dropped into a chair and set his tape recorder on the table. "So what is it you wanna tell me?"

"You interviewed Agatha Wells more than once."

Addison leaned back in his chair, causing the springs to squeak. "I meant what do you wanna tell me that I don't already know."

"Where did you meet?"

"Why does it matter?"

"She accosted Holly."

Addison's smug expression slipped for just a second. "I doubt that."

"And why is that?"

"Agatha Wells is disappointed in Holly for her lies and theatrics, but I get the impression she still very much cares about her."

"Then you don't have very good instincts. She cornered Holly in a public bathroom and threatened her, but you probably know all about that since you're the person who called her to let her know Holly was at the bar."

Addison tilted his head, smugness returning. "What makes you think I had anything to do with it?"

"Because you were there, and you know how to contact her."

"Who I call is my business. And did anyone actually witness this threat? Because for all I know, it's just a product of Holly's overactive imagination."

Marx resisted the urge to slap some sense into the man. He was eating up Agatha's lies and regurgitating them all over the place. "Do you believe everythin' Collin's mother tells you?"

Addison crossed his arms over his protruding gut. "Not everything. I don't believe her son was the innocent Boy Scout she makes him out to be, but she does make some valid points."

Marx pressed his hands to the table top, leaning. "She told Holly that if she didn't take the money she was offerin' and disappear, she would pay somebody to *help* her disappear. And just to make sure Holly understood what she meant by that, she reminded her that girls like her disappear all the time and end up dead in shallow graves."

Addison's eyes narrowed. "That doesn't sound like the woman I've spoken with."

"Agatha Wells is a box of crazy disguised by nice wrappin' paper. You just have to be around her long enough to notice." He tossed the printout of Victor Wells's social media posts on the table in front of him. "Her husband figured it out and finally left her."

Addison picked up the paper and studied the contents. "I've seen these. Divorce makes people bitter, and they say all kinds of things."

"Does it also make them turn on their own child? He believes, without a doubt, that his son is guilty."

"I'll admit, that one makes me wonder."

"Collin and his mother lie as easily as they breathe. Does any of what they're sayin' really match up with what you've seen from Holly?"

Addison crossed his arms and leaned back in the chair again. "I saw her go into a bar."

"Did you see *why* she went into that bar, or did you just assume it was to drink and flirt with people?" Marx paused, waiting for him to dispute it, but he didn't. "She went there to comfort a friend. She didn't drink, unless you count Dr. Pepper, and you can question anybody who was in that bar and they'll tell you that she didn't flirt with anybody."

Addison frowned.

"If all of this—the abduction, the trial—is Holly's vindictive way of gettin' back at Collin for somethin', then why isn't she tellin' her story to the media? Why isn't she sharin' the details that would rip his reputation to pieces? She's certainly had time to work them out, so why not use them to her advantage?"

Addison said nothing, which was a good sign. If he didn't have a snide retort, maybe Marx was getting through to him.

"Collin Wells did abduct her, and his mother did threaten her last night at the bar. There's somethin' wrong with that family, Addison. When they want somethin', there is nothin' they won't do to get it, even if it means manipulatin' some gullible soul into doin' their dirty work. Don't be a pawn for them."

Addison's nostrils flared. "Even if you're right, what do you expect me to do?"

"Tell me where to find Agatha Wells."

"And become known as someone who gives up information about my sources? That's journalism suicide." He tilted his head, considering a new angle. "But I'll consider it for an exclusive with Holly."

Marx scoffed. "After the way you dragged her name through the mud? Not a chance."

"If there's nothing in it for me, then why should I help?"

"Because it's the right thing to do."

Addison laughed. "No one cares about the 'right thing' anymore, Detective. Except maybe you."

"Agatha Wells is gonna send somebody to hurt Holly, possibly kill her. Do you want that on your conscience?"

Addison ran his tongue along the insides of his lips, his fingers tapping his biceps. "I can't tell you where she's staying. We met at a coffee shop of her choice."

"What about a phone number?"

Addison pulled his phone from his pocket and set it on the table, tapping the screen to open up his contacts. He gestured to Agatha Wells's number. "Help yourself."

"I'd like you to call her. Set up a meetin'."

"And if she's as crazy as you want me to think she is, the moment she finds out I turned on her, she'll kill me."

"You really think I would send you to meet with her alone?" Did the guy think it was his first day on the job? "Call her."

Addison grabbed his phone with a grimace. "I don't like you."

"Don't worry, the feelin's mutual."

Addison dialed the number and put the phone on speaker. An automated voice picked up the connection. "We're sorry. The number you dialed has been disconnected and is no longer in service."

Marx bit back a curse. How was he going to find Collin's mother when she was ahead of him at every turn?

Addison ended the call, confusion stamped on his face. "I don't know why she would disconnect her number."

"Because she got what she wanted from you, and she doesn't need you anymore." Marx walked to the window, trying to figure out his next move. "Do you have any idea who she might contract to come after Holly?"

Addison rocked in the chair again, and the springs let out another cringe-worthy screech. "The last time I spoke with Wells—Collin, not Agatha—he mentioned receiving a lot of letters. Fans, critics, men and women who are in love with him. Maybe he mentioned them to his mother too."

Marx turned toward him with interest. High-profile cases like this one tended to draw the desperate and insane out of the shadows.

He should've considered that Collin might receive letters. He was attractive and charming enough to inspire followers, which meant Agatha Wells had a pool of disturbed individuals to choose from.

24

$\mathcal{S}$hannon had an hour lunch break before court resumed, and she was going to stretch out on her sofa. Hopefully a little rest would help her concentrate in the courtroom this afternoon.

She dropped onto the buttery leather cushions, but she barely had a chance to stretch out her legs when her cell vibrated with an incoming text. The sender was programmed into her contact list as "Carson's Attorney."

Drew Carson was supposed to be at the courthouse in an hour, so why was his lawyer contacting her? And with a text message, no less. Blatantly unprofessional. She tapped the screen of her phone to open the message:

> Hello, Ms. Marx. I'm contacting you on behalf of Mr. Carson. It seems he's decided not to testify. I explained the consequences for reneging on the deal you offered him, but he's adamant that he will not be taking the stand.

Shannon stared at the message in disbelief. Testifying reduced Carson's sentence from twenty years to twelve—a pittance for attempted kidnapping and attempted murder. Why would he throw that away?

Unless Collin had gotten to him.

But how? Shannon had gone to great lengths to ensure that Carson was held in a separate area of the county jail than Collin. Their paths should never have crossed, and he was fairly isolated from the other inmates for his own protection.

Maybe it was just a case of cold feet.

Shannon swung her legs off the couch. She needed to request a continuance from the judge so she could find out what in the world was going on with her witness.

Before she could pick up her office phone, her cell rang. Rick was calling, probably to fill her in on his interview with Addison.

She would have to call him back. She placed the call to the judge, apologizing for the last-minute request and explaining the circumstances.

Tipper sighed at the inconvenience but granted her a continuance until Thursday morning.

She called Rick back, and he answered on the second ring. "Sorry, I wasn't ignoring your call."

She cringed as the words left her mouth. For the first two years of their separation, she ignored every one of his phone calls, watching with anguish in her heart until his name stopped flashing across the screen.

"I needed to call the judge," she explained.

"Everythin' all right?"

"Carson just backed out of our agreement. He's refusing to testify. The judge granted a continuance, so I'm going to the jail to find out what's going on."

"I'm comin' with you."

She huffed. "I don't need a police escort. I'm not a helpless damsel. I can—"

"Take care of yourself, yes, I know. If I had a nickel for every time Holly told me that, I'd be able to afford a nicer car. But it's not about that. Addison said Collin has been receivin' letters from admirers. I think the name of the person Agatha hired might be in those letters."

"I would say that's more likely than her finding and hiring someone on the street."

"Do I need a warrant to search his cell?"

"No. Trial detainees aren't entitled to fourth amendment rights, but you'll need official jail personnel with you for the search."

"Good. I'll be by to pick you up in twenty minutes."

The line disconnected, and Shannon sighed. This day was not going at all the way she planned.

. . . .

The corrections officer opened the door to Collin's cell, and Shannon followed Rick into the small room. Charcoal sketches were taped to the wall, and Shannon's gaze fixed on the detailed drawing of a small bird, no doubt the one Mr. Burdock was supposed to deliver.

Another sketch focused on almond-shaped eyes filled with tears. Shannon recognized those eyes. Collin had captured Holly's pain and fear with disturbing perfection, as though his memory hadn't degraded one bit over the past ten months.

She folded her arms against the chill lingering at the base of her spine and glanced at Rick, who had been drawn in by the artwork as well. A muscle flexed his jaw as he studied the drawing of a faceless girl huddled in a corner, the bruises on her skin depicted by dark smudges.

"Why are these pictures on his wall?" he demanded.

The guard shrugged. "There's no rule against him hanging his art."

"They're drawin's of his victim."

"They all look pretty vague to me. Unless they're pornographic, we don't usually bother to take them down."

Rick's fingers flexed at his sides, and Shannon caught his hand when he reached toward the artwork. As much as he might want to rip them off the wall and shred them into confetti, it would only supply Collin with more ammunition to use against them in court.

"Just leave them. It's not worth the potential consequences, especially when he can just draw more."

Begrudgingly, he dropped his arm and turned his attention to the small metal table attached to the wall. It was covered with law books, notepads, and a sketchbook.

Shannon flipped through the law books, searching for anything interesting between the pages, but she found nothing but a few torn strips of paper used as place markers. The sketchpad was filled with more of the same artwork, though the deeper she went, the more disturbing the sketches became.

Disgusted, she closed the cover. "Any sign of the letters?"

"Only place left to check is under the mattress." Rick lifted one corner of it and felt along the surface. He found them at the other end. "There's gotta be thirty letters here."

"Hopefully they're not all from different people."

"What are you doing?"

Shannon and Rick turned to see Collin in the hall, one of the guards gripping him by the elbow. Now that afternoon court proceedings had been canceled, he was being escorted back to his cell.

"We're goin' through your stuff," Rick replied. "What's it look like?"

Collin turned on the guard monitoring their search. "You can't just let them go through my things. She's trying to prosecute me."

"That's only a problem if you have something in there that proves your guilt," the guard pointed out. "Do you?"

Collin pressed his lips together.

"We found what we came for." Rick held up the bundle of letters and led the way out of the cramped cell.

211

Collin's eyebrows drew together in confusion. "I don't know what you hope to find with those."

"The name of the person your mother hired to kill Holly."

"My mother would never hire someone to kill Holly. She knows—"

"How obsessed you are with her?"

"She knows how much Holly means to me."

"I guess you don't know your mother that well. Don't suppose you wanna tell me where she's hidin' out."

Collin rolled his eyes. "My mother's not exactly intelligent, Detective. If you look hard enough, you'll find her."

Rick grunted, probably in distaste of how easily Collin insulted his own mother. The man had no respect for anyone but himself. "Thanks for the names and addresses."

They started down the hall when Collin called out, "I'm sorry to hear about your witness not showing, but if you're here to change his mind, it's not going to work."

Shannon paused and looked back at him, uncertainty unfurling in her stomach. She'd requested that Carson be kept out of the general population for his own protection, but what if Collin had found another way to get to him? A way to pass along a threat, unnoticed by the guards?

Rick pressed a gentle hand to her back, propelling her forward, and they made their way to the visitation lounge, where Carson was supposed to meet with them. Shannon glanced at the men scattered around the room, but none of them were her cagey witness. Where was he?

Flustered, she marched back to the reception area to speak with the officer who was supposed to pass along her request for a meeting.

She approached the glass. "Excuse me. I requested to meet with Drew Carson."

"Sorry, but Mr. Carson doesn't wanna see you. Either of you."

"That's ridiculous. He's my witness."

The officer shrugged. "Yeah, he said come back in a couple weeks and he'll listen to what you have to say."

"A couple of weeks?" She turned to Rick. "This doesn't make sense. I agreed to reduce his sentence from twenty years to twelve if he testified against Collin. He wouldn't just throw that away."

"Unless somebody persuaded him that silence was in his best interest." Rick held his badge up to the glass. "I'd like to see Drew Carson's visitor log for the past month please."

The corrections officer clicked a few keys and then printed out a single sheet of paper, sliding it through the narrow opening beneath the glass. "He's not exactly a popular guy."

Shannon peered over Rick's shoulder at the short list of names. His most recent visitor was three days ago. Agatha Wells.

Shannon squeezed her eyes shut and dropped her forehead against Rick's shoulder. How many of her witnesses had Agatha Wells intimidated? And how many more would she threaten before they could catch her?

25

*J*ordan pulled the pizza from the oven and placed it on the counter, his attention drifting toward the nearest window of his apartment.

Holly stood in front of it, arms wrapped around her waist, her long red hair pulled over one shoulder. There was a vulnerability to her posture—a frightened girl staring out the window at an overwhelming world—and it made him want to wrap his arms around her.

But that was a line he couldn't cross, not until she was ready.

He prayed the day would come that she would trust him the way she trusted Marx, that she would curl up with him beneath a blanket on the couch and let him hold her. Just hold her. Some days it was almost unbearable being within arm's reach and unable to touch her.

She'd been the unshakeable one when they were children, brave beyond reason, and he wanted to strangle the life out of the man who taught her fear.

Except he'd tried that, and it didn't go as planned. He tossed the oven mitt on the counter and cleared his throat. "Dinner's ready."

Holly glanced at him over her shoulder, her eyes heavy with too much emotion. "It smells amazing, but I'm not really hungry right now. You go ahead."

Her cheekbones had become more defined over the past week, and he had no intention of letting her skip another meal.

"I made pizza . . . from scratch, which took hours, and then loaded it up with mushrooms and pineapple"—her favorite toppings—"and you're refusing to eat it?"

She opened her mouth, an apology on her lips, then paused, eyes narrowing. "Are you trying to guilt-trip me?"

"Would I do something like that?"

"Yes."

He smiled. "Okay, yeah, I probably would, but I would enjoy my pizza a lot more if we had it together."

She turned away from the window. "I'll sit with you while you eat. Now that you have a kitchen table and chairs."

"And a rug." He gestured to the rectangle of material near the front door.

Her eyebrows knitted. "That's a doormat."

"It said rug on the tag."

"It lied to you."

He grinned and carried two plates of pizza to the table. He'd had this apartment for almost a year, and he was still collecting the basic pieces of furniture.

He pulled out a chair for Holly and bowed theatrically. "Milady."

She cracked a small smile, a pale imitation of her usual one that could light up a room, but he would take it. "So now that you have a rug"—she air-quoted the last word— "what's the next big thing on your home furnishing list?"

He dropped into the chair across from her. "I was thinking a really nice can opener, for all those highly nutritious meals I eat right out of the can."

For a moment, Holly just stared at him, and then she laughed—a sweet sound interspersed with quiet snorts. He adored it.

"A can opener doesn't count."

"Hey, I'm a guy. I don't . . . furnish. I have a couch, a bed, my kickboxing bag. What else could I possibly need?"

She picked at a piece of pineapple. "Pillows."

"Pillows. Are we talking fuzzy, sparkly purple pillows?" Like the dozen she had in her bedroom at Marx's apartment. She had more pillows than floor space. "Because I have a manly reputation to uphold, and the moment Sam sees a sparkly pillow on my couch, it's all over."

Sam lived five apartments down, and they worked out together almost every day.

Holly flicked the pineapple around on her plate. "Maybe."

"Tell you what, when we furnish *your* place, I'll help you pick out a hundred pillows."

He'd dropped by to inspect her apartment the other day, and it needed a lot of work. He wasn't worried about the windows—the landlord would replace those—and cleaning up a year's worth of mildew and cobwebs would only take a couple of days.

His biggest concern was the apartment's design. The moment he set foot inside and switched on the light, he was transported back to that warehouse room where Holly was kept. The stained cement floor, the metal door, the single bulb on the ceiling, the exposed stone blocks of the walls.

Most of the apartment walls had been covered with drywall, but one—the one that stretched the length of the entire space and wrapped around the alcove where Holly's bed rested—still retained the original blocks.

The similarities to that warehouse room were unmistakable, and Jordan had a feeling it was intentional. Another one of Collin's mind games. Marx and Sam were going to help him give the place a facelift: add some more drywall to cover all the stone, carpet the floor, add a few more lights.

"I don't think I'll be moving back to my place anytime soon," Holly said, still playing with the same piece of pineapple.

"Repairs should only take a couple months."

"That's not what I mean." She sighed and dropped her hands into her lap. "If the entire trial is hanging on my testimony, then Collin is winning."

By all appearances, the outcome was leaning in Collin's favor, but Jordan didn't want to confirm her fears. He also wouldn't lie to her. Maybe they just needed to take a break from anything that pertained to the trial. If he could distract her from her anxiety, she might be more willing to eat something.

He scooped both plates off the table and tucked them into the fridge, along with the leftovers. "Change of plans. Grab your coat."

She shot him a puzzled look. "Where are we going?"

"Someplace that'll help you get your mind off things."

. . . .

Skaters glided across the outdoor ring of ice, some so graceful that they could've been floating. Holly wasn't going to be one of those people. She was going to be the person who spent more time on her butt than her feet.

She rubbed her mittens together. "I'm not sure this is a good idea."

Jordan finished tying the lace on her ice skate, and looked up at her. "I won't let you fall."

"What if I slip, and I trip you, and we both fall?"

The smile that curved his lips brought out his dimples. "You're gonna be fine." He stood, balancing on the narrow blades of his skates, and offered his hands. "Come on."

Reluctantly, Holly placed her hands in his, and he pulled her to her feet. She wobbled, and he slid his hands up to her elbows to steady her.

"You good?"

"No." She was about to walk out onto the biggest frozen puddle she'd ever seen . . . with knives under her feet. What could possibly go wrong?

219

He laughed and led her toward the rink, one slow step at a time. "Just hold on to me."

Anxiety fluttered through her stomach the moment her skates hit the ice, and she clutched desperately at Jordan's forearms. She was not coordinated enough for this.

Jordan just smiled and skated backward, pulling her along with him. "Keep your ankles straight."

She looked down at the skates. Were her ankles straight? She couldn't see them, but they felt straight. "Okay. Now what?"

"Just relax."

Her awkward movements became graceful as she followed his lead. The people passing by them faded into the background as he swayed, pulling her into a slow and rhythmic dance across the ice.

She looked up at him through the glitter of snowflakes on her eyelashes, and caught him watching her. The look in his eyes made her heart flutter, and the heat that gathered in her cheeks felt hot enough to melt the ice around them.

She'd seen that look before, the day he considered leaning in to kiss her. But it was something more than desire; it was . . .

A camera flash broke into her thoughts, and she looked in the direction it had come from, unease stirring inside her. She searched the spectators for anyone who seemed fixated on the two of them, but she saw no one.

It was probably just a parent capturing precious moments of their child, but she couldn't shake the feeling that they were being watched.

"You're doing good," Jordan said, his voice dragging her attention back to him.

She wasn't doing anything. She was just along for the glide. "When did you learn to ice-skate?"

"I had a lot of alone time after you disappeared, and skating on old Mr. Hansen's pond helped pass the winters. I almost fell through the ice once."

Her eyes widened. "You could've died."

"Yeah, but I didn't."

Holly's blades hit a groove, and the fragile balance she'd been clinging to vanished. Her feet went in different directions, and an embarrassing sound somewhere between a yelp and a squeak escaped her.

Jordan tried to hold on to her arms, but his fingers slipped off her coat. He locked an arm around her waist, halting her clumsy tumble toward the ice, and pulled her back to her feet. "Wow, that was almost spectacular."

Her heart thundered in her chest, and she tried to catch her breath. "This probably would've been easier to learn when I was little."

Amusement lightened Jordan's voice. "I hate to break it to you, but you're still little."

"Ha-ha." The top of her head might only reach his shoulders, but that had nothing to do with her being short and everything to do with him being gigantically tall.

She started to straighten her legs and put a little space between them, but his arm was still clasped around her waist, holding her close. A spark of fear ignited in her stomach. She was stuck. *Trapped*, the fear whispered, but she banished that thought.

Jordan would let her go. All she had to do was ask. "Um, Jordan . . ."

He must have heard the discomfort in her voice, because he released her, withdrawing slowly so he didn't upset her newfound balance. "Sorry." He circled around to face her, keeping his body at a distance to give her the space he knew she preferred.

Sometimes she felt guilty for needing that space, but she didn't have the greatest history with men, especially the ones who were attracted to her. Every inch between her and them gave her an advantage if things went badly.

But Jordan was different. He would never hurt her, never force her to do things she didn't want to do. Logically she understood that, but there was so much more to it than logic.

She opened her mouth to apologize for being . . . complicated, but he spoke before she could. "Why don't we grab something warm to drink and then try again."

She followed his attention to the concession stand. "Do you think they have hot chocolate?"

"It's a concession stand, Holly. They all have hot chocolate. I don't know about marshmallows, though."

She reached into her coat pocket and pulled out her Ziploc stuffed with marshmallows. "I'm good."

He laughed. "Somehow I'm not surprised."

He offered his hand and she took it, holding on tight as she skated back to the wall opening on unsteady legs. She almost wiped out a second time, but he had scary-fast reflexes. Holly breathed a sigh of relief when they left the ice and she plopped onto a bench.

She was going to figure out this ice-skating thing. Just maybe not tonight.

26

Shannon fidgeted with her keys as Rick escorted her up the front steps to her house.

It had been nice spending the afternoon and evening with him, even if part of that time was at the county jail. She wanted to invite him in, and possibly to stay the night. Rick would probably accept the invitation without hesitation, but she couldn't give him hope for something between them without giving him all the facts.

Before anything more than these cordial and polite interactions could exist between them, he needed to know the truth behind her decision to divorce him.

Telling him now was a terrifying prospect. The truth could mend the rift between them, or it could push them further apart.

There were two things that Rick had told her he would never forgive: infidelity and dishonesty. His father had been unfaithful and secretive, and his decisions sent pain rippling through Rick's entire family.

Shannon had done what she thought was best for the man she loved, but it required prolonged dishonesty.

Now that she had him back in her life, even if not in the way she hoped for, she was afraid to lose even these small moments between them.

Maybe if you tell him the truth, it will make things right, her heart reasoned, even as her mind disagreed. *Tell him and he'll never forgive you. You'll lose all the progress the two of you have made.* Her heart immediately countered with inarguable truth: *Is it really progress if it's built on a lie?*

Her heart and mind could never agree; they were opposing counsel forever arguing their points in an imaginary courtroom.

For nearly six months before she filed for divorce, her inner dialogue had been a complete catastrophe—heart and mind tearing her in different directions. Never mind her hormones.

Her mind had won that battle, if this lonely life she now lived could be called winning.

She closed her fingers over her keys and steeled herself. "I know you have a lot of work to do, analyzing those letters and running down addresses, but would you like to come in for a few minutes? There's something we need to discuss."

. . . .

Marx draped his coat over the back of a bar stool at the kitchen island and sat down as Shannon put water on to boil.

It felt strange being in this house. They had spent years transforming it into a home—painting the walls, pulling up the old carpet, replacing damaged baseboards. Now he was no longer a part of it, and that knowledge left a dull ache in his chest.

How had things gone so wrong?

"I hope tea is all right." Shannon pulled two mugs from the cupboard, placing tea bags in them.

Marx interlaced his fingers on the countertop and watched her. She was still so beautiful—the olive tint to her skin, the silkiness of her hair, the way her curves . . .

"Rick."

"Hmm?" He lifted his eyes to hers as she turned toward him.

Her lips quirked into a teasing smile. "Were you staring at me?"

He inhaled slowly, considering his reply, then exhaled. "I might've been."

"That explains why you didn't hear my question."

"You asked a question?"

She laughed softly. "I did, actually. I'm guessing by your parting question for Collin that we still have no idea where his mother is. Sully hasn't been able to find anything?"

"Unfortunately no. She hasn't used her credit card or an ATM in the past month, and before that, she bounced around from one motel to another every few days. They don't have any family in the area, so wherever she's stayin', she's payin' cash."

"There can't be that many establishments that would accept cash payments. There's no protection for them if the guest causes damage."

"You'd be surprised how many places cater to people who don't wanna be noticed."

She poured water into each mug, then placed one in front of him. "I suppose."

He wrapped his hands around the warm ceramic, the heat soothing the chill in his fingers. "So what's on your mind?"

Shannon leaned against the opposite counter, gripping her mug of tea with both hands. "It's about us."

Dread settled in his chest. This was where she pushed him away, deciding it would be better if they didn't see or talk to each other anymore. He didn't think his heart could handle that again. "I know you have priorities, but things don't have to go back to the way they were. If you want more space, I can do that, but don't cut me out of your life again."

She dropped her eyes to her tea. "At the time, I thought cutting ties would be better, that if I was no longer a part of your life, you would have an easier time moving on. I wanted you to be happy."

"Happy." Did that word really just leave her mouth? "The love of my life left me after twenty years, and you thought I would be happy?"

Her lips parted soundlessly, and the length of time it took her to find her words told him they were going to be an excuse. "It's more complicated than that."

"It's not complicated. You wanted to focus on your career, you didn't want kids, you didn't love me anymore, you hated my job—"

"I still hate your job. It's dangerous, and I was always worried you wouldn't come home at the end of the day."

"So you divorced me to make sure I *never* came home at the end of the day. Makes perfect sense."

"I don't want to fight. I just want to explain."

He picked up his mug to taste the tea. "I'm listenin'."

"I never stopped loving you."

He paused with the mug halfway to his mouth. He must not have heard her correctly, because her words didn't fit with the cold disregard she'd treated him with the past three years. "Come again?"

"You heard me."

"I distinctly remember you sayin'—"

"I lied."

He set the mug carefully back onto the marble countertop. He wasn't sure whether to be hurt or relieved that she supposedly still loved him. In the end, she still walked away and destroyed their marriage. "But everythin' else was true."

She kicked off her high heels and stretched her toes on the cool tile floor, giving herself a moment to think. "I did worry about you every night with your job, and I did want to become the district attorney. But I could've pursued my career and worried about you while still sharing a life with you."

He sat back in the chair, his head spinning. "If it wasn't about love and it wasn't about your career—or mine—then why?"

Moisture gathered in her eyes. "I did what I did because I love you."

"You realize that makes no sense."

She brought the mug of tea to her lips, but her mind was elsewhere. "I knew that if I left you with any hope of a future for us, you would cling to it, so I told you what you needed to hear."

"So breakin' my heart was premeditated. That makes everythin' better."

She frowned at his sarcasm. "I never wanted to hurt you. This whole mess was about making things better for you."

"Better how? I was happily married before you handed over those divorce papers."

She released a frustrated breath and walked to the kitchen window, staring out at the fenced-in backyard. "You weren't happy, Rick. I saw the pain and longing in your eyes every time you saw a father playing with his child. You wanted a family, and I was the reason we were never going to have one. Because of who I am, because I'm too much like my mother."

"You are nothin' like your mother." That woman had been too absorbed in her own selfish desires to care for a child. Without a father in the picture, Shannon had practically raised herself.

Shannon studied her reflection in the window. "I see her staring back at me with each passing day."

"You never would've abandoned or neglected a child, and you certainly wouldn't have left them to starve."

"Not physically. But emotionally . . . I'm just not built to be a mother. I don't have maternal instincts, Rick. Our child would've hungered for an affection and connection I'm not capable of."

Marx stood, but kept a hand on the back of the chair. "I think if you had just tried . . ."

She shook her head. "I would've been cold and distant just like she was. I know that now even more than I did then. But you . . . you would've been an amazing father." She turned toward him, her face damp with tears. "I wanted that for you. I wanted you to experience the joy I was holding you back from."

Disbelief and anger churned through him. "So you left me?!"

"I did what was best for you."

"That should've been my choice to make!"

"If I had talked to you about it, you would've made the wrong choice."

"I would've chosen you!"

"Exactly."

His temper boiled. "You had no right to make that decision for me, to rip apart my life. You didn't even talk to me. You didn't ask me what I wanted."

"Rick—"

He held up a hand to cut her off. He didn't want to hear any more excuses for what she'd done. "You summarily decided that you knew best, and that is not how a relationship works, Shannon. The moment we said our vows, our life decisions were supposed to be made together."

Her voice hitched. "I'm sorry, Rick."

Right now, her apologies meant nothing. "I need to go home and check on Holly. Lock your door and reset the alarm after I leave."

She looked like she wanted to protest, but he didn't care at the moment. He grabbed his coat from the back of the chair and walked out.

27

*S*hannon opened the folder in front of her and skimmed her notes, but the words faded to the back of her mind as her thoughts lingered on the conversation with Rick last night.

She'd hoped that the truth might mend their relationship, but it only widened the rift between them, the distance so great that she doubted there was anything she could say or do now to bridge the chasm.

The way Rick looked at her before he left, as though she'd betrayed him, made her wish she had ignored her heart and kept the truth to herself.

She loved him more than anything in this world, and letting him go was the most selfless thing she could think to do. Yet somehow, by trying to improve his life, she had made a mess of things.

With a sigh, she closed the folder, her heart heavy. There was nothing she could do to fix her mistakes now.

Judge Tipper cleared his throat. "Ms. Marx, you were granted a continuance until this morning so that you could sort out the issue with your witness, Mr."— his gaze dropped to a document in front of him— "Carson. Were you able to do so?"

Shannon stood, and she could feel Collin's smug gaze on her. "He will not be testifying at this time, your honor."

"Very well. You may call your next witness."

"The state calls Jace Walker to the stand."

The courtroom door opened, and Jace wheeled into the room and up the ramp onto the witness stand with a grimace of determination fit for a hockey match. She locked her wheels and straightened her shoulders, trying to appear undaunted by the number of eyes watching her.

"Ms. Walker, you come from a fairly wealthy family, and you could live just about anywhere. Why did you choose to live in a lower income area of the city?"

Jace shrugged her shoulders. "I could live wherever I want with my parents' money, sure, but I wanna stand on my own two feet. Metaphorically speaking, because I can't actually stand."

Some of the jurors smiled, drawn to her open humor and engaging personality.

"And you live in the same apartment complex as Holly Cross?"

"Yeah. I was actually there the day she moved in, and I was super excited because I thought maybe we could be friends. I offered to help her move her stuff in, but all she had was a duffel bag. Literally, like a few pairs of clothes stuffed into a bag. That was it."

"That seems unusual."

"Right? That's what I thought. So I asked her where the rest of her stuff was, and she said she didn't have anything else."

Shannon considered how to phrase her next question. "You said you wanted to be friends with Holly. How did that work out?"

"Well, she's my best friend." Her gaze slid past Shannon to land on Jordan, who sat just behind the defense table, and she added with an air of teasing smugness, "And I'm hers."

Jordan lifted an amused eyebrow, and Shannon resisted the urge to roll her eyes at their squabbling over who got to be Holly's best friend.

"But it didn't start out very well," Jace continued. "It took a month to get her to even interact with me, and several more before she trusted me. Holly's kind of like a mouse. All cute and adorable, but super cautious, and you kind of have to lure her out of her safe hidey-hole with treats. Preferably marshmallows."

A few laughs rippled through the courtroom, and Jace blew out a tense breath, trying to rein in her nervous rambling.

"And how long have you two been friends?"

"About . . . two-ish years, I guess."

Shannon cringed inwardly. They had talked about Jace being precise with her answers, and *ish* did not qualify as precise. "You mentioned that she's cautious."

"Yeah, I noticed that right away."

She launched into a description of the timid girl who moved into the apartment complex. Holly hid inside her basement apartment like it was a fortress, and it was rare for her to open the door when someone knocked.

When she finally began to let down her guard and nurture a friendship with Jace, her peculiarities became more obvious. She frequently looked over her shoulder when they were out in public, as though she thought someone might be watching her, and she avoided all social media and digital trails, just as Sully had mentioned.

"A few weeks after we started hanging out, I took a picture of her for my phone's caller ID, and she freaked. I mean, tears in the eyes, begging me to delete it and not put it on the internet. I asked why, but she wouldn't tell me, and she was super spooked over the next few days."

"You think she was afraid of someone?"

"Yeah." Jace thrust a finger toward Collin. "That creep."

Tipper cleared his throat. "No name-calling in my courtroom, Ms. Walker."

"I thought I was supposed to tell the truth. The whole truth. Didn't I just swear to that?"

A few more laughs passed through the courtroom, and Tipper sighed. "Continue, counselor."

Shannon inclined her head gratefully. "When did you first meet Collin Wells?"

"In February of last year, at the ice arena. I play sled hockey with some other disabled athletes, and Holly came to watch the game. I know she doesn't care about hockey—she doesn't even like sports—but she comes to support me. I was actually trying to steal the puck from one of my opponents, when I saw him."

"When you saw Collin Wells," Shannon clarified. "How did you know what he looked like, if you had never met him before?"

"My boyfriend is a cop, one of the three trying to keep Holly safe after her foster brother came snooping around, and he had a picture. I took it so I would know what he looks like if he showed up."

"What happened at the ice rink?"

"Jordan . . . do you guys know Jordan?" Jace looked at the jurors, and then pointed to him. "He's the blue-eyed one that looks like he just stepped off the set of a surfer movie."

Shannon cleared her throat, reminding Jace to stay on topic.

"Right, well, he was standing between Collin and Holly, and Holly was up against the plexiglass wall surrounding the rink. I've never seen her so scared. She was frozen in place, gripping the railing, and trembling. A few of my friends and I got off the ice to help, and I told Collin to back off and stop harassing my friend."

"Did he?"

"No. I mean, he did, but he first said something to scare Holly even more. He said, 'I'm building you a box for old times' sake.' I didn't understand it at the time."

"But you did later?"

Moisture gathered on her lashes, leaving a mascara-coated imprint of them on her cheeks. "Yeah. I understood a lot of things later, like why my friend was so nervous and so on guard all the time."

"It must have been hard for you the night that she was taken."

"I was so scared I was gonna lose her and Sam both." She sniffled. "Sam was bleeding to death, and I knew Collin must have Holly."

"And you were abducted just three days later."

She sniffed and wiped her nose with the sleeve of her shirt. "I was coming home from the hospital to change when someone hit me on the back of the head. And then I woke up gagged and blindfolded."

"Did you see who hit you?"

"No, but I remember voices."

"Whose voice do you remember?"

Jace pointed at Collin again. "His. He carried me into some room and locked me in. I don't know how long I was in there, but when he came to get me, he took me to where he was keeping Holly. That's when I realized what he meant when he told her he was building her a box. She was locked inside it when he brought me into the room."

"If you were blindfolded, how do you know she was locked in a box?"

"I didn't realize there was anyone in it when he first set me on top of it, but then he said she was in time-out and knocked on the lid. And I heard her voice inside."

"What happened in that room?"

Jace swallowed. "He kept me blindfolded, but he removed the gag. He told me I was there because of Holly, that she had trouble sharing her feelings, and I was gonna help with that. He was gonna make her talk by hurting me."

"Did he hurt you?" Shannon asked.

Jace yanked up her shirt sleeve and showed Shannon and the jury the scars on her arm, each one about the size of a quarter. "He burned me with a lighter. One of those old ones with the lid that snaps open and shut." She pulled her sleeve back down, and her voice trembled with emotion as she admitted, "Sometimes I still hear that sound when I'm trying to sleep."

"He said you were there to help Holly share her feelings. What did he mean by that?"

"He wanted to know how much pain she was in. I could tell by his voice that he enjoyed it. All of it. Holly told him that it hurt to breathe, and that she just wanted the pain to stop. But that wasn't enough. He wanted to hear her say that she was afraid of him, of whatever else he was gonna do to her." She seared Collin with a glare. "There is something very wrong with you."

To Shannon's surprise, Collin didn't object. He just tilted his head, as if he were considering her words.

"What happened after Holly told Mr. Wells what he wanted to hear?" Shannon asked.

"He dragged me out of the room and gagged me again. Then he wrapped something around my neck and said we were gonna play a game. He was . . ." She rubbed her throat. "He was gonna hang me."

Shannon gave her a moment to work through her emotions before asking, "And what happened next?"

"I heard Holly crying, begging him to stop." Jace's breath trembled under the pressure of tears as she inhaled. "He was hurting her."

"And you recognize the man who hurt you as Collin Wells?"

"Yes, I know his voice."

"No further questions at this time, Your Honor." Shannon took her seat.

"You know my voice," Collin said, almost mockingly, as he walked toward her. "Interesting, considering we've only met once. I don't count the restaurant, since you arrived as I was being wrongfully arrested and escorted out. But, as you mentioned, we met at the ice rink. If you can identify my voice from that very brief interaction, then you must have phenomenal voice recognition skills."

Shannon had expected him to do his research on the reliability of voice recognition. It was less reliable than eyewitness testimony, and it was seldom utilized in the courtroom. Unfortunately, there was no other option when the victim had been blindfolded.

Collin approached the witness stand. "So, according to what you just told the court, you didn't see who abducted you, and you were blindfolded the entire time you were held captive. Is that correct?"

Jace regarded him with fear and irritation. "That's a stupid question. You heard the whole conversation."

"Yes or no, Ms. Walker," Tipper instructed, sounding mildly exasperated.

"Well, obviously it's a yes."

"So what you're saying is that you never saw me, but you believe it was me based on my voice, which you had only heard once before," Collin summarized.

"Yeah."

He held up a voice recorder. "I'd like you to tell me which one of these voices is mine, if you can."

He pressed play and a voice resounded through the room: "It is better to risk saving a guilty person than to condemn an innocent one."

The voice sounded deep and gravelly, but then a different voice spoke, this one higher and wispy. Ten distinctly different voices recited the same quote by Voltaire.

Collin stopped the recorder. "Can you identify which, if any, of these voices are mine?"

Jace hesitated, her brow furrowed in confusion. "Um." She glanced at Shannon and then back at the recorder in Wells's hand. "Can I hear them again?"

Collin played the recording again, and Shannon listened carefully.

240

"None. None of them are your voice," Jace said when he stopped the tape again.

"Final answer?"

She swallowed nervously. "Yes."

Collin smiled. "All of them are my voice. And the guard present while I recorded them can attest to that."

Shannon sprang to her feet. "Objection, Your Honor. Not only is a recorded voice automatically altered by the quality of the recording equipment, complicating an accurate identification, but it's a trick question. The defendant's phrasing, 'Can you identify which, if any, of these voices are mine?' presupposes that either none or only one of the recorded samples is correct. There was no option for 'all of the above.' It was a question meant to confuse and fluster the witness."

"There was no sinister intent in the phrasing of my question," Collin argued. "My point is, voices are easy to manipulate. A slight accent, a varying intonation, a raising or lowering of pitch. The littlest change can make a voice unrecognizable. Considering my life is hanging in the balance here, I would like a more accurate means of identification than voice recognition."

Tipper fisted his hands beneath his chin as he considered both sides of the argument.

"Your Honor, all of these audio samples may be a product of the defendant's vocal cords, but not one of them depicts his natural voice. My witness heard the voice of her captor, and she identified it as the one we've been listening to for the past four days." She gestured to

Collin. "These recordings are irrelevant, and the defendant is just trying to muddy the waters."

Tipper looked at Collin. "She makes a valid point, Mr. Wells. I'm inclined to agree with the prosecution on this one. Jury will disregard the defendant's argument that pertains to the voice recorder."

Tipper's call seemed to surprise Collin, but he recovered quickly. "Ms. Walker, you said when you realized Holly was missing that I must have had her. You assumed it was me who took her, and while blindfolded and afraid, you assumed I must have been the person responsible for your abduction and assault as well, when in fact it was Ms. Glass who brought you to the warehouse."

"She may have brought me there, but you're the one who hurt me, and you're the one who hurt Holly."

Collin's eyes twitched with irritation, but he waved at the witness stand and declared, "No further questions," before dropping back into his chair.

28

*S*hannon readjusted the bobby pin in her hair to capture the wayward strand that had come loose this morning, and then stared at her reflection in the bathroom mirror.

She hadn't questioned her abilities in the courtroom in almost ten years. She had opposed defense attorneys ranging from highly skilled—such as Mr. Burdock—to public defenders who could barely navigate a law book.

Collin Wells was a different breed entirely. He might not know the law inside and out, but he was frighteningly intelligent and ruthless.

In his arrogance, he probably believed he would never get caught for what he did to those girls, but Shannon couldn't shake the feeling that he'd planned for the possibility of a trial.

She sighed and turned on the faucet, letting the water warm. She watched the stream of water as it circled the drain, a perfect visual representation of her case.

"Don't be so pessimistic," she whispered to herself.

She still had several witnesses to call, and it was possible that not every juror was buying Collin's act. All it took was one voice of reason among the twelve to shift the tide.

The bathroom door opened, but she didn't pay much attention until someone approached her from behind.

A flash of blonde hair and a hooded sweatshirt were all that registered before a hand grabbed the back of her head and slammed her face into the mirror.

The impact sent pain splintering through Shannon's skull, and her vision blurred. Before she could gather her scrambled thoughts and react, her attacker slammed her head into the mirror again.

Her legs buckled, and she crumpled to the bathroom floor. The ceiling tiles warped above her, like a kaleidoscope, and she groaned.

A distorted figure leaned into her vision. "Please," a husky female voice said. "Let the case die so you don't have to."

Please. That one word snagged in Shannon's mind. The woman had just tried to crack her skull open, and she was pleading with her. And then the rest of the sentence registered through the haze of pain: *Let the case die so you don't have to.*

The woman could kill her right now, and there was nothing Shannon could do.

"Please," her attacker repeated, her voice laced with desperation. "Just let it die."

And then she was gone.

Shannon pressed a hand to her head, a warm liquid gathering between her fingers. Blood. Where was it all coming from?

The bathroom door opened again, and a fresh wave of terror washed through her. Her attacker was coming back to finish her off.

Get up, Shannon. Get up. But she couldn't seem to draw her sprawled limbs together. The effort left black dots dancing in her vision.

Someone gasped and then shouted, "Hey, we need an ambulance! Someone's hurt!"

A blurry face appeared above her, and Shannon tried to focus, but blackness crawled across the woman's features, and within seconds, everything disappeared.

· · · ·

The ache thundered between Shannon's ears, worse than any migraine she'd ever had.

She stared at the bathroom mirror as she sat against the wall. Cracks rippled outward from where her forehead had connected, and blood stained the glass.

A paramedic dabbed at the gash on her forehead with a cotton swab, his expression pinched. "We really should take you to the hospital."

Being transported from the courthouse to the hospital in an ambulance wouldn't exactly be discreet, and the last thing she wanted was for the media to catch wind of this.

Before she could protest, the bathroom door swung open, and Rick pushed his way past the officers.

"Shannon." He crouched beside her, fear and anger fighting for control of his expression. "Are you all right?"

After the way things ended last night, he was the last person she expected to see. No, on second thought, the redhead who sank to her knees beside him was the last person she expected to see in the courthouse bathroom.

What was Holly doing here? The courtroom was packed with reporters and journalists, and if they caught sight of her, it would be a madhouse. Shannon frowned at Rick. "You shouldn't have brought her here."

"She was in the break room at the precinct, and you try tellin' her she can't come when somebody she cares about is hurt," he shot back, a growl in his voice.

"How did you even know . . ."

"Shawn called. He said you were attacked."

Her assistant. The poor man was probably pacing the hallway outside the bathroom in a near panic.

Holly shifted closer, her complexion growing paler with concern. "Are you okay? There's a lot of blood."

"I'm all right."

The paramedic sat back on his heels, clearly annoyed. "You're not all right. You have a concussion, and I think you need stitches."

Rick stood. "Sounds like we're goin' to the hospital."

The paramedic grunted. "Good luck with that. She's refusing to get in the ambulance."

Holly fished the keys out of Rick's jacket pocket. "I could drive her."

Shannon grimaced. If Holly drove her to the hospital, they would probably arrive with more injuries than they left with. "As much as I appreciate the offer, Holly, I don't think . . ."

Rick snatched the keys from Holly. "I'll drive."

Glancing between Rick's determined expression and the worry shining in Holly's eyes, Shannon sighed, surrendering to her fate of hospital gowns and prodding doctors.

. . . .

Marx paced outside the examination room, anger fueling his steps. He and Shannon might have some problems to work through, but that didn't make him care about her any less, and it infuriated him that someone had hurt her.

Sully was reviewing the security tapes for the courthouse, trying to find an angle that captured the attacker's face. Unfortunately, the woman seemed familiar with where the cameras were placed, because her head was always positioned in a way that concealed her face.

Blonde with a hooded sweatshirt, around five foot four, but too slender to be Agatha Wells. The woman was shorter than Shannon by four inches, but she'd caught her by surprise.

"She's gonna be okay, Marx."

Holly sat in one of the two chairs beside the wall, gripping the edge of the seat. She hated hospitals. They reminded her of the days after her assault, but she wanted to be here for him . . . and for Shannon. When *she* was in the hospital, in surgery for hours, Shannon had been the one sitting in that chair, comforting him with her presence.

He was blessed to have such compassionate girls in his life.

"I know she'll be all right. I just wish I could figure out who attacked her."

The woman told Shannon to let the case die, the same words that had been written in the anonymous letter that came with the flowers. He would bet his pension that Agatha Wells was behind the flowers, which meant she was connected to whoever attacked Shannon.

A doctor exited the examination room and looked between them. "I'm looking for Ms. Marx's family."

Marx swallowed. He couldn't claim to be Shannon's family any longer. Before he could figure out how to respond, Holly popped out of her chair and appeared beside him.

"That's us. How is she?"

The doctor considered the two of them, probably noticing that neither of them shared any physical characteristics with Shannon. "She needed a few stitches, and she has a pretty bad concussion, but otherwise she's all right. I would recommend a few days of rest."

Marx bit back a scoff. "She's in the middle of a criminal trial. She's not gonna rest until the verdict's in."

"I see." The doctor hugged the clipboard to his chest. "She may experience severe headaches and dizzy spells, along with nausea and excessive tiredness. But it's the dizzy spells that concern me. I would feel more comfortable if someone was around to look after her while she's *not resting*."

"We'll keep an eye on her." Holly rocked forward on her toes as she eyed the doorway behind him. "Can we see her now? Is she good to go?"

"I don't think we could keep her a second longer if we wanted to. She's all yours." The doctor strode away to attend to other patients.

Marx followed Holly into the room, which had three curtained-off sections. Shannon's irritated mumbling came through the curtain area to their right.

"Perfectly fine . . . a ridiculous waste of time . . . hideous hospital gowns."

Holly pulled her lips between her teeth to restrain a smile, then cleared her throat. "Knock, knock."

The curtain whooshed open, and Shannon sat there on the edge of the bed, popping the last few buttons of her blazer into place. "The doctor says I'm perfectly fine, and I can go home."

She slipped her feet into her high heels and stood. She was barely upright before she swayed, a look of disorientation flashing across her face.

Marx caught her shoulders to steady her, and lowered her back onto the bed. "The doctor said you're fine, hmm?"

She pressed a hand to her head. "Perfectly."

"You should stay and let the nurses monitor you."

"I am not staying in this place. I'm going home to my couch and a pint of Häagen-Dazs."

Marx sighed. Why did God give him such hardheaded, stubborn women to love?

29

Shannon melted onto the cushions of her couch and rested her head on the back of it. She felt drained, and everything from the back of her neck to the roots of her hair throbbed.

Under the circumstances, the judge had offered to postpone proceedings until Monday, but Shannon had every intention of being in court tomorrow, even if she needed a bucket beside her table to throw up in.

The nausea was unbelievable. She pressed a hand to her stomach and closed her eyes.

The events in the bathroom came rushing back—the feeling of a hand gripping the back of her head, the moment just before her face hit the glass, when she realized there was nothing she could do to stop the impact.

She'd been threatened numerous times, but she'd never been attacked before.

Sweat broke out on her scalp as the woman's threat echoed in her mind: *Please, let the case die so you don't have to.*

The quiet thumping of cabinets drew her back to her living room, and she looked toward the kitchen, anxiety tapping along her nerves. But then she remembered she had company.

She'd grown so used to being alone that the sound of someone else in her home was unnatural.

Holly shuffled into the room a moment later with two mugs of hot chocolate in her hands, and the steamy aroma of peppermint and cocoa filled the air.

"I found peppermint oil and thought it might go good with hot chocolate. But you don't have any marshmallows." She set the mugs on the coffee table in front of the sofa.

"I suppose I'll have to remedy that."

Holly grabbed the knitted throw blanket and offered it to Shannon before sitting down in the armchair. She tucked her hands between her thighs and tried to work up the nerve to say something. "You should let someone else prosecute Collin."

The idea had occurred to Shannon nine months ago, but now she was too invested in the lives of the people this trial would affect to hand the reins off to someone else. "I'm the most qualified person to handle this case."

Holly pulled her lips between her teeth. "Then I wanna drop the charges against him so no one has to prosecute him."

Shannon shifted on the cushions to better see the young woman. "I'm going to pretend I didn't hear that, because you know what it would mean if he went free."

Holly fidgeted anxiously in the chair. "I do."

"He would come after you again. After Rick, Samuel, Jordan, maybe even Jace."

"No, I can protect them. I can . . . I can make everyone safe."

"By running away?" Shannon sighed sympathetically. "I'm sorry, honey, but that's not a solution. It's a desperate act that will only delay the inevitable."

"I have to do something."

"All you have to do is tell the truth in front of the jury. You don't need to worry about anything else."

"But I do." Tears glittered in Holly's eyes as she looked out the front window at Rick, who was on the phone. "Marx loves you. He's already lost two people he loves because of me. I don't want you to be the third."

She was talking about Jacob and Matt. Jacob had died in the line of duty while trying to protect Holly from Edward Billings, and Matt's illegal activities had put him on the opposite side of the law. When he pulled a gun on Holly, Rick had no choice but to shoot him.

"You didn't cause their deaths, Holly, and what happened today in that bathroom is not your fault."

"The only reason someone attacked you is because you're prosecuting Collin for what he did to me."

"And for what he did to Jace and Rachel." Though, without Holly, she doubted she would've pursued charges against Collin for those crimes. They were too difficult to prove on their own. "I know you feel like you're somehow responsible for what happened to me, but the only person to blame is the person who attacked me."

"Putting him in prison isn't worth people getting hurt."

"It is if the alternative is letting him go so that he can attack and kill more innocents." She paused to gather her thoughts. "When I became a prosecutor, I knew there would be risks. Anytime you challenge the evil in this world, it fights back. Sometimes it gets the upper hand, but we can't just give up when that happens. We have to fight even harder."

"What if they try to kill you next time?"

As terrifying as that possibility was, Shannon couldn't let it stop her from doing her job. "I'm going to see this case through because it's the right thing to do, regardless of the danger. And I need you to promise me that you'll give me that chance."

Holly hesitated. When she made a promise, it was as binding as a legal contract. She never went back on her word. "Okay, I promise."

Shannon would rest easier knowing that the girl wasn't going to bolt in the middle of the night and disappear.

The front door opened, and Holly dried her face with the sleeves of her sweatshirt. "I'm gonna grab you a pillow from upstairs so you can sleep down here. With your dizziness, it'll be safer if you don't go up and down the stairs."

Holly climbed out of the chair and disappeared from the room, the soft tap of her feet receding up the staircase.

Rick paused in the archway, a bewildered frown on his face as he watched Holly's retreating figure, then continued into the living room. "Everythin' all right?"

"She's worried about me."

He tapped his phone against his palm, his expression grim. "Understandable. You could've been killed today."

Thankfully, the woman only seemed interested in scaring her.

"I got permission for a protective detail. An officer should be here shortly."

Shannon massaged her forehead and stared at the ceiling. She couldn't argue this time.

"How's your headache?"

"Worse than the night I passed my bar exam and partied until three in the morning." She barely remembered that night, but she would never forget the hangover the next day.

"I'm sorry this happened."

"I should've been paying more attention."

"You were in a courthouse bathroom. There was no reason to suspect somebody would be crazy enough to attack you there."

Holly returned with a pillow, the reading glasses from Shannon's nightstand, the sweatshirt she'd left lying on the bed, and a pair of slippers. "I didn't wanna dig through your drawers for more comfortable pants, but I found your sweatshirt."

"*My* sweatshirt," Rick corrected, eyeing his old Yankees sweatshirt that had been in the laundry hamper when he moved out. "But you always wore it more than me anyway." It was an obvious attempt to lighten the mood, but he didn't smile.

The tension from their conversation in the kitchen last night lingered between them. It was more unbearable than the pain in Shannon's head, but she didn't know how to fix it.

Rick walked to the window and brushed aside the curtains. "Patrol car's here. Holly, you ready to go? We should let Shannon get some rest."

Holly plopped down in the armchair again, wiggling into a comfortable position. "I'm gonna stay the night."

Shannon blinked. She didn't recall discussing that or issuing an invitation.

Rick let the curtain fall shut. "I don't think that's a good idea, sweetheart."

Holly grabbed her mug of hot chocolate from the coffee table and held it in her lap. "There's an officer guarding the house, so we'll be safe. And the doctor said Shannon needs someone to keep an eye on her tonight."

"I don't have the guest room made up." Shannon knew it was a halfhearted excuse, but she didn't have any other reason to refuse Holly's help.

"That's okay. I'll probably be awake most of the night anyway."

Shannon puzzled over her statement before remembering that she suffered from night terrors. According to Rick, she scarcely slept.

Rick sighed and rubbed the back of his neck in displeasure. "Okay, then I'm stayin' too. Shannon, since you're sleepin' on the couch tonight, I'll take your room."

Our room, she thought wistfully.

"I'll let the officer know we're plannin' to stay. No sense in two of us bein' here tonight." He left the room, the suffocating tension following him out.

Shannon released a heavy breath and slumped on the couch. This was going to be a long night.

· · · ·

Marx sat in the dimly lit kitchen with a cup of coffee and the stack of letters from Collin's admirers.

He needed something to keep his mind off the conversation that had taken place in this house last night.

Deception was one of only a few things he struggled to forgive. He'd seen firsthand how it could destroy a family. Shannon knew that, and still she decided to lie.

She reasoned it was for his own good, but that was nothing but a justification. If she had just told him the truth, they could've worked things out. He never would've agreed to a divorce.

He tapped a finger on the mug as he tried to make out the chaotic handwriting of the letter he held. He thought *his* penmanship was bad, but this letter looked like it had been written by a drunk chicken that was occasionally zapped by a cattle prod, sending the lines veering wildly.

He was never going to be able to decipher it, so he moved on to the next one. He'd gotten through a third of the stack last night, and a little more than that this morning, which only left him a handful to go through now.

Several letters were penned by the same people, and he stacked those together.

One thing became clear as he worked his way down to the last letter: there were a lot of desperately lonely people in the world. But only one of the senders concerned him.

Molly, a woman who sent Collin five letters over the past several months, was deeply in love with him. She expressed a desire to be the only woman in his life. There was no direct reference to Holly, but she alluded to "that girl" on several occasions, calling her toxic. But it was her comment in the latest letter that truly unnerved him:

> I know how much she means to you, but
> I won't share you with her. She has to go.

There was no mistaking the inherent threat in those words. She wanted Holly out of the picture so she could be the sole focus of Collin's attention.

But there was a hard line between longing for something and taking steps to make it happen. He couldn't tell from Molly's letters if she was willing to cross that line or not. But if she was willing, and Agatha hired her to stop Holly from making it into that courthouse, then he had less than two days to find her.

There was no last name listed on the envelope, but Molly did provide a PO box so that Collin could write back to her. He would need a warrant to find out more information on the person renting the box, and for that he would have to wait until morning.

As he restacked the letters, it occurred to him how unnaturally quiet the house was. Shannon was asleep on the couch, and the last time he saw Holly, she was curled up in the armchair, fighting back giggles as she read one of her silly novels. Silence meant she was likely up to some kind of mischief.

He pushed back his chair and went to look for her. He was surprised to find her sitting at the top of the staircase, flipping leisurely through a photo album that rested in her lap.

Where had she found that? It was obvious by the faded outlines on the walls that Shannon had removed all the pictures of them, so he doubted she would leave an album lying around.

He climbed the steps and settled down beside her. "Where'd you dig this up?"

"I found it in a kitchen drawer earlier, when I was making hot chocolate."

He lifted an eyebrow. "You were snoopin'?"

Holly straightened her shoulders indignantly. "No. I was looking for marshmallows, but Shannon's weird and doesn't have any. I know I should've left it where it was, but . . ." She shrugged. "I was curious."

"Naturally."

She turned the page, the plastic over the pictures crinkling. There were so many memories preserved in this book, moments he'd clung desperately to over the past three years—the sound of Shannon's laughter when she was so tired that everything was funny, their first Christmas as newlyweds, the time she dyed all of his clothes a pale purple because she didn't separate the whites.

Holly touched the picture of Shannon in her wedding dress. "She looked beautiful."

"Yes she did." He'd forgotten to breathe when she started down the aisle—an ethereal beauty in her long white gown, black hair curled around her shoulders, gray eyes reflecting the light.

She turned to another page, admiring the candid shots. "You guys were so happy." She looked over at him. "What happened?"

Marx rested his elbows on his knees and rubbed his hands together. "I wanted kids. She didn't. That was always somewhat of a strain on our marriage."

Holly closed the album and listened intently.

"When she said she was leavin', a small part of me suspected it had somethin' to do with our disagreement over startin' a family, but she didn't mention that. She handed me the divorce papers with a string of lies attached—I don't love you anymore, I hate your job, I wanna focus on my career. But the truth is, she thought I was unhappy without children, so she left me in the hope that I would fall in love with somebody else and start a family."

Holly tilted her head, thoughtful. "But she still loves you."

"So she says, but you don't leave somebody you love."

Holly's expression turned guarded, and she looked down at her hands on the album. "You do if you think it's the best thing for them."

Marx had an uneasy feeling in the pit of his stomach that they weren't just talking about Shannon anymore. "Holly—"

"If she really believed she was causing your unhappiness, then letting you go was probably the most loving thing she could think to do. Was it right for her to do that? Probably not. But sometimes love causes people to do the wrong thing for the right reasons."

He couldn't deny that he was guilty of that on occasion.

Holly shifted, angling her body toward him. "Shannon loved you enough to give you up, to give you another chance at a family, probably knowing that if you found one, she would spend the rest of her life without the man she loves."

"She lied to me, Holly."

"Why do you think she would do that?"

"She knew I wouldn't sign the divorce papers if I knew the real reason. So she said she didn't love me, knowin' I would never force a woman to stay with me if she didn't want to. In the end, all she managed to do was to make both of us miserable."

Holly rested her head on his shoulder. "I'm sorry."

He wrapped an arm around her, pulling her close. "At least somethin' good came out of her leavin' me."

"What's that?"

"I did find a family." He kissed the top of her head, and she smiled up at him.

If things had worked out between him and Shannon, or if he'd been granted the children he so desperately wanted, he wasn't sure there would've been enough room in his heart or his life for Holly.

It was his longing for a daughter that let him see the sweet and innocent girl sitting on the curb outside that park. Without that longing, he might have treated her with the same polite detachment he did all other victims.

He never would've invited her to stay with him if he still lived with Shannon, and he certainly wouldn't have offered a reward for information to find a victim he'd helped once upon a time.

Holly likely would've died in that warehouse, her last moments filled with fear and hopelessness.

Grief gripped him as he considered the possibility, and he didn't realize his arm had tightened around Holly until she squirmed and protested, "Um . . . you're kind of squeezing me."

He loosened his hold. "Sorry."

She looked up, her eyes shimmering with concern. "What's wrong? Why do you look sad?"

"I'm not sad. I'm just thinkin'."

Sitting on these steps with Holly, reflecting on what might've been, he was grateful beyond words that God hadn't given him children when he asked for them.

His heart still ached for the lost years with Shannon, for every night that he fell asleep with his arms wrapped around a pillow instead of his wife, and every morning he woke up alone in an empty bed. But he would accept that pain and so much more if it meant having this amazing girl in his life.

He hugged her closer. "I love you, sweet pea."

"I love you too," she said, offering him a sweet smile. "So maybe now that Shannon told you the truth, you two can ..." She twirled her hands, and he pretended confusion.

"Play charades?"

She rolled her eyes. "Work things out."

He narrowed his eyes, suspicion threading through him. "Why are we really here tonight? Is it actually because Shannon needs help? Or are you tryin' to play matchmaker?"

Mischief glittered in her eyes. "I plead the fifth."

"Mmm hmm. Keep your little nose out of it, cupid."

She hopped to her feet, the album clutched to her chest. "No promises." She flitted down the steps like a matchmaking cherub, and disappeared into the living room.

30

*S*hannon twisted the paper clip between her fingers as she tried to ignore the earthquake between her ears.

The ambient noise of the courtroom echoed inside her head, and the overhead lights burned straight down her retinal nerve into the pain center of her brain.

Her migraine medication barely scratched the surface of the ache, and it took all of her willpower not to slip on her sunglasses and bury her face in her arms.

That would look professional.

Rick insisted that she accept the judge's offer of a continuance and stay home, but she wasn't going to postpone this case for a bump on the head. Every day that this trial dragged on was another day that Holly had to live with fear and uncertainty.

"It's a shame what happened yesterday."

Shannon squinted up at the man who had spoken.

Collin stood beside her table with his hands in his pockets, looking as relaxed as ever. "It seems no place is safe these days. Not even a courthouse." His gaze drifted to the bandage on her forehead. "That's a nasty bump. Anyone else would be at home, resting. Yet you decided to come to court."

Shannon pushed to her feet; she would not let this man tower over her. "That's how invested I am in putting you away for the rest of your life."

"Lofty goals for someone whose case is crumbling."

"You're overconfident."

"And you're scared." His gaze slid over her, lingering in a way that exacerbated the nausea in her stomach. "You're surprisingly attractive for a woman your age."

She stiffened her spine, determined not to show fear. He was hardly the first defendant who tried to intimidate her with inappropriate glances and suggestive comments.

"While I appreciate the compliment, we both know I'm too much woman for you. You prefer the petite ones, because it's harder for them to fight back."

His smile spread into a grin. "How is our sweet little Holly?"

"You can find that out for yourself when she arrives for her testimony tomorrow."

The amusement slid off his face. "She won't show. She's too scared."

"You have a habit of underestimating her. The last time you did that, she stabbed you in the leg with a piece of glass and nearly killed you."

His mask of humanity slipped for just an instant, and she glimpsed something that left a chill in her soul. Now she understood what Holly meant when she described her foster brother as darkness wrapped in human skin, and she fought the urge to take a step back.

Collin opened his mouth, but before he could speak, a door opened and the jury filed in. He swallowed his words and walked back to his table.

Shannon let out a breath and sank into her chair, shaken by the interaction. She grabbed her pen and tried to focus her thoughts on something she could control—the questions she had prepared for her next witness.

"Ms. Marx," Judge Tipper called, demanding her attention. "Are you sure you're well enough to proceed today?"

She stood, pressing her fingertips to the tabletop to maintain her balance as a wave of dizziness crested over her. "I am, Your Honor."

"If that changes, please don't hesitate to inform me. You may call your witness."

"The state calls Detective Richard Marx."

It had been a long time since a case required her to call Rick as a witness, but she doubted his temperament under pressure had improved over the years. In fact, given the personal nature of this case, and the unresolved issues between the two of them, he would probably be a ticking time bomb on the witness stand.

The rear doors parted, and Rick walked in. Her ex-husband was a good-looking man when he dressed in jeans and a T-shirt, but when he donned slacks and the dark blue button-up she'd bought him years ago, he was breathtakingly handsome.

He offered her a reproving glance as he passed by, still perturbed that she ignored his advice, and made his way to the front of the room.

Shannon didn't miss the hard set of his jaw as the clerk swore him in. He was already in a bad mood, and she hadn't even asked a question yet.

She let out a breath that was very nearly a sigh as she approached the witness stand. "Good morning, Detective."

He nodded curtly. "Mornin'."

She walked him through the questions she asked every law enforcement officer—how long he'd been with the department and how many years he'd served in his current position.

Rick was a veteran detective with an excellent solve rate—he closed more cases than most of his colleagues at the department. But he also had a reputation as a hothead; his short fuse landed him on the bench more than once, but the jury didn't need to know that.

"How did you meet Holly Cross?" Shannon asked.

"I was called to the scene of a homicide." He described his surprise when he learned that the dead body wasn't the assault victim but one of her attackers. He was even more surprised when a patrol officer pointed out the petite victim sitting on a curb, wrapped in a blanket.

From a distance, she looked more tired than traumatized, but her demeanor changed the moment he approached, becoming more guarded and anxious. Even after he identified himself as an officer, she kept her distance from him, watching him closely with her wide, perceptive eyes.

"Holly started out as just another case for you, the victim of a crime that needed solving, but she quickly became more than that, didn't she?" Shannon asked.

"I wouldn't say quickly—it took months to earn her trust—but yes, she became more than just another case."

"But it wasn't a romantic connection that developed between you."

"No. My relationship with Holly is more paternal. We're not related, but . . ."

Shannon's throat tightened at the deeply personal subject. "But you've always wanted a daughter."

He looked away from her, clearly still upset about their discussion the other night. "Yes. Over the years, I've imagined what my daughter would be like. Compassionate, thoughtful, determined, sweet-natured, honest. Everythin' Holly is."

"You love her."

"More every day."

Shannon was grateful that Rick had found Holly, though the young woman wasn't what she had in mind when she left him. She was far from a new wife and little children, but she brought an undeniable amount of joy into Rick's life.

"In February of last year, you invited Holly to stay in your apartment. What inspired that decision?"

"I knew that if I didn't give her someplace safe to stay, she would run away and disappear."

"Can you tell the court about the circumstances leading up to your decision?"

The chair creaked as Rick shifted. "Holly and I were in the middle of one of her drivin' lessons—I'm teachin' her to drive—when I was called to a homicide. Holly's apartment was in the opposite direction of the scene, so she came with me, and I instructed her to stay in the car until I was done. After I finished up at the crime scene, I drove her home. When we pulled up to the curb outside of her apartment, a man was leanin' against her front door."

"Did you recognize the man?"

"Yes. His name is Collin Wells. The moment Holly saw him, she froze in fear. I told her to stay put, that I would take care of the situation. I stepped out of the car to explain to Collin that he wasn't welcome and that he needed to leave, but he insisted that he was there for a long overdue visit with his 'little sister,' whom he also referred to as an 'old flame.'"

Shannon nodded and immediately regretted the gesture. It sent the room swirling. She placed a hand on the witness stand to steady herself. "And did Holly stay put as you instructed?"

"She did, until Collin said that he might stay in New York City and visit her again. That's when she jumped out of the car and took off. Holly's a bit faster

269

than I am, so Officer Barrera—who had stepped out of the main apartment buildin' to join us just moments before—went after her. He called me to let me know where she was, and I picked her up. She was so scared that she refused to go home."

"So you took her back to your place?"

Rick nodded. "I did. She's been stayin' in the spare bedroom."

"Is it true that her apartment was broken into the following morning?"

"Yes. The thief broke in through a rear window and took all of Holly's clothes, as well as the glass from the broken window."

Curiosity flickered across the faces of some of the jurors. Thieves weren't known for cleaning up after themselves. But Collin had plans for that broken glass.

"The thief," Rick continued, "left a note in the box where Holly kept her more personal items that said, 'How does it feel?'"

A phrase Collin favored when tormenting his victims.

"Were Holly's missing clothes ever found?"

"They were recovered from a storage closet in the warehouse where she was held."

"Did you have a suspect?"

"Collin Wells was spotted lurkin' around the apartment the mornin' of the break-in."

Shannon cast a pointed look at the jury, silently urging them to take note. "Mr. Wells was loitering around Holly's apartment just before the break-in. Her clothes were stolen during that break-in, and they ended up in the very warehouse where she was later kept against her will. The same warehouse where Mr. Wells was found. That certainly doesn't seem like a—"

A camera flash from the back of the room sent pain lancing through her eye sockets into her brain, and she pressed a hand to her head.

"Shannon." Rick placed a hand over hers and stood. "Are you all right?"

"I'm . . ." Another series of flashes scrambled her ability to think.

"Turn off those camera flashes!" Tipper demanded, and Shannon was silently grateful to him even as the volume of his voice ricocheted off the inside of her skull. "Ms. Marx, are you able to continue or do you require a recess?"

Shannon massaged the skin above her eyes before letting her hand drop back to her side. "I'm well enough to continue, Your Honor. Thank you."

Rick shot her a look of frustration mixed with concern as he dropped back into his chair. It was possible that he was right, and she should've accepted the offer of a continuance, but there was no sense in it now. She was already here.

She cleared her throat and tried to pull her thoughts together. "Did Mr. Wells attempt to contact Holly while she was staying with you?"

"He did." Rick interlaced his fingers on the edge of the witness stand. "Holly received phone calls from him on multiple occasions as well as text messages."

"Objection, Your Honor," Collin declared. "If there's some evidence linking me to a phone or phone number that placed those calls and sent those messages to Holly's phone, I wasn't made aware of it."

Tipper raised his eyebrows at Shannon. "Ms. Marx? Is there evidence that specifically links Mr. Wells to the number that contacted Ms. Cross?"

"No, Your Honor."

Collin had used multiple burner phones not only to protect himself from legal consequences but to keep Holly from being able to block his number.

"Then rephrase."

She pressed her lips together in irritation, but didn't argue. "What lead you to believe Collin Wells was the caller on these occasions, Detective?"

"Holly identified his voice."

"When Holly reported these phone calls to you, did she disclose what the caller said?"

"She did, and I documented each call." Rick listed the date and time of each phone call Holly received, including the one on her birthday—confirming Samuel's version of events that night. "The one that concerned me the most was the one she received while in the break room of the police department. Someone called her phone four times within a span of two minutes. When she answered, the caller said, 'someone didn't come home last night.' When she didn't respond, the caller asked, 'you're too scared to speak, aren't you? Does the sound of my voice make you shiver in anticipation of pain? Do you start thinkin' about all the times I held you down and . . .' and then Holly hung up."

Shannon felt a little nauseous as he recited the phone call. Collin enjoyed terrifying his victims. "And she identified that voice as belonging to the defendant?"

"She did."

She decided not to ask him about the anonymous text messages Holly received, since they couldn't directly connect Collin to any of them. Instead, she moved on to the next line of questioning. "Did Mr. Wells make an appearance at any point?"

"His first appearance was at Holly's apartment in February. He made a second appearance when he showed up at the ice rink, where Holly was visitin' with friends. Then at an apartment buildin' when Holly was with me and Officer Barrera. At a restaurant where we gathered for a party. In the parkin' lot outside of her gym. And then at Officer Barrera's place of residence."

"How did Holly react to his presence?"

"I wasn't there for every one of his uninvited visits, but what I witnessed, and what was reported to me, was that she was absolutely terrified. At her apartment, and at the apartment downtown with me and Officer Barrera, she tried to run as fast and as far from Wells as possible. At the restaurant, when I found her in the hallway leadin' to the restrooms, Wells had her pinned against the wall, and she was so petrified she couldn't move."

"So in your professional opinion, as a detective trained to read the subtleties of human interaction, these visits weren't friendly?"

"No," Rick said flatly. "They were threatenin'."

Collin sighed, as if it burdened him to have to speak again. "Objection. I never issued any threats."

"Not overtly," Rick shot back.

"Veiled threats are subjective, Detective," Collin replied. "If I said you might not make it home tonight, it could mean your car might break down, you might get called to another crime scene, or maybe you'll spend the night in a hotel."

"Knowin' you, it would mean you enlisted somebody to stab me at a traffic light," Rick replied icily.

Tipper raised his gavel, intending to quell the argument by slamming it down, but he thought better of it. "Ms. Marx, control your witness."

"Apologies, Your Honor." She lasered Rick with a warning look. He needed to control his temper. "As a consequence of these visits from Mr. Wells, Detective, what did you advise Holly to do?"

"Request an order of protection."

"An order of protection is granted when there is sufficient proof that an individual poses a physical or psychological threat to another, correct?"

"Yes."

"And it was granted, prohibiting Mr. Wells from coming within five hundred feet of Holly. Did he, to your knowledge, ever violate that protection order?"

"Yes, by approachin' Holly outside the gym as she was leavin', and then at Officer Barrera's apartment. Both incidents took place *after* the order of protection was delivered to Mr. Wells."

"Hmm," Shannon said thoughtfully. "Officer Barrera's apartment, where she disappeared."

Rick's eyes hardened. "Where she was *taken*."

"She was missing for four days, and you had no leads to help you track her down. How did you eventually find her?"

"I offered a thousand-dollar reward for information leadin' to her location, and a witness came forward to tell us he saw a woman matchin' Holly's description tryin' to escape from an abandoned warehouse."

Shannon remembered seeing the announcement on television. Rick had been devastated and desperate as he stood in front of the cameras, pleading for someone to speak up.

It had taken the witness four days to come forward, and even then, he tried to withhold the information until the reward was in his hands. Rick nearly put the man through a window for withholding Holly's location.

"So you and a team of officers followed the tip to the warehouse," Shannon said. "And what did you find?"

"We found a woman lyin' dead on the lower level, and on the second floor, I found Jace Walker. There was a black bag over her head, fixed in place with duct tape around her mouth and neck. Her arms were taped behind her back, and there was a noose around her neck."

"Jace Walker, the young lady in the wheelchair," Shannon said to remind the jury.

"Yes. She disappeared three days after Holly was taken."

"Was Holly being held where the witness claimed to have seen her?

"Yes."

Shannon gestured for him to continue. Rick shifted in his seat and then proceeded to describe the scene that still haunted him. A trail of broken glass had led him to the room where Holly was being held, and when he opened the door, he found two bodies lying motionless on the floor. Collin was unconscious, bleeding from a wound in his thigh, and Holly was barely breathing, her skin nearly as cold and gray as the cement floor beneath her.

"She'd been beaten so badly she . . ." Rick lifted his eyes to the ceiling and blew out a breath of grief. "She nearly died. She was in a coma for eight days."

"And Mr. Wells?"

A vein in Rick's neck throbbed with barely suppressed rage. "He was on top of her when she stabbed him with a piece of glass. She managed to nick his femoral artery before he wrapped his hands around her throat and choked her unconscious."

"Thank you, Detective. I have no further questions."

. . . .

Collin stood and slowly buttoned his suit jacket. "I know you're a busy man, Detective, and I don't want to keep you too long when you have actual crimes to investigate, so I'll try to be brief."

Shannon's grip on her pencil tightened, and she saw the same anger flicker through Rick's eyes. Collin had just suggested to the jury that what he'd done to Holly wasn't an actual crime.

"Your wife . . . excuse me, *ex-wife*, questioned you about the events leading up to and surrounding Holly's abduction. I don't dispute that I showed up at Holly's apartment, or at the restaurant, or that I was found in the warehouse with her. But there are a few details you glossed over in your retelling of events, details I think the jury needs to know."

He gripped his wrist behind his back and walked around the edge of the desk.

"When you pulled up to the curb in front of Holly's apartment the day I first stopped by to visit, she was in the passenger seat of your car. Did she get out and ask me to leave?"

"No."

"So she requested that you ask me to leave?"

Rick's voice deepened with irritation. "No. She—" Collin cut in before he could explain that Holly had been too scared to speak.

"Meaning *you* decided that I should leave, and if I remember correctly, you threatened to 'redecorate the pavement with the insides of my head' if I visited her."

Shannon closed her eyes with an inward groan. That certainly sounded like something Rick would say.

"Do you recall that conversation, Detective?"

"It sounds vaguely familiar."

"And this from a man with a badge, someone sworn to uphold the law and protect the innocent." Collin threw his arms out to his sides. "Do I have a criminal record I'm unaware of, one that makes me deserving of threats from law enforcement?"

"Nobody has a criminal record until they get caught. That doesn't mean they haven't committed crimes."

"So that's a no, then. I have no criminal record."

"Not at the moment, no."

"And that day at Holly's apartment, I made no aggressive gestures. Yet you approached me with rudeness and threats of violence." He tilted his head, as though in thought. "I get the sense that you disliked me before we even met."

"*Dislike* is puttin' it mildly."

"How would you put it?"

"Is there a stronger word than despise?"

Shannon barely resisted the urge to drop her head on the desk. He had to be honest on the stand, but did he have to be so volatile?

Collin smiled. "Remind me to send you a thesaurus for Christmas next year."

278

Quiet laughter rippled through the jury box.

"After my visit that day, Holly moved in with you. Was that your idea or hers?"

"Mine."

"I thought so. And the order of protection keeping me away from her . . . also your idea?"

Rick's eyes narrowed with suspicion. "I didn't originally suggest it. That was Officer Barrera. But after conferrin' with Shannon, I recommended it to Holly."

"You talked her into it. Did you also tell her not to accept any calls from me or go anywhere alone where we might be able to see each other?"

"I did."

"And during these visits that you were so determined to prevent from happening, did I ever *overtly* threaten Holly? Did I ever put my hands on her?"

A muscle flexed in Rick's jaw. "No, because we wouldn't let you get that close to her."

"Really?" Collin challenged. "Because I was alone in the hallway with her at the restaurant, and despite your previous statement that I had her pinned to the wall, I didn't threaten or touch her in any way. You can confirm that with her. And she didn't ask me to leave then either."

"What's your point?"

"I appreciate you asking," Collin said with a smile. "My *point*, Detective, is that you took a family reunion and turned it into an unnecessarily tense situation that only continued to escalate."

Rick sat forward, anger sharpening his voice. "Unnecessarily tense situation? Holly was terrified of you because you raped her."

"Did she tell you I raped her? Specifically those words?"

Shannon pressed her lips together. She wanted to object to the question, but it wasn't out of line.

Holly had never spoken those words, because she couldn't seem to push them from her throat. She settled for euphemisms like "he hurt me," but they all knew she was referring to wounds much deeper than cuts and bruises.

Collin leaned on the witness stand, his face mere inches from Rick's. "Well, Detective, did she tell you I raped her, or did you just assume?"

Shannon rose to object before Rick could do something rash like slam Collin's head off the witness stand. "Your Honor, the defendant is intentionally trying to provoke my witness to anger."

Tipper sighed. "Mr. Wells, take a step back. Detective, answer the question."

Collin raised his hands and retreated. "Apologies, Your Honor. Detective?"

"No," Rick gritted out. "Holly didn't use those exact words."

"Hmm. Do you often paraphrase her words—or lack thereof—Detective? I ask because it's my understanding that you're the officer who took her statement regarding her abduction, a statement that paints me in a very bad light."

"I didn't influence her victim statement, if that's what you're askin'."

Collin grunted thoughtfully. "You have quite the reputation in the police department. You're well-known for your solve rate. Rumor has it, you frequently elicit a signed confession from your suspects."

Rick stared at him with disinterest.

"It can't be easy to persuade someone to confess to a crime, considering the consequences they know they'll be facing."

"We're all trained to interview suspects."

"Yes, but some are more skilled than others." He grabbed a folder from his desk and opened it. "And then there's your temper, the short fuse you're also well-known for."

Shannon uncrossed her legs and sat up straighter. Collin had managed to get his hands on Rick's personnel file.

"This last spring, you physically assaulted a suspect in a parking lot. And before that, you nearly threw a witness through a window at the police department because he didn't answer your question fast enough."

"He knew where you were holdin' Holly, and he was more interested in reward money than savin' her life."

"So if you don't like someone, it's okay to verbally and physically attack them?"

"I never said that."

"Maybe not with your words, but when you threw me up against the wall at the restaurant and then onto the floor, the message was loud and clear." Collin tossed the folder back onto his desk. "How should an order of protection be delivered, Detective?"

Rick hesitated, and Shannon frowned. It was a simple enough question, one he'd answered in court before. Maybe the sudden shift in topic had caught him by surprise.

"The order is served, and the man or woman against whom the order is placed is given time to respond appropriately," Rick finally answered.

"Time to respond appropriately," Collin repeated as he strolled away from the stand, tapping a finger against his lips. "And how long did you give me, Detective?"

Rick said nothing.

"When I came to the restaurant to order something for dinner, didn't you throw me up against the wall, force the papers into my hand, and then immediately arrest me?"

Rick's neck flushed, and he glanced at Shannon. Without him saying a word, she knew Collin was telling the truth. How could he be so rash and foolish?

"That . . . might have happened."

"That *did* happen, Detective," Collin amended. "You arrested me without cause because you were angry and determined to have Holly all to yourse—"

"Objection!" Shannon cut in. "That comment is completely out of line."

Collin held up his hands before Tipper could respond. "Apologies. I can rephrase." When Tipper nodded his consent, Collin asked, "Did you or did you not arrest me without cause, Detective?"

"I arrested you to keep Holly safe."

"Oh, I have no doubt that's what you told her, and I have no doubt that she believed you. Holly has always been very impressionable. Especially when it comes to an older male influence. As most of you know"—Collin turned to the jury—"Holly's father was murdered when she was nine and she was orphaned. She's always craved a father figure to take care of her. And you, Detective, a man who always wanted children, stepped into that role with no resistance."

"My relationship with Holly has nothin' to do with—"

"You manipulated her, using the same skills you use every time you step into an interrogation room. We've already established that you're a persuasive man. If you can convince a hardened criminal to throw away his future by signing a confession, influencing the perception of one desperate young woman craving a father figure wouldn't take much effort."

Shannon shot to her feet again. "Objection! He can't just accuse a decorated detective of manipulating a witness in a criminal trial."

"Be careful of the accusations you're flinging around, Mr. Wells," Tipper warned.

Collin bowed his head in acquiescence. "Detective, have you ever convinced Holly to accept something she didn't believe was true?"

"No, I haven't."

"Holly feels things very deeply. Have you ever used her emotions to influence her behavior or decisions?"

Rick narrowed his eyes. "Sometimes she's impulsive and reckless with her safety, so I remind her that I love her, and her recklessness worries me. She's usually more careful after that."

"Have you ever pushed her into a decision or made a decision for her that she didn't agree with?"

"There have been times when I needed to make a decision for her safety that I knew she wouldn't like."

"Like moving her into your guest room?"

"I didn't force her to come stay with me. I offered; she accepted."

"You convinced her that it was in her best interest. You invited an impressionable young woman into your home under a pretense of *safety*, then proceeded to influence her perceptions and control her decisions. You had her escorted everywhere she went, forbade her from seeing me or speaking with me. And you accuse *me* of imprisoning her?"

Shannon started to object, but Rick and Collin shouted over her.

"Holly is welcome to leave whenever she wants, and . . ."

". . . turned her against me."

284

" . . . keep her safe from you!"

". . . finally got the daughter you thought you could never have, and you made sure no one could take her away from you."

Shannon pressed fingers to her temples as Judge Tipper pounded his gavel, desperately trying to be heard over the shouting men.

"Quiet!" He slammed his gavel one last time, the thump echoing in the silence that descended over the courtroom. "Detective, you are out of warnings. One more outburst, and I will hold you in contempt of court. Mr. Wells, you crossed a lot of lines with your arguments this morning."

"I apologize, Your—"

"I don't care about your empty apologies. This is a court of law, not an episode of Jerry Springer. I won't have yelling matches and childish squabbling in my courtroom. Now, if you're quite finished with the witness, sit down and be quiet."

The reprimand didn't seem to bother Collin as he returned to his seat. He'd gotten his point across.

Tipper set down his gavel and leaned back in his chair. "Jury will disregard the last minute of bickering. Ms. Marx, you may call your next witness, and they better be more behaved than this one."

31

"The State calls Detective Michael Everly to the stand," Shannon announced.

Michael sat on one of the benches close to the double doors, and he rose when she called his name. Michael was the physical epitome of average: brown hair, brown eyes, with no distinguishing features. But it was his integrity and faith that set him apart from the crowd.

He rubbed his hands together as he passed by the counsel tables, a nervous gesture that Collin no doubt noticed as well. Michael had only been a detective for four years, and this was his first time testifying in a case of this magnitude.

Shannon waited for him to get comfortable on the witness stand. "Good morning, Detective Everly."

He tipped his head. "Good morning."

She rounded her desk, hoping that she wouldn't be struck by another dizzy spell. "I hear you and your wife are expecting."

Michael's entire countenance changed as love and pride overshadowed his nervousness. "A little girl. She's due to make her appearance in nine days."

For just a moment, the joy in his face made Shannon wonder if she'd made a mistake all those years

286

ago when she decided not to have children. "Do you have a name picked out?"

"The doctors told us we couldn't have children biologically, so we decided that since our baby was conceived by the grace of God, we would call her Grace."

"That's a lovely choice." Now that the conversation about his family put Michael at ease, she redirected his attention to the matter at hand. She questioned him about his career to assure the jury that he was both experienced and reliable. He'd been with the NYPD for sixteen years, four of those years as a detective, and he had no reprimands on his record. "How did you come to be involved in Holly's case?"

"Detective Marx was called away for a family emergency in Georgia. For the duration of his leave, I was assigned to cover his ongoing cases. When an envelope addressed to him arrived, marked urgent, I opened it, expecting it to pertain to one of the cases I was overseeing. But . . . it didn't."

"What was inside the envelope?"

"A DVD, a sort of home video." Michael licked his lips with hesitation. Although he and Shannon both knew that the distorted male figure in the video was Collin Wells, neither of them could say that in open court. "Someone had filmed a gir . . . excuse me, a young woman being abused."

"What kind of abuse? Physical, emotional, sexual?"

The chair creaked as Michael shifted uncomfortably. "All of the above."

"How did you identify the victim in the video?"

"Her attacker—whose face and voice were digitally distorted—called her by her first name. Still, even though I had seen Holly around the department, I didn't put it together until Detective Marx returned and identified her."

"What role did you play in the investigation that ensued?"

"Initially I hit the ground running with a lot of other people in the department, searching the city and trying to track down possible witnesses."

"Witnesses, but not suspects?"

"We had a suspect—Collin Wells." He directed the jury's attention to the defense table. "We just didn't know where to find him or anyone who could tell us where he was holding Holly. He doesn't have a residence here in New York City, but we didn't have any luck tracking him to a hotel either."

"Then how did you eventually find her?"

"On the fourth day that she was missing, a witness came forward with a tip that led us to an abandoned warehouse in the Bronx."

Shannon nodded. "You and several other officers, including Detective Richard Marx, entered the warehouse to look for Holly. Can you tell us what happened?"

"We were all gathered in the alley . . ."

Shannon hadn't been present for the raid on the warehouse, but as he described the events, she could envision it taking place.

Michael hovered in the alley along with the other officers, sweat beading across his forehead and under his arms despite the chilly March evening. There was no way to know who or what was behind the door they were about to open. The windows were boarded over, and the witness whose information had sent them here was a drug addict.

As his eyes swept the alley, he prayed that God would shield them and lead them to the two missing girls. Holly Cross had been missing for four days, and her friend Jace Walker had disappeared just last night. There was nothing to indicate the two abductions were connected—the girls were distinctly different in appearance—but Detective Marx was convinced the same person was involved.

One of the Emergency Service Unit officers opened the rusted sliding door, and Michael's grip tightened on his gun. They poured into the dark warehouse, flashlight beams bouncing in every direction.

Michael's heart slammed into his rib cage when he saw a woman lying on the floor not twenty feet in front of them, blood pooling around her head. She wasn't one of the girls they were looking for. Michael looked up at the loft railing that she must have fallen over, and then back at the body.

She was beyond help, so they left her where she was and branched out to search the warehouse. Michael was brushing aside a layer of cobwebs hanging in a second floor doorway when he heard Marx's desperate voice bellow from clear across the warehouse.

"Get me an ambulance now!"

Michael turned and sprinted toward the voice. As he drew closer, Marx shouted again.

"Ten minutes?! She doesn't have ten minutes! She can't breathe!"

Fear pulsed through Michael's veins. One of the girls was dying. He spotted another officer standing beside a victim sitting on the floor—Jace Walker—and he realized that Holly was the one who was dying.

Michael skidded to a stop alongside the other officer, watching as Marx carried Holly's limp, bruised body down the steps. "What's her condition?"

"Critical," the officer replied, barely audible over Jace's screams for her friend.

A few seconds after Marx and Jordan rushed out of the building, a series of car doors slammed. Michael frowned. "Where are the EMTs?"

The officer's face turned grim. "The ambulance was rerouted to a crash site. Multiple casualties. The next one is ten minutes out. Marx is taking her to the hospital in his car, but . . . I don't think she's gonna make it."

The officer's callous speculation added fuel to Jace's distress, and she covered her face, sobbing. "She has to make it. She has to."

Michael glared at the officer and crouched in front of the crying woman. "If anyone can get Holly the help she needs, it's Marx. He won't let anything get in his way." He visually checked her over. "How are you? Are you hurt?"

She looked at him through the strips of oily black hair hanging over her face. "Is he dead? Please tell me he's dead."

Michael looked past her to the body lying on the floor of one of the open rooms. "I don't know. I'll check."

He stood and walked toward the room with the light on. Before he even reached the doorway, he saw the blood pooling across the cement. Collin Wells was unconscious on the floor, and an officer pressed a wadded up cloth to his thigh, trying to staunch the bleeding.

"How's he doing?"

The man nodded toward the shard of bloody glass lying on the floor. "I think the girl nicked an artery. Unfortunately, the pervert's probably gonna make it."

Michael's gaze traveled past the scattered clothes to the camera recording the events, and a wave of nausea washed over him. Collin had been making a third video when Holly stabbed him in the thigh with a hunk of glass.

"Check that out," the officer said, directing his attention to the wooden box in the far corner.

Michael stepped carefully around the evidence on the floor, pulled on a glove, and studied the box. There was an open padlock resting on the latch, and a hole about the size of a dime drilled into the bottom of the lid. Carefully, he opened the lid to peer inside. He stared at the long, ragged grooves along the inside of the lid where someone had raked at it with their fingernails, and swallowed the bile that crept up his throat. Collin had forced Holly into the box and locked it.

Shannon broke into his story with a question. "Whose fingerprints were on the padlock?"

"We found the same set of prints on the padlock for the box and the padlock for the door, and those prints belong to Collin Wells."

"Did you find Mr. Wells's fingerprints anywhere else at the scene?"

Michael listed off the numerous places Collin's fingerprints had been found, including the video camera, the bat, and various items in the storage closet. The closet was packed with enough food and water to sustain two people for six months, along with hygiene products, blankets, and clothes.

"Let's go back to the abduction site—Officer Barrera's apartment," Shannon said. "How was Holly taken without being seen?"

"We reviewed camera footage from the area," Michael began. "And there was no way she could've been carried out of the building without being seen. She would've had to be inside something."

Shannon grabbed a photo from her folder of a figure dragging a rolling suitcase out of the side door of the apartment building. "Something like this suitcase?"

"We suspect so, yes. Holly is small enough that she would fit inside. And here in the man's opposite hand is a bat that looks strikingly similar to the one found at the warehouse."

Shannon handed the photo to the bailiff to pass along to the jury. "So at the same time Holly disappears, a suitcase big enough to hold her is wheeled out of the building by a man carrying the bat that disappeared from Officer Barrera's apartment and showed up at the warehouse, where it was then used for what purpose?"

Michael swallowed uncomfortably. "Bruises on Holly's body suggested she was beaten with a long, cylindrical object."

A few of the jurors looked horrified, and they didn't even know the extent of the injuries that beating had caused.

"Do you believe Holly was specifically targeted by the man who took her, or was she simply a victim of opportunity?" Shannon asked.

"She was targeted. Her apartment was broken into a month and a half before her abduction and all of her clothes were stolen. We found every stolen article of clothing in that storage closet, as well as her travel bag, which she had taken with her to Officer Barrera's apartment."

"So you believe that the man who abducted her had been stalking her for at least a month and half?"

"Yes."

"Are you aware that Holly took out an order of protection against Collin Wells because he was stalking her?" She directed everyone's attention to Collin, who adopted a pained expression.

"Detective Marx informed me of that fact after she went missing."

Shannon smiled. "No further questions. Thank you, Detective Everly."

. . . .

Collin cleared his throat as he stood. "That was certainly a lot of information. I commend you for being able to remember it all." He moved around his desk and out onto the floor as if it were a stage. "Sixteen years with the police department, but only four years as a detective. Many officers graduate to detective within six to eight years. Why did it take you twelve?"

Shannon expected that question to arise. Michael was the primary detective on Holly's case. Any defense attorney would try to discredit him.

"The longer I worked the streets as a patrol officer, the more experience and knowledge I gained about people. I was in no rush to cut that opportunity short."

"I see. You were assigned as the primary detective on Holly's case, correct?"

"After she was found, yes."

"But Detective Marx remained involved?"

"He didn't process the scene or handle any of the evidence. He stayed at the hospital with Holly, and I kept him apprised of the investigation."

"You said Detective Marx told you I was stalking Holly—a claim which I wholeheartedly refute. Is he also the one who suggested me as a suspect?"

"Yes."

Collin looked around the courtroom before asking, "Your only suspect? Did you even consider anyone else? I mean, there are a lot of people in New York City."

"We investigate the most obvious angle first. Holly was scared of you, and she had a protection order against you, which made you the most likely suspect."

"Did Holly tell you I was the person who abducted her when you interviewed her at the hospital?"

"I didn't interview Holly."

"Oh, that's right. Detective Marx took Holly's statement at the hospital. But as the primary detective on the case, wasn't that your job?"

"We made an exception," Michael said. "After what Holly had just been through, we thought it would be easier for her to confide in someone she trusts."

"Would I be wrong in assuming Detective Marx insisted on being the person to take her statement?"

"I don't recall if he insisted or not, but there were very few members of law enforcement that Holly trusted at the time. Detective Marx was the obvious choice."

Collin grunted in thought. "I see. Were you at least present when she gave her statement, or was he alone with her at the time?"

"Holly wouldn't have been comfortable with anyone else in the room."

"Is that a yes or a no?"

"Yes, she was alone with him."

Collin slid his hands into the pockets of his slacks. "Let's talk about the rape kit. Surely if I raped Holly, as the charges against me suggest, my DNA would've been recovered during the exam. Was it?"

Shannon caught Michael's concerned glance. No exam had been performed because Holly was in a coma and couldn't consent. Shannon had pushed for one, but Rick, the only person listed as next of kin, refused to subject Holly to something he knew she wouldn't want. In the end, they believed the videos would suffice.

Michael cleared his throat. "No sexual assault exam was done."

Collin frowned. "That seems unusual. Was it an oversight by the police and hospital staff, or did someone make the call not to have an exam performed?"

"Holly was in a coma, so the decision was made by the person listed as her next of kin."

"And who is that?"

Michael paused before answering. "Detective Richard Marx."

Collin feigned surprise. "You're telling me that a seasoned detective, a man who knows the importance of evidence in a trial, denied an evidence-gathering exam?"

"Holly doesn't like people touching her. He knew she wouldn't want the exam."

"Or he knew it would exonerate me of the rape charge."

Shannon shot to her feet. "Objection. The defendant seems more interested in slandering a decorated detective than he does in proving his own innocence."

Collin held up his hands. "I'm moving on, Your Honor." When Tipper nodded, Collin shifted topics. "Detective Everly, the bat found at the warehouse, did it belong to officer Barrera?"

"Officer Barrera identified it as his, yes."

"You insinuated that my prints were on the bat because I"—he air-quoted with his fingers—"beat Holly. If the jury will recall, this is also the bat that I used to hit Drew Carson over the back of the head, when he had Holly at gunpoint. In order to save her life. If this is the bat that came from Officer Barrera's apartment, then of course my prints are on it."

Michael's lips thinned, but he said nothing.

"Is it possible that whoever abducted Holly from Officer Barrera's apartment also took the bat to the warehouse?"

"Is that a trick question?"

Collin smiled. "No, it isn't. A yes or no will suffice."

"Yes, it's possible."

"And my fingerprints in the warehouse—do they confirm that I held Holly captive, or simply that I was present in the warehouse at some point in time?"

"Your prints on the padlocks suggest you were responsible for her captivity and torture."

297

"I'm not asking about the padlocks yet, Detective. Just my prints in the warehouse in general."

"They confirm that you were present in the warehouse at some time in the near past."

Collin nodded. "And this person who supposedly dragged Holly off in a suitcase—can you see their face in the photo?"

"No."

"Can you see any distinguishable features at all?"

"He's average height."

"He?" Wells took the photo from the bailiff and showed it to the jury again. "Does anyone else see a *he* in this picture? Because I can't see enough to determine if it's a man or a woman." He set the photo in front of Michael. "How about you? Can you be one hundred percent certain it's a man?"

Michael stared at the image for a long moment, unwilling to answer. "Not one hundred percent, no."

"Did you find a suitcase with my fingerprints on it?" He didn't wait for Michael to answer. "Of course not, because this isn't me." He smacked a hand on the photo for dramatic emphasis. "I had no idea Holly was even missing until I saw her picture on the news. I assumed, when I left Officer Barrera's apartment, she would be fine. I started looking for her the moment I realized she was missing. I've never been much of a believer, but it was nothing short of divine intervention that I stumbled across the warehouse where she was being held."

Michael's eyes narrowed, and Shannon suspected it was the reference to divine intervention. He was a devout Christian, and Collin was using it to get under his skin.

"I was about to give up, but then I heard a woman screaming. What would you do if you heard a woman screaming inside an abandoned building, Detective?"

"I would go in to help her."

"Which is exactly what I did, and I saw much the same as you—a woman lying dead on the floor, several empty rooms. Then I heard another scream. I searched everywhere, calling out, hoping it was Holly. Hoping I could—"

"Objection, Your Honor. This isn't a platform for his monologue."

Before Tipper could open his mouth, Collin said, "I'm laying the foundation for my question, Judge. It is relevant."

To Shannon's irritation, Tipper waved him on.

"During my search, I came to a padlocked door. If you realized that the screaming woman was trapped behind that padlocked door, what would you do, Detective?"

"Try to find the key or bolt cutters."

"Again, exactly what I did. It took me a while to reason out that the dead woman might have the key on her, and I ran down to check, finding it in her pocket. Now, is it possible that my fingerprints on the padlocks

299

were from my effort to unlock the room and set Holly free from the box?"

"Yes, it's possible," Michael said reluctantly. "But that doesn't explain your fingerprints on the video camera or the items in the storage closet."

"I was frantic to find Holly. I did pick up the camera to see what was going on, and I remember a storage closet—it was one of the rooms I searched—but I'm not a trained detective. I'm not conscious of everything I touch when I walk into a room, especially when I'm stressed and worried." Collin paused, and then asked, "Were my prints on everything in the storage closet?"

"No."

"Were there prints on the other items in the storage closet?"

Michael ran his tongue over his top teeth as he delayed answering. "Yes, there were prints on the other items in the closet."

"Whose prints?"

"There were multiple prints."

Collin smiled just a little. "Detective, whose prints were on the items in the closet? Specifically."

"There were several unidentified prints, probably belonging to the employees who unpacked and stocked the products at the grocery store. But there was one set of identifiable prints found on nearly every food and hygiene item in the closet, and they belonged to Rachel Glass."

Collin raised his eyebrows and looked around the courtroom. "Rachel Glass. The dead woman who was in the warehouse before I even found Holly? The woman who burned down the women's shelter and murdered seven people? That Rachel Glass?"

"Yes," Michael gritted out. "That Rachel Glass."

"Well, that is interesting." Collin cocked his head, his expression pensive. "How about transportation? How did Holly get to the warehouse?"

"We found a red Honda parked two blocks from the warehouse, and we suspect it was the vehicle used to transport her. The car had been reported stolen."

"Stolen by whom? When?"

Michael looked down at his lap and exhaled slowly. "It was stolen the night the shelter was burned down, and hair and fingerprints belonging to Rachel Glass were found in the front of the car."

"Were my prints in the car?"

"No."

"So Rachel stocked the supplies in the storage closet of the building where Holly was kept, and you believe Holly at some point was transported in the car that Rachel stole." Collin pretended surprise. "I'm seeing a very obvious line between point A and B, and yet you seem to have missed it, Detective."

"Rachel Glass's fingerprints were nowhere else at the scene. Just yours and some unidentifiable prints probably belonging to trespassers."

"But couldn't she have worn gloves? In fact, if I remember correctly . . . ." He walked back to his table and

301

rifled through a folder on his desk. He pulled out a document, which he proceeded to read. He gave Rachel's description before reaching the vital parts. "Contents on her person: black jeans, black boots, black leather gloves." He looked up at Michael. "She was wearing gloves when her body was found at the scene."

Michael shrugged, and Collin smiled confidently.

"So, Detective, is it possible that Rachel Glass, who appears to have bought the groceries and stocked them in the closet, who was at the scene when I arrived, who likely had Holly in her stolen car at some point, and who left no fingerprints at the scene because she was wearing gloves, held Holly captive in that warehouse?"

Michael cast Shannon a desperate look. If he said yes, he would give the jury reasonable doubt, but he couldn't say no. The fact of the matter was, it was possible even if they all knew it wasn't the truth.

"I think it's possible there were two people involved in Holly's captivity, and I believe you were one of them," he said.

The smile slid off Collin's face. That wasn't the answer he was hoping for. "I see. And you're basing that on what?"

Michael leaned forward, leveling a hard gaze at him. "The victim identified you as her attacker, and Rachel Glass as your accomplice. Also, the manual bruising on Holly's body, specifically her throat, came from hands too large to be Rachel's. You wanna paint yourself as the hero who searched for her for days and then rescued her from a terrible situation? What hero

302

rescues a woman and then throws her on the floor and tries to force himself on her?"

Collin tapped irritated fingers on the edge of the witness stand, trying to maintain an appearance of calm. "No further questions at this time, Your Honor." He walked back to his table and dropped into the chair.

Tipper nodded. "At this time, we will recess until nine o'clock tomorrow morning."

32

*M*arx waited along the back wall of the courtroom as Shannon gathered her belongings.

She was furious with him right now, and he couldn't blame her. She'd been blindsided by the details of the protection order.

He hadn't intended for things to go the way they did that day in the restaurant, but when he came back into the building to find Holly terrified and trapped against the wall by Collin's body, he snapped.

The only thing that mattered to him in that moment was protecting her. He could've given Collin the protection order and sent him on his way, but he knew that piece of paper wouldn't deter him. Arresting him seemed like the best option at the time.

Shannon grabbed her briefcase off the table and strode toward him, practically flaying him with her eyes. "You should've told me about the situation with the protection order."

He pushed away from the wall. "I know."

"And you should really consider some anger management therapy. Your temper up there was ridiculous."

"I know that too."

"Your outbursts could've landed you in contempt of court. You do realize that Holly won't set foot in this room without you."

He *did* realize that, but Collin had a way of getting under his skin. "I'm sorry."

She sighed, some of her anger fading. "I'm sorry too. I hate that I had to bring up the issue of children in front of everyone. I know it's a painful topic, especially after our . . . discussion the other night."

He still hadn't worked out quite how to feel about their heated conversation. He was still hurt, still a little angry, but he could see her perspective more clearly now.

He pulled open one of the double doors and held it for her. "I understand why you had to bring it up. It's not uncommon for men my age to be attracted to younger women. The jury needed to know why I see her differently."

Her phone chimed, and she pulled it from her purse to check the message. "Shawn was able to procure the warrant you requested for the post office box."

Good. If he could find out who the box was registered to, presumably a woman named Molly, then maybe he could track down the person targeting Holly and eliminate the threat before her testimony tomorrow morning.

A uniformed officer approached, nodding to Marx before directing his attention to Shannon. "Are you ready, ma'am?"

Shannon's mouth turned down at the *ma'am*, but she nodded. "I am, thank you." She offered Marx a tense smile. "I'll see you tomorrow morning."

Marx's phone rang, but he watched the officer escort Shannon from the courthouse before answering. "Marx."

"Detective." There was an undertone of stress to the familiar voice.

"Addison?"

"I need you to meet me."

Marx needed to grab his warrant and visit the post office before it closed. He didn't have the time or the patience to deal with a self-absorbed journalist. "I'm busy. What do you want?"

"It's about Holly. I think she's in danger."

. . . .

Addison Miles slouched in a plastic chair much too small for a man his size, and held a bag of frozen carrots to the back of his head.

Marx took in the pink-and-tan apartment building in front of him—the complex designed more like a motel, with an outdoor stairwell leading to the second story—and then returned his attention to Addison as he stepped onto the sidewalk.

"What happened to you?"

Addison winced as he looked up. "Someone hit me from behind."

The blow to the head must have knocked him off his feet, because his left eye was swollen, probably from the impact with the floor. Marx supposed he should have sympathy for the man, but he couldn't seem to muster anything more than irritation, disgust, and contempt.

"I really hope there's more to this story, because if not, I have somewhere else to be."

Addison lowered the dripping bag of carrots, outrage tinging his voice. "I was attacked."

"I somehow doubt it was unprovoked."

"What's that supposed to mean?"

"You irritate people." He folded his arms. "Now explain to me how you bein' attacked has anythin' to do with Holly."

Addison frowned. "After we talked, and you accused me of calling Agatha Wells to let her know Holly was at the bar, I started thinking. I didn't call her, but Mina was with me. She knew Holly was at the bar."

"Who is Mina?"

"My photographer. My last guy quit. He said the work was too dangerous. Mina's skills are subpar, but I had to take what I could get." He returned the pack of frozen vegetables to his head. "Anyway, I tried calling her several times. I wanted to know why she was talking to my sources without me. I hired her to take pictures, not highjack my stories."

Marx's patience were wearing thin. "And?"

"She ignored all my phone calls, so I decided to drop by tonight, confront her face-to-face. I was about to knock, when I heard voices coming from inside. Mina wanted to know why someone wasn't writing her back, why he didn't seem to notice her. I pounded on the door, and when she opened it, I pushed my way in to see if I was right about my suspicions."

Marx stared at him, confounded by the man's behavior. "You forced your way into a woman's apartment, and you're upset that she hit you?"

"I told you I heard voices, and Mina wasn't talking to herself—though I wouldn't put that past her. There was someone else in the apartment. When I let myself in, Agatha Wells was standing right there in the living room."

That got Marx's attention. "You're sure?"

"I've met with the woman more than once. I know what she looks like. I think she's been staying with Mina. I don't know for how long. Maybe since we first interviewed her three months ago."

That would explain why the police couldn't find out where she was staying. She was hiding with someone who wasn't even on their radar.

"I demanded to know what was going on. I asked Agatha about the threats against Holly, and the next thing I know, Mina's clubbing me across the back of the head, and I'm waking up on her living room floor. I knew Mina was a little off when I hired her, but this is . . ." He gestured to the open doorway beside him.

Marx pushed the door the rest of the way open and stepped inside the small apartment. At first glance it seemed like an ordinary space with sparse furniture and faded carpet, until he turned to see the wall across from the couch.

Most people had a television or a fireplace. Mina had covered the entire wall in a collage of cutout pictures. Collin's face was everywhere, sometimes whole and sometimes spliced in half and connected to a woman's face.

"Well, that's disturbin'." Marx pointed to the female half of the spliced image as Addison stumbled in behind him. "Who's this?"

"That's Mina."

Marx frowned at the letters plastered above the pictures, spelling out the phrase: *Collin & Molly Forever*. "If this is Mina's apartment, and her face is all over this wall with Collin, then who is Molly?"

Addison shrugged. "I don't know."

"And you're sure it was Mina who hit you?"

"Positive."

Marx scanned the rest of the collage, noting several images of Holly. There was one of her outside the remains of the women's shelter, her expression mournful. Another of her standing in front of a shelf lined with books. Sitting in a coffee shop sipping hot chocolate. Ice skating with Jordan. Getting her hair trimmed at the salon with Jace. Outside the bar where she met up with Sam.

"I wasn't even with Mina when she took most of these. She's been following Holly on her own time," Addison explained. "Backstabber."

Marx's gut twisted. How long had this woman been watching Holly? *Why* was she watching Holly?

He pulled a glove from his pocket and opened what appeared to be a scrapbook on the shelf in front of him. He studied the close-up snapshot of an eye— almond shaped, with rings of root-beer brown and golden honey. He'd stared into those eyes more times than he could count.

He flipped the page to find strands of carrot-red hair trapped inside the protective sheet of plastic. His eyes bounced back to the picture of Holly at the hair salon. Mina had slipped in and collected the strands the beautician had snipped?

What was wrong with this woman?

Addison peered over his shoulder. "Is that . . . human hair?"

"I think it's Holly's hair."

"That's disgusting."

Marx turned a few more pages of the album before closing it. He examined the other items on the shelf, finding a notebook. The first page was lined with the same two words: Molly Wells.

Molly. Could this be the same Molly who was writing letters to Collin in prison? The woman who wanted Holly out of the picture?

Marx flipped through the pages of the notebook, watching the signature evolve until he recognized the curly "M" and the "y" with an exaggerated tail.

He fished his cell phone from his pocket and pulled up the picture he'd taken of the most recent letter

Molly sent to Collin. He compared the style of the signature scrawled across the bottom of the letter with the name written in the notebook. Identical.

Was Molly sharing this apartment with Mina and Agatha, or . . .

"That's Mina's handwriting," Addison said, crowding Marx so he could see the notebook.

"You're sure?"

"Yeah, but I don't know why she's writing 'Molly Wells.' That's just . . . weird."

It looked like Marx wouldn't need to visit the post office after all, because Molly and Mina were the same person.

His gaze snagged on strands of blonde hair hanging out of a box, and he lifted the lid to find a wig. The woman who attacked Shannon at the courthouse had long blonde hair.

"Is Mina familiar with where the cameras are in the courthouse?"

"Probably. We cover a lot of stories there."

Marx closed the box and looked at Addison. "You had no idea your photographer was this disturbed?"

"Like I said, I knew Mina was a little strange when I hired her, but I didn't realize she was crazy."

Marx eyed the package of frozen carrots the man was still holding against his head. "I guess I don't have to ask if she's violent."

He had no idea what was going on in Mina's mind right now, but if Agatha Wells was whispering in her ear, Addison was right: Holly was in danger.

Marx made a few calls—first to Sully, to request any information he could find on Addison's photographer, then to Michael and CSU. They needed to tear this place apart and figure out Mina's plan before she set it in motion.

· · · ·

Marx sat in the driver's seat of his car outside his apartment building, studying the photo of the woman Sully texted to his phone. Mina Baldwin was in her midthirties with black hair, dark eyes, and rows of piercings that followed the arch of her eyebrows.

Marx couldn't recall ever meeting her before, but she looked vaguely familiar, so he must have seen her.

Sully was still working on pulling her background information, but Marx had put out a BOLO with her name, alias, photo, and vehicle registration. Every squad car on the street was on the lookout for her.

There was nothing more he could do tonight except comfort Holly, who was going to be an anxious wreck the night before her testimony.

He climbed out of his car and shut the door, starting up the sidewalk to his apartment building. Something crunched beneath his shoe, and he lifted his foot to see a dark smudge on the pavement. The sidewalk and street were littered with brown and yellow pebble-like objects.

He bent to pick one up. It was an M&M. Before the meaning behind the candy could register, something smacked the top of his head.

"What in the . . ."

He rubbed at his stinging scalp, then looked down at the offending yellow M&M. Another one hit the pavement about ten feet away, and he tracked it back to the top of his apartment building.

"Holly!"

A pale face peered hesitantly over the edge of the roof.

"What in the world are you doin'?"

There was a pause before she said, "Nothing," and then disappeared from view again.

Marx shook his head at the candy littering the ground around him and headed into the building, climbing the eight flights of steps to the roof. He pushed open the rusty door and stepped out into the darkness.

Holly sat cross-legged on a blanket with a jar of candy nestled between her thighs, close enough to the edge of the roof to make him nervous.

He dropped down beside her, groaning as his body protested against the hard surface, and rested his arms across his knees. "Should I be worried that I keep findin' you up here?"

She rummaged through the jar for another handful of candy, and tossed two more pieces. "I can't leave the building without someone guarding me, so up here is the safest option for fresh air."

"I see you cracked open the rainy-day fund."

"Seemed like a good time."

Her testimony was in twelve hours, and he knew she must be counting down the minutes until she had to see her foster brother again.

"You wanna talk about it?"

She released a trembling sigh and pulled her eyes away from the lights glittering in the distance to look at him. "I'm not sure I can do this."

"You're not givin' yourself enough credit."

She shook her head. "Nothing good ever comes from being in the same room with that man. It's only ever humiliation and pain, and I just . . ."

"I know that talkin' about what he did to you will be hard, sweetheart, but you can do this. And I'm gonna be there the entire time."

She hurled another piece of candy over the edge. "Something's gonna go wrong. I can feel it."

Marx thought about Mina. There was a good chance she would try to attack Holly outside the courthouse tomorrow. And he couldn't be sure she was the only person Agatha Wells hired. "There's always the chance that things won't go as smoothly as we hope, but no matter what happens, you get up on that stand and do the best that you can."

"What if I panic?"

"Then you panic. We'll deal with it." He offered his hand to comfort her, but instead of placing her fingers in his, she sprinkled a few M&M's into his palm.

He smiled. They sat together in silence, staring at the lights in the distance and tossing yellow and brown candy off the roof until the jar was empty.

33

*H*olly could still feel the coldness of the cement floor beneath her back, stealing the warmth from her body, as she stood in front of the bedroom mirror. The night terror that had woken her still lingered in the back of her mind as she prepared for court.

She tugged the hem of her sweater lower over her dress pants and studied her reflection.

She was covered from her collarbone to her toes, and yet she felt naked. That nightmare, so vivid, transported her back to that inescapable room, the place where Collin stripped away more than her clothes; he stripped away pieces of her soul, and she was still trying to get them back.

Every day that she felt more secure in her body, that she broke through a relationship barrier, that she found joy despite the excruciating memories—that was a day she defeated Collin. One small battle at a time.

But this was different.

Confronting Collin in person . . .

A tremor swept through her at the thought. She didn't want to see him again, let alone talk to him, but she didn't have a choice. If she refused, and Collin went free, how many more people would he hurt?

She had to do this. For the people she loved. For the women and children in that shelter. For every person whose life he *had* and would destroy.

She swallowed and wrapped her arms around her stomach, her eyes trailing to the closet as she pondered another layer. Maybe just one more sweater would . . .

She shoved the thought from her mind before it could give strength to her insecurities. She always felt naked and vulnerable when Collin looked at her, and there weren't enough clothes in the world to change that.

The only thing that did have the power to change it was her faith in God. She squeezed her eyes shut and whispered a prayer.

"Heavenly Father." She bit her bottom lip to keep it from quivering. "Clothe me in the dignity he tried to take away. Dress me in strength so I can speak the truth." Tears spilled down her cheeks as everything in her, body and soul, cried out to God. "Wrap me in layers of your peace."

She opened her eyes and brushed the dampness from her cheeks.

Was this how David felt when God called him to take a stand against a seemingly unstoppable enemy? Did he tremble at the knowledge that no one before him had been able to take down the giant? Did he pray for strength and courage with every step as he marched into that battle?

A knock on the bedroom door drew Holly from her thoughts, and she turned to see Marx in the doorway.

317

He wore a bulletproof vest over his sweater, and a second smaller one hung from his left hand. "You ready, sweetheart?"

She released a shivery breath and glanced at her reflection one last time. With God on one side of her and Marx on the other, she could confront her giant.

. . . .

The courthouse steps were crowded with people from every walk of life, and any of them could be a threat.

Marx scanned the rows of faces, hoping to spot Mina. He had no doubt she was nearby, waiting for the right moment, but he didn't see her. No one else set off warning bells, but there was no way to know how many people Agatha Wells had hired.

He opened the passenger door of his car, and camera flashes ignited behind him.

Holly shrank down in the seat, eyes wide as she stared at the swarm of people waiting to bombard her with questions. "Why are there so many people?"

"Just focus on the doors at the top of the steps." He offered her his hand.

After a long moment of hesitation, she placed her icy fingers in his, and he helped her out of the car. Shielding her with his body, he double-checked her bulletproof vest.

If Mina opened fire and a bullet hit her, the impact would likely break a rib or two, but she would survive.

"Okay, you ready?"

She glanced at Sam and Jordan, who were waiting to help escort her up the steps, and then at the crowd. She stiffened. "That's—"

He followed her attention to Addison, who lingered on the fringes of the crowd. "We'll keep an eye on him. Let's get you in there." He shut the car door and nodded to Sam.

Pushing his way into the crowd, Sam cleared a path for them to follow. The moment the media caught sight of Holly's vest, they began firing questions:

"Holly, why are you wearing a police vest?"

"Is she in danger? Did someone threaten—"

"Are you expecting a shooter?"

One reporter asked a rude question and shoved a microphone in front of Holly's face. Marx slapped it away. "Back off."

These people disgusted him.

There was a time and a place for the media, but this wasn't it. Accosting victims with painful, personal questions on the steps of a courthouse wasn't news; it was indecency.

Addison shouldered his way through the crowd, checking the faces of the women he bumped into. Marx locked eyes with him, but the bushy-haired journalist shook his head. None of them were Mina.

"Holly!" a reporter called out. "Is it true that you and Wells dated in the past?"

Holly stiffened, and Marx whispered, "Just ignore them, sweetheart."

He studied the faces around them, trying to anticipate which direction the threat would come from.

A sudden movement to his right caught his attention, and he didn't have time to process the details as a figure lunged toward them. A camera flash glinted off the knife in the attacker's hand, and Marx barely had time to pull Holly out of the path of the blade aimed at her throat.

It sliced across his arm, but the pain barely registered.

As the attacker regained her footing, his brain quickly catalogued her details: pale, red hair, female . . . with a camera hanging on a strap around her neck.

The woman sliced at him again, screaming savagely, but Jordan dove toward her, hitting her arm to deflect the thrust. "Get Holly inside!"

Chaos erupted and bystanders scrambled for safety. Marx tried to shield Holly from the frantic stampede and flailing limbs as he maneuvered her up the steps.

She twisted in his arms to see behind them. "Jordan. We have to help him."

"He'll be fine. I need you inside. Now."

"But she has a knife!" Holly stumbled, her concern for Jordan slowing them down.

Desperate to get her to safety, Marx wrapped an arm around her waist and picked her up. He hauled her up the last five steps and through the doors into the courthouse.

Before the doors closed, he heard Sam shout, "Drop the knife and get on the ground!"

. . . .

Shannon checked the time again, and then looked toward the rear doors. Restlessness was spreading through the courtroom—voices whispering, chairs creaking—and a nervous sweat gathered along her hairline.

Judge Tipper made a phlegmy sound of impatience in the back of his throat. "Ms. Marx, if you can't produce your witness—"

"She's just running late, Your Honor."

Or running away. Holly was due in the courtroom ten minutes ago. If she'd gotten scared and taken off . . .

"If I could beg the court's patience for another few minutes, I'm sure she'll be here."

"Five minutes, Ms. Marx. If she's not in my courtroom by then, we're moving on."

"Thank you, Your Honor." She scooped her cell off the table to text Rick, when one of the rear doors opened.

The grim expression on her assistant's face as he walked briskly down the aisle toward the front of the room *without* the witness she'd sent him to find, ignited a spark of dread in the pit of her stomach. Something was wrong.

He leaned across the bar and whispered, "We have a problem. A woman with a knife attacked the group coming into the courthouse."

Shannon's fingers went cold, and she nearly dropped her phone. "Is anyone hurt?"

"One of the officers escorting her was wounded." He hesitated to continue, and fear crushed the breath from her lungs.

"Rick." She pressed a hand against the table to steady herself. "How bad?"

"No one knows yet. Paramedics are on the way."

She nodded, forcing herself to breathe. If no one knew how badly Rick was hurt, then he wasn't bleeding out on the courthouse steps. "Okay. And Holly?"

"Ms. Cross was moved to a guarded conference room until law enforcement can secure the scene."

The poor girl was probably an emotional disaster. As if the impending confrontation with her foster brother weren't terrifying enough, she was attacked before she could even enter the building.

Pulling herself together, Shannon turned toward the judge. "Your Honor, I request a recess."

Tipper's mood grew even more sour. "You're making a lot of requests, counselor. You better have a good reason."

"Someone just tried to murder my witness on the front steps of the courthouse."

Gasps rippled through the room, and Collin sat straighter in his chair, an expression of concern on his face that looked disconcertingly genuine.

Tipper slammed his gavel to quiet the room. "Attend to your witness, Ms. Marx. We'll reconvene in thirty minutes."

Shannon thanked him, hastily gathered up her things, and followed her assistant, Shawn, out of the courtroom. "Which room?"

"Lower level."

She stripped off the heels that were slowing her down, and hurried down the stairs in her stockings. She spotted the two security officers standing guard in front of a conference room before her feet left the last stair.

She pulled her ID from her briefcase and showed it to them. "Is my witness in there? A red-haired girl, petite?"

One of the officers nodded. "Yes, ma'am. The detective escorting her is in there with her."

"I would like to see them."

Shawn touched her shoulder to grab her attention. "I'm gonna speak with the police, see what else I can find out."

"Thank you."

The officer opened the door, letting her into the room. Rick sat in one of the cushioned chairs, but he stood when she entered.

Relief washed over her, and she dropped her briefcase onto the table before throwing her arms around his neck. Despite the news that it may have been him wounded in the attack, he was alive and whole.

"You're all right."

323

He folded his arms around her, the warmth of his breath on her neck easing the knot of fear in her stomach. "I'm always all right."

She rested her forehead against his, their lips a hairsbreadth apart. "You had me worried."

"I promise I'm fine. But if this is what happens when you worry, feel free to worry more often."

She huffed a laugh and drew back to look him over more thoroughly. There was a rough bandage wrapped around his forearm. "What happened?"

"It's just a scratch."

She studied the wrapping and the dried blood on his arm. "A scratch? Really?"

"I already had this argument with Holly." He pulled his arm from her grip. "I was not stabbed, I don't need stitches, and I am not goin' to a hospital."

Her eyebrows lifted. "All right." She turned her attention to the young woman pacing along the far wall like a caged tiger. "How's she doing?"

"She's scared. And she's angry with me. She wanted to help Jordan when the woman went after him with the knife, but I wouldn't let her."

"There was nothing she could've done."

"I know that, and you know that, but Mighty Mouse over there is determined to protect everybody she cares about, even if she can't possibly win the fight."

Shannon smiled. "Can you blame her? It took her almost nineteen years to find people she could trust, people who mean it when they say they love her. She's going to fight to keep them, with everything she has."

"I suppose." He rubbed absently at his bandaged arm. "What's goin' on with the trial?"

"The judge granted me a brief recess so I could check on the two of you. We're due to reconvene in twenty minutes." She crossed her arms. "What happened?"

She listened as he explained the series of events that led them to this moment, and she couldn't help but look at Holly. If Rick's reflexes had been a second slower, this kindhearted girl, who loved marshmallows and hot chocolate, would be dead.

Shannon dealt with murder and death in the courtroom on a regular basis, but it was easier to distance herself from a photograph, from a person she'd heard about but never met. Imagining someone she knew, someone she'd come to adore, vanishing in an instant of violence made her queasy.

"Hey." Rick touched the side of her face. "You all right?"

She dragged her eyes back to him. "Just remembering why I never let myself get emotionally entangled with witnesses and victims."

Rick's expression softened. "She's all right. Everybody's fine."

"If you had been a second slower . . ."

"We would be preparin' for a funeral rather than a testimony, I know." A shadow of pain passed behind his eyes as he looked at Holly. He had so much love for her. "But you can't live life afraid to let people in because you might lose them."

Or hurt them, she thought, which was exactly what she'd done to him, the one person she allowed herself to love. But now wasn't the time to dwell on that.

"I'm not sure Wells had anything to do with this attack."

Rick arched an eyebrow at her abrupt change in subject, but he didn't call her out on it. "I don't think he did either."

"He seemed genuinely concerned when I announced that someone tried to kill Holly."

"If he was concerned, it was because somebody just tried to destroy his favorite toy, and he's not done playin' with her yet."

Shannon shuddered at the disturbing thought. She would never understand how one human being could so easily dehumanize another.

A knock on the door, followed by her assistant's voice, reminded Shannon that they were short on time. "Thank you, Shawn." She walked over to Holly. "Are you ready?"

Holly wrapped her arms around herself. "I'm not sure I'll ever be ready to see him again."

"I know." Shannon tucked a few strands of hair behind Holly's ears, surprising herself. She had never been an affectionate person, but comforting this young woman whose eyes sparkled with fear and vulnerability felt oddly natural. "But you'll be perfectly safe in that courtroom. He can't touch you."

Holly pulled her bottom lip between her teeth and nodded distractedly.

"Though I don't think this enormous bulletproof vest is the best fashion statement for the courtroom," Shannon said, giving the edge of the armor a teasing tug.

Holly smiled. "I kinda like it."

Shannon slid Rick a look, and he smiled. He'd told her that she would have a hard time getting Holly into the courtroom without body armor.

He cleared his throat. "I'll take care of it. We'll see you in a few minutes."

"All right." She offered Holly a smile she hoped was reassuring, and headed for the door.

As she left, she overheard Holly's protest that she wanted to wear the vest during her testimony, followed by Rick's explanation that it only stopped bullets, not painful questions.

34

*H*olly stretched and twisted the sleeves of her sweater as she took her seat on the witness stand.

The sweater was designed to be formfitting, but with anxiety eating away at her appetite these past few weeks, it hung loosely from her slender frame.

The weight loss emphasized her fine bones and large eyes, and with her porcelain pale skin, she looked as fragile as a china doll.

Shannon caught Rick's eye, silently expressing her concern. This testimony was going to be intense, and Holly already looked as though she might faint and fall out of the chair.

Rick whispered a few words of reassurance to Holly, pressed something into her trembling hand, and then found his seat behind Shannon.

She leaned over the bar and whispered, "Is she all right?"

"The man who brutalized her is sittin' twenty feet away, so no, she's not all right."

Shannon scowled at his snarky response. "I'm aware of that, but she looks pale."

"She's always pale. Here." He handed her a thick, purple band.

"What's this for?"

"For when she breaks the first one." He leaned back without any further explanation, and shot Collin a murderous look.

Shannon set the band on her desk and silently prayed that they would all make it through this testimony intact and—she looked from Rick to Collin—alive.

She grabbed a folder from her desk before approaching the witness stand. "Holly, would you like a glass of water before we get started?"

Holly shook her head. "Can we just . . . get this over with? I don't like it here."

Holly had avoided looking at the defense table since she entered the courtroom, but Shannon had no doubt she could feel the attention of the predator just feet away.

Shannon glanced over her shoulder at the defense table. Sure enough, Collin was watching Holly with the intensity of a cat stalking its prey. He looked disturbingly hungry.

She moved a few inches to the left, using her body to block the defense table from Holly's view. "Can you tell the court how you know Collin Wells?"

Holly's gaze never left her lap. "He's . . . he was . . . my foster brother. When I was . . . fourteen, I was placed with his family."

"Would you say that you have a normal brother-sister relationship?"

"I don't know what a normal brother-sister relationship is supposed to look like. But . . . if what he

329

did to me is considered *normal* . . . no girl should ever be cursed with a brother."

Shannon knew about the horrors that shaped the eleven months Holly lived with the defendant's family, and what she wouldn't give to enlighten the jury.

"When you moved on from that foster home, did you have any intention of maintaining contact with your foster brother?"

"No. I just wanted him to leave me alone. I moved a lot, trying to hide from him, but he always found me."

A virtual ghost, Sully had called her, a young woman who went to impossible lengths to disappear. A few of the jurors glanced at the defense table, no doubt remembering his words.

"How did you feel when he showed up on your doorstep?" Shannon asked.

"Scared."

"Why were you so scared?"

"Because he . . ." Holly twisted and tugged at a purple band in her hands, a twin to the one Rick had just handed Shannon. "He hurt me the last time he found me, and I . . . I was afraid he might hurt me again."

"Objection," Collin called out, and the sound of his voice echoing through the nearly empty courtroom sent a visible jolt of fear through Holly.

Shannon reached into the witness box and placed a hand over Holly's, hoping to reassure her that she was safe.

Collin pushed to his feet. "If I found and hurt Holly before, I would like the police report to be shared with the court."

There was no police report because Holly never filed one, a fact Collin would've uncovered during his attempts to find her.

Shannon tried to counter his objection. "Those events happened out of state, Your Honor. I'm merely referencing—"

"A fictional event," Collin cut in. "There's no police report because there was no attack."

"Thousands of sex crimes go unreported each year. It doesn't mean they didn't happen."

"You're using false allegations to smear my reputation in front of the jury."

"Your reputation is hardly my concern, Mr. Wells. My concern is justice for the people you victimized."

Tipper thumped his gavel, bringing an abrupt end to the exchange. "That's enough." He looked between them. "Sit down, Mr. Wells. As for you, Ms. Marx, I trust you know that you cannot use an assault that was never reported or documented as a means to convince the jury that the defendant is guilty of *this* assault."

"I'm merely trying to establish why the witness felt frightened, Your Honor. Nothing more."

Tipper nodded and waved a hand. "Continue."

Shannon released Holly's hand and took a step back, physically and emotionally. "Holly, you stated that you were afraid the defendant might hurt you again. Did he?"

Holly's answer was so soft that it was barely audible. "Yes."

"I understand that you were at Officer Barrera's apartment the night you were abducted. Can you tell us what you remember?"

"I was alone on the couch while Sam . . . I mean, Officer Barrera was in another room, talking to his sister, and there was this sound, like a lock being picked. And then the door opened."

Holly described the evening with surprising clarity—Drew Carson barging in and shooting Samuel, the moment she leaped onto his back to protect her wounded friend from a second bullet, the struggle with Drew that eventually ended with her on the floor at gunpoint.

"Drew aimed the gun at my head, and I remember thinking, 'I'm gonna die, but it could be worse.' And then . . . it was."

"What made things worse?"

"Collin walked into the apartment. He hit Drew with the bat, and then he . . ." Holly trailed off, her eyes lifting, when one of the rear doors opened with a soft groan.

Jordan slipped in and started down the aisle, not even pausing when Tipper cleared his throat. "This is a closed court, young man."

"He's a close friend to the witness, Your Honor," Shannon explained, though she wasn't happy to see him in the courtroom.

Jordan reclaimed his spot on the bench directly behind the defense table, and Collin sprang to his feet. "Your Honor, this man is dangerous. He tried to strangle me in my hospital bed."

Shannon crossed her arms. "I would like to see the police report for that incident."

Collin glared at her. "The officers who witnessed the attack covered for him."

"By your logic then, if there's no police report, the attack never occurred."

Tipper rubbed at his chin. "You can't have it both ways, Mr. Wells. If the witness is comfortable with the gentleman's presence, he's welcome to stay."

Shannon turned to Holly to confirm that she didn't mind Jordan being in the room. They were going to be discussing some deeply personal details. Holly fidgeted in the chair, then nodded.

"Okay, let's talk about what happened after Wells struck Drew Carson."

"He . . . hit me with the bat." She grazed her cheekbone with her fingertips. "I just remember pain in my head, and then . . . I passed out."

Shannon motioned for her assistant to grab the first photograph from the folder on the table. He handed it to the bailiff, who passed it on to the jury.

"This photograph was taken at the hospital on March 22, after Holly was stabilized. The bruising along the left side of her face is from the impact of the bat. The doctor said it was amazing that her cheekbone didn't shatter." She let the jury examine the photo while she proceeded to the next question. "You stated that you passed out after Mr. Wells hit you. What's the next thing you remember?"

Holly tugged harder at the rubber band, her anxiety climbing. "I woke up . . . in that place."

Shannon pulled a photograph from the folder she'd brought with her, this one depicting a dingy room with stone block walls, a stained cement floor, and a lone bulb caged in wire on the ceiling.

She showed it to Holly. "This place?"

Holly glanced at the chilling image and then away. "Yes."

Shannon passed the image along to the jury. "How long did Collin Wells keep you locked in that room?"

"It felt . . . like an eternity, but"—she drew in a trembling breath and released it—"I was told it was only four days."

Four days *would've* been an eternity in that horrific place. Never knowing when the next cycle of abuse would come. It amazed Shannon that Holly had managed to survive.

"And when you woke up in that room, were you alone?"

"No." Holly rubbed at the tip of her nose with the sleeve of her sweater, her voice stuffy with tears. "Collin was . . . he was there."

"What was he doing?"

Seconds of silence ticked by, and just when Shannon thought she wouldn't answer, Holly choked out, "He was . . . on top of me. I tried to push him off, but I . . . I . . ."

Shannon placed a hand on the witness stand and lowered her voice so that only Holly could hear her. "It's okay."

Holly had fought as hard as she could, but Collin had the physical advantage.

"What did he do while he was on top of you?"

"He wrapped his hand around my throat, and I couldn't breathe."

"Did he say anything to you while he had his hand around your throat?"

"He said, 'I've missed this,' and then . . ." Her lips trembled, and she pulled them between her teeth, trying to gather the courage. "And then he k-kissed me."

A bench creaked, and Shannon looked over her shoulder. Jordan had leaned forward, elbows on his knees, a mixture of pain and anger on his face. This was only the beginning; Shannon's questions had barely grazed the surface of the violence that happened in that room.

"Let's talk about the first night you were there, Holly."

Shannon gently probed for details, slowly building the story for the jury.

Some of the night was a blur—stretches of time blotted out by emotional trauma—but much of the physical and verbal abuse was still sharp in Holly's memory.

In some ways, the verbal abuse had been more brutal than the beating that left her with a broken wrist and fractured ribs. The cruel words designed to tear down her spirit lingered long after her bones and bruises healed.

No man will ever love a woman as broken and used as you. You're worthless. You're like the kicked puppy that everyone feels sorry for but nobody really wants.

There was more to that night, but Holly wasn't ready to talk about the sexual assault. Shannon tiptoed around the topic, gleaning important details of the events surrounding it.

She circled back to the baseball bat from Samuel's apartment, and Holly grew a few shades paler when Shannon probed about how it had been used to break her bones. She reminded the jury that Collin's fingerprints were on it, and then moved on to the events that followed the sexual assault.

"What happened after Wells left the room?"

"He locked the door. Turned off the light. He always turned it off after he left. It was so . . . dark and so cold, I couldn't stop shaking."

Shannon suspected that had more to do with the trauma than the temperature. "And what did you do then?"

"I . . . um, I curled up on the floor, trying to stay warm."

As Shannon suspected she would, she deliberately skipped the most important detail. "You're leaving something out, Holly." When the young woman looked up at her, her honey-brown eyes liquid with tears, she asked gently, "Where were your clothes?"

The question sent the tears spilling over, and when she answered, her voice was so soft that Shannon wasn't sure the jurors could hear her. "Everywhere." She drew in a hiccupping breath. "I had to . . . to put them back on."

Shannon hesitated and then asked the question she knew would be met with resistance. "Why were your clothes *off*, Holly?"

Holly twisted the band in her hands so tightly that it snapped, making her flinch.

Rick had told Shannon this might happen. She walked to her desk to retrieve the spare band he'd given her, and the expression of helplessness on his face as he watched Holly struggle made Shannon's heart break.

Rick was a protector, and being unable to help the people he loved, especially the women he loved, was not something he handled well.

She walked back to the stand and offered Holly the purple band. "I know this is difficult, and it's hard to talk about—"

"I don't wanna talk about it."

"I know, but holding the truth inside and refusing to acknowledge it doesn't undo what happened. It just makes the wound that much deeper."

337

Holly twisted the new band in her lap. "He hurt me."

Shannon pursed her lips. Holly was never going to say the word, especially with a roomful of people. "When you say Collin Wells hurt you, do you mean he raped you?"

Holly choked on a sob and tried to wipe the tears from her face, but they were flowing too quickly.

Shannon offered her a tissue. "I just need you to answer with a yes or a no. You don't have to elaborate. Did the defendant rape you while he held you captive in that warehouse?"

For a moment, Holly looked as though she might throw up right there in the witness box. It took her three gasping tries to form the single word. "Yes."

Shannon breathed a sigh of relief. Ideally the victim would provide more detail, but she would take what she could get. "Okay, that's it. We're done talking about that, and we're moving on, all right?"

Holly nodded as she struggled to regain control of her breathing. Shannon gave her a moment to pull herself together before broaching the next subject.

"This room where you were kept, was there a bed? Blankets? Access to a bathroom?"

Holly drew in a quavering breath. "There was no bed. No . . . mattress or cot, and I just had my clothes to keep me warm. But there was a . . . a bucket for when I needed . . . to go."

Shannon glanced at the jurors, unsurprised to see compassion and even anger on some of their faces.

C.C. Warrens

Holly experienced something no human being should ever have to.

"Did you ever leave that room?"

"I convinced him to take me to the bathroom. I got away from him and ran toward the steps leading downstairs, but I had to stop because there was broken glass all over at the top of the steps. That's when I realized why he took my shoes and left me barefoot."

"In case you tried to escape."

Holly nodded. "He said . . . the glass was from my apartment windows. Someone broke into my apartment in February, and they swept up all the glass from the broken window and took it with them. It didn't make sense, but then, in that warehouse . . ." She cleared her throat softly. "Collin said it was poetic that I was trapped by my own windows."

"What did you do?"

"I pulled off my sweater and cleared a path. And then I ran down the steps toward an exit, but . . . the door was jammed, and I didn't have enough time to squeeze through."

"What happened?"

"He caught me, carried me back upstairs, and threw me into the room. I banged on the door and screamed for help until my voice gave out." Fresh tears trickled down her cheeks. "But no one came."

The heartbreaking truth was that someone heard her crying out for help, saw her trying to escape through that old, rusted door, and chose to do nothing. Until Rick offered a reward for information. Only then did the

339

man come forward with the information that led them to Holly.

"Was there anyone else in the warehouse?"

"Not at first. But then . . . one time after he left, I heard a voice that didn't belong to him."

"And who did that voice belong to?"

"Rachel Glass."

"What happened to Rachel Glass in that warehouse?" Shannon asked.

"She thought we were friends, and she wanted to see me. Collin brought me out of the room, and I tried to convince her to get help, but . . . he pushed her over the railing. He made me watch her die, and there was . . ." Her voice broke under the weight of grief. "There was nothing I could do."

"I'm so sorry you had to see that happen."

"She wasn't a bad person. She was just . . . scared and confused, and she didn't deserve to die."

Shannon nodded understandingly. "What happened next?"

"I passed out, and when I woke up . . . I was in the box."

With a bit of prompting, Holly described her experiences in the box, from the moment she first woke up inside and hyperventilated in panic to the moment Jace was brought into the room.

Her version of events supported Jace's testimony, down to the clicking sound of a lighter.

"Why do you think he brought Jace into the room?"

"Because I wasn't giving him what he wanted."

"And what did he want?"

The rhythm of Holly's breathing changed, becoming more agitated. "To know . . . things."

"What kinds of things?"

Holly glanced toward Collin, but Shannon kept her body angled between them like a protective shield. "When he . . . when . . ." She blew out a slow breath, trying to calm her anxiety. "When he was hurting me, he would ask . . . 'how does it feel?' He wanted to know how much pain I was in and how scared I was." She hugged herself, trying not to choke on her own tears. "I told him what he wanted to hear so he would stop hurting Jace."

"Why do you think he wanted to know those things?"

"Because he . . . likes it."

"So, you were under the impression that Mr. Wells enjoyed your pain and fear," she said. "That it excited him."

Holly's voice shook as she answered, "Yes."

All eyes flickered toward Collin, who sat at his desk with the air of a man watching a fascinating play unfold. Shannon half expected an objection, but he didn't even twitch.

Shannon walked her through the events that followed: Jace being dragged away, Collin pulling her out of the box.

"My legs were numb from being all twisted up, and I couldn't stand," Holly said. "He dropped me, and when I hit the floor, it felt like knives stabbing into my chest. I blacked out from the pain."

"And when your awareness returned, what was happening?"

Holly had to fight to get the words out. "He was . . . on top of me again."

"But you were able to fight back this time, weren't you?"

"With a piece of glass."

"Where did the glass come from?"

"The top of the steps. When I used my sweater to clear a path, some of the broken glass must have gotten caught in the material. After Collin threw me back in that room, I shook out my sweater and wrapped it around myself, trying to stay warm. I didn't even notice the glass until . . . until he was on top of me again, and . . ."

Holly's words stalled, and she twisted the purple band so tightly around her fingers that it would probably leave rings indented in her skin.

Shannon suspected she was caught up in the memories of sexual abuse, so she lowered her voice to a soothing whisper. "We're discussing what *you* did in this moment; not what Wells was doing, okay?"

Holly swallowed, and the band loosened around her fingers. "Okay."

"What did you do with the piece of glass?"

"I grabbed it, and then I stabbed him in the leg with it. I tried to stab him again, but he caught my wrist.

And then he choked me. I don't remember anything after that."

"You don't remember Detective Marx finding you?"

"No."

"You were in critical condition." Shannon pulled a document from the folder in her hands. "When you arrived at the hospital, you had three broken ribs, two collapsed lungs, internal bleeding, severe abdominal bruising, as well as severe bruising on your neck and extremities, and a broken wrist."

Horror rippled across the faces of some of the jurors.

"Was the defendant the person who caused those injuries?"

Holly nodded. "Yes."

Shannon closed the folder. "Thank you, Holly. I know that was difficult, and I appreciate you being willing to speak the truth." She turned to the judge. "Your Honor, if I might make a request."

"Let's hear it."

"Given the witness's level of fear toward the defendant, I request that he remain behind his desk during cross-examination."

Collin stood. "Now you're angling for sympathy from the jury. I've never been a threat to Holly."

"Considering we're here to prove otherwise, I think it's a reasonable request," Shannon interjected.

Tipper rubbed at his chin. "I agree. Mr. Wells, you will remain behind your desk for the duration of this testimony."

The corners of Collin's eyes twitched, the expression of irritation so subtle that Shannon doubted anyone else noticed. "Of course, Your Honor."

Shannon thanked the judge and returned to her seat, hoping that the physical distance between Collin and the witness box would be enough to keep Holly from dissolving into panic.

35

*C*ollin straightened his suit. "It's good to see you, Holly. You look beautiful today."

All the color drained from Holly's face, and Shannon sprang to her feet in outrage. "Your Honor …"

Tipper held up a hand, stopping her objection before she could finish it. "Mr. Wells, you will refrain from commenting on the witness's physical appearance."

Collin dipped his head. "Apologies, Your Honor. I was just trying to be polite."

He donned a compassionate and remorseful expression so flawless that Shannon doubted anyone would recognize it for what it was—a skillfully constructed mask. It unnerved Shannon that someone incapable of empathy or remorse could feign the emotions so expertly.

"You have every right to be afraid of me, Holly. I know I hurt you, and I can't even begin to apologize for that. I wish …"

He licked his lips, an odd gesture that didn't seem to fit with the image he was projecting. Shannon glanced at Holly, whose breathing had grown shallower and more rapid. She was petrified, and Collin was enjoying every moment of it.

The realization turned Shannon's stomach.

"I wish I could erase the fear in your eyes and wipe away the memories that haunt both of us," he continued. "I lost control of myself that day at the warehouse. I understand that what I did was wrong, but what I don't understand is why you're misleading the jury this way. I know you're upset with me, and rightfully so, but I would never do what you're claiming. A rash action in a moment of extreme emotion, yes—not unlike your good detective here." He gestured to Rick. "But kidnapping? Torture?"

He pulled a stack of pictures from a folder and started to step away from his desk, but his movement was halted by a trifecta of reactions: Holly's flinch, the judge clearing his throat, and the ominous creak of the bench behind him as Jordan shifted forward.

Irritation flickered across his face, then vanished beneath his veneer. He didn't appreciate being chained to his desk.

He held up the photos for both Holly and the jury to see, and slowly flipped through them. "This is what you're accusing me of doing to you?"

Holly's complexion turned a sickly shade of gray as Collin displayed the photos of her injuries for everyone in the room.

"Strangulation, beatings, sexual abuse? I have no doubt that you were abducted and forced to endure unimaginable cruelties, but I didn't do these things to you. I'll gladly pay for the crimes I committed, but not these . . . lies."

Rick placed a hand on Shannon's shoulder and leaned close, keeping his voice low. "I thought you said he wasn't gonna vilify her."

"He won't."

He would have to find a way to defend himself without destroying the jury's belief that Holly was innocent.

Collin dropped the pictures back onto his desk. "You told prosecution that I hit you with a bat the night you were abducted from Officer Barrera's apartment, correct?"

Holly swallowed and tried to find her voice. "Y-you did."

"Why would I do that?"

She lifted her chin just a fraction and pressed her shoulders back. "Because I would've . . . fought you when you took me, s-so . . . you knocked me out."

"I didn't come there to hurt you or take you, Holly. I just wanted to sort out that restraining order misunderstanding. I came to talk to you, knowing that you were staying with a cop, and that I might get arrested. But I needed to understand what was going on."

Shannon folded her arms over her stomach, irritation prickling beneath her composure. If Carson had been willing to testify, she would be able to refute his argument.

"When I got there, the door was open, and I saw a man pointing a gun at you. I didn't come there with the intention of hurting anyone, so I didn't have a

347

weapon. I grabbed the closest thing to me—a baseball bat by the door—and hit the guy with it."

He sighed and shoved his hands into the pockets of his slacks.

"I'm not proud of what happened next. But I didn't want to be blamed for the cop bleeding to death on the floor, so I did the only thing I could think of—I ran. Maybe if I hadn't left you there alone . . ." He looked down and pinched the bridge of his nose, as though fighting back tears. "Maybe you wouldn't have been taken."

Holly gaped at him in disbelief. "You . . . you're the one who took me."

"Do you actually remember me *taking* you, or is that a scenario suggested to you by someone else?"

Holly sputtered soundlessly for a moment, then looked past Shannon at Rick.

Collin made a show of turning toward him so the jury could follow his attention. "Let me guess, Detective Marx told you I took you."

Holly shook her head. "You were there . . . at the apartment and—"

"If you remember me abducting you, how did it happen? Did I throw you over my shoulder like a fireman and carry you out?"

"I . . . I don't know."

"Well, maybe you know if I took the elevator or the steps."

Holly shook her head, frustration leaving her breaths uneven and jerky.

"Did I put you in the trunk of my car, or did I lay you out across the backseat?"

"I don't—"

"You don't know that either?" He paused for effect. "You don't know because it didn't happen, Holly." When she drew in a breath to protest, he said, "Don't misunderstand. I'm not saying you fabricated the abduction. I've seen the pictures. I have no doubt you were taken. What I'm saying is, I'm not the person who took you, and you were probably unconscious when someone else did. Which brings me to my next question. How much do you weigh?"

She shifted in her seat. "I don't know."

"I would guess you're around a hundred pounds. If I remember correctly, it's about six floors from Officer Barrera's apartment to the ground floor, and given how petite you are, is it possible a woman could've carried you down those steps?"

"I . . . don't know."

"I do. It's been documented that a woman can carry a full grown man over her shoulders in what's known as a fireman's carry. Surely, if a five-foot-four woman can carry a two-hundred-pound man out of a burning building or off a battlefield, she could carry you easily. One might say you're a bit of a lightweight by comparison."

He pulled another photo from the folders on his desk and held it up for the court. It was a headshot of a brunette with blue eyes.

"This is Rachel Glass, my supposed accomplice. Some of you may know her better from the crime scene photo with blonde hair." He pulled out that photo as well. "Do you know this woman, Holly?"

Holly averted her eyes from the graphic photo. "Yes."

"When you were held captive, you reported hearing a voice outside the room that wasn't mine. Was that Rachel Glass's voice?"

"Yes, but—"

"Rachel Glass developed an unhealthy fixation with you, don't you think?"

Holly's eyes darted toward Rick again as she desperately sought guidance. "I'm not sure."

"Well, let's take a look at the facts." He held up his left hand and bent down a finger for each fact he listed. "She burned down the shelter where you both spent time. She attacked you in a bathroom and tried to abduct the girl you were looking after." He bent a third finger down. "She followed you in a stolen vehicle. She attempted to kill your boyfriend with that same vehicle while you were present. She abducted your best friend. I seem to be running out of fingers."

A few of the jurors chuckled.

He raised his right hand and continued listing the facts. "It was her voice you heard outside your room at the warehouse. You admit to seeing her in the warehouse in your statement. And she was found dead in that very building. Eight reasons that prove her guilt, but you're blaming me."

"Rachel didn't hurt me. You . . ." She struggled to get the words out. "You . . . hit me, you . . ."

"Raped you?"

Holly flinched and tears spilled down her cheeks.

"There's no DNA, no rape kit. You can't just accuse a guy of something that horrific without proof, Holly. Yes, I lost my head after I found you in that warehouse. I hurt you, but that was the only time I touched you."

Holly paled even more. "You're lying."

"I don't need to lie, because I have facts and evidence on my side. Rachel Glass was obsessed with you. That obsession led her to abduct you from Officer Barrera's apartment and hold you someplace where she could have you all to herself. She tormented you, tortured you. By the time I found you, she had already fallen over the railing to her death, and you were locked in a box."

Holly shook her head. "No."

"I can't help but think, after everything Detective Marx has manipulated you into doing, that he has something to do with this tale of kidnapping and abuse. He saw an opportunity to blame me, to shift Rachel's unspeakable actions onto me when he found me in that warehouse, and he took it. Is it possible your story is so full of holes, so sparse on details, because it's a fabrication based on one man's prejudice against me?"

Rick shot to his feet, but Shannon spoke first. "Objection! He's suggesting that a witness is committing perjury and accusing a detective of falsifying a report and manipulating a victim."

"I'm not accusing her of perjury," Collin said. "I'm suggesting she was manipulated while vulnerable and traumatized, and she believes what she's saying is true because it was fed to her by a man she trusts."

"That's ridiculous!"

"He took her statement with no other witnesses, and he wasn't even the detective assigned to her case. She doesn't make a move without him!"

Tipper slammed his gavel. "You two and your bickering are giving me a headache." He turned to Holly, who was watching the exchange with wide eyes. "You don't have to answer that question, Ms. Cross. Mr. Wells, take care not to make unfounded accusations against a detective of the New York City Police Department or you might just find yourself in a slander lawsuit."

"Of course." He nodded regally. "I'm sure Holly would appreciate a break if prosecution has no more questions for her."

Shannon cast him a sharp glare before addressing the judge. "Redirect, Your Honor."

Tipper nodded. "The witness is yours, Ms. Marx."

Shannon didn't bother to approach the witness stand because she only had two questions. "Holly, did Detective Marx influence the statement you provided after you woke up in the hospital?"

Holly shook her head. "No."

"The statement and testimony you gave were entirely based on your recollection?"

"Yes."

"No further questions," Shannon announced.

Tipper looked at Holly. "You may step down, young lady."

Rick approached the witness stand, ready to lead Holly from the courtroom.

Collin gestured toward them. "What did I tell you, ladies and gentlemen? She doesn't make a move without him."

Tipper slammed his gavel. "Mr. Wells, you're trying my patience with your outbursts. The jury will disregard the defendant's last statement."

Whether his accusations were acknowledged or stricken from the record, the human mind can't erase what it hears, and Shannon could see the silent judgment from select members of the jury as they watched Rick escort Holly out of the courtroom.

36

*M*arx studied the woman in the interrogation room through the one-way mirror.

It was eerie how similar she looked to Holly. Her carrot-red hair was even cut in the same style and length, but her eyes were more brown than honey.

"Creepy," Michael said from beside him.

"Mmm hmm." Marx opened the file Sully had handed him the moment he walked into the precinct, and reviewed it a second time.

The woman picking at her fingernails ten feet in front of them looked nothing like the one pictured in the file.

Both women were five three and in their midthirties, but the details diverged from there. The woman in the file had black hair, was about sixty pounds overweight, with multiple facial piercings.

"Are we sure this is even the same woman?" Michael looked between the file photo and their suspect.

"Fingerprints don't lie. This young lady's name is Mina Baldwin, and she has a record for theft, assault, and stalkin'."

"She changed her entire appearance."

"I'd like to know why." Marx closed the folder and walked into the interrogation room, Michael on his heels.

Mina straightened in her chair, her brown eyes sweeping over them before landing on Marx. "I'm so glad you're here." She lifted her cuffed wrists. "Can you please take these off?"

Marx pulled out the interrogation room chair and draped his suit jacket over the back of it. "No."

A puzzled frown formed between her eyebrows. "Are you mad at me?"

"You did cut me with a knife."

"That was an accident. I wasn't aiming for you."

Marx sat down. "No, you were aimin' for Holly. I just got in the way."

She scrunched her nose. "Sorry. You forgive me, right?"

Marx narrowed his eyes—not at the request for forgiveness, but the mannerism that reminded him of Holly. "We'll talk about forgiveness later. Right now I'd like to talk about you." He opened the folder. "Says here you steal things, Mina."

"My name's Molly."

"Not accordin' to your birth certificate."

She shrugged. "It must be a typographical error."

"A typographical error," Marx repeated slowly. He looked at Michael, keeping Mina in the corner of his vision. "You know, I don't think Holly would know the word typographical."

Mina fidgeted in her chair, seeming flustered by his statement. "Typo, I meant typo."

355

Marx leaned back in his chair and crossed his arms. "It must be hard pretendin' to be somebody you're not."

She offered him a wide-eyed look. "I don't know what you mean."

"Stealin' an identity is easy enough, but physically tryin' to be that person? No matter how long you study them, you never quite know all the details."

What concerned him was that he had no idea how long the woman had been watching Holly.

"You're not making sense. You've had a long day. You're probably tired."

"See that right there?" Marx pointed at her. "That compassion—there was somethin' off about it. For Holly it comes naturally. Not for you."

Mina's lips tightened.

"Before today, we might've thought you changed your appearance out of admiration, to support Holly for stepping up and fighting back," Michael said. "But seeing as you tried to stab her, I'm thinking you want her gone so you can be her. Question is why?"

"Why what?"

"Why would you wanna be a girl who was recently tortured by a psychopath, a girl whose entire life has been a nightmare?"

Anger sparked in Mina's eyes. "He's not a psychopath. He's just . . . misunderstood."

Marx snorted in disgust. "Oh, I understand him just fine. He's an animal wrapped in human skin."

Mina slapped the table. "You don't know him like I do!"

"He's been locked up for months. How could you possibly know him?"

"We write letters to each other. He's brilliant and witty, and he loves me."

"Love doesn't require you to change everything about yourself." Michael pointed to her photo. "Why erase this beautiful person to become someone you're not?"

Mina slapped the folder off the table. "Nothing about her is beautiful. She's hideous, useless. I've chewed gum worth more than her."

Marx's stomach knotted. People didn't inherently hate themselves—it was learned from other people's mistreatment—which meant someone had likely flung those cruel words at her before. "Mina—"

"Molly. My name is Molly."

Marx hesitated, unsure whether or not he should play into her delusion. "There is nothin' hideous or worthless about Mina Baldwin."

"I hate her." She bared her teeth in a snarl. "I *hate* her."

"You could've cut and dyed your hair, joined a gym, a church—any number of things to feel better about yourself. Why mimic Holly?"

"She has no idea how lucky she is."

"How exactly is she lucky?"

"He loves her. She's his whole world, and she doesn't even care."

357

"You're talkin' about Collin?"

Mina leaned forward and lowered her voice, as though to impart a secret. "I've seen her with other men. Holding hands while ice skating, going to bars. How can she do that to him?"

Marx glanced at Michael, who looked as bemused as he felt. "Holly was never in a relationship with Collin. He attacked her."

Mina laughed as she sat back in her chair, the sound slightly unhinged. "Is that what she told you? She lied. Collin has always loved her, but Holly . . . she just plays with him."

"How long have you been watchin' Holly?"

She shrugged. "A while. Long enough to know that she doesn't deserve Collin's love and affection."

"So you decided to kill her?"

"No. I never planned to kill her. I just wanted him to see me, to love me." She pressed her hands to her chest. "He looked right through me the day I met him, and I knew I had to change. I had to make him notice me." She played with the ends of her red hair. "And now he does."

Marx exchanged a concerned look with Michael. This woman was clinically insane. There was no other way to explain why she was so desperate to gain the attention of a man who tortures women.

"Did you attack Shannon Marx in the courthouse bathroom?" Marx asked.

Mina's mouth turned down at the corners. "She won't stop trying to punish Collin for things he didn't do. She was warned."

So she shoved Shannon's face into a mirror? Marx's fingers clenched into fists, and he had to fight to keep his anger in check.

Michael glanced at him and, seeing how close he was to exploding on the woman, took the lead on the questions. "When did you meet Collin?"

"August 2nd, six p.m. Addison took me along when he went to visit him in jail, and that day, I knew we were meant to be. We've been writing love letters to each other ever since."

Except no letters from Collin had been found in her apartment. She may have written them to him, but he didn't appear to have written back. Michael decided not to address that particular issue.

"This was shortly after you started working for Addison."

"I followed his blog for a long time, and I . . ." She laughed a little. "I feel silly, but for a time, I thought *he* and I were meant to be together. Of course, that was before I read about Collin and realized the truth."

"How did you meet Addison?"

"Oh, well . . . I was reading his blog, and he mentioned that his cameraman quit after being attacked. I love taking pictures—just like Holly does—so I applied for the job."

"Did he know you were gonna attack Holly at the courthouse?"

"No. I told you, killing her was never my plan."

Michael frowned. "Never *your* plan. But it was someone's plan."

Mina's lips sputtered soundlessly before she managed to speak. "I . . . I don't really wanna talk about this. Could I have hot chocolate? With marshmallows? I love—"

Marx slammed a hand on the table so hard she jumped in her chair. "You are not Holly! Quit actin' like her."

Tears flooded her eyes, and she regarded him with caution. "You *are* angry with me. I knew it."

Marx clenched his teeth. "I just want answers, Mina."

"Stop calling me that!"

Michael leaned over and whispered, "We might get more answers if we play along with her beliefs instead of trying to break them."

Marx didn't want to play into her delusions, but confronting her didn't seem to be working. "Fine."

Michael pushed back his chair. "Molly, I'll grab you a hot chocolate. Do you want something to eat?"

Her face brightened, all anxiety draining away. "I would love some peanut butter crackers."

Apparently she was unaware of Holly's aversion to peanut butter. Collin had forced her to eat it during her captivity, and ever since, the smell of peanuts made her gag.

Michael smiled. "Coming right up." He slipped out to grab her snack.

Marx stared at her, trying to find the will to treat this woman with the love and patience he afforded Holly. "I know you don't wanna talk about what happened on the courthouse steps . . . sweetheart." He nearly choked on that last word. "But it's important."

She relaxed a little more. "You called me sweetheart. Is that because you love me?"

Marx swallowed. "You said you didn't plan to hurt Holly, but you tried to stab her. Whose idea was that?"

"There's only room for one love in Collin's life. That's what she said, and she's right."

"She who?"

"His mother, of course. She wants what's best for him, and that's me. I would be loyal and loving."

"But you would have to kill Holly for that to happen."

"As long as she's alive, she's the one his heart will want. But his mother's right—she's toxic. Just look where he is because of her."

Marx tapped his fingers on the table. "I understand she was stayin' with you."

"It's not true what they say about mother-in-laws. Agatha's wonderful. When we talked to her a few months ago, she knew I'd been writing to Collin, she knew how much I love him. She said she wanted to get to know me more. She said she would bless our relationship if I . . . got rid of Holly." Tears glittered in her eyes. "But I failed. She's gonna take back her blessing, and we're never gonna be together."

"Where is Agatha Wells?"

She covered her face and choked on a sob.

"Did she hire anybody else to come after Holly?"

Mina folded forward in her chair, sobbing and mumbling about "needing him."

"Mina . . . Molly, I need you to answer me. Did Mrs. Wells hire anybody else?"

She was too lost in her own grief to answer. Marx sat back in his chair, exasperated. He needed to find Agatha Wells, but he had no idea where to start.

37

*M*arx's gaze swept over the Sunday morning congregation as the pastor delivered his message.

He was more focused on protecting Holly than he was on the lesson. Her testimony might be over, but that didn't mean she was safe.

Mina was in custody, and there was no proof that anyone else intended to come after Holly, but he doubted Collin's mother would just let her son's accuser walk away without consequence.

He didn't see her in the crowd, but that didn't mean she wasn't there. It was a large church, and the rows were crowded with people.

Holly started dragging him to church almost every Sunday after he became a Christian. She enjoyed the worship band and disco lights on the ceiling. Personally, he preferred hymnal music to screeching guitars and deafening bass, but he doubted there was a hymnal in the entire building. Everything was projected onto screens.

"Sometimes it's easy to think that, simply because we can't see it, the Almighty doesn't have a plan," Pastor Greg said from the front of the room, capturing Marx's attention.

With one thing after another going wrong with the trial, Marx had begun to wonder if God truly intended to bring order out of this mess. Michael was certain that they would all understand when God was ready for them to understand, but Marx didn't share his certainty.

"But the truth is, God always has a plan—a plan to prosper His people, to give them hope and a future," Pastor Greg continued.

Marx glanced at Holly, who scribbled the pastor's words down on her pamphlet with a bright pink pen, and underlined the word *always*.

Her eyebrows pinched in contemplation, and she was no doubt wondering if that Bible verse applied to her current situation.

Surely, God's plan involved Collin being convicted of his crimes and sentenced to life in prison. Letting him free would mean nothing but misery and pain for Holly.

Marx didn't think he could continue to put his faith and trust in a God who would allow that to happen.

38

*M*onday morning arrived with yet another surprise.

Shannon had called all of her witnesses last week, and it was now time for opposing counsel to do the same. Armed with the list Burdock provided, she had prepared a thorough cross-examination for each witness, but Collin had amended the list this morning.

Shannon studied the updated document, bemused, then glanced across the courtroom at the defense table. What was Collin thinking?

Tipper, equally confounded by the unexpected change, frowned at Collin. "Mr. Wells, are you certain you want to call *no* witnesses? This is your time to make your case."

Collin rose to address the judge. "To be honest, Your Honor, the prosecution has proven my innocence better than any witness I could call."

His words sent fiery indignation scorching through Shannon, and the court document crinkled around the tightening grip of her fingers.

And yet, doubt stretched through the back of her mind. Unless he truly believed she failed to convince the jury of his guilt, why would he forfeit his right to call witnesses? Did his arrogant comment have a basis in truth?

"I would be remiss in my duties if I didn't inform you that your decision is irregular and unwise," Tipper explained.

"I appreciate your input, Your Honor."

"You understand that you cannot argue a mistrial on these grounds. You've been given ample opportunity and time to gather witnesses for your defense."

"I understand, Your Honor, and I will stay the course I've chosen. I trust the jury to make the right decision based on the information they have."

Tipper sighed. "Very well. We'll move into closing arguments then, if the prosecution is prepared."

Shannon would've preferred a bit more time, but she could manage. She rose and clasped her hands in front of her. "I am, Your Honor."

With his gesture of permission, she rounded her desk to address the jury.

"A good magician can make you believe in magic. He can convince you that what he is showing you is truth, when in reality it's nothing more than a well-rehearsed illusion. If he can keep you distracted, then you're too mesmerized by the illusion to focus on the truth behind the trick. Collin Wells is an illusionist. He wants you looking everywhere but at him, because if you fix your attention on him long enough, his true nature might come into focus."

She gestured to Collin, imploring each of the jurors to look deeper than his outward appearance.

"He's spinning creative stories of witness confusion and police conspiracies, hoping you won't realize that his charming and civilized appearance is nothing more than a disguise. Collin Wells is a predator. He's not some harmless, innocent soul who's been wrongly accused. This man stalked a young woman across state lines and continued to terrorize her at every opportunity. He savored the fear he caused with his phone calls, texts, and unwelcome visits, but when that fear was no longer enough to sate his appetite, he abducted Holly."

She walked the length of the jury box as she continued.

"He locked her in that cold, windowless room for four days with nothing but a bucket and the clothes on her back. Clothes he tore from her body with each assault, leaving her to re-dress in agony and shame."

The foreman, a balding man in his fifties, blinked rapidly and dropped his eyes, the expression on his face muddled with too many emotions.

Shannon was certain she caught a flicker of empathy before he ducked his head. Empathy stemmed from experience—he must have known someone who had been through a similarly terrible ordeal. Shannon hated that he or someone in his life had suffered, but maybe that tragedy would inspire him to be harder on Collin.

"Wells beat Holly so badly that he broke bones. She died on the way to the hospital, her lungs collapsing as air and blood filled her chest cavity. The doctors were able to revive her, but it took six hours to repair the internal damage. And even then, she spent eight days in a coma. Collin Wells did that to her—with his fists, his feet, with a bat covered in his fingerprints. A bat he stole from Officer Barrera's apartment the night he stuffed Holly into a suitcase and wheeled her right out the door."

Collin shifted in his chair, no doubt eager for his turn to speak.

"I don't deny that Wells had help. He manipulated several people into participating in his plan, but the fact of the matter is, he is the one who committed the acts of violence. He did not abduct Jace Walker, but he did hold her against her will. He did bind her, burn her, and wrap a noose around her neck. She identified his voice. He did push Rachel Glass over that railing when she was no longer of use to him. Holly witnessed it. He *did* abduct, abuse, and rape Holly. She testified to it in excruciating detail."

Shannon locked eyes with each of the jurors.

"The defendant will no doubt deliver a beautiful speech when it's his time to address you, and in that speech will be a convincing story that shifts the blame onto everyone else and leaves him guiltless. I implore you to keep the evidence in mind. His fingerprints—and only his fingerprints—were recovered from the padlocks of both the room and the box where Holly was held captive. His fingerprints were on the bat used to break her bones. And his fingerprints were on the video camera that was used to record videos so violent that you're not permitted to see them."

"Ms. Marx!" Tipper objected.

Shannon muttered an apology, not a word of which she meant, then resumed her closing argument. "You've met Holly, the young woman whose friends describe her as warmhearted and timid, the girl who only wants what everyone in this room wants—a chance to live her life without fear. It was very difficult for her to come here and describe her pain to a room full of strangers, but she was willing to do it in the hope that you would help her. Because as long as Collin Wells is allowed to roam free, Holly will live a life caged by fear. She will have no choice but to disappear, to become that invisible girl the police had such a difficult time tracking down. No one should have to live that way."

She interlaced her fingers in front of her.

"I'm asking you to look beyond the defendant's polished appearance and well-thought-out story and see the truth. He's a predator. He's taken lives and he's destroyed them, and he needs to be held accountable. Thank you."

She returned to her seat, praying that her words had made a difference.

· · · ·

Collin let out a heavy breath as he approached the jury box. "That's certainly a tough act to follow." He ran a hand over his hair and looked back at Shannon. "I'm not sure what offends me more—the defamation of my character or the blatant disregard for facts."

Shannon folded her arms. What disregard for facts was he referring to?

"The prosecution's job was to prove beyond a shadow of a doubt that I'm guilty of all of these terrible things. Apparently the only way she can do that is by ignoring all the evidence that points to Rachel Glass."

Shannon uncrossed her legs and sat forward, anxiety flaring in her stomach. He was really going to try to pin this entire case on the woman he murdered.

"The woman had an unhealthy obsession with my foster sister. I assume it started when they were staying at the battered women's shelter together. Rachel burned that shelter to the ground, intentionally killing seven people. She stole a car, which the police suspect was later used to transport Holly to the warehouse. Her height, weight, and clothing choices match the unidentifiable figure dragging a suitcase—presumably with Holly's body in it—out of Officer Barrera's apartment building the night Holly went missing."

Collin paced in front of the jury box.

"Rachel Glass was capable of murdering seven women and children. She was capable of abducting Jace Walker. She stocked a warehouse with six months' worth of food and hygiene supplies—an act of premeditation. I don't care what the prosecution believes. I *know* that Rachel Glass abducted my foster sister. I *know* that she held her captive and beat her so badly that she nearly killed her. I *know* that Rachel Glass locked Holly in a wooden box, because I had to rifle through her pockets for the key!" He tapped a finger on the frame of the jury box. "I recognize that I'm not innocent. When I found Holly in that warehouse, trapped in that box, I didn't react the way I should've. I should've immediately called an ambulance. I should've called the police. But I was so overwhelmed with emotion . . ."

He turned his back on the jurors and walked a few feet away, rubbing a hand over his eyes as if to wipe away tears.

He sniffed before continuing. "Holly was injured and vulnerable when Detective Marx took her statement. Detective Marx, who threatened to shoot me in the head, who falsely arrested me, who had some kind of vendetta against me the moment I tried to reconnect with Holly. I know that he influenced Holly's statement, that he twisted her perception of the events at the warehouse. I know because I didn't do those things, and Holly would never say that I did without a powerful, outside influence."

He pressed both hands to the jury box, leaning forward, as he swept his gaze over the faces of the jurors.

"The question is, what happens now? Can you really convict me of these . . . heinous acts when so much of the evidence points to someone else? Someone prone to violence and obsessive behavior? Can you really say beyond a shadow of a doubt that I'm guilty?"

He shrugged and backed away.

371

"I leave that in your very capable hands. Thank you for your time." He cast Shannon a discreetly smug glance as he passed by, and she clenched her teeth.

"At this time, we will break for jury deliberation. We will reconvene when a verdict has been reached."

Tipper slammed his gavel, and the jurors rose. Usually by the end of closing arguments, Shannon had some idea which way the verdict was leaning, but several of the jurors looked overwhelmed and lost as they filed out of the room.

. . . .

Holly nudged the step stool over in front of the kitchen cabinets and climbed on top of it, reaching for another glass mixing bowl.

Baking was always a good distraction, especially now as she anxiously waited for the jury to decide on a verdict—a decision that could take hours, even days, according to Shannon. It was a good thing Holly had plenty of flour, butter, and eggs to keep her busy.

Some of her baking adventures over the past few months had turned out a little wonky, but every new recipe and every new . . . mishap taught her more about the process.

She now knew the reason why you mix chocolate chunks into the batter with a spoon instead of an electric mixer. Some of those little chocolate chunks exploded out of the mixing bowl like shrapnel.

Where was that other bowl? She stood on her toes and scanned the shelves.

"Be careful, baby, I don't want you to fall," Ms. Martha said, her sweet Southern voice pouring from the laptop speakers.

Jordan had set up a video connection on her laptop so she could bake with Ms. Martha. She might not be able to go back to Georgia and hide from the fear and anxiety of this trial, but even the sound of Ms. Martha's loving voice was soothing.

Mr. Gus, however, sounded perpetually grouchy. "For cryin' out loud, Martha, the girl's a grown adult. Quit treatin' her like a child."

"You just mind your business, Augustus. Us girls are bakin'."

"You're not bakin'. You're talkin' to a screen."

"You spend the whole day sittin' on your rear, watchin' a screen, so don't you start with me."

Holly smiled as she listened to their conversation. Marx's parents were always bickering, but somehow they managed to do it with affection.

Holly snatched the large bowl from the second shelf and hopped down. Ms. Martha insisted that she separate the dry ingredients from the wet ingredients, though she didn't understand why. They would all end up in the same bowl eventually.

"Why on earth does Richie put everythin' so high up when he knows you're so tiny?" Ms. Martha demanded, disapproval in her voice. "It's discourteous."

Holly scowled as she set the bowl on the counter. "I'm not that tiny." Plenty of people needed to use step stools to reach things. "And he has a specific spot for everything."

"Well, all right then. Let's start by creamin' the butter. Go ahead and dump it into the mixin' bowl."

Jordan came up behind her as she scraped the butter into the bowl with a knife. "What kind of cookies are we making?"

"Gingersnaps."

Ms. Martha waved the recipe card in front of the camera. "My boy loves soft gingersnap cookies. With a little extra sprinkle of sugar."

Holly's lips twitched as she fought back a smile. Sugar was the nickname she'd given Marx a couple of months after they met. She'd been drifting in and out of consciousness at the time, and one of the few things she remembered from that unpleasant experience was a man reassuring her, in a Southern accent as sweet as sugar, that she would be all right.

The front door opened and Marx stepped in, his face unreadable. "Hey, sweet pea." He nodded to Jordan and then to the computer screen. "Hi, Mama."

He didn't go through his normal routine of dropping his keys on the side table and hanging his coat on the hook by the door, which meant he didn't intend to stay.

Holly's insides coiled into nervous knots. "Is it time?"

"Mmm hmm. Shannon just called to let me know the jury is ready to announce the verdict."

Holly felt like she might be sick. It only took them eight hours to come to a decision that would affect the rest of her life. What if they decided in Collin's favor?

She didn't realize she was squeezing the butter knife until Jordan gently pried it from her fingers. "It's gonna be okay, Holly."

She nodded stiffly. "Um . . . I'm . . . I'm gonna get my coat." She paused, then turned back to the laptop to say a quick good-bye to Marx's parents before slipping into her room.

As she bent to grab her dress shoes, her eyes caught on the pink-and-purple bag tucked beneath her bed—her travel bag. Her heart throbbed in her chest at the thought of leaving everyone and everything she loved behind.

But it was just a contingency. There was a chance she wouldn't even need it.

Lord, please work things out for us.

It was a prayer she had muttered many times over the past nine days, but she had no idea if or when God would bring an end to this storm.

She grabbed the heel of one of her black ballet flats, then glanced at her sneakers. If things went sideways, sneakers were a lot easier to run in.

39

*M*arx wrapped an arm around Holly's shoulders and pulled her against his side as they waited for the jury to deliver the verdict. He didn't have to look at her to know she was dreading this moment. He could feel the frightened tremors rippling through her body.

"Foreman, has the jury reached a verdict on the charges against the defendant?" the judge asked.

A balding man in his fifties rose in the witness box. "We have, Your Honor." He referenced the sheet of paper in his hands. "In the case of the State of New York versus Collin Victor Wells, on the count of murder in the first degree, we find the defendant not guilty."

Marx had expected that pronouncement, given the lack of evidence, but Holly sucked in a sharp breath.

She looked up at him, her brown eyes shining with confusion and fear. "But he killed her. They can't just—"

"Shh," he said gently, rubbing her arm and trying to soothe her.

The foreman glanced toward them, then back at the paper in his hands. "On the count of assault in the third degree"—the charge Shannon brought against Collin for his mistreatment of Jace—"we find the defendant not guilty."

Sam shifted beside Marx, his expression as hard as granite. His girlfriend still had nightmares about the events in that warehouse, but there would be no justice for it.

"On the count of assault in the first degree . . ." The foreman grimaced, as though dissatisfied with the decision the jury had come to. They all had to agree on a verdict, but that agreement was sometimes reluctant. "We find the defendant . . . not guilty."

Marx gripped the back of the bench in front of him, having a difficult time absorbing that verdict. *Not* guilty. Collin had nearly killed Holly, and Shannon had provided medical reports and photographic evidence for the jury. How could they be so blind to the truth right in front of them?

"On the count of kidnapping . . ."

Holly's body pressed more heavily against Marx, and her fingers clutched at his shirt, gripping a fistful of the material.

The foreman's gaze flickered toward them, and the regret shining in his eyes twisted Marx's guts into knots.

No, don't say it.

"We find the defendant not guilty."

The whimper of disbelief and anguish that escaped Holly's throat shredded Marx's heart. Her legs turned liquid, and he tried to keep her on her feet.

The foreman hesitated, Holly's grief seeming to affect him more than the others. If Marx had to guess, the man had a daughter around Holly's age.

"Foreman, please continue," Tipper instructed.

The foreman cleared his throat. "On the count of rape, we, uh . . . we find the defendant not guilty."

Collin glanced back at Holly, amusement sparkling in his eyes, and she struggled to draw in a breath, her lungs constricting in panic. Marx wanted to pound Collin into the floorboards, but he set aside his anger and focused on Holly.

"Breathe, sweetheart."

She slipped out of his arms and shot out of the courtroom like a bullet. Gasps rippled through the room, and the foreman fumbled over his words as he tried to read off another verdict.

Marx nodded to Collin and silently mouthed to Jordan, "Watch him."

Jordan nodded, even as he glanced in the direction Holly had fled.

Marx threw open the courtroom door and burst into the nearly empty hallway, searching for a flicker of red hair or a purple sweatshirt, but Holly was nowhere in sight.

Her frantic flight from the courtroom wouldn't have gone unnoticed.

Marx approached a woman on her cell phone. "Excuse me."

She frowned at the interruption, then noticed the badge clipped to his belt. "Hang on a minute." She pulled the phone away from her ear. "Can I help you with something?"

"Did you see a red-haired girl come through here a minute ago?"

"Hard to miss her. She looked pretty panicked." She nodded down the hall. "She went that way, but I didn't see where she went from there."

"Thank you."

The bathrooms were in that direction, and he hoped Holly was just camped out in one of the stalls, working through her emotions.

She had a peculiar habit of hiding in bathrooms when she was scared or hurt. Marx suspected it had something to do with the night she tried to overdose on pills when she was fifteen. As she lay dying on the bathroom floor of her foster home, she felt God's presence. When she shared that moment with Marx, she said it was the first time she remembered feeling safe. It made perfect sense to him that she would seek that safe space whenever her world felt upside-down.

He tapped on the women's room door. "Anybody in there?"

He pressed an ear to the door, listening for the sound of distressed sobs or retching. Holly's stomach was deeply intertwined with her emotions, and after the devastating verdicts the jury just delivered, he wouldn't be surprised if she was dry-heaving into a toilet.

When no one answered, he pushed open the door and peered inside. "Holly?"

There was no one at the sink, and as he stepped inside and nudged open one stall after another, his stomach knotted. They were all empty.

He swore and pulled out his phone, dialing Holly's number. "Come on, baby, pick up." The call rang through to voice mail. He tried again, with the same result. "Holly, I need you to call me and tell me where you are. I know you're scared, but please . . . just call me."

He snapped his phone shut. Where would she go? Something inside him whispered with urgency, *Home. Go home.*

He wrenched open the bathroom door and rushed back into the hall just as Sam came sprinting toward him.

"Where is she?"

Marx shook his head. "I don't know, and she's not takin' my calls. I'm gonna head back to my apartment, see if she's there. Grab Jordan and start checkin' everywhere you think she might go."

"What about Collin?"

"He's not my concern right now. Holly is out there alone, and his deranged mother is still unaccounted for."

Sam's eyebrows pinched with concern. "Holly already testified. Do you really think she'll still go after her?"

"I think I don't wanna take that chance. Call me if you figure out where she might be."

Marx sprinted out of the courthouse, praying he didn't get caught in rush hour traffic.

· · · ·

It took too long for Marx to reach his apartment, and he ran up the steps, taking them two at a time.

"Holly," he called out, breathless, as he threw open his apartment door.

Most of the lights were on, which he would expect given Holly's anxiety level, but there was an unusual quietness in the air, an emptiness that didn't belong.

He hurried to Holly's room and pushed open the door. Riley lay in the center of the bed, snout buried in one of Holly's fuzzy, green slippers, a mournful gleam in his eyes.

Marx's gaze moved past him to the empty space on the nightstand where a picture of Holly's family always sat.

He rounded the bed to check the drawer, which had been left open. Various journals and pens remained in the drawer, but her Bible was gone, along with the butcher knife she always kept for protection.

"Lord, please no."

Dropping to his knees, he checked under the bed for her duffel bag. He'd bought her a pink one with purple flowers, something to replace the one sitting in an evidence locker at the precinct.

A streak of clean floor surrounded by dust was the only sign that the duffel had been there.

Marx rested his forehead against the bed, anger and grief wrapping around his heart.

Holly was gone.

A warm nose nudged the side of his face, and something crunched beneath Riley's front leg as he shifted on the mattress. Marx looked up. Was that a sheet of paper?

He tugged it free and unfolded it, his heart skipping when he recognized Holly's handwriting:

> I love you. I hope you know that. You mean more to me than anyone in this world, and I have to keep you safe. The court is going to let Collin go, and if I stay, he'll hurt all of you. Or worse. So please don't come looking for me. Just let me go. And please take care of Riley. I love you.
> ~Holly~

The tears building in Marx's chest spilled from his eyes. She was cutting ties and disappearing, with no intention of ever coming back.

She didn't have much money, which meant she wouldn't get far, and she would have to choose between food and a safe place to sleep. She wouldn't survive on the streets for long. Her heart was too big, and she would step into the wrong situation to help someone, but there would be no one there to help *her*.

He pulled out his phone and sent her a text:

Baby, please tell me where you are.

He waited, but no reply came. He snapped his phone shut and squeezed it in his fist to keep from throwing it across the room.

He stood and glared up at the ceiling. "This is your fault. Every day, she writes to you in that journal of hers. *Dear Jesus*. Well, where are you? Through all this mess, when she needed you, where were you? Where are your promises of hope and a future? Huh? Is this her future? Misery, pain, and fear? Is this all you have to offer?"

He swatted the lamp off the nightstand.

"You were supposed to protect her!" Fresh tears fell, and the strength drained from his voice. "I was supposed to protect her."

Now she was gone, and he had no idea how to find her. Even if he checked into every means of public transportation out of the city, he would never catch up to her in time. And that was assuming she didn't just hitchhike.

"Where do I even start, Lord?" He scrubbed a hand over his eyes and looked down at the open nightstand drawer.

His attention snagged on the sparkle-covered jewelry box. He remembered that particular box, because it held the ankle bracelet he'd given Holly as a gift this past spring.

She'd been terrified that Collin would escape custody, or that something would go wrong with the trial, and he would come after her again. The bracelet was meant as a comfort, to assure Holly that if Collin grabbed her again, they would be able to find her quickly.

To anyone who didn't know what to look for, it was a simple charm bracelet, but embedded in one of the charms was a GPS tracker.

His heart leaped with renewed hope, and he snatched up the box, popping it open. Empty. She was still wearing it.

40

*H*olly hugged her travel bag to her stomach as she sat on the outdoor bench, waiting for the bus.

She wasn't even sure where she was going—someplace far from New York. Virginia, maybe? She glanced at the ticket in her hand, but through her tears, the destination was little more than a smudge.

She didn't want to leave behind everyone and everything she loved, but what other choice did she have?

Any minute now, Collin would be released from jail. She never should've trusted the justice system.

Disappearing was the only way to protect herself and the people she loved. They might want her to stay, but she wouldn't make them targets by hiding behind them. Not again.

Her phone chimed with an incoming text message, and she wiped her eyes to clear her vision. It was from Marx:

Baby, please tell me where you are.

She pulled her lower lip between her teeth to keep it from trembling and turned off her phone. Her heart couldn't tolerate another voice mail or text message; it was still so raw.

She dried her face with her coat sleeve and sighed. Where was her bus? It should've been here by—

Something cold and hard pressed into the back of her neck, and she stilled at the familiar feeling of a gun against her skin.

A moist whisper slipped into her ear, and the familiar voice sent a shiver down her spine. "There are a lot of innocent people here, and I don't have the best aim, so let's not make a scene."

Holly's heart staggered faster, and she looked around at the other women, men, and children waiting for the bus.

"Hand me the phone."

Holly hesitated, and the barrel of the gun pressed harder against the back of her neck. She flinched, and passed the cell phone over her shoulder.

"Good girl. Now, let's take a little stroll on this lovely evening."

. . . .

Marx slammed his car door and surveyed the row of buses. According to the GPS locator on Sam's phone, Holly was here somewhere. "Sam, Jordan, search the buses bein' loaded. I'm gonna check inside."

They split up, and Marx pushed his way past people waiting in line to purchase tickets. He showed his badge to the employee behind the glass.

"I need to find a girl who purchased a bus ticket within the past hour."

The man blinked slowly. "You're kidding, right? Do you know how many women . . ." When Marx showed him a picture of Holly, he trailed off, recognition crossing his face. "Oh, her. Yeah, I remember her. Miss I-don't-care-where-I-go-as-long-as-it's-far-from-here. That's what she said when I asked where she wanted to go."

"And?"

The man shrugged. "I don't know. She was crying. I figured she had a bad breakup with her boyfriend."

Marx barely resisted the urge to pull the man through the narrow opening of glass and shake him. "Where did she decide to go? What destination is on her ticket?"

"Oh. Virginia, I think." He tapped a few keys on his keyboard. "But that bus left ten minutes ago."

Marx squeezed his eyes shut. He'd missed her by ten minutes. He headed back outside to the loading area. People filed onto buses headed all over the country. A flash of pink caught his eye—a pink duffel bag with purple flowers was slung over a man's shoulder.

Heart thundering faster in his chest, Marx rushed forward, catching the man by the sleeve before he could board the bus to Ohio. "Where'd you get this bag?"

The man's eyes widened, and he froze momentarily. "Um . . ."

The bus driver turned in his seat. "Come on, we're on a schedule here, and you're holding up the line."

Marx yanked the guy *out* of line and shoved him up against the side of the bus. "The redhead you took this bag from—where is she?"

The man tried to push Marx's hand away. "Get your hands off me, or I'm gonna call the cops."

Marx shoved his badge into the man's face. "Answer my question."

"Ah, man." The guy dropped his head back against the bus with a thump. "You gotta believe me, I didn't take the bag from anyone. She left it sitting on a bench."

"For how long?"

"I don't know. Ten minutes? She wandered off with some old woman and didn't come back."

Agatha Wells had beaten them here, and she had Holly.

The man pulled the strap of the duffel over his head and offered it to Marx. "Here's the, um, the bag. Can I go now?"

Marx snatched it and glared at him. "Get out of my sight."

The man scrambled onto the bus. Marx carried the bag back to his car, meeting Jordan and Sam along the way.

"Holly's not on any of the buses," Jordan said, his voice laced with worry.

"Agatha Wells took her."

"What?!" Jordan shouted. "When? And where did she take her?"

"About ten minutes ago." Marx dropped Holly's bag into the backseat and climbed behind the wheel. "Sam, where's she at?"

Sam dropped into the passenger seat, refreshing the map on his phone. "Holly's GPS tracker says she's less than . . ."

A gunshot cracked through the night, the sound echoing from the salvage yard less than a block away. Fear slugged Marx in the chest.

Holly.

. . . .

Holly pressed her back flat against the cargo container and listened for the crunch of approaching footsteps on the snow-glazed asphalt.

Mrs. Wells had ordered her through the torn fence into the unlit salvage yard, but when she tried to follow, the jagged edges of the fence snagged her bulky winter coat.

Holly took advantage of that small blessing and darted into the maze of scrap metal and broken appliances.

A gunshot sliced through the air behind her, the bullet so close that it buzzed past her ear and pinged off a dismembered truck.

Panic tried to edge its way into her thoughts now, as she looked around at the mounds of scrap and debris. Of course her foster mother would bring her here, to dispose of her with the rest of the unwanted trash.

She used to wonder where Collin learned his disregard for human life, but as his mother hunted her through this metal graveyard, it all finally made sense.

A sliver of moonlight peeked between the sheet of dark clouds, and she lifted her eyes to the heavens, a silent prayer springing to her lips. "Even though I walk through the valley of the shadow of death, I will fear no evil. For you are with me."

Something to her right thumped, sending a fresh ripple of fear through her, and she held her breath.

"Hiding is pointless, my dear."

Holly's pulse jumped. The shadow of death was on the other side of the cargo container.

God, I don't wanna die here, shot and left to bleed out in the trunk of some filthy old car.

There were too many things in this life she still wanted to do. She wanted to learn to ice-skate, to go on a date, maybe fall in love. She was not going to die here. She flexed her fingers around the hunk of metal in her hands, preparing for a fight.

Mrs. Wells released an exaggerated sigh. "If I can't find you, you know I'll just hire someone who can."

Holly swallowed, the sound seeming to echo in the silence that followed Mrs. Wells's words. Why was she doing this?

Holly was no threat to her son now; the jury had already decided he was innocent. Her plan was to disappear, someplace Collin would never find her, which was exactly what Mrs. Wells had wanted.

"I'm not a terrible person, Holly. I don't *want* to do this. But you've left me no choice."

Holly inched backward, barely lifting her feet from the ground as she retreated from her crazy foster mother's voice.

She'd always suspected the woman was unhinged, but something—maybe the risk of her son being sent to prison—had shattered whatever remained of her fragile grip on sanity.

"The way you taunt my boy . . . as long as you're alive, you're an irresistible temptation to him. As his mother, I have to protect him from that."

Tears burned Holly's eyes. Her life mattered so little to this woman that she would snuff it out just so her son wouldn't be *tempted.*

Mrs. Wells came into view, and Holly ducked around the far side of the container, her heart throbbing in her temples. Her foot slipped on a patch of ice, and she gasped as she tried to keep from falling.

"I hear you." Another gunshot ripped through the night, and Holly bit back a startled scream.

She shrank into the shadows of a gutted car, gripping her slender chunk of metal as if it were a shield.

"Holly," Mrs. Wells called out, impatience coloring her voice. She rounded the enormous metal box, her foot landing on the same patch of black ice that had nearly taken Holly to the ground.

She slipped, windmilling her arms in an effort to keep her balance.

It was now or never. Holly sprang from her hiding place and brought the metal bar down on her foster mother's forearm.

Mrs. Wells screamed, and the gun flew from her grasp and skidded across the ground. She clutched at Holly's jacket as she fell, and Holly went down with her, their bodies landing in a tangle of limbs.

Holly fixed her sights on the gun. If she could get to it first, she would take away her foster mother's only weapon against her. Ignoring the sting of the gritty asphalt and debris cutting into her palms and knees, Holly scrambled for it. A hand grabbed at her ankle, but she jerked her leg free and wrapped her fingers around the gun.

Mrs. Wells pushed herself into a sitting position, and Holly scooted away from her, raising the gun. "Stay away from me."

Mrs. Wells groaned and cradled the arm Holly had struck. "I should've just poisoned you. It would've been simpler."

Holly's hands trembled as she held the loaded weapon. "What did I ever do to make you hate me so much?"

"You infected my boy's mind, and he's been obsessed with you ever since. And now you've ruined his future."

Ruined his future? He wasn't even going to prison. "Did you . . . did you pay that woman to attack us at the courthouse?"

Her lips slid into a chilling smile. "Oh, I didn't have to pay her a cent. She's in love with my son. Of course, homely as she is, she doesn't have a chance."

She grabbed the pipe Holly had dropped and started to push herself to her feet.

Holly shook the gun at her when she stepped forward. "I said stay away from me."

"We both know you're not going to shoot me."

Holly could pull the trigger and claim self-defense. The law would probably let it slide. But taking a life, even the life of someone who hated her and wanted her dead, wasn't something she could forgive herself for.

"She might not shoot you, but we will." Marx stepped out of the darkness with Sam and Jordan behind him. "Drop the pipe. And I will not say it twice."

With a smoldering glare, Mrs. Wells let the pipe clatter to the ground. "Look at you three, just as obsessed with her as my son."

Marx holstered his weapon as Sam moved in to arrest her. "There's a difference between obsession and love."

Mrs. Wells scoffed as Sam led her away, the two of them disappearing back into the veil of darkness.

Holly's eyes flooded with tears of relief as Marx crouched beside her. "She is . . . the worst foster mother. Ever."

"I can't argue that." Marx took the gun from her trembling fingers and handed it off to Jordan. He looked her over, grimacing at her bloody hands and knees, then pulled her into a hug.

As if someone flipped a switch, all of her energy drained out of her, and she melted against him, breathing in the scent of his cologne. *Safe.*

He squeezed her, as though afraid she might dissolve. "What did I tell you about runnin' away?"

She choked on a sob. "I can't stay."

He pulled back and cupped her face. "Yes you can."

"I tried it your way, and they didn't believe me. They're gonna let him go, and . . . it's gonna happen all over again. I . . . I can't . . ."

"It is not gonna happen all over again." He brushed the tears from her face with his thumbs. "He pled guilty to two charges—sexual battery and misdemeanor assault. The judge is gonna sentence him in the mornin'."

"But what if the judge decides he's been in jail long enough? Sometimes that happens."

"Sweetheart, I promise you, no matter what the judge decides"—he glanced at Jordan, whose expression was oddly grim—"Collin is not walkin' out of that courthouse a free man."

Something about the way he said that sent unease crawling through her stomach. "What does that mean?"

He paused for a moment. "It means that I will protect the ones I love with everythin' I have."

No, he couldn't mean . . .

"Now let's get you home so I can take a look at these cuts." He stood and pulled her to her feet. "It looks like you have some bits of gravel and glass embedded in them."

She couldn't care less about the ache in her hands and knees. Marx was going to do something that could potentially ruin his life. "Marx—"

"We're done talkin' about this. Whether you decide to stay or run off to Virginia, my decision doesn't change."

She looked at Jordan. "You can't let him do this."

Jordan tucked his hands into his jacket pockets. "I'm sorry, Holly, but in this instance, I agree with Marx."

Anger flushed her face. "Well, Sam would agree with me."

"Collin abducted Sam's girlfriend, tortured his friend, had him shot, and would do it all again in a heartbeat. Sam understands," Marx explained.

They had all discussed this without her?

She hugged herself. "I don't want you to do this." Every life he was forced to take in the line of duty weighed on him, and she didn't want Collin's death to add to that crushing burden.

"I know. Let's pray I don't have to." He wrapped an arm around her shoulders. "Now, am I takin' you home or am I takin' you back to the bus station?"

Tears spilled down her face. There was nothing she could say—or do, apparently—that was going to change his mind.

She rested her head against his chest, her heart breaking at the thought of tomorrow. "Home. I wanna go home."

41

*M*arx pinched the sliver of glass in Holly's palm with a pair of tweezers and, trying to be gentle, worked it loose. He dropped it into a bowl, along with the other bits of gravel and glass he'd dug out of her skin.

"I think that's the last one." He inspected both of her hands again. "But do me a favor and don't crawl on your hands and knees through any more junkyards."

She offered him a tired smile. "It's not really on my to-do list."

Dousing a cotton ball in peroxide, he dabbed at the small punctures and scrapes that peppered her skin.

"You know, I *can* do this myself."

"I'm aware." But he had no intention of sitting aside while she tended to her own wounds, minor as they were. He could've lost her tonight; one well-placed bullet was all it would've taken.

He needed to take care of her right now, to protect her, even if the only threats were broken glass and infection.

She sat stiffly as he used his fingers to widen the torn fabric of her jeans and applied peroxide to her knees. "I'm gonna put some antibiotic ointment on your hands and wrap them, just to make sure they don't get infected."

"You're fussing."

"I have a right to fuss. You ran off and nearly got yourself killed."

She dropped her hands into her lap. "Mummifying me with gauze isn't gonna fix that."

"You're lucky I don't mummify you with bubble wrap. I've seen rookie cops get into fewer scrapes than you."

"You mean on their first day?"

"No, their first year."

"Oh." Reluctantly, she held out her hands, letting him apply the antibiotic. "I know you're mad at me for leaving, and . . . that's okay. I'm still kind of mad at you for using that GPS tracker to find me after I asked you not to look for me."

"I did what I had to do."

"No, you did what you thought was right. So did I."

Irritation prickled beneath his skin. "What would you have done if we hadn't shown up? Would you have shot your foster mother?"

"I . . ."

"She was gonna come at you with a pipe. Would you have killed her to save yourself?"

Holly swallowed and dropped her eyes. "No."

"Then I stand by my previous statement. I did what I had to do. You can be mad at me if you want. All that matters to me is that you're still alive."

She looked at him, her eyes shining. "I was just trying to keep you safe."

He sighed. "Baby, I don't need you to keep me safe."

"That's what people do when they love each other."

"Runnin' off and puttin' yourself at risk isn't gonna protect either of us. If you want what's best for me, then you need to protect my heart."

Her eyebrows knitted. "What do you mean?"

"You, sweet pea. You are my heart. The light of my dismal life. The best thing you can do for me is to stay put and stay safe." To lighten the heavy mood, he added, "And quit tiltin' my pictures."

She snorted back a laugh and leaned her forehead against his.

"I mean it," he said. "You tilt my pictures one more time, and I will put all the hot chocolate mugs on the top shelf, beyond your tiny reach."

She sniffled and released a shuddering breath. He could tell by how heavily she leaned against him that she was worn out, and with Collin's sentencing tomorrow, she was probably still scared.

"Why don't you go get some rest, sweetheart."

She drew back. "I'm not tired."

"You can barely sit up straight. You're properly medicated and mummified, so go rest. Lie down and read a book or somethin'." She was so exhausted that he doubted she would be awake long enough to read a paragraph.

He stood and pulled her to her feet. She gave him a quick hug, and he planted a gentle kiss into her hair.

"I love you, sweetheart."

"I love you too." She stretched onto her toes to kiss his cheek, then shuffled off to the bedroom.

He rubbed at his eyes and walked into the kitchen to put on a pot of coffee. He had no intention of sleeping tonight. Until Collin was . . . taken care of, Holly was a flight risk.

He filled the coffee pot and leaned against the counter, his heart conflicted. He'd taken more lives in the line of duty than he wanted to remember, but each time he pulled the trigger, it was to protect himself or someone else. He'd never planned to take a life.

Until now.

Collin was a darkness that should have never existed on this earth—an embodiment of evil that destroyed every life it touched.

Holly was still trying to rise from the ashes and rebuild. Not for the first time, but the third, fourth, fifth. Collin had ripped apart her life so many times that it was a wonder she had the strength and will to keep moving forward.

Holly would tell him that her strength came from God, that He walked beside her in the aftermath, lighting a path through the shadows of grief, and bracing her arms as she pushed aside the barriers that tried to keep her trapped in brokenness.

"Lord, I know Holly was your baby before she was mine, that you loved her before I ever knew her. But you brought her into my life, knowin' she would mean the world to me. And right now, Lord, I need you to help me protect her."

He gripped the edges of the counter and looked down at the tiles of his kitchen floor.

"Nothin' has gone right with this trial, and tomorrow, that spineless judge is gonna sentence Collin. I know it's gonna be a slap on the wrist. Months, if anythin' at all. I need you to step in, to make things right. Because if Collin is allowed to walk out of that courthouse tomorrow mornin' . . . I'm gonna fix it the only way I know how."

He just hoped God would forgive him.

A knock on the apartment door interrupted his thoughts, and he pushed away from the counter. Who was bothering him at this hour?

He strode to the front door and peered through the peephole, surprised to find Shannon standing in the hall. Disarming the alarm and unsnapping the dead bolt, he opened the door.

Her dark hair was twisted into a messy bun on top of her head, and she was dressed in jeans and his old sweatshirt. He always loved the way she looked in his shirts.

"Hey." He gestured for her to come in. "You're out late. Everythin' all right?"

She brushed past him, the aroma of lavender and vanilla teasing his senses. "I wanted to check on Holly."

"I told you she's fine." He'd called Shannon to fill her in as soon as Holly was safe in his car. "And she's probably asleep by now."

Shannon glanced at the first aid supplies on the coffee table, concern seeping into her voice. "You're sure she's all right?"

"Minor cuts and bruises." He shut the door quietly. "What are your plans for Mina and Agatha?"

Shannon perched on the arm of the couch. "Honestly, I don't want to pursue prison time for Mina. I think she needs help, and the best place for her is a psychiatric institution. As for Collin's mother, I'm going to prosecute her for anything and everything I can— witness intimidation, attempted murder, and conspiracy to commit murder. That woman's an atrocious human being."

"Yes she is. I just hope she's not as convincin' as her son in front of a jury. That family certainly knows how to spin a story."

Shannon sighed. "I'm sorry, Rick. I knew things were going to be difficult when I took this case, but I really thought . . . I really tried to . . ."

"I know."

She shook her head. "I've never seen so much go wrong. If I didn't know better, I'd swear some invisible force was fighting against us at every turn."

Marx grunted, deciding not to comment on that point. "What are our chances tomorrow?"

"At most, fourteen months."

"And at worst?"

"At worst . . . time served."

Marx dropped onto the couch, a grim acceptance settling in his bones. "You mean there's a chance that he could be released tomorrow."

Shannon opened her mouth, then closed it without speaking. Marx nodded at her silent confirmation: yes, there was a chance.

"All we can do at this point is hope for the best." Shannon rose from the arm of the couch. "I should get going. I just wanted to check in and make sure everyone was all right."

Rick caught her wrist in a gentle grip, stopping her before she could reach the door. "Please stay."

"Rick—"

"If you were tellin' me the truth, and the only reason you left me was because I wanted children, then don't go. I don't need children. I need my wife."

She licked her lips, searching for a reply. "I broke your heart. I lied to you. You deserve—"

"Don't tell me I deserve better. Three years ago, you unanimously decided that I would be better off without you, that I deserved somethin' other than what I had. That decision was wrong, Shannon. So, why don't you let me decide what's best for me, and stay."

Tears gathered in her eyes. "How can you just . . ."

"Forgive you?" He caressed her wrist with his thumb.

"After the way I treated you, after everything I put you through."

"I've learned that sometimes the best blessin's come from the most heartbreakin' situations." He glanced at Holly's bedroom door. "If you hadn't left me, I don't think I would've had room in my heart or my life for Holly."

Shannon sat back down on the arm of the couch. "Of course you would have."

He shook his head. "I would've helped her, like any good cop, and then I would've moved on."

He would've missed out on so much.

"Holly talks about God bringin' beauty from ashes. When you made that decision three years ago, you shattered my life. God brought Holly into that miserable mess and reminded me that there's still hope and joy in this world."

Shannon wrapped her fingers around his. "I'm glad for that."

"I won't pretend that these years apart were easy, but I'm not angry anymore."

"I'm sorry I caused you so much pain."

He let out a long breath. "It's over and done with. Just answer one question for me. Do you still love me?"

"I never stopped loving you, Richard Damascus Marx."

His throat tightened, and hope blossomed in his chest. "Then let me hold you tonight. I could really use the company."

She looked as though she might object, but then she nudged her way onto the cushion beside him. "I didn't bring a change of clothes."

"You can go to court in jeans and a sweatshirt. Who's gonna mind?"

She laughed softly. "The judge."

He cupped her face, his thumbs brushing lightly over her lips as his fingertips slid into the wisps of hair around her ears. "I've missed you."

She pressed her forehead against his, their lips less than an inch apart. "I've missed you too."

Her familiar warmth ignited a fire inside him, and he pressed his lips to hers, savoring the long overdue moment. With effort, he reined in his desires. He needed her comfort and companionship tonight more than he needed anything else.

He readjusted on the couch, and she curled against him, her body molding to his as if they were made for each other. He rested his chin on the top of her head and held her tight.

Even if the events in the courtroom tomorrow morning ended with him in prison for the rest of his life, he would have this moment to cherish.

42

*J*udge Tipper tapped his fingers as his gaze swept from one side of the courtroom to the other. "I've given a lot of thought to this case."

Shannon twisted the pencil in her hand and glanced at her cell phone sitting on the desk. She'd been expecting a call or even a text this morning, but nothing had come through.

"It's been quite some time since I had a case this emotionally heated, and despite the jury's verdicts, I'm hard-pressed to ignore what I've seen and heard as I bring sentencing."

One of the double doors at the back of the courtroom opened, and Shannon snuck a glance. It was just the spectator who'd left a few minutes ago returning to his seat.

As her attention moved back toward the front of the room, it snagged on Rick. He stood behind her, hugging a pale and anxious Holly to his side. He must have thought she might try to bolt out of the courtroom again, because he made sure she was surrounded: him on one side, Jordan on the other, and Samuel just behind her in case she scrambled over the bench.

"I haven't come to this decision lightly," Tipper continued, laying the foundation for what would no doubt be a pitiful sentence.

Shannon's pulse jumped when she noticed the bulge scarcely concealed by Rick's jacket. Was he wearing his gun? Law enforcement wasn't required to pass through the metal detector that kept weapons out of a courtroom if they were on duty and protecting a witness. But the threats against Holly had been handled, so why had he brought it?

She met his eyes, silently questioning, and what she saw there chilled her: apology mixed with steely determination. No. She glanced at Collin and then back at Rick. No, he wouldn't.

He had a clear line of sight to the defense table, but if he shot Collin, he would be arrested and prosecuted. As a cop, he would be lucky to survive a day in prison. He had to know that. Shannon tried to communicate her objection with a subtle shake of her head, but Rick only pressed his lips together and hugged Holly tighter.

"Mr. Wells, you pled guilty to the charges of sexual battery and misdemeanor assault," Tipper continued, drawing Shannon's attention back to the front of the courtroom.

She tried to concentrate on the judge's words, but they were barely more than static beneath the rapid pounding of her heart in her ears. She wanted to snatch up her phone and make a call, one last desperate effort to change these circumstances, but she couldn't.

"You understand the heinous nature of these crimes you committed against Ms. Cross."

Collin lowered his head, as though ashamed of his actions. "I do, Your Honor."

"You've expressed remorse for these crimes throughout the trial, expressions I believe to be sincere. Given that, the likelihood that you will repeat these offenses is remote."

Remote? The word nearly burst from Shannon's lips. The man was a repeat offender if ever she'd seen one. She chanced a look over her shoulder at Rick, who looked like he was about a second away from losing his temper.

She wanted to beg him not to do this. She'd just gotten him back, and she couldn't lose him like this.

"However," Tipper said, snapping Shannon's attention back to him.

However? Tipper was not a *however* kind of judge.

"I cannot ignore the traumatic impact your actions had on the victim, Mr. Wells. For that reason, I'm sentencing you to the maximum permitted time of eighteen months, minus time served."

Minus time served meant he would spend nine more months behind bars. With good behavior, he could be out in three. It didn't even scratch the surface of what this monster deserved.

She cast a cautious glance at Rick. His usually bright green eyes had darkened with something perilously close to rage, but he made no move to draw his weapon. Yet.

Holly stared down at her shoes, silent tears of grief shining on her cheeks. She'd expected this.

"You will be required to see a counselor for one hour every week," Tipper announced. "During which time I hope you remedy whatever misguided feelings you have for Ms. Cross. You will have no contact with her— either written or spoken—for the duration of your sentence."

He lifted his gavel to declare the matter closed, when the rear doors opened and a man with a detective's badge dangling around his neck walked in, flanked by two men who appeared to be marshals.

Shannon recognized the detective from his file, and she nearly wilted into her chair with relief.

It was about time.

· · · ·

Detective Liam Duggard's gaze flickered over the crowded benches as the judge finished announcing the defendant's sentence, and his eyes snagged on the young woman who swayed under the pronouncement. He couldn't see her face, but her build was exactly the same. She turned to look back at him, along with everyone else in the courtroom, and Liam's heart twisted in his chest.

Purity.

After years of searching, he'd begun to fear that he would never find her, that she'd been swallowed up by the world, and then he saw the media coverage for a missing girl this past spring. Liam had compared his grainy black-and-white security camera photo with the colored media headshot, almost certain it was the same girl.

The problem was, he was the only one who could see the resemblance. He requested time off to come to New York City, but his boss denied it. She didn't want his "obsession" causing an incident that would reflect poorly on her precinct.

And then six months ago, the call came, confirming Liam's suspicions that Holly Cross was Purity, and that her rapist had followed her across state lines and attacked her again.

It was New York City's DA, Shannon Marx, who reached out. She contacted Liam's boss and the district attorney, urging them to revisit Purity's case, as well as several unsolved crimes that had been handled by other precincts. She claimed the man responsible for a number of assaults in the state of Pennsylvania was sitting in her county jail, awaiting trial.

Liam's DA was reluctant to expend the time and resources it would take to organize a court case without absolute proof that the man in New York's custody was the man they were looking for. Shannon Marx provided them with the missing piece: Collin Wells's DNA.

Even with that essential piece of the puzzle, it took months to organize everything. Between the different jurisdictions handling the crimes, reluctant victims and witnesses, and unprocessed evidence, they had a mess to sort through.

He caught sight of Shannon, who looked both relieved and irritated by his presence, as he strode up the aisle. Right . . . he was supposed to call this morning to let her know if he was coming.

He paused at the gate dividing the courtroom and called out, "Your Honor, may I approach?"

The judge leaned back, frowning. "What's the meaning of this interruption? Who are you?"

"Forgive me, Your Honor. I'm Detective Liam Duggard, Pennsylvania PD. And these"—he gestured to the two people behind him—"are federal marshals. We have an order of extradition for Mr. Collin Wells."

He saw the defendant jerk in surprise and barely restrained a smile. Collin Wells was a good-looking man with a perfect complexion and an expensive suit. He looked like a trust fund kid rather than a psychopath who enjoyed beating on girls, but the facts spoke for themselves.

"On what charges?" the judge demanded.

"For the false imprisonment, assault, and rape of ten women in the state of Pennsylvania, including Ms. Holly Cross."

The judge blanched, as though he'd been slapped across the face, and looked toward Holly. Liam glanced toward her too. She looked small and terrified as she trembled in the older man's arms, and Liam couldn't fathom how anyone could look at her and fail to see the truth—that the defendant was the monster she claimed he was.

The judge cleared his throat and straightened in his chair. "I assume you have evidence to support this . . . claim."

411

He didn't say *outlandish* claim, but the skepticism in his tone was undeniable. He had just sentenced a serial rapist to eighteen months in prison, and he didn't want to be wrong.

"Yes, Your Honor, we do. Not only do we have witness statements from nine of the ten victims, we have conclusive DNA evidence linking Mr. Wells to all ten rapes."

Holly's statement was the only one they didn't have. If the nurses at Mercy Hospital hadn't been able to convince her that a sexual assault kit was necessary to rule out internal injuries, they would have nothing.

Strain tightened the skin around the judge's mouth. "This is a very unorthodox way to go about this, Detective. You could've waited until after everything was concluded."

Liam scoffed inwardly. The judge clearly wanted everyone out of the room so he wouldn't have to suffer the embarrassment of being wrong in front of so many witnesses.

"I apologize, Your Honor. But as the defendant has a tendency to disappear, we didn't want to take any chances by delaying."

Irritation and fear sharpened Collin Wells's voice. "This is ridiculous. You can't do this. I didn't attack anyone."

Liam held up the file in his left hand. "I have pictures. Would you like to see them, Your Honor?"

The judge motioned him forward, and Liam approached with the extradition order and the folder of victim photos. He handed them over and stepped back.

Liam watched the judge's face closely as he carefully flipped through the photos. His Adam's apple bobbed as he swallowed repeatedly, as if fighting back the urge to vomit.

Liam took one more step back just in case. "May we take him off your hands, Your Honor?"

With one last thick swallow, the judge closed the folder and pierced Wells with a look of disgust. "You put on quite a show." He handed the folder back to Liam. "Get this animal out of my courtroom."

"Happily." Liam strolled over to Wells, who looked tense enough to implode. "You know, I made a promise to myself three years ago that I was gonna find you and make you pay."

"For what?"

Liam handcuffed Wells's wrists behind his back. "Little pink shoes, bloody footprints, and a disappearing girl." When Wells's gaze moved to Holly, Liam grunted. "Yeah, that's the one. I figured you'd remember." He gripped his arm and dragged him toward the aisle, pausing beside Shannon. "I don't know if anyone's said it yet, but thanks. If you hadn't reached out . . . ."

She nodded briskly. "I assume DA Jefferies has everything in order?"

"He does. Mr. Wells will be arraigned Friday morning, and assuming he decides to plead not guilty, the trial shouldn't be too far behind. Everyone wants this done and over with, even if that means shuffling around some dates on the courthouse calendar."

Wells smiled, smugness creeping into his expression. "Your case isn't going to hold up."

"Ten cases, actually, and you don't have a dead woman to blame this time." Liam jerked him further down the aisle.

Several men lined the walkway, and Holly stood among them. She looked like she wanted to say something, so Liam hauled Wells to a stop, keeping a firm grip on him, and gave her a minute to work up her nerve.

The older man behind her offered a hand. "Detective Marx." The other two introduced themselves as Sam and Jordan. There seemed to be an unspoken yet collective decision to fill the silence while Holly tried to find her words.

She bit her bottom lip to keep it from trembling along with the rest of her body, then asked in a soft voice, "He's going to prison?"

"With the evidence we have, he'll be in prison for a very long time. He won't be able to hurt any more women."

She hugged herself, clearly terrified to be this close to her attacker, and tried to keep her shoulders straight. "Are you gonna lock him in a small room with no windows?"

Liam hadn't been present for the trial, so he didn't know all of the details, but he suspected Wells had kept her in a place very similar to what she just described. "Probably for the rest of his life."

Tears spilled down her cheeks, but she lifted her chin and stared at Wells, icy resolve shifting behind her eyes. "How does it feel?"

Liam's gaze slid past her to Marx, whose eyebrows lifted. Wells didn't seem to appreciate the question; he leaned forward, words on his lips, but Liam jerked him back at the same moment Jordan stepped in front of Holly.

The blond man's eyes smoldered with pent-up fury, and it seeped into his quiet voice. "Touch her and you won't make it to Pennsylvania."

Wells sneered at Jordan. "Don't take your anger out on me just because you couldn't protect your little girlfriend."

Liam glanced at Jordan's hands as they curled into fists. "Let's not make a scene."

Wells twisted, his attention fixed on Holly. "You think you're safe, *Little Bird*. But you'll never be safe."

Marx wrapped his arms around her from behind, holding her protectively. "You should be more worried about your own safety. There are a lot of predators in prison, and you'll be lucky if you survive."

Fear flashed through Wells's eyes.

"I'm gonna follow you guys to the border," Jordan said. "Just in case something goes wrong." He looked as though he hoped something would go wrong.

"I'm coming too," Sam volunteered.

Two federal marshals, two cops, and a man whose anger may or may not stem from romantic interest in Holly? Any escape attempt by Wells would be suicide.

It comforted Liam to know that, even though he hadn't been able to help Holly three years ago, she was safe now. He had no doubt that these three men would protect her with their lives.

Epilogue

Two Months Later

The aroma of taco beef filled Holly's small apartment, and she mixed the skillet of deliciousness on her stove top, desperately trying not to burn it.

She added water to the beef to provide a little moisture and—oh no, that was too much. Now it was a taco moat.

Steam plumed from the skillet, and she hissed inward through her teeth, waving an oven mitt through the cloud. She didn't want to break in the smoke alarms her first week back in her apartment.

Her home was more than she could've ever hoped for. When Jordan said they would fix it up, she took that to mean cleaning and replacing the windows. But the three amazing men in her life did so much more than that.

The floor, formerly a chilly cement, was now a warm wood vinyl that didn't turn her toes to popsicles in the winter, and the walls alternated between creamy beige and eggplant purple—her favorite color. There were six round lights on the ceiling, and she loved the warm glow that filled the room every time she flipped the light switch.

A knock came from the front door, and she glanced at the digital clock on the microwave. No one was supposed to be here for another fifteen minutes.

She turned off the burner for the taco beef and grabbed one of the folding metal chairs from the kitchen table, intending to drag it over in front of the sink so she could look out the window and see who was at the door.

Then she remembered that she didn't have to. When the guys remodeled her apartment, they added a peephole to the door exactly at her eye level.

Riley beat her to the door, sniffing and barking at whoever stood on the other side. Holly, trying not to get knocked over by his tail-wagging enthusiasm, peered through the peephole to see Jordan standing on her patio. Jace and Sam lingered at the top of the cement steps behind him.

Jace cleared her throat with emphasis. "We're not crazies. You can open the door."

Holly grinned—she loved her friends—and unbolted the door, swinging it open. "Hey guys."

Jordan held up a tub of Rocky Road ice cream. "I brought dessert." He lifted the plastic bag in his other hand. "And marshmallows, sprinkles, and chocolate syrup to go on top."

It had been a while since she had a Jolly sundae, and it sounded perfect. She widened the door. "You may enter with your bag of tasty treats."

Jordan swept past her with the groceries. "Where's Little J?"

Holly pointed to the couch, where her chunky gray cat sat, glaring at the people intruding on his space. "Riley keeps trying to bond with him, but he doesn't seem too interested."

"They'll warm up to each other." Jordan set the food on the small kitchen table. The square card table wasn't going to be big enough to accommodate six people, but she had an abundance of pillows they could spread out on the living room floor.

Jordan, true to his word, had taken her shopping and helped her pick out a variety of pillows, most of them in various shades of purple and pink.

Sam stepped inside and handed Holly a cardboard box. "I brought Monopoly."

Oh boy. Games and Jace were a dangerous combination. She was competitive to a fault, and she didn't understand the concept of playing "just for fun."

Jace threw her hands up behind Sam. "The only thing I brought is my amazing self."

Holly laughed and set the game on the kitchen counter. "That's all any of you needed to bring."

Sam grabbed the board that was resting against the outside of the apartment and laid it down over the steps, creating a makeshift ramp for Jace to use. She cruised down it, through the front door, and into the kitchen.

"Oh yeah, I love this floor." She spun her wheelchair in a circle. "And these guys wanted to do carpet."

Holly tucked her fingers into the back pockets of her jeans and smiled wryly. "I was thinking about adding some rugs."

Jace's eyes narrowed, the blue of her irises vanishing amidst the black eyeliner and mascara-lengthened lashes. "If you add death traps to this floor, I am never coming to visit."

Holly laughed. Jace hated rugs because they got caught in her wheels, and she ended up spinning in place. "Just kidding." She gestured to the other side of the room. "But pillows."

"Score!" Jace sped across the room and scooped up a pillow, punching it with a fist as she eyed Jordan. "Let's see what you got, second-place best friend."

Holly's cheeks warmed. Would they ever stop competing for best-friend status?

Jordan strolled into the living room and snatched up one of the pink pillows, accepting her challenge. "You're on, as long as your boyfriend doesn't beat me up when I win."

Both of them looked at Sam, whose eyebrows lifted. "If you two wanna wail on each other with pillows like children, feel free."

Jace launched into action, pummeling Jordan's midsection.

Holly shook her head and walked back to the patio to move the board off the steps and back up against the side of the building. She dusted off her hands and started to close the door when a maroon car parked along the curb.

There was still a ding on the front bumper from where it had been . . . spontaneously attacked by a handicap sign. Marx climbed out and rounded the car to open the passenger door, offering Shannon a hand.

They had come together. That was a hopeful sign that things were improving between them.

Shannon descended the steps first, and Holly threw her arms around her before she could even step inside. "Hi!"

The poised lawyer stiffened, apparently surprised by the affectionate gesture, then hugged Holly back. "Hi."

Holly released her and stepped back, tucking her hair behind her ears. "Thanks for coming."

"I appreciate you inviting me."

"It's nothing super fancy." Nothing befitting Shannon's elegance. "Just tacos and ice cream."

Shannon cocked her head with interest at the living room brawl. "And pillow fights?"

Holly smiled sheepishly. "Yep."

"Hey, sweet pea." Marx came through the open doorway and set a vase of colorful flowers on the counter to his left. "Your apartment-warmin' gift."

Holly couldn't care less about the beautiful bouquet of flowers. It had been nearly a week since she last saw Marx, and she missed him. And judging by the way he hugged her up onto her toes when she threw her arms around him, he missed her too.

He squeezed her tight. "I know you have your own place, but I expect you to come visit me at least once a week."

She smiled. "Who else is gonna fill your rainy-day jar with nasty brown and yellow M&M's?"

"You do realize that beneath the colored shell, they're all brown."

"They taste different."

He snorted in amusement and lowered her feet back to the floor. "You're imaginin' things."

Still tucked beneath one of Marx's arms, Holly looked between him and Shannon. "So are you two . . . back together now?"

Shannon reached over and took Marx's free hand, twining her fingers through his. "We're thinking about getting married again."

Excitement bubbled up in Holly, and she tried to keep it from overflowing. "I think that's a great idea, and there's plenty of time today."

Marx laughed. "We can't just get married today. We have to set a date."

Oh, um . . . "How about Friday? I can take pictures."

She'd only ever photographed one wedding, and while it was a nice ceremony, the couple and everyone in attendance were strangers to her. Photographing and preserving Marx and Shannon's wedding would be beautiful and personal.

"I'm sorry, Holly," Shannon began. "But you can't take the pictures of our wedding."

Holly's hopes crumbled. "Oh."

Maybe they didn't think she would do a good job, or maybe . . . she wasn't invited. That possibility sent a stab of pain through her chest. After the public trial, her presence would probably draw unwanted attention.

"It would be difficult for you to photograph the ceremony while you're standing beside me as my maid of honor," Shannon said, and Holly gaped at her, certain she'd misunderstood.

"Your what?"

"My maid of honor."

Holly looked around. "Me?" That position was reserved for sisters and best friends, neither of which Holly was to Shannon.

"Yes, you," Shannon said on a laugh.

Fresh excitement bubbled inside Holly, and she threw her arms around Shannon again. "I would love that." Then something occurred to her: weddings had dress codes. She drew back. "Can I wear jeans?"

"Well," Shannon said, glancing at Marx, "I bought this beautiful yellow dress and—"

Holly scrunched her nose in disgust. "Why would you buy a yellow dress?"

Shannon sighed. "Apparently it was a mistake I will never be making again. Jeans are okay."

"Holly," Sam said, drawing everyone's attention to the stove. He held the lid to her skillet in one hand and studied the contents of the pan. "You know there's only enough meat in here for three people."

She frowned and shuffled over. "No, there's enough for everyone to have a taco."

He lifted an eyebrow. "*A* taco? As in one?"

She shifted with uncertainty at his tone, and glanced at everyone else. "Yeah."

"No one ever eats just one taco."

"I do."

"Because you're pint-sized," Marx commented, and she scowled at him. "Maybe we should call out for some rice with chips and salsa. And some cheese dip for Holly."

"On it." Sam stepped outside where it was quieter.

Holly frowned at the skillet of meat. She should've realized that the guys would eat more than that.

Shannon checked her phone and then tucked it back into the rear pocket of her jeans. "We have company coming. He should be here any minute."

Company? Holly's apartment was already stuffed to bursting with people, and she hadn't made enough food for everyone. "Who else is coming?"

Shannon pressed her lips together. "Detective Liam Duggard."

Jordan voiced the single question that ping-ponged around in Holly's mind. "Why is he coming here?"

"He wants to speak with Holly in person."

Something must have gone wrong, and he was coming here to warn her. Holly leaned against the counter and hugged her stomach, trying to quiet the anxious fluttering.

The Pennsylvania trial was closed to the public, and no one had any idea what was happening behind those sealed doors. The jury could've acquitted Collin, or he could've escaped.

Jordan stepped closer and reached out to comfort her, but paused with his hand a hairsbreadth from her arm. "It's gonna be okay, Holly."

Holly stared down at her slippers as the awful possibilities whirled through her mind.

"He didn't give you any indication why he's comin'?" Marx asked.

"No. He just said that he needs to talk to Holly. I could try calling the district attorney, see if the trial concluded."

A door closed softly, drawing everyone's attention to the unfamiliar car parked along the curb. The large man who stepped onto the sidewalk was the same one who swept into the courtroom with two federal marshals.

Holly shifted uneasily. "Should I . . ."

"Stay put. I'll talk to him." Marx ran a gentle hand over Holly's hair, reassuring her that he would take care of the situation, and then bounded up the steps onto the sidewalk to intercept the detective.

Holly watched with growing dread as the two men spoke in low tones. Marx tapped his fingers on his belt as he glanced over his shoulder at the apartment, indecision on his face.

What was happening?

Riley nudged between Jordan and Holly, and pressed against her side, offering comfort as her anxiety climbed. She dropped a hand and sank her fingers into his thick fur.

Marx leveled a warning look at the detective as he said something else, and the man nodded. Marx spun on his heel and returned to the apartment, the Pennsylvania detective just steps behind him.

Detective Duggard dipped his head to fit through the low-hanging doorway, and then unfolded his enormous frame in her kitchen, making her one-room apartment feel even smaller.

"Hello, Holly." He looked at her like he knew her, like she mattered to him, but she didn't know him outside of that brief interaction in the courtroom.

"Hi."

"I know we didn't get to talk much in the courtroom, but my name's Liam." He offered his hand, and she glanced at it, her fingers digging harder into Riley's fur.

Riley let out a rumbling growl, warning the newcomer to keep his distance, and Liam promptly dropped his hand.

"I'm the detective who worked your case in Pennsylvania."

Holly's eyebrows pinched. "I never talked to the police in Pennsylvania. How did you even know something happened?"

"A nurse from the hospital called after you were admitted, but you disappeared before I could get there. I searched for you and found the condo where you were living."

Her throat tightened. She'd barely escaped her home that night. She managed to grab the scissors she kept under the bed and cut the zip ties from her wrists. Collin caught her as she staggered out of the bedroom, and she stabbed him with the scissors and pushed him down the steps. She slipped and nearly fell in his blood at the bottom, but she managed to stumble out the door and onto the sidewalk.

Twice she'd stabbed Collin—once with scissors and once with a chunk of glass—and still he'd survived. If she didn't know better, she would think he was immortal.

"If I can ask," Liam began. "Where did you go after you left the hospital?"

Holly pulled on her lower lip with her teeth. "One of the nurses gave me some clothes and a little bit of money. I took a bus as far as I could, and then hitchhiked to New York City. Eventually I found a women's shelter and stayed there for a while." Her eyes burned with tears as she thought about the fire that had scorched through it. "But it's gone now."

Liam nodded. "I'm sorry for everything you've been through. I can't even imagine. But I want you to know that I never stopped looking for you."

Holly was surprised that anyone had bothered to look for her. She'd been invisible, a transient with no friends or family to notice if she disappeared. "Thank you for . . . caring. But even if you had found me, you wouldn't have been able to help me."

"I would've tried."

Staring into his blue eyes, filled with warmth and compassion, she believed him. He would've tried to protect her from Collin.

Jordan folded his arms and shifted the conversation out of the past and into the present. "Why are you here?"

"Right. Sorry to just pop in out of the blue, but the trial's over, and I wanted you"—he tipped his head toward Holly— "all of you, to know how things turned out before it hits the news."

Holly swallowed, her throat dry. "Please tell me your judge and jury were smarter than ours, that they didn't let him go." She didn't think she could handle that.

"Collin Wells isn't going anywhere," Liam said. "He was convicted on all ten counts of false imprisonment, rape, and assault. The judge sentenced him to life in prison without the possibility of parole."

Liam's words seemed so impossible that Holly struggled to absorb them. *Life in prison.* He was never getting out. Collin could never touch her again.

The relief slammed into her with so much force that she slid down the cupboards to a crouch, fresh tears burning across her vision.

Safe. She was finally safe.

"I'm sorry," Liam said. "I thought that would be good news."

"It is good news," Marx assured him. "You just told her she doesn't have to spend the rest of her life in fear. She's overwhelmed."

Holly wiped at her face and drew in a shuddering breath. For the first time, she could truly plan her life.

She was going to solve mysteries with Jordan, help plan a wedding for Marx and Shannon, plant a flower garden, learn to ice-skate.

She was going to throw open the doors and windows and live every moment like the gift it was meant to be.

Dear Reader

Some of you are probably thinking that this is the end of Holly, Marx, and the gang, but not to worry! Their stories will continue on in the fourth Holly Novel.

I wanted to express my thanks to all of you who took precious time out of your day to read this novel. If this is the first book you've read by me, I hope you'll go back and start the journey at *Criss Cross*. The experience is so much richer when you watch the characters and relationships grow.

If you think you would enjoy excerpts from future books (as well as publication dates and the occasional short story about my life), I would love for you to sign up for my newsletter. I send this out maybe four times a year, so no worries—I won't be bombarding your inbox.

If you're not an email kind of soul, then you can find updates on book progress and interactive questions on my Facebook or Instagram page or on my website. If you want to chat with other readers about my books, check out the Facebook group "C.C. Warrens' readers: Mysteries, Mischief, and Marshmallows." And yes, if you were wondering, Holly is the inspiration for that title!

If you love these stories, I hope you'll take a moment to share your thoughts and feelings on Amazon, Goodreads, and Bookbub. I know everyone asks you to write reviews, and if you're an avid reader like me, that's a lot of reviews. But trust me when I say, as an author who has poured out her heart into every book she's ever written, your reviews are cherished.

I would love to hear from you, so feel free to reach out through any of my social media sites, my website, or through email. Have a beautiful day!

About the Author

C.C. Warrens grew up in a small town in Ohio. Never a social butterfly, she enjoyed painting, sketching, and writing, with the occasional foray into theater acting. Writing has always been a heartfelt passion, and she has learned that the best way to write a book is to go for a walk with her husband. That is where the characters—from their odd personalities to the things that make them bubble over with anger—come to life.

How to Connect

Facebook: https://www.facebook.com/ccwarrens/
Website: https://www.ccwarrensbooks.com/
Email: ccwarrens@yahoo.com

Made in the USA
Las Vegas, NV
12 September 2024

95189298R00256